MW01223075

My Courage Rises

✦ ✦ ✦

BONNIE HERRON

EAST PARK PUBLISHING
VICTORIA, CANADA

Library and Archives Canada Cataloguing in Publication

Herron, Bonnie, author
My courage rises / Bonnie Herron.

ISBN: 978-0-992033-80-4 (pbk.)

I. Title.
PS8615.E77M83 2014   C813'.6   C2013-904980-0

Cover and text design by Fiona Raven

First Printing 2014
Printed in the USA

Published by
East Park Publishing
Victoria, Canada

www.MyCourageRises.com

. . . for every person
who rises above intimidation,
with, or without, the inspiration
of Jane Austen

Part 1

1 ... Attack

*U*sing her torn knickers, Fiona wiped away blood and semen from her inner thighs. She squatted down beside the trail and dug a hole, scraping away the soft forest floor with her bare hands. She dropped in her knickers, filled in the hole, and covered it over with dirt and leaves. She stood up, immobilized momentarily, as she looked down at the grave of her virginity.

With these bloody knickers, I'm burying my memories of this horrible, humiliating night. Nobody will ever know what happened to me. Nobody. That bastard!

She hoped she could avoid seeing anyone, as she made her way out of the trees, across the open field, and through the town toward her place. She nearly succeeded. But, as she passed by the home of her best friend, Katie Montgomery, Katie's voice sounded out.

"Fiona! Come in! Mum's out. I'll make tea. . . . God! You look awful. What happened to your hair? Turn around. Why are twigs and leaves . . . they're tangled into your hair. What's going on? And what's that in your hand?"

Katie's rapid-fire questions gave Fiona a few seconds to calm herself and prepare to lie to her best friend. As she stepped up onto the porch to join Katie, she tried to sound cheerful.

"I got into the University of Edinburgh! My teacher's training at Moray House starts in September, finally."

"Congrats, lass, I knew you'd do it. So what that you had to wait two years. You're only twenty. You'll still be the first person in your family to graduate from University. I'm happy for you."

Fiona was silent, which wasn't normal when she was with Katie. So, Katie pressed her.

"You've answered only one of my questions. Now, tell me, what the devil happened to your hair?"

Again, Fiona didn't respond.

"Let's go inside. Maybe a cup of tea will loosen your tongue."

Fiona sat down on the sofa while Katie went into the kitchen to make the tea. The moment Katie left the room Fiona put her head in her hands. Overwhelming emotion forced tears from her intense blue eyes down onto her cheeks. She tried to stifle a sob, placing one hand over her mouth and nose.

How could I let myself get raped? I'm fit. I play field hockey. I'm intelligent. I won a scholarship. Everybody in town knows I'm tough, mentally and physically. What if he brags about his conquest tonight? Everyone will think I let him do it. Nobody'd believe I was weak or stupid enough to let this happen.

When Katie came back with the tea, she set the tea tray on the coffee table in front of her distraught friend. She sat down on the sofa and put her arm around Fiona's shoulders. Fiona struggled to control herself.

"I can't tell you what happened to me. I know. I must look awful. Don't tell anyone, Katie. I can't talk about it. Just . . . take my word for it. I'm fine. Don't pressure me to explain. Can I trust you to do that, Katie, please?"

"Yes, of course. I can see you're determined to keep your secret. But, it won't last. Something is tearing you up. Eventually, you'll need to face it. Don't you trust me enough to help you through this?"

Fiona held her breath, as she considered Katie's offer to unburden herself. She attempted to get up, but she was shaking. She sat back down. In spite of her resolution not to tell anyone, the need to share the burden of her heavy emotion was overwhelming. Of all the people she knew, Katie was the one person she could trust with her humiliating secret. She sat up straight, wiped her eyes, and turned to look into Katie's eyes.

"He grabbed me from behind."

2 ... In her own words

I don't know how long he stood behind me. I was reading my letter at the edge of the loch. Darkness was falling. A cool breeze rustled the leaves on the trees behind me. I didn't hear him approach. I was holding the letter up toward the fading light, with my arms slightly away from my body, when he made his move.

He shot his hands up under my arms and squeezed my breasts so hard I shouted out from the pain. I was shocked. I couldn't believe what was happening. I screamed, 'Stop. Let go of me!' I twisted away from him. He lost his grip on my breasts and grabbed for my shoulder, tearing my sweater off my arm. I had just enough momentum to escape from his grip. I heard him curse as I ran away from him. Oh, Katie! I could hear his steps pounding along the trail as he chased me. I ran as fast as I could.

But, he was faster. He tackled me from behind. We both fell to the ground. He flipped me over, keeping a grip on my lower body with his knee. Then, he straddled me as if he were mounting a horse! He grabbed my flailing arms and pinned them over my head with one hand. He fumbled with my clothing. His head was down and I couldn't see his face under the visor of his cap. I kept shouting 'Stop.' He ignored my cries, reached up under my skirt, and tore off my knickers. No matter how hard I tried, Katie, I couldn't get out from under him. He was too strong. I kept my eyes closed. I thought, if I didn't see his face, he might not kill me. Suddenly, he spoke.

'Fiona, you know you want me.'

I opened my eyes. It was Jeremy MacAndrews, Laird

MacAndrews' son, sitting astride me! He had a twisted smile on his face. He was enjoying my fear! . . . the fear on my face! I screamed at him, 'I have never wanted you, Jeremy! That day will never come!' He smiled. Now he could hear the fear in my voice too. I struggled to get out from under him, shouting all the while. But, the more I protested, the more aroused I could feel him becoming. I tried begging. That didn't work either. He forced himself inside me, finally closing his eyes and throwing his head back as he climaxed. He seemed not to hear me crying or feel the resistance of my body. I was a virgin, Katie, a virgin!"

Fiona spoke faster and louder as she described the rape. She didn't seem to realize that she'd stood up and was pacing back and forth in front of the coffee table. When she stopped speaking, she continued to breathe rapidly. Exhausted, and emotionally drained, she looked back at the sofa, where Katie sat with tears streaming down her face. Fiona sat back down beside her friend.

"God! This is terrible, Fiona. But you know, dearie, don't you, it's not your fault. You could never overpower Jeremy. He's exceptionally strong. He and his football mates on the University team are all like that. You did the right thing. You survived the attack. The bastard didn't beat you or kill you."

"No, but he did rape me, didn't he? I'm so angry. I want him to pay for this. He was so smug, so certain he'd done nothing wrong. Before he left me there in the woods, bloody and ruined, he said, 'I'll see you in Edinburgh, lovely Fiona. I'm sure we'll be enjoying sweet love regularly. I know you liked it. You must have. . . . all that screaming in ecstasy when I gave you what you wanted. See you at school.'"

Katie began muttering curses, as Fiona related Jeremy's threatening words. Fiona continued in a sarcastic tone of voice.

"Katie, you know how much power his family has. Even if anyone believed he did this to me, nobody could do anything about it. His father, our supremely important, Laird Edward

MacAndrews, the exalted Baron of Glenheather, owns everything and everyone for miles around here. He'd never believe his spoiled son is a twisted rapist."

"I'm afraid you're right there, Fiona dear."

"God. What about my promise to Billy? We agreed to wait, to keep our virginity, until we marry after the war. Years of self-denial . . . . denying Billy, too, wasted. My first experience isn't making love with my husband. Instead, it's rape by a spoiled, despicable creep with no recourse possible. Worse yet, I can't be honest with Billy. I'll never tell a soul about this. And, neither will you. Jeremy probably has other conquests. Maybe he won't bother talking about me, the lowly daughter of one of his father's tenants."

"I promise I'll never tell a soul."

"Thank you, Katie. You're a dear friend. I'm trusting you with this awful secret. Now, I have to hurry home, in case my parents and sister leave early from the social at the Kirk. I don't want them to see me looking like this and start to ask questions. I'll see you tomorrow."

Fiona stepped out onto the Montgomery's porch and came face to face with her parents and her sister, as they rounded the corner in front of Katie's house, on their way home.

3 ... Suspicions

"Saints preserve us, Fiona! What happened? Come walk with us, lassie. Tell us how you got to lookin' such a mess."

Fiona's Mum, Kathleen, had spotted her as soon as she stepped out onto Katie Montgomery's porch. Fiona composed herself. She would need to be careful. These were the three people who knew her best. They knew when she was telling the truth. She laughed, and said casually,

"Nothing much. We had a great game of pick up field hockey. Katie and I won. High schoolers sure think they're the best at everything, don't they? We showed them twenty-year olds can outplay them. Do I look that bad?"

"Ah Fiona, that competitive spirit o' yours will be the end o' you. Surely, you'll want to stop that kind o' roughhousin' when you get to the University."

Ian, Fiona's father, just smiled and shook his head. Her sister, Brigit, said nothing. She glared at Fiona, as usual.

The Gilman family climbed the outside staircase at the back of the Marysburgh General Store, to their living quarters above. Under the light at the top of the stairs, seventeen-year-old Brigit, following Fiona, noticed smears of dried blood on the back of Fiona's leg. She thought it was odd that there were no other scrapes or cuts from the field hockey triumph, given the sorry state of Fiona's hair. Excited that she might have something on Fiona, she said,

"What really happened tonight, Fiona? You're lying. I know it."

Fiona ignored her sister, rushed to the bathroom ahead of everyone and washed herself quickly. She came across the blood smears while she was washing. She hoped she could explain them away as a result of the scrimmage, if Brigit brought it up again. It would be dangerous for her, if Brigit were ever to find out about the rape. She was mean spirited and very jealous of Fiona. Where Brigit had experienced much kindness from her elder sister, she had returned Fiona's kindness with resentment.

The family's general store was busy the next morning. Fiona was glad she could keep her mind occupied, as she attempted to cope in the aftermath of Jeremy's attack. She carefully arranged food on the shelves and organized the yard goods, thread, lace, and other sewing items on the large tables in the store. Several mothers came in to choose finely-woven fabrics for their daughters' new clothing. Fiona used her knowledge of Scottish tradition and the latest fashions to help them match their tastes to their mostly limited budgets, without any customer losing her dignity. But, here was someone just entering the store that didn't have a daughter with her, someone that Fiona was very glad to see.

"Ah, Mrs. MacDougall. Here for fabric, then?"

"Aye, Fiona. It seems that Johnny McCauley was serious after all when he asked me to go to his niece's wedding with him. You'd think he'd find some younger woman to keep him company. I dinna know what he sees in me, but I guess I'll be findin' out soon, won't I?

Bess MacDougall was the long-time choir director at the Kirk, a lonely widow whose only daughter had married young and moved to Canada. Bess had taken a great liking to Fiona, whose sunny disposition and wonderful singing voice made her job as the choir director much easier.

"Fancy tartan or just plain wool, Mrs. D?"

"I'll have this plain, lightweight wool for the dress. Why don't we make a shawl in the McCauley tartan? That'll give poor Johnny a fright, won't it? He'll think I'm lookin' to him for a husband!"

At these words, both women laughed. The thought of feisty Mrs. MacDougall dating Johnny McCauley, the town's shyest bachelor, was hilarious to both of them. Fiona was grateful for this little bit of fun. It distracted her, for a few moments, from her terrible ordeal of the evening before.

Fiona had become skilled at constructing both traditional and modern clothing, often using her own designs. Over the next two weeks, she spent many hours on this new project, to help keep her anxiety at bay. So far, she hadn't heard any gossip about her, or Jeremy, for that matter. She hoped to keep it that way. She was relieved to overhear from a customer conversation that Jeremy had returned to the university in Edinburgh, for pre-season football training.

When she wasn't working or sewing, Fiona discussed the attack with Katie several times. Katie's support and understanding helped her deal with the crippling emotion that came in waves, whenever memories of the attack intruded into her thoughts. It seemed, though, that nobody knew about it. So, she relaxed and began to look forward to University in Edinburgh.

Several weeks after the rape, Fiona went to Katie's for lunch. Katie looked unwell, as she contributed her own lamentations to their conversation.

"This blessed curse. Why has God given me the heaviest periods? Is it so I can spend all my time and effort on monthly supplies, worrying about leakage, and be inconvenienced as much as possible?"

As Katie spoke, Fiona suddenly sat up straight. She felt a sickening ripple of fear roll through her body.

My period! When was it? Why don't I remember? When was it supposed to be?

Katie was alarmed by the look on Fiona's face.

"What's wrong, Fiona? Why are you looking like that?"

"My period. I haven't . . . since Jeremy . . . . I'm never late. Oh my God!"

4 ... Consequences

Fiona was terrified. Surely, she'd missed a period because she was distressed in the wake of Jeremy's attack. But, now that she thought about it, her breasts were newly sensitive and she'd been sick to her stomach a few times in the past week.

At first, everyone at home was alarmed that she might have come down with the Spanish Flu. It was often a fatal illness and it had been rampant in the UK and many other countries, since the spring of 1918. Once the town doctor said she didn't have Spanish Flu, she relaxed. So did the rest of the family. If they knew that her sickness was due to a pregnancy, their sympathy would turn instantly, to incrimination. She was certain of that.

As it was, Dr. Johnston, who had attended her mother when Fiona was born, and ever since, eyed her suspiciously, but he held his tongue. He did, however, advise her parents that she should delay her move to Edinburgh, because of a new and wide-spread outbreak of the Spanish flu, in that city.

Good. Maybe Jeremy MacAndrews will get the flu and die. The world would be well rid of him. But, I'm probably not that lucky. He's already ruined my anticipation about moving to Edinburgh, Spanish flu or no Spanish flu. His parting words still haunt me. I just know he'll try to come after me in Edinburgh.

Prompted by Jeremy's threatening words running through her mind, Fiona agreed with her parents. She'd wait until January, to move to Edinburgh. Surely, the flu outbreak would be over by then and maybe the Great War as well, she told them.

But, what if I really am pregnant, repulsively so, with Jeremy's child? I can only fake the flu for so long. My parents will think

I've been promiscuous; nobody will believe I was raped. And, what about the life inside me? What would I do with a baby? Such unwanted children are a financial burden to the family. Their unwed mothers are shamed and rejected by the whole community. Getting rid of the baby is unthinkable, even if I did know how to go about it. Worse yet, what do I say to Billy?

As the weeks dragged on, Fiona calculated that she had missed another period. She was certain she must be pregnant. There was little time to decide what to do. After much agonizing and many private tears, she decided to write to Billy. He was recuperating in a London hospital, where a special surgical team had worked on his wounded leg.

Billy and Fiona had been friends since primary school. She trusted him more than anyone in the world. He might not consider marrying her after he found out about Jeremy. But, she knew he was an honourable person who would give her the best advice he could, under the circumstances. All she could do was hope he'd help her. She took her chance and wrote to him.

Dear Billy,

I was so happy to get your last letter. You're coming home at last. I passed your Mum in town the other day. She's very excited about your return. She'd been fretting that you might go directly to Glasgow to continue your apprenticeship.

I have some news, Billy. I hardly know how to tell you. I don't want you to think poorly of me, because of what I have to say. Something terrible has happened. I know of no other way to say it than just to get it out. I was raped by Jeremy MacAndrews when I walked down by the loch one evening.

I'm so sorry to give you this awful news, Billy, dear. I waited for you. I wanted to be only yours. Now, our plan is ruined. I'm not hurt, just extremely angry and very ashamed. I feel it's my fault. I should've been more careful. But, you know how much my quiet times near the great loch mean to me. He sneaked up on me when I was enjoying the peaceful sounds of the woods and the water before sunset. It was stupid of me to get caught alone down there. I just wanted to think about university in Edinburgh and our wonderful future together.

I'm afraid there's more bad news. I need to tell you now, before you come home. God must be angry with me. He's punished me with a lasting reminder of Jeremy's attack. I'm going to have a baby, Billy, Jeremy's baby. I'm so sorry to give you this unwelcome news.

I'll understand if you care never to speak to me again or want anything to do with me. But, please, at least help me with some kind of plan to get away to have the baby. Nobody here in Marysburgh can know about this. I'd be ruined and so would my family. You, too, would be ridiculed. I could never keep the baby. It would remind me of Jeremy and his despicable act, every day of my life. I won't do that.

I'll understand if you'd be willing to help me, only as a friend. I'll understand if you don't want a future wife who's had another man's child. Please, Billy, will you help me?

I've not told Mum and Daddie yet. I'm sure Daddie will want to kill me and Mum will think I'm a grand disappointment.

I'm so alone with this secret, Billy. Katie Montgomery is the only person who knows about this horrible situation. There's nobody else I can tell. Please help me.

Love, Fiona

Fiona's letter reached Billy in London, as he was recovering from his final surgery. He had suffered severe leg wounds when he pulled several of his fellow infantrymen out of firing range, during one of the endless, bloody battles in France, as the Allies pushed toward victory. The surgeons had saved his leg, but the damage to his leg muscles and nerves meant he couldn't return to the war. He was awarded a medal for bravery. He'd be honourably discharged and sent home, once his wounds healed.

From his hospital bed, he wrote back to Fiona immediately. He'd been thrilled to hear from her and ripped open her letter, only to be shocked at her news. He said he'd trembled with rage at Jeremy, before he surrendered to the anguish he felt for her, for himself, and even for the innocent life inside her.

Billy took some time after receiving Fiona's news, to calm down, clear his head, and think practically about their options. She had to get away from Jeremy's vicinity and anyone she knew in their town. He devised a plan.

His mum's younger sister, his Aunt Helen Brody, lived in Glasgow. Her husband, Robert, was killed in the war. They'd longed for children but were unable to have them. Billy would contact Aunt Helen, to ask if Fiona could stay with her until the baby was born. He'd also ask her, whether or not she'd consider raising the baby as her own. In his letter, he outlined this plan and offered Fiona his support.

'Fiona, I understand why you wouldn't want to be reminded of Jeremy by seeing his child every day for the rest of your life. And I know you, Fiona, dearie. You'd not make the baby an orphan, by turning it over to the social welfare people, or to the busybodies of the local Kirk charity. If my plan works, it would benefit you, the baby, and my Aunt Helen. Nobody in Marysburgh would be the wiser.'

He ended his letter by encouraging Fiona to tell her parents about Jeremy's attack and the unwelcome result, for all of them. He'd come to know Fiona's father very well; he knew Ian Gilman was a good man, who did not allow anyone to take advantage of him, if he could help it. He was also very intelligent and would know better than to confront Jeremy or Laird MacAndrews. He'd be careful not to expose the family to retribution from these powerful people.

Billy signed his letter, 'With much love, my Dear Fiona. I'll send word to you after I go and speak to Aunt Helen.'

Well, at least he still seems to be able to stand me, even after the rape. I'm so lucky to have him. I'll pray for Helen Brody to take me in, at the least, even if she doesn't want the baby. Otherwise, I'll simply be ruined.

5 ... *Discovery*

*F*iona sat alone in her room. She was finding it increasingly difficult to hide her condition from her parents and especially from Brigit, who shared a room with her. She avoided tight clothing and left her skirt fasteners undone beneath her sweaters, to hide her slowly thickening middle. Brigit was embittered by her own plain looks, when compared with her older sister. She was thickly built, with the short, stocky frame of her paternal great grandmother. Unlike Fiona, Brigit had a somber disposition. She was an average student who was terrible at sports. So far, nobody had asked her on a date.

Fiona tried to stop worrying about hearing from Billy, stood up, and went into the bathroom for her turn at a Saturday night bath. She was stepping into the warm water when Brigit barged into the room.

"Oh, you're in here. Sorry. My, you're getting fat, aren't you? You'll stop getting looks from the boys, if you keep eating so hearty, won't you?"

"Get out! Will you never respect my privacy, Brigit?"

Brigit didn't argue and left the room. But, her curiosity was peaked. Fiona's 'fatness' looked a lot like the belly of a neighbor woman that Brigit remembered seeing. She'd babysat for the neighbour early in her pregnancy.

On Monday, Brigit went to the library after school, to try to get a look at one of the medical books. Hopefully, there would be at least one picture with an explanation attached. She sneaked by the librarian who was helping another student and went straight to the 'adults only' shelf that was filled with medical books. There, she found the evidence she needed. She decided to keep her discovery to herself for the time being. She'd use it to her advantage or, at the very least, to Fiona's detriment, later on.

To the great relief of the people of Europe and the Americas, Armistice was achieved on November 11, 1918. The Great War was over, finally. Good news for Fiona continued, when a telegram from Billy arrived the last week of November. He'd visited with his aunt in Glasgow who had said 'yes,' and 'yes.' Nobody but Fiona knew what he meant. He'd arrive home in Marysburgh on December 2, on the noon train.

Fiona was very excited about Billy's arrival. They'd leave Marysburgh for Glasgow together, the day after he got home. She couldn't postpone telling her parents of her predicament any longer. She must tell them, now. That evening, after Brigit left to visit a friend, she approached them downstairs as they were closing up the store.

"Mum, Daddie, I need to talk to you. Now . . . tonight."

"We're just closing the store. We'll be up in a few minutes. Put the kettle on, will you?"

"Sure, Mum. You saw Billy's telegram, didn't you"?

"Aye, we did. It's grand he's comin' home."

Fiona went upstairs to prepare the tea. She was quite sure her father would require a stiffer drink, once he heard what she had to say. She was terrified her mother wouldn't understand or that both of them would judge her harshly. Her fear increased even more when she considered the beliefs of her father, and his efforts to serve as a good example at the Kirk. Well, there was nothing she could do to avoid the conversation now. She heard them come up the stairs and enter the room behind her.

Fiona turned toward her parents and started speaking straight on, as she handed her mum a cup of tea. She avoided looking into her father's eyes, as she began to speak.

"Billy knows something happened here while he was away.

I wrote to him and told him. He has been very understanding . . . and . . . and, he thinks you'll like the plan he's come up with, to fix the problem that was brought on us all, from outside either of our families."

"Fiona, you're speaking in riddles! What the devil are you saying? Is Billy alright? Has something else happened to him?"

Kathleen Gilman was alarmed by her daughter's unusually vague statements. Ian remained calm, but he had a look of deep concern on his face. He kept his voice calm and addressed his obviously distraught daughter.

"Fiona, just get to the point, lassie. What is it? What's wrong? Just tell us."

"Mum, Daddie, back in August, I was in the forest beside the loch. I was attacked. The attacker was Jeremy MacAndrews. Now, I'm expecting his baby. I'm so sorry, so ashamed. I know I'm a huge disappointment to you both."

Fiona was overcome by tears of sadness and guilt for bringing this shame on her family. She was afraid for herself and for them. Billy's plan sounded so much easier when she read it. Now that she was living it, she couldn't speak for all the crying—both hers and Kathleen's.

Ian got up and went to the cabinet, where he poured himself a large glass of whiskey. He appeared, barely, to be containing his emotions, as Fiona looked up at him through her tears. He tried to speak, but his emotions overwhelmed him. His love for his daughter, mixed with feelings of rage and frustration toward her attacker, left him momentarily mute. He went back to his chair and sat quietly sipping his drink, until he could control himself. He was helpless to undo Jeremy's attack on his precious daughter. He vowed to himself that somehow, he'd get even with this spoiled, rich, obviously disturbed, and irresponsible criminal, as soon as the opportunity presented itself. Finally, he spoke.

"This is bad news, for all of us. Fiona, ye said Billy had a plan. What is it?"

"Billy's Aunt Helen, his Mum's sister, in Glasgow, has agreed to let me live with her until the baby's born. Then she'll adopt the baby. We . . ."

"Fiona! That baby's our grandchild! Don't you want your son or daughter to be raised by your own family?"

"Now, now, my dear wife, I know ye're upset, my Kathleen. But, we can't raise an illegitimate child, especially a child of the Laird's blood. The Church is very clear on morality. No matter whose fault this is, we'd all be ruined."

"Daddie's right, Mum. I know this child is my flesh and blood. But, to me, it's a MacAndrews first, Jeremy's child. It's a child of rape. That's how I'll always see it. Why would I let our family be disgraced and discriminated against by the whole town? We'd be judged by the Minister, and the other members of the Kirk. And for what? For a MacAndrews? This child, too, would suffer from torment for being illegitimate, if the townspeople knew where it came from.

Fiona's parents could see she was getting worked up. Her voice got louder and her speech got faster, as she went on. They decided to let her get her emotions out. After all, she'd been living with this awful secret for months now. They waited patiently, as she continued.

"Putting up with an arrogant and condescending Laird, living our lives as his tenants is one thing. But, having a child by his despicable, rapist son and raising it in full view of everyone, is unthinkable. Besides, Jeremy will probably brag about his conquest, making sure everyone hears about his 'achievement' without his having to pay one shilling for his child. You know that's the truth and so do I.

Billy's Aunt is a loving, childless woman, widowed by this dreadful war. Nobody in Glasgow would know where the child came from. He or she would have a wonderful home with many advantages that we couldn't provide, under these circumstances."

"But . . . Fiona, dear, what about the Spanish Flu? You know Glasgow was the first place in the UK to get it. All summer, they sprayed the streets with chemicals and wore masks. Why would you expose yourself or the baby to the likes o' that scourge?"

"Because the alternative of staying here to bear the shame is worse, Mum, that's why. Besides, Billy's Aunt Helen says they seem to have it under control."

They heard footsteps on the stairs and decided to wait until the next day to carry on with their conversation. All three were exhausted emotionally—the two women from crying and Ian from fighting with himself to stay calm when all he wanted to do was get his shotgun out of the bedroom closet and shoot Jeremy MacAndrews.

The next morning, Kathleen Gilman entered her daughters' room as soon as Brigit left for school. She sat down on the side of Fiona's bed, placing a tray of soda biscuits and a glass of warm milk on the table beside the bed.

"Here, Fiona, eat these soda biscuits before you rise. They should help with the nausea. I'm so sorry I didn't notice before, darlin' why you were feeling poorly."

"It's not your fault, Mum. I've been hiding my condition carefully, until I could figure something out. I let out my clothes so you wouldn't notice.

Oh Mum. I'm so sorry to cause this mess for our whole family. I'm embarrassed and ashamed. I'm afraid that severe judgments could come down on our family from the Minister and our neighbours. You, Daddie, and Brigit will suffer because of me. I hope I can get away from here before anyone finds out what happened."

"Fiona, it's not only our reputation that concerns me. It breaks my heart to know that a child o' half our blood won't be with our family. Nevertheless, we understand why you don't want Jeremy's child in your life to remind you of its father. Daddie and I support your decision. Billy's aunt will adopt and raise the child. But, Fiona, we hope you won't come to regret your decision, once some time has passed."

"I doubt I'll ever regret not having Jeremy's child in my life. My biggest regret is that Billy won't be getting a pure bride. I'm very worried about his reaction to that. His plan sounds like it will work if he can accept me as I'll be, after the child is born— his intended wife, but with a stain. He seems accepting of the situation, but I'm anxious to see his face and feel his reassuring arms around me."

As she spoke, Fiona saw that her mother looked at her with empathy and compassion, for the terrible circumstances she faced. Kathleen Leary was from one of the Irish Catholic families that came to Marysburgh when the shipyards were set up. Her family had been disappointed when she fell in love with Ian Gilman, a full-blooded Scot—and a faithful member of the Church of Scotland to boot. Kathleen was accustomed to conflict where love was concerned, which resulted in her becoming a very tolerant, very understanding parent. Fiona knew her mother was grateful, at least, that she hadn't considered trying to abort the pregnancy. Kathleen had convinced her girls that abortion was simply murder, regardless of whether or not rape was a factor.

"Along with all of that to worry about, I also regret not being able to take my scholarship. I so wanted to make you and Daddie proud parents of a university graduate."

"I can see you're concerned about Billy's reaction, but I don't think you need to worry on that account. You'll see that when he gets here, I'm sure of it. As for the scholarship, I'm disappointed for you, Fiona, about your ruined plans for university. But, think of it this way. You're giving life to a child who will be loved. That's a grand thing to do. I'm proud of you, my gel, for the young woman you are. No matter what happens, Daddie and I are proud of you. Don't you be forgettin' that."

Fiona had applied, two years earlier, to have her scholarship postponed, by The Edinburgh Provincial Committee, who'd taken over responsibility for training teachers from the Church. She was needed to help her parents run the store, which supplied the demands of the naval base nearby and the shipbuilders in the area, during the Great War. But, the war was over now. She was expected to take the scholarship, or lose it.

The possibility of applying for an additional extension was out of the question now. Even the hint of a scandal, particularly the pregnancy of an unwed young woman, tainted by rumours of rape, would certainly lead to horrified reactions from Committee members, who considered it their duty to see to the morals of all young women who wanted to teach their children. The Church wasn't officially in charge, but, the influence of the Church was still very much in play. Thanks to Jeremy, Fiona would never be able to afford to live her dream of becoming a teacher.

"Ah, my darlin,' but what is done is done. As for your embarrassment at being forced into intimacy with Jeremy MacAndrews, I know you couldn't help it. I'm sorry you suffered at the hands o' that coward. There, there. Don't fret. I love you with all my being, my first born child. I know you'll make the right decisions. Daddie and I will help you as much as we can."

Brigit stood outside the bedroom door, shallow breathing so they wouldn't hear her, while she eavesdropped on her mother and sister. She'd forgotten a book for school and returned home to get it. She hadn't wanted anyone to know she was back. She entered the building from the back, outside stairs and crept quietly toward the room she shared with Fiona. Alerted by the hushed voices of Fiona and her mother as they talked, she moved closer so she could hear. She couldn't believe her good luck. Here was the oh-so-perfect daughter confessing to having a

MacAndrews baby in her. What a scandal! At last, she'd gained an advantage over the sister she had envied for as long as she could remember.

6 ... *Betrayal*

Billy McGinnis arrived in Marysburgh on the train the next morning. Fiona met him at the station looking radiant— partly from the pregnancy and partly because she was overjoyed to see Billy. She was well aware that he'd always admired her voluminous dark hair and intense blue eyes; this day they were complemented by her rosy cheeks. She admired Billy's familiar, handsome face, topped by his fair, wavy hair that had grown out during his stay in the hospital. From the earliest days of their relationship, she'd joked with him that he was tall, blonde, and handsome. He limped as he moved his lanky frame toward her along the platform, assisted by a cane. Smiling, he stabilized himself, hooked the cane over his forearm, and held out his arms to her.

"Fiona, you're lovely, lass, lovelier than ever."

Fiona walked into his embrace and wrapped her arms around his neck. It was such a relief to feel Billy's strong arms around her. She was so very grateful for his love and understanding. She couldn't help weeping silently as he held her.

"I won't pretend there's no reason to cry, my sweet Fiona. I've been worried about you. But, I see that your father hasn't killed you, as you predicted in your letter. And, I'll wager that your Mum's been understanding. She must have been relieved that you planned to give birth, not get rid of the baby."

"Aye, she was. She keeps to her Catholic beliefs. I'm pleased I could give her that, anyway. She and Daddie are disappointed about university. But, they support our plan to move to Glasgow."

"Good. Now, let's get going to my folks' place. We won't tell them about your condition today. Let's give them this afternoon to enjoy having their son back from the Great War, before we drop the news on them. I'll tell them before we leave for Glasgow."

Megan and William McGinnis Sr. owned *The McGinnis Drinking Establishment* in the center of town. Billy was their only child, born when they were both in their early thirties. His parents were happy to have produced a decent fellow. They were proud of his bravery under fire and relieved that he, unlike so many others from their town, had survived the Great War.

Meg and William had wanted Billy to work with them in the family's pub, eventually taking it over. But, Billy had an inquisitive mind. He was interested in mechanical things. Had he been from a wealthier family, he would have gone up to university to become a mechanical engineer. Instead, he apprenticed for steam engineering until 1915, when, looking older than his seventeen years, he suddenly enlisted in the British Army. Now, at twenty, he would finish his apprenticeship in Glasgow, hoping that there'd be work for journeymen of his trade in post-war Scotland.

Billy held Fiona's hand as they walked into the pub.

"Good day to you both, Mr. and Mrs. McGinnis!"

"Billy!"

Meg and William rushed over to the young couple. Meg embraced her son. William shook his son's hand as he spoke.

"Thanks be tae God for savin' ye in this awful war."

Meg realized, as she put her arm around Fiona's shoulder, that she hadn't seen her lately.

"Fiona, where've you been hiding? The store must be keeping you busy. Sit down, both of you, and have a pint with us."

Meg, older sister to Billy's Aunt Helen Brody, came from the well-to-do Muir family. The family had the means to educate their daughters in good schools, with the expectation that they'd marry someone of their own social station, preferably from Inverness. But, Meg fell madly in love with William McGinnis and followed her heart, marrying him and living in Marysburgh far away from her family home. Helen, on the other hand, met most of their parents' expectations when she married Robert Brody and moved to Glasgow.

Fiona and Billy spent a pleasant early afternoon with his folks. They took their leave in time to arrive at the Marysburgh General Store for tea. As they left the pub together, Billy mentioned to his parents that he wanted to speak to them, on a serious matter, before he left for Glasgow the next day.

"That sounds ominous, Billy. I hope you have good news for us," replied his mum.

Ian and Kathleen Gilman were elated when they saw Billy and Fiona enter the store. Ian directed Brigit to mind the store while he and Kathleen went with the young couple upstairs to the parlor. After greetings and hugs, when they were all settled near the fire, Ian handed Billy a glass of whiskey.

"How're your folks, Billy?"

"They're healthy, thanks. The business is going well too."

"Good. Ye must send our regards tae them."

"I will."

The two men talked for a few minutes about Billy's healing wounds, business at the store, and their relief that the war was over. Fiona and Kathleen soaked up these moments with their men, loving them even more as they watched them speak so easily with each other. Their mutual respect would be an advantage as all of them dealt with the next few months. But soon, they saw the expression on Billy's face change, sobering, as he turned his chair to look directly at Ian.

"Ian, about Fiona . . ."

"Nae, Billy, not just now. Ye young people should enjoy yourselves for one evenin'. After all, as Harry Lauder sings, 'It's a braw bricht moonlicht nicht' and tomorrow will come soon enough. Away with ye both, then. Tomorrow, after you've said goodbye tae your folks, we'll meet at two o'clock here. There'll be plenty of time for discussin' arrangements before ye and Fiona take the early evenin' train tae Glasgow."

Fiona and Billy left for their walk in the early winter moon-light, passing through the store downstairs, on their way out. Brigit, seething with resentment, watched them coming down the stairs holding hands. She was stuck with minding the store, while the precious Fiona and her boyfriend were treated as equals by her parents. They all seemed to get along so well, while she was ignored. She had to put up with the customers, made up of annoying townspeople, drunken sailors from the nearby naval base, and workers from the shipyards who shopped at the store wearing their dirty work clothes, while the lovely Fiona enjoyed herself.

By the time her father came downstairs to relieve her, Brigit was smoldering with bitterness. She gave him a dirty look and stomped out of the store. She'd show all of them just how much power she had in this family. She rushed to the home of her nearest classmate, where she began to reveal Fiona's situation, one juicy morsel of gossip at a time.

The next morning people in the town were talking about Fiona and her alleged baby. Kathleen and Ian noticed furtive glances between local customers as they shopped in the store. Both parents grew increasingly worried that something had gone wrong.

Meanwhile, Billy was at home packing up the civilian clothes he'd need for his apprenticeship and his new life in Glasgow. He'd rented a room at the home of his employer, Jack Murray, where he'd live while they waited for Fiona to have the baby. He'd be relieved when she was settled at Aunt Helen's.

Billy's thoughts were interrupted, when his mum barged into his room, ranting. Expressions of anger, mixed with disbelief, alternated on her face and in her voice.

"Is it true, Billy? Is Fiona having the child of another man? Do you know whose child it is? It's the Laird's son's child, that's who! Did she even tell you she'd been with Jeremy MacAndrews? I just can't believe . . . ."

"It's alright, Mum. I know about the child. And yes, Jeremy MacAndrews did force himself on Fiona."

"What? Oh, poor Fiona! And that wicked laird-in-training! If this were the old days and ways of the clans, her father and yours wouldn't hesitate to kill him. This just can't be happening to her, Billy, to you, to all of us . . . ."

She finally stopped. Billy had quickly finished packing his Army duffle bag, while his mother carried on. So, someone had leaked the damaging news. He should have known their plans were going too smoothly. Obviously, someone had found out their secret. And, he had a pretty good idea who it was. But, he'd deal with the traitor after he calmed his mum. He could understand that she was upset. He must tell her, now, what his plans were for Fiona and the baby. He closed his bag, turned toward his mum, and placed his hand on her shoulder.

"Mum, I'm sorry we didn't tell you sooner. Fiona is moving to Glasgow. Aunt Helen has agreed to take her in. She'll adopt the baby as soon as it's born. Don't look so dismayed, Mum. You know how lonely Aunt Helen's been since Uncle Robert was killed in Belgium. They tried so long to have children of their own. She'll make a wonderful mother. I promised her we wouldn't tell anyone about our plans until arrangements had been made for the adoption.

Fiona and I didn't want anyone else to know. I had planned to tell you both before I left for Glasgow today. I should've known someone would blab Fiona's secret before we could leave town."

Meg McGinnis was dumbstruck. Her sister had always been secretive, but this was unbelievable! Here she was, adopting the child of Meg's intended daughter-in law! After a few moments, she calmed down a bit.

"What if the child is actually yours? How do you know it isn't our own flesh and blood?"

"Mum, Fiona was raped by Jeremy MacAndrews. I was still on the continent. There's no chance that the child is mine or anyone else's. Fiona was a virgin when she was raped. What we do know is that the child is Fiona's and that Fiona will one day be my wife. We'll need to give Aunt Helen some time. I'm sure she'll write to you as soon as Fiona is settled in with her."

Meg had tears in her eyes when he finished speaking. She hugged her son, this honourable man, and left to break the news to his father. A few minutes later, William Sr. came to Billy's room and held out his hand to Billy.

"I'm proud of ye, Son. God will reward ye for your responsible and honorable behavior. We love Fiona and wish the best for the both of ye. Let us know if ye need anything, when ye get to Glasgow. Say goodbye to Fiona for us, won't ye?"

With relief, Billy shook William's hand.

"Thank you. We'll be fine. It's good to know you and Mum are behind us."

Throughout the discussions with his parents, Billy managed to conceal his increasing anger at Brigit. It must be she who overheard the news that Fiona was having a baby. She must have told her mates. Who else could it be? He hugged his folks, bid them goodbye, strapped on his bag, and headed over to Fiona's place, itching for a confrontation with Brigit.

7 ... *Escape*

*B*illy arrived at the store just as Brigit was coming out the front door of the store. He stepped up onto the porch, as she locked the door behind her. Fighting to keep control of his temper, he began to question her.

"Brigit, my mum heard some gossip about Fiona from a neighbor. What do you know about it?"

"Why ask me? Since when do you pay me any heed? You usually ignore me. Who said I told anybody anything?"

"No other person could know the words that are spoken in this house. You've always been jealous of Fiona . . ."

"Fine. So what? What if I did tell my best mate about the perfect Fiona's disgusting tricks? How could I ken that she'd tell anyone else? Fiona probably chased after Jeremy anyway. He's always looked at her. It's her own fault and nobody else's she's got that baby in her."

She was getting angry. Her voice grew louder as she shouted at Billy.

"She'll get what she deserves now, an illegitimate baby and no husband! All my mates say you'll leave her now that she's shown what a trollop she is!"

It took much strength for Billy to stop himself from slapping her right there on the porch. But, he held his temper so the scene wouldn't escalate further out here in front of the store. He stepped closer to her, looked down, and spoke directly into her face in a cold tone of voice, while his emotions raged inside.

"I'll not speak to you again, Brigit, ever. Fiona deserves a better sister. You'll not be welcomed in our home, ever, and you are not to address either me or Fiona again. I hope, for your own sake, that you pray for forgiveness from God, for your vile actions toward a sister who always treated you well. You've damaged the reputation of your whole family."

He walked past her, around to the back outside staircase. He knew he'd have to tell Fiona and her parents about Brigit's betrayal.

Earlier that day, while Billy was at home packing, Ian and Kathleen had surprised Fiona with a special going-away gift. Ian was obviously delighted with himself, as he called to Fiona, holding the surprise behind his back. She knew something was up, from the look on her father's face.

"Fiona, Mum and I want you to have this gift. We've been savin' for it so you could go off to the University of Edinburgh in style. But, that's no matter. You're moving away to Glasgow and we want you to have it. We hope you like it, bonny lass."

He handed Fiona a Gladstone Kit Bag, made of rich, soft brown leather. He watched as his daughter's eyes opened wide. The bag had brass clips that closed the top. Brass buckles adorned the straps that fastened over the top to keep the closing secure. Fiona was overwhelmed when she saw the gorgeous bag. She couldn't stop tears from welling up in her eyes.

"Oh! Thank you . . . thank you. . . . I can't believe it! Nobody in this family's ever had a travelling bag like this. But, it's too expensive. I can't keep it."

"Nonsense, Fiona. Daddie's been waiting two years to give you this bag. He started saving for it when you finished school and agreed to delay your plans for university. We couldn't have managed the store, these last two years of the Great War without your help, dearie. We know you've made a big sacrifice and we want you to know we appreciate it. We've been hiding the bag since we bought it last summer, in Glasgow. Now, hurry up and get your bag packed before Billy arrives."

After thanking and embracing her parents, Fiona started packing. By teatime, she waited in the parlor with her parents, for the sound of Billy's footsteps on the back stairs. When she heard him approach, she got up, ready to give him a big hug as soon as he walked into the room.

But, when she saw his face, she knew something was wrong. She didn't know, yet, that the town was talking about her. She just knew something was wrong. Ian greeted Billy, before she could say anything.

"Ah, Billy, here you are. Fiona's ready to go. Sit ye doon for a wee bit. I have somethin' tae give ye."

He picked up an envelope from the table and handed it to Billy.

"Here, Son, we want ye tae have this. It's the money we've been savin' for Fiona tae take with her tae the university. You probably know that the costs tae live in Glasgow have gone way up. Even tea and scones cost more than they did before the war. And, ye'll need money tae pay for tram tickets to visit Fiona. There're enough there tae get your Aunt Helen a nice gift, too, for her kindness tae Fiona."

"Ian, Kathleen, thank you. Fiona and I appreciate your offer. I won't take the money for me, but I accept it gratefully for Fiona—she'll need some visiting this long winter. The money will allow me to take Fiona out for tea, a few times. I promise you she'll not want for anything while she's at Aunt Helen's. Thank you from the both of us.

Now, I have some news. My Mum told me there's talk in town about the baby and the fact that it's Jeremy's."

At the sound of these words, the faces of Fiona and Kathleen looked stricken, while Ian's face darkened, reflecting his brewing anger. He'd been bothered all along that their secret might get out before Fiona could leave town. He was well aware, too, that Brigit had been jealous of Fiona all her life. She had a tendency to sneak around or barge in whenever other members of the household tried to enjoy a quiet moment together. She must be the tattler. She must have overheard the three of them talking about Fiona's predicament the other night.

"I'll murder her!"

He stood up quickly from his chair. The chair fell backwards and clattered loudly as it hit the floor.

"Ian! You'll do no such thing! I know you must be thinkin' tis Brigit who talked, but don't you think . . ."

Billy interjected.

"Sorry, Kathleen. I've already heard from Brigit's own mouth that she's the sinner here. I'll tell you both right now. I've spoken the last words I'll ever speak to her. There's no forgiving this kind of betrayal."

He turned to Fiona and took her hand, as he spoke tenderly to her.

"You'll hold your head up high, lass, no matter what happens. You and I will go to the train as we planned. We'll leave the gossips to themselves."

Kathleen could feel her tears rolling down her face. She knew how difficult it would be to repel cruel remarks and nosy questions that would surely come from the townspeople. The stigma attached to having a daughter who was pregnant and not married would be a lasting sentence for the family, especially at the Kirk. She tried to smile, for Fiona's sake. There would be plenty of time to deal with the condemnation of their family, after Billy and Fiona left.

Billy hugged Kathleen, shook Ian's hand, and walked over to where Fiona's new Gladstone bag sat on the floor by the doorway.

"What's this, then? Is it yours?"

"Aye, Billy, a gift from my parents to send me off in style. Do you like it?"

"It suits you perfectly, my lovely lass. Now, let's get to the train. It won't wait for us, if we're late. We still need to buy tickets."

"Tickets are in the envelope with the money, Billy. That's the least Fiona's Mum and I could do. Take good care of yourself and Fiona, Billy. We'll miss you both."

Fiona hugged and kissed her parents. Then Billy wrapped his arms around Fiona, who had started to cry. He soothed her by whispering in her ear:

"Everything will be fine, my sweet Fiona. We'll get through this together. Try to think about how happy we'll be making Aunt Helen. She told me she thinks of you as an angel sent to give her the child she always wanted. Hold onto that, Fiona, and your worries will be fewer. We must go now."

They walked down the steps. Billy had strapped on his British Army duffle bag. He carried Fiona's Gladstone bag in one hand, while he leaned on his cane with the other. They ignored Brigit as they passed her on the front porch of the store. Stepping onto the street, Fiona put her arm through Billy's. Neither of them looked back, as they held their heads high and walked toward the train.

8 ... Glasgow

The train trip to Glasgow relaxed Fiona. She and Billy walked along the aisle until they found two seats together—a window seat for Fiona and the seat beside her on the aisle for Billy. At first, they travelled in silence, relieved to relax after an emotionally-charged day. The rhythm of the moving train was soothing. It wasn't long before Fiona took out her sketch book.

Lately, she'd been creating more of her own clothing designs, testing them out on a few customers of her family's store. She concentrated on her newest designs until Billy tapped her on the shoulder and announced that they were at Cardross Station. Fiona recognized it from the pictures she'd seen. She remembered from her school history class that Robert the Bruce died there many years earlier.

Further along the route toward Glasgow, Billy again pointed out a sight that Fiona was especially interested in seeing.

"Fiona, look! Here's what you've been waiting to see. It's the clock tower for the Singer Manufacturing Company at Clydebank. Look at the lights."

"They're brilliant! I'd love to visit that factory. Ever since Mrs. MacDougall gave me her used sewing machine, with its signature, red "S" trademark, I've wanted to see how they're made. I'm sure they're making improvements all the time. I'd like to see what's coming next."

"My Aunt Helen knows how to sew and she'll have the latest machine. You might not need your mum to send your old machine to Glasgow. Either way, I'll take you to Clydebank to see the factory, once you're moved in."

"Grand! I'll hold you to that, Mr. McGinnis."

"I'm sure you will. My father told me something interesting about the Singer factory. He said there are so many folk working there, the builders can't keep up with the need for housing at Clydebank. So, workers for the Singer factory and also the two big shipbuilding companies travel back and forth from Glasgow every day, even on Sundays. As you'd expect, anyone's working on Sunday has greatly angered the leaders of the Church of Scotland. But, in spite of protests by the clergy, the trains continue to run, seven days a week. It'll be easy for us to get a train to the factory. We'll use a bit of your father's money. He'd like that. "

"Yes, he would, Billy, he surely would."

Fiona went back to her sketchbook while Billy spoke quietly to a soldier who sat across the aisle, until the train pulled into Glasgow.

War machinery was evident everywhere in the streets of Glasgow as Fiona and Billy stepped off the train. They were met by the smells and sounds of military vehicles, cars, horses and carriages, mixed together with people talking, shouting, and celebrating. These past few weeks following the end of the Great War had been hectic. Although thousands of military troops were still stranded in Europe awaiting transport, many soldiers had come home, joining those who were wounded in earlier battles. Mothers, fathers, sons, and daughters gathered at the train station, waiting to greet their loved ones, grateful they had a survivor to meet.

To Fiona, these sensual reminders of war stood in great contrast to the cheery Christmas decorations in the shop windows and on the streets. She looked out the window as the tram made its way along Argyle Street toward Helen Brody's home in the West End. She was excited by the number of shops that lined both sides of the streets in the center of town. Just seeing the shops gave her a kind of hope. Maybe Aunt Helen would take her to some of these shops to buy fabrics. She planned to keep developing her clothing design and dressmaking skills, with the hope of finding a few clients and earning a bit of money. It would be nice to have a profitable distraction during the long wait for the birth of this child.

They arrived in front of Aunt Helen's terraced home. It was a much grander dwelling than Fiona had seen, in her family's neighborhood, or other areas of Marysburgh. They climbed the steps and rang the bell.

Aunt Helen, herself, opened the door immediately. She must have been watching for them through the window. She was a tall, lean woman, barely forty, with regular features and warm, deep brown eyes. Her dark hair was neatly styled in the latest fashion, drawn back from her angular face. She was dressed in a tailored, charcoal grey silk suit, as if she were expecting very important people this evening. She smiled warmly at them both and immediately reached out to take Billy's hands. He was her only nephew. Fiona could see, by the look on her face, how much she cared for him.

"Aunt Helen, we're finally here. I've brought my dear Fiona."

Helen saw Fiona offer her hand, and she offered her own. She invited them into the house.

"Welcome, Fiona. I hope you'll feel comfortable and happy here, in your new home. You must be tired from the trip. Come right in. You can lie down for a wee while, if you like. Billy and I will catch up on the news from Marysburgh while you rest. It's just this way."

"Thanks Mrs. Brody. It's been a long, emotional day."

In her nervousness at meeting the woman who'd rescued her from her trying circumstances, Fiona fretted that she might not get along with her, or she'd feel judged. She was relieved and grateful that she liked Helen Brody immediately. Already, she felt welcome in her new, temporary home. She noticed Helen's refined manner. Billy had told her that his aunt had an extensive library and was an avid reader. Helen also worked with the Women's Suffrage movement. Fiona was sure she could learn a lot from this generous woman.

"I'll show you upstairs, Fiona. And, please call me Helen, or Aunt Helen, if you like."

She took Fiona by the hand while Billy followed them up the stairs, carrying her bag. It had been a trying day for all of them. Billy put Fiona's bag down, kissed her on the cheek, and closed the bedroom door, as he walked out of the room behind Helen.

Fiona could hear Helen and Billy chatting as they went back downstairs. As she lay there in the dark, she thought how lucky she was to have Billy and his Aunt Helen. She closed her eyes, confident that something good would come from this situation for all of them.

Billy relayed to his Aunt the details of their turbulent morning in Marysburgh. Helen was surprised that Brigit could be so cruel to her sister. She asked Billy about her own sister, his mum, Meg McGinnis.

"Billy, I feel badly for keeping your dear mum in the dark about our quickly-concocted plan. Was she very angry?"

"Aye. But, I think she was more disappointed at being left out. It's too bad that Brigit blabbed the news all over town before I told Mum about our arrangements for Fiona. She's very happy that you'll finally have a child to love. She asked me to give you her best. Will you write to her soon?"

"Yes, I will. But, first, thank you, Billy, for bringing this lovely girl and the wee bairn she carries into my life. I'll love this child as my own. Your mum, and any other family members who wish to love the child too, will be most welcome."

With Fiona moved into Helen's, Billy made his way to a more ordinary part of town, to his rented room at his new employer's house. The wartime rent freeze had been lifted and many landlords were taking advantage of their ability to over-charge for rent. Billy was lucky he'd pay a modest rate for room and board to his new landlord.

The door of the well-worn-looking house was opened by a smiling Jack Murray. He was a sturdy man in his fifties, with a full head of white hair, weathered cheeks, and bushy white eyebrows. Billy had been highly recommended to Jack, by his former employer, as a hardworking, intelligent young man. News of Billy's recent medal for bravery added to the respect that Jack already had for Billy.

"Welcome tae ye, Billy McGinnis."

Jack shook Billy's hand vigorously, as he stepped through the doorway, returning Jack's smile.

"We've saved a room for ye as promised. We're mighty glad tae see ye."

"Thanks, Jack. I'm glad to meet you too. I can't wait to get started on the job."

Just then, Billy saw a small face peep out from behind Jack's legs.

"Who's tha', Pappy?"

"It's Billy McGinnis, Geordie."

"Billy, here's ma wee grandson, Geordie, just turned three years old. He's the image of my son, who didna survive the war. His mum died givin' him life, so Geordie lives with us."

Billy held out his hand. The wee boy imitated his Pappy, shaking Billy's hand with gusto. Both men laughed, just as Jeannie Murray came around the corner. She still had the blonde hair of her youth, with streaks of grey. She was pleasantly plump, making her look younger than she was.

"Nanny, Nanny, look, we ha' a man here tae visit us. He's Billy."

Jack smiled at the boy's comments.

"And here's the luv of my life. Jeannie, meet Billy McGinnis. He's finally arrived, in plenty of time for Christmas."

Jeannie liked Billy the moment she saw him. His upright, military posture, in spite of the cane he leaned on, and the remnants of his grown-out military haircut reminded her of her lost son. She walked right up to him and hugged him.

"Welcome, Billy McGinnis. Jack is glad tae get ye. Ye must make yourself at home. I've saved ye some supper. But first, you'll want tae get those bags up tae the room. Geordie will show ye."

Billy gladly followed the wee boy; he was relieved to know that he'd be comfortable in the home of these warm, friendly folk.

Early the following morning, Billy and Jack left for work. Billy didn't have a chance to do anything but work for the rest of the week. He worried about Fiona, wondering how she was getting along with Aunt Helen. But, he knew she'd be well cared for. He decided to concentrate on his apprenticeship training, rather than on worrying. They'd made the move to Glasgow now, and nothing could send them back to Marysburgh for the time being. He'd write to his parents as soon as he got a moment. He'd let them know everything was working out just fine, so far.

9 ... New folk

*H*elen Muir had been a top student at the University of Edinburgh, where she met and later married Robert Brody. When her husband was killed in the war, Helen became the owner of their extensive library. She was glad to share her home with Fiona, a bright, curious young woman, with whom she could discuss the library's many books, essays, and geographical accounts of Scotland and other parts of the world. For her part, Fiona was thrilled to have access to such intellectual resources and company, particularly because her opportunity to attend university had been ruined by Jeremy MacAndrews.

The two women became friends easily. Helen asked Fiona to call her Helen, not Aunt Helen, which put their relationship on a more equal footing. During the first week of Fiona's stay, the two women talked over the physical care that Fiona would need before the baby's arrival. Helen arranged to have Fiona examined at the West End Branch of the Glasgow Royal Maternity and Women's Hospital. Excellent maternity care was available, because of the pioneering work of such well-known female physicians as Elsie Inglis, who had died in the past year. Helen explained to Fiona that Dr. Inglis and other female physicians had improved the conditions for mothers and their children, with advances such as anesthetics, milk depots, and examinations for infants. She was determined to see that Fiona had the advantages of securing a safe delivery and a healthy child. By providing such support for Fiona, Helen felt that she was participating in the life of this new baby, the baby who would be hers, even though she wouldn't give birth.

At the end of their second week together, Helen offered Fiona a chance to visit a place she'd long wanted to see.

"Would you like to go to the *Willow Tea Rooms* on Sauchiehall Street this week?"

"Yes, please! Definitely, thank you, Helen. I've read all about Charles Rennie Mackintosh, our extremely talented Scottish architect, and those lovely tearooms he designed for Kate Cranston. I'd love to see every one of his modern buildings."

"They're grand, Fiona. Now that the doctor's pronounced you and the baby healthy, a visit to the *Tearooms* will be a nice reward for you. All you've done since you got here is read, rest, and walk. You must be bored by now. I know you'll like the *Tearooms*. There's a wonderful glass frieze in the window and a sumptuous décor. We'll sip tea in the *Salon de luxe*, sitting on elegant, high-backed chairs, surrounded by extravagance."

"What a treat! I can't wait."

This first visit to the *Willow Tearooms* would be the first of many pleasant excursions for Fiona and Helen. After tea, they walked around the corner to see Mackintosh's spectacular, Glasgow School of Art, with its highly stylized mosaics and the awe-inspiring stained glass window in the lobby. Fiona admired, particularly, the modern, curved pieces of art that served as handles on the huge, dark wooden entrance doors of the School.

The week following their visit to the *Tearooms*, Christmas was near. Fiona, Billy, and Helen had an unexpectedly warm and wonderful Christmas, because of their association with the Murray clan. While Helen's place was quiet, populated only by the two women and visited by the housekeeper, Violet, the milkman, and Helen's friends, who came off and on for tea, the Murray household, where Billy stayed, was a lively opposite. First, Jack and Jeannie's identical twin daughters were home for the holidays from Dundee where they worked as weavers at a mill. As well, Jack had three brothers and Jeannie had two sisters who all had children of their own. The Murray house was the largest of the family homes, constantly busy with people. Many suppers at the Murray home included extra guests from the clan or from families who worked with Jack.

Fiona first met the Murrays on Christmas Eve, when everyone gathered to celebrate the season before they gathered the next day to celebrate it again. As he and Fiona walked toward the Murray's front door, Billy reassured her that she'd find them hospitable, generous, and non-judgmental. Jack, smiling, as usual, welcomed them both and quickly offered to take Fiona's coat.

Jack, Billy, and Fiona were still standing inside the doorway, when Geordie ran into the vestibule shouting,

"Where's the wee bairn? There's s'posed tae be a baby. Where ha' ye put it?"

"Geordie, come here tae Nanny. Leave Fiona alone."

Turning to Fiona, Jeannie Murray apologized.

"I hardly ken wha' we'll do wi' tha' wee boy! I hope ye'll forgive him."

"No harm done. Glad to meet you, Mrs. Murray. Thanks for inviting me."

"Call us Jeannie and Jack, dearie. We're havin' such a grand time gettin' to know yer Billy. Wha' a worker! Such a handsome young man tae boot."

"I like him too! I couldn't do without him, Jeannie."

Jack showed Fiona into the living room where she immediately felt at ease. A few warmly-coloured, well-worn carpets of faded yellows and greens were spread around the dark wood floors. Comfortable looking easy chairs in dark greens and burgundies along with a huge, overstuffed sofa, added to the room's cozy appearance. Mismatched lamps of various sizes throughout the room shed soft yellow light onto faces that Fiona could barely distinguish. Delicious aromas of roasting meat and sugary, hot desserts floated past her as she walked into the room and sat on the sofa. These sensual delights were enhanced by the sounds of lively Scottish tunes playing in the background.

As Fiona sat down on the sofa, two young women, as alike as anyone had ever seen, rushed over to sit with her, one on each side. She knew they must be Jack and Jeannie's identical twin daughters, but she wasn't prepared for their rapid rate of speech and their intertwined sentences. They examined her with wide-eyed scrutiny.

"So, ye're the lucky gel tha's so attached to our Billy."

"Aye, and who are you?"

"Auch, I'm sorry. I'm Tess. I'm older. She's Taylor, born four minutes after me."

Their bright young faces were so alike that Fiona found herself staring at each twin in turn, looking for a distinguishing difference. They were slightly plump, with round faces, curly, short blonde hair, and light blue eyes. Their skin was freckled, with a ruddy undertone. They were dressed exactly alike, wearing full skirted dresses, decorated with shawls made of the Murray tartan.

As Tess prattled on, Fiona could see that this elder twin did most of the speaking. Taylor, it seemed, was the quieter one. When Tess finally got up to go into the kitchen, Taylor spoke to her.

"Are ye plannin' to work, after the bairn is born?"

"Aye, sooner than that. I want to get a few dressmaking clients. Billy's Aunt Helen has a few friends that might hire me. You'll meet her tomorrow at dinner. What're you reading?"

"A wee book of the songs and poems of Robbie Burns. I love tae read it."

"Did you study Burns at school?"

"Aye, but we both, Tess and me, left school tae get jobs. Mum and Daddie needed our help during the war. Our brother,

George, was killed and we've taken in Geordie. I suppose ye found that out the hard way when ye came in. He's such a lively wee lad.

I loved school. I wanted tae stay. But, our Daddie said tha' lassies, in his family, canna stay at school past the required age. Mum tried tae convince Daddie I should stay. But, he didna change his mind."

"I know how you feel. I planned to go to university in Edinburgh, but. . . the baby . . . . Anyway, I had to give that up."

"Tha's too bad, Fiona. Ye'll ha' the wee bairn tae keep ye busy, won't ye?"

"Well . . . that's a long story. It'll keep for another time when . . . "

Billy interjected. "What's so serious over here, you two young lasses?"

"Books. Reading. Taylor's a serious reader like me. Taylor, I'll lend you a few books, if you like. I'll bring them tomorrow."

Taylor smiled and nodded, while Billy reached out and took Fiona's hands to help her to her feet.

"That's a fine idea, Fiona. Now, let's go into the kitchen. The rest of the family wants to meet you. Happy Christmas, Taylor."

As they walked toward the kitchen, the noise grew louder. Fiona had never seen so many folk packed into one room. Some played instruments, some sat, some stood, and all of them sang. From the adjacent room, Jeannie Murray pounded away on the piano in accompaniment. Fiona and Billy squeezed in, while everyone was finishing the final chorus of Harry Lauder's *Wee Deoch an Doris*. They joined in, grateful that these warm, lively people made them feel right at home.

10 ... A proposal

After Christmas Eve dinner with the Murray clan, Billy took Fiona back to Helen's. While they rode along on the tram, he filled her in on the state of his trade and how it could affect them in the coming year.

He started by telling her he was relieved to be employed. Thanks be to God that he lived through the war and would soon have his Journeyman's ticket. His trade would be needed as long as the Clydebank factories and shipbuilders had enough business. Many returning soldiers haven't been so fortunate. They're out of work and scrambling to find places to rent when they come to Glasgow. Many men do find work at Clydebank, where they labor for long hours, before taking the train back into Glasgow. There, they consider themselves fortunate to rent very expensive, terribly rundown flats. Opportunistic landlords and employers were ignoring workers' requests. No amount of complaining to the government, for better living or working conditions, has helped. Billy's tone of voice became ominous as he continued to speak about the difficult post-war working conditions.

"There's trouble coming, Fiona. You and Helen be careful when you're out. Don't get in anybody's way. Don't draw attention to yourselves. D' you get my meaning, lass"?

"Aye, Billy, I do."

They got off the tram and walked toward Helen's house. Fiona carried on their conversation about conditions for returning soldiers.

"It's terrible. Men who fought for the country work long hours, for little pay, if they find work at all! It's just as bad that they go back to empty, overpriced flats, alone. The only good thing about the situation is that working men can send a little money back home, for their wives and children."

"True, but, the situation is dire, Fiona. Many folk are getting desperate. You never know when their frustration will get the best of them."

"I'll be careful, Billy."

He took her arm as they climbed the steps to Helen's front door. He leaned down to kiss her on the lips, lingering a bit longer than he usually did. It was difficult for him to contain himself, when he loved her so much.

She responded to his kiss, overwhelmed by her love for this kind and decent man. In spite of the growing child of another man in her belly, Fiona was actually grateful for her circumstances just now. What more could anyone in her position expect? Here, with Billy, she felt very lucky.

"Goodnight, my dear laddie. Happy Christmas. I'll see you tomorrow at 3:00 when we all go back to the Murray's for supper. What's this . . . ?"

"A small gift to remind you how much I love ye, lass. Open it now, if you wish."

"If I wish? Of course I wish!"

Excited, Fiona took the small, square box from his hand. She was shaking with excitement. She untied the pretty ribbon and lifted the lid. She was shocked at the beauty of the ring inside the box. It was a brilliant blue, rectangular shaped, sapphire stone, with a border of tiny diamonds all around it, set into a white gold band. It was the most dazzling blue stone she had ever seen.

"Billy! Where? How? Oh, my God, what IS this, Mr. McGinnis?"

"Well, Miss Gilman, it's from my mum. She's been saving it for when we became officially engaged. I love you, Fiona. Will you have me, my bonny lass? Will you marry me?"

"Yes, yes, yes!"

Fiona threw her arms around his neck. As she did so, the box dropped on the step and they both scrambled to get it, laughing at the same time.

"So that's what ye really think of my offer, Miss Gilman."

He retrieved the ring and carefully placed it on her finger. Fiona laughed at his gentle sarcasm and rewrapped her arms about him, her love for Billy causing her eyes to fill with tears.

"You said your mum gave you this ring. It's not hers, is it? I've never seen her wear it."

"It was my grandmother's ring. Aunt Helen will recognize it. It was left to my mum when their mother died. She wanted to give it to us all along, as soon as I got home. But, when we left Marysburgh in such a hurry, after the gossip began, she was so upset she forgot about it. She sent it to me with a friend who was coming to Glasgow. I got it only last night, just in time to give it to you today, my sweet Fiona."

"Thank you, Billy. I'm thrilled to accept this engagement ring. I'll wear it proudly. It's reassuring to know you still love me . . . want me to be your wife . . . after Jeremy. I love you, Billy."

She turned her face up to his and kissed him tenderly on the lips.

"I'm a lucky man to have you. Now, you'd best get inside. It's cold out here. The light's still on in the library. Show your ring to Helen. She already knows how much I love you."

After a final, long kiss, Billy waited while she unlocked the door, waving high with her left hand facing him, so that the ring would reflect the light from the porch. She blew him a kiss as she closed the door.

Fiona went to bed exhausted, but exhilarated after displaying her fabulous ring for Helen and accepting her congratulations. She was overcome with gratitude to God, who must, she thought, have a special purpose for her. Otherwise, why would she deserve a man like Billy to take care of her?

She resolved to call her Mum and Daddie at the store in Marysburgh with the news of her engagement to Billy, at last. They wouldn't publish their engagement, according to the forms of the Established Church of Scotland, until a date was set. But, Fiona knew her parents would be overjoyed at the news of their promise to each other. Finally, she drifted off to sleep, satisfied that this was the best Christmas Eve of her life. Well, other than having Jeremy's baby growing inside her. But, that would end and she would still have Billy.

On Christmas day, a telegram of congratulations arrived from Fiona's parents. Billy had telephoned them at the store, finalizing their consent. They were very pleased for both young people. In fact, everyone close to Fiona, with the exception of her sister, Brigit, had been waiting politely and hoping that Billy would be able to reconcile Fiona's pregnancy by Jeremy MacAndrews, with his long-standing intention to ask Fiona to be his wife. Their closest friends and relatives were relieved at the news of their official engagement.

What Kathleen and Ian didn't tell Billy and would never tell Fiona is the reaction by the Minister, members of their Kirk, and many townspeople, to the rumours of Fiona's pregnancy. Dirty looks, noses in the air as people passed them on the way in and out of church, and cold, curt tones of voice, replaced friendly, neighbourly banter. These changes came from people who had formerly called themselves friends of the Gilmans.

The worst reaction came when a group of long-standing members of the Kirk signed a petition to have Ian removed, from his position as Church Officer. But, the Minister must have finally consulted his Bible, or God directly, about such treatment of a man who'd been a pillar of the Kirk all of his adult life. He refused the request and admonished the requestors, telling them to act like good Christians, to forgive, rather than to incriminate their fellow believers. Fiona's parents were determined she'd never learn of these unpleasant circumstances that followed her exit from Marysburgh.

Back in Glasgow, Christmas dinner at the Murray house was a joyful experience. Everyone admired Fiona's ring and wished the couple well. Helen, too, enjoyed herself immensely. She wasn't accustomed to the noise level of the chaotic environment, in which everyone ate, drank, talked, and sang, and in which new people were readily accepted. Her experience was one of quiet, formal Christmas dinners at home with Robert and a few close friends.

When Helen was introduced to Geordie, she bent down and told him she was honored to meet him, for he had the same last name as the Duke of Athol. He was duly impressed, smiling and standing straighter. They formed an instant connection. Helen was more than ready to mother a child. She enjoyed getting to know this little boy.

At the end of the evening, Helen told Fiona and Billy it was the most enjoyable Christmas she could remember, since Robert's death. She hadn't realized just how lonely she'd been, until she met Fiona and this wonderful Murray clan. Surely, she thought, 1919 would be the best year of their lives.

11 ... Caught in a riot

Five weeks later, Billy was hard at work, learning as much as he could, as fast as he could, about steam engineering. Jack's business involved making and installing parts for steam engines used by shipbuilders in Clydebank and other, regional shipbuilding companies. He rented a workshop in Glasgow, but most of the work was done at Clydebank. On Friday, January 31, Billy and Jack travelled to Clydebank on an early morning train.

That same day, in Glasgow, Helen and Fiona had an appointment to meet with a new dressmaking client for Fiona. They'd meet at her home, where she'd select a fabric from the swatches Fiona carried with her. After taking a few measurements, Fiona and Helen would go to a shop on Sauchiehall Street to purchase the fabric, on their way home.

The client lived just past George Square, an area that the two women had been to before. They took the tram down Argyle Street and enjoyed the walk over to George Square. Normally, the square was quiet and empty in the early morning. But, this day it was unusually crowded.

Fiona and Helen noticed several groups of men, standing around talking, while many others streamed into the Square. They could hear raised male voices from another part of the square. They hurried across the square to the client's street and went about their business quickly. By the time they got back to George Square, they were met by a wall of angry men, shouting loudly. Some men held up signs that protested working conditions.

The two women were alarmed by the noise, the pushing, the shoving, and the sound of bottles flying through the air, like flying weapons. In the distance, they could see City of Glasgow policemen, batons in hand, attempting to control the crowd, beating unruly men with their truncheons. The two women hurried through the square. They heard the roar of the crowd when someone attempted to read The Riot Act, but was quickly cut off. Suddenly, somebody pushed into Fiona. She was hurled forward onto the cobblestone surface of the square.

Alarmed, Helen shouted over the noise around them,

"Oh no! Fiona! Are you hurt?"

Fiona was a bit dazed, unsure of what had happened. She knew only that she was lifted up immediately from behind, under both arms, and hoisted to her feet. Helen stood in front of her staring, with a look of horror on her face. She waited for Fiona to speak. Instead, a young man shouted.

"Are ye alright, Miss? Are ye hurt?"

"I don't think so. What happened?"

Fiona could hardly be heard over the growing racket in the street. The young man gestured that this was no place for the two women today. He helped them to the edge of the square, holding onto Fiona's arm.

"Thank you, I can take her from here."

Fiona's rescuer nodded and then disappeared back into the crowd. Fiona and Helen walked slowly away toward the tram on Argyle Street. The tram stop at George Square was blocked with rioters and police. Helen supported Fiona as they went.

Fiona was shaken; she became more distressed as they walked. Both women were concerned about the safety of the baby, as well as their own. It was an odd moment, when Fiona realized that she felt very protective of this child within her. She hadn't changed her mind about keeping the baby. It was still Jeremy MacAndrews' offspring, after all. But, she knew just how important the baby was to Helen's happiness and she wanted to deliver it safely to her. Only then, would she and Billy be able to start their life together.

When they arrived home, Helen insisted on contacting the Women's Hospital to arrange for Fiona to be checked over. She thought Fiona's fall might have done harm to her, or the baby, or both. Fiona, too, thought it best to be cautious, although she felt better once they got home.

Out at Clydebank, Billy and Jack, working in separate areas, heard about the riot in George Square. A few men came to relieve the very few workers who'd shown up for work at Clydebank. Jack wasn't completely surprised. The tension had been building for weeks. He was greatly concerned that his business would fall into hard times if such political unrest continued. It would likely bring military reprisals and more work stoppages.

For his part, Billy was all the more appreciative of his apprenticeship and his reasonable accommodation at Jack's home. He could handle the long working hours. He was young. But, he'd be glad to finish his training at the end of June. Once he got his Journeyman's Ticket, he and Fiona would marry and establish their own home, somewhere that conditions were more favourable.

In the midst of hearing about the riot in George Square, Billy remembered Fiona's mentioning that she had a meeting with a new dressmaking client this very morning. Worse yet, he realized she and Helen would have crossed through George Square, to get to the client's home. Horrified, he hurried across the huge plant and found Jack. He'd leave on the next train back into Glasgow, to make sure Fiona and Helen were safe.

Once he was on the train, Billy realized he was also concerned for the safety of the baby. It wasn't that he had any feelings for the babe, exactly, but he knew how important this wee person was to Helen. He owed her for taking such good care of Fiona.

He admitted to himself, too, that the babe was Fiona's flesh and blood, wanted or not, and for that reason too, he wished no harm to the wee soul.

By the time Billy raced up the steps at Helen's home, and banged on the door, Fiona had already been checked out at the hospital. Helen opened the door.

"Billy. What're you doing here? What . . . ."

"Where's Fiona? Are you two alright? Were you in George Square? Were you there today?"

Helen remained calm as she invited Billy into the house. She led him to the library, where Fiona was having tea, sitting in her reading chair. She'd found several leather-bound first editions of Jane Austen's novels on Helen's book shelves. Reading this particular author, today, calmed her and provided a pleasant distraction from her frightening experience in George Square. She was wrapped up warmly in a blanket with her feet up on a stool.

"Fiona, are you hurt? Something happened, didn't it?"

"Yes, Billy, but I'm fine and so is the baby. We were caught in George Square when the pushing and shoving escalated. I was knocked down, but nothing's broken. I've a few scrapes on my hands, where I tried to break my fall and a small cut on one knee. The doctor said I was lucky I wasn't trampled. Many others were. They flooded into the hospital while I was there. I'm sorry you were worried."

"You went to hospital?"

"Yes, but we're fine."

"Are you sure?"

"Yes, I'm sure!"

He left the doorway, where he'd been standing while he interrogated her. He walked over to Fiona's chair, sat on the overstuffed arm, and took her hand. He couldn't take it if something happened to her. He just couldn't. Helen brought in more tea, but Billy had a better idea.

"I'd prefer a wee drop of whiskey, if ye don't mind, Helen."

The two women smiled at that remark, taking a bit of tension out of the room. The three of them enjoyed a fine supper together that evening, an unusual treat for a week day. Billy asked Fiona if she'd like to get out of Glasgow and take a short train ride to the Singer Manufacturing plant, as soon as she felt better.

"Yes! I would! The doctor told me not to walk around too much this week end. After that, I should be fine. I'd love to see the plant. They'll have the latest models in the show room. But, Billy, can you get time off work, with rioting going on?"

"I'll work the weekend and some extra hours on Monday. Jack owes me. He said so when I worked today, instead of going to George Square, like so many other lads. So, it's settled. I'll pick you up at ten on Tuesday morning. There's no need to get up too early."

By Tuesday, Fiona was feeling back to normal. She didn't seem to have any ill effects from her fall during the riot. She enjoyed the train ride, as always. When they arrived at the Singer plant, she and Billy took the short tour. They were amazed by the high level of productivity in the factory and by some of the new advances on the latest machines. They ate their lunch, lovingly packed and sent along with Billy, by Jeannie Murray, along with her best wishes for Fiona. Later in the afternoon, they boarded the train back to Glasgow, enjoying their time together as they held hands on the train. Neither of them could know that it would be their last day together.

12 ... Tragedy

A cold, early February wind rushed into the vestibule as Helen opened the door a crack. She was surprised to see Jack Murray standing on her doorstep.

"Jack, what are you doing here at this hour? Is Billy with you? Come in. It's freezing outside."

Helen pulled her robe closer around her slim body as she showed Jack in. He was alone. She closed the door and led Jack into the library.

Where the devil was Violet? She must be out the back getting wood for the fireplace.

"Sit down, Jack, you look terrible. Fiona's still asleep. She went to bed happily weary, from her outing to Clydebank yesterday with Billy."

Jack looked anxious. He hadn't spoken yet, causing Helen to become anxious too. "I'll fetch us some tea."

When Helen returned with the tea, she seated herself across from Jack, waiting for him to speak.

"Helen, there ha' been a terrible accident. I am very sorry tae tell ye, that Billy is dead."

Helen's face drained of all color. She felt sick to her stomach.

"What? I beg your pardon? He survived the Great War. He escaped from Europe without getting the Spanish Flu there, or here. He can't be dead! There must be some mistake. He's my only nephew, my sister's only child, and Fiona's beloved fiancé. This simply can't be true! How do you know this?"

"It was an accident, 'tis my fault. After he brought Fiona home yesterday, I asked him tae go back tae Clydebank for the late shift. We're behind, ye see. So many workers staged tha' protest in George Square. They didna come to work. Billy offered tae help us catch up.

The police inspector said Billy climbed atop a large piece of machinery, to make an adjustment. The lad who usually does this wasna at work. They think Billy must ha' lost his balance, likely because the leg he injured in the war buckled and couldna hold him. He fell, smashing his head on the concrete floor below. It was all over in an instant. He didna suffer long, only a fraction of a second as he fell. They didna find him until the shift break, in the middle of the night, when a worker came tae collect him for tea. Auch, Helen, I'm so sorry. It's a tragedy for your family and for Fiona too."

Helen was in shock. She couldn't speak. They both sat there, listening to the Westminster clock, ticking away on the mantle. Action was impossible for Helen. Jack had to do something. He got up and poured the tea. As he handed the cup to Helen, they heard footsteps on the stairs. Fiona. She would need Jack's strength now, the feel of a strong man's arms about her, someone to hold her the way that Billy would have held her.

"Helen, Fiona's comin' doon the stairs. We'll need tae tell her. Do you want me tae do tha'?"

Tears streamed down Helen's face. All she could do was nod.

Well rested and energetic, Fiona saw Jack first, as she walked into the library.

"Jack! What are you doing here so early? Where's Billy?"

The look on Jack's face registered, alarming Fiona. She glanced at Helen, who was now weeping openly.

"Oh God! Tell me, somebody tell me! Where's . . ."

She began to sway. Jack leaped up to steady her.

"Sit ye doon, lassie, here, beside me on the sofa."

He led her to the seat and carefully sat down beside her. He took a deep breath and told her the awful truth.

"Billy's gone, Fiona. 'Twas an accident at Clydebank. The police say his injured leg must have buckled. He fell from a piece of machinery onto the concrete floor. He didna suffer. He died instantly, helpin' others, doin' his job, makin' up for others who hadna done theirs."

Jack paused, to let his words sink in. Fiona was stunned, staring straight ahead. When she didn't speak, Jack continued.

"He was a happy man, Fiona, deeply in love wi' ye. He was very excited about your plans tae marry. He spoke of nothin' but you, at supper last night. Nobody could get a word in edgewise. Imagine tha' in our household! He couldna stop talkin' aboot ye and how much he loves ye."

Jack put his arm around Fiona. She allowed her head to drop onto his shoulder as the shock settled over her. She began to weep quietly but was very soon shaking. Jack held her, while she got the first of her many tears shed. Her mind was racing. All she could think of was how Billy must have felt as he fell.

Did he know he'd die? Did he have hope that something would cushion his fall? Was he mad at himself for losing his balance, or for climbing up on top of the machinery in the first place? He knew his leg might not be strong enough, didn't he? How could he do that? Had the war taught him to be overly brave, to the point of being reckless?

Oh, Billy! I'll never see you looking at me with love in your eyes, you'll never hold me again, and we'll never have the children we talked about. There won't be a wedding. I'm alone.

Just then, the baby kicked, jerking Fiona back into her reality.

I'm not alone. No, it's worse than that. I'm saddled with Jeremy MacAndrews' baby, an intrusive presence within me. I need to think about Billy. The greatest love of my life has died, leaving me without his tender touch, his gentle kisses, and the promise of our future together. I need to grieve for Billy. I don't need to be reminded of my rape and this unwanted child, at a time like this. How could God have visited such horrible things on me? I'm a good person, not a criminal, not vicious, not thoughtless. Billy was a gentle man, one of the decent people, honorable, responsible, always determined to do the right thing. Why did this happen to us?

"Fiona . . . Fiona."

Helen spoke softly, as she touched Fiona's shoulder, having regained her own composure for the moment.

"Say goodbye to Jack and let's go upstairs. You'll need rest."

Fiona turned to Jack as he got up.

"Where is he? Where's my Billy? I need to see him."

"Nae, Lassie, ye canna see him yet. The police are involved and they must wait for the medical examiner. I will let ye both know when ye can see him. Now, I'll help ye up the stairs before I go."

That afternoon, Fiona called her parents. Helen said they had telephoned while she was asleep, having heard the terrible news from Billy's parents.

"Hello, Daddie. It's Fiona."

She could hear her father say, "Kathleen, Fiona's on the phone."

"My sweet lass, we're so sorry tae hear about our Billy. We all loved him; he was a fine young man. This is tragic, for us all, but especially for you, Fiona. How're ye gettin' along, my gel?"

"I think I'm still in shock, Daddie. I can't believe I won't see him again. I don't know what I'll do."

Fiona could hear her Mum's voice, insisting on having the phone.

"Fiona, darlin' you'll come home, that's what you'll do. You'll be needin' your own family to help you through this awful time."

"Mum, I know you and Daddie love me and support me. But, I'm going to stay with Helen for the time being. Jack Murray said the medical examiner is involved. They don't know when Billy's body will be released. His parents will be notified when that happens. I'll be able to see him here, in Glasgow.

I won't be coming to Marysburgh for Billy's funeral anyway. I'm showing well beyond any doubt now. My presence there would stir up the gossip again. That would just make the situation worse for all of us. I know this isn't what you want to hear, and it's probably shocking to you. But, I can assure you that Aunt Helen, who was very close to Billy, will help me get through this . . . this awful time."

Disappointed, Kathleen wished her daughter well. How she'd love to take Fiona into her arms and hold her. But, she admired Fiona's courage, in the face of her awful misfortunes. She was impressed that Fiona was strong enough to make up her mind and stick to it. In fact, in the face of adversity, this daughter of hers seemed to get stronger. Everyone didn't have her courage or her strength of character. She'd need it.

13 ... Forensics and a funeral

The comfort of communal grieving, at the funeral of their loved one, was not to be for some time, for the McGinnis and Gilman families. Billy's death had occurred at work, apparently without a witness. The police consulted John Glaister, who was the Chair of Forensic Medicine and Public Health at the University of Glasgow. There would be an autopsy and an investigation into Billy's death. There were suspicions that perhaps Billy's fellow workers, the George Square rioters, who'd refused to work their shift at the shipyard the night Billy died, might be connected, in some way, to his death. As well, the shipbuilding company wanted to be absolved of any blame for the accident, either directly or indirectly.

While the investigation continued, Billy's body remained in Glasgow. Once the autopsy was completed, Fiona, Helen, and Billy's parents were allowed to view his body. Helen held onto Fiona's arm, while William McGinnis supported Meg. They watched as the sheet was lifted away from Billy's face.

Fiona saw immediately that someone had carefully combed Billy's blond, wavy hair. His face was as white as the sheet that covered him. Beside her, Meg wept and she could see William's hands shaking. Fiona's eyes filled with tears. She turned away, grateful for Helen's support as they left the room. This was the last time Fiona would see Billy's face. But, she'd carry her memories and her love for him for the rest of her life. She was sure she'd never be able to love anyone else, as much as she loved Billy.

Dr. Glaister concluded that Billy's blood contained no lethal toxins. He hadn't been drinking alcohol and he had no injuries other than those that could be explained by the fall. The police investigation into the company's procedures, and interviews with the few workers who were on shift that night left no alternative, but to declare Billy's death an unfortunate accident. With nobody to blame for her loss, Fiona was forced to accept that Billy was simply not meant to be with her. She'd have to learn to let him go and try to get on with her life.

Billy's funeral was held in Marysburgh several weeks after his death. Fiona looked after Geordie Murray, while Helen and the Murrays travelled to Marysburgh. William McGinnis had asked Jack if he'd be one of the speakers at the wake. He could tell everyone about the last few months of Billy's life in Glasgow. Jack was honored to oblige. The Murrays gladly accepted a room above the pub. Helen stayed with Billy's parents. She'd try to comfort her sister, Meg, and her brother-in-law, William, as best she could.

Helen insisted on buying train tickets for the Murrays. It was the least she could do for their kindness to Billy and to Fiona, who would give birth to Helen's child. Jack protested, but he took the tickets in the end.

When Helen returned to Glasgow, after the funeral and the lively wake, at *The McGinnis Drinking Establishment*, she shared her experiences with Fiona, as soon as Jack and Jeannie left with Geordie.

"How did you get on with Geordie, Fiona?"

"He's a lively, endearing child. But, it's a relief to send him home with his grandparents. He kept my mind off Billy, at least some of the time, with his non-stop chattering. Violet kept him amused while I rested in the afternoons. So, that's enough about Geordie, Helen. I'm ready to hear about my dear Billy's funeral."

"First, Fiona, anyone who asked about your absence was told you're overcome with grief, at the sudden death of your fiancé. The distress caused by the investigation into his death has made you ill. I put off anyone who pressed me for more information, by adding that you'd developed a small dressmaking business which was helping you to stay occupied and sane, in the aftermath of Billy's death. Even the most suspicious of the nosy gossips agreed that it was important for you to retain your clients. You'd be needing an income to support yourself, now that you won't be married.

Ah, Fiona, the funeral was very moving. Billy would have been touched by the heartfelt reaction to the life he lived and the kind of person he was. Meg and William know everyone in town, of course. The Kirk was filled to overflowing with neighbors, classmates from school, some of whom were in their naval uniforms, and Billy's army mates from the war. William stood as soon as the soldiers began to enter the church, causing everyone to rise.

There were many soldiers, Fiona. So many are grievously injured. Some, missing legs, came into the Kirk in wheelchairs, or on crutches. Some limped, leaning on canes. Others had pinned up the empty arms of their uniforms. Some are burned; we could see shreds of fine hair straggling down from under their caps. Some are blind, having been caught in the mustard gas attacks.

God. It was overwhelming . . . so touching to see these brave men, all honouring Billy. They stood at attention when the piper led in the flag-draped casket, carried by six townspeople, including your father. The soldiers saluted, or did the best they could, to honor their fallen comrade. His unit mates wept openly as they stood there."

Fiona took in Helen's words silently, her eyes filling with tears as she listened. She was grateful to hear how much Billy's fellow soldiers respected and loved him. When he came home from the war, he wasn't willing to talk about his wartime experiences with her. The emotions of these men were a testament to the special bond they had with Billy. It seems that nobody, except those who were there, would ever be able to understand what the war was like.

"I don't think I can hear any more about the service just now, Helen. It's simply too sad. Tell me about the wake."

They talked for another hour about Jack's speech and the funny stories many people told about Billy. Helen said his primary school teacher gave a talk, remembering how special Billy was and how other children followed him even then. He'd protected the younger children from older bullies. This comment reminded Fiona that Billy had been her protector too. Now he was gone.

Fiona went to bed that night somewhat relieved the funeral was over. Billy was at rest in the graveyard of their familiar Kirk. She'd visit his grave as soon as this baby was born and given away to Helen.

Helen hadn't told Fiona everything. She withheld from her the most disturbing event at the funeral. She didn't want to upset Fiona by describing the appearance of Jeremy MacAndrews and his father, Laird MacAndrews. That news could wait until tomorrow.

Fiona awoke, already crying. She'd been dreaming of Billy as he was when they were children at school. She'd loved him for a very long time. In the dream, many happy scenes seemed real. She saw their first kiss, saying goodbye each time he took the train away from home to go back to war, arriving home at the station, proposing to her on Helen's front porch, and their final day together at Clydebank, a happy day, when both of them were full of hopes and plans for their future together.

But, the last image in Fiona's dream was Billy's white face as he lay, lifeless, in the morgue. As much as she hadn't wanted to see him that way, she'd taken the advice of her mum, Kathleen, who'd told her it was important to see a loved one's body, to confirm, in your mind, that the person was really dead. She'd told Fiona the mind can play tricks on a grieving person, one who's only too willing to rationalize away the reality of death and pretend that the death must have been a dream.

Mum was right. I can't pretend Billy is alive. It really was Billy's face on that body in the morgue. It's a devastating reality.

As she got up, washed, and dressed, Fiona realized that she wouldn't feel any better about Billy until she had the baby and went back home to visit his grave. She needed to see his final resting place, to say goodbye, to tell him how much she missed him. But, for the next few months, she'd just have to wait.

"Good morning, Helen."

"Good morning, Fiona dear. How did you sleep?"

Fiona told Helen about her dreams and her decision to go back to Marysburgh, to visit Billy's grave, as soon as the baby was born. After breakfast, they took their tea in the library, where Fiona could sit with her feet up, in her favorite chair. Helen waited until Fiona was comfortable and then began to relate the rest of the news from Billy's funeral.

"Fiona, something happened after Billy's funeral that you'll need to know about from me, before anyone else brings it up."

Fiona looked at her, apprehension showing on her face.

"Is it bad . . . more bad news? How could anything be worse than Billy being dead? I don't think I can bear anything else. Are my parents OK?"

"Yes, Fiona. Your parents are fine. Let me get this out and then we can decide what, if anything, we need to do. The funeral was ending. Everyone stood, as the casket was carried out of the church, followed by those of us in the first few rows. As we neared the back of the church, we saw Laird MacAndrews. Beside him, stood Jeremy MacAndrews. The Laird had a firm grip on his son's arm. Jeremy looked very uncomfortable and his father looked very determined. We proceeded to the graveside. We didn't see the MacAndrews men again, until everyone began to leave the graveyard.

I was standing near the grave, with your parents. Your father caught sight of the MacAndrews pair. He turned, and addressed the Laird, asking if he might speak to his son. MacAndrews nodded. He released Jeremy's arm, as he turned away to express his condolences to Meg and William. I overheard the conversation between your father and Jeremy.

'Why are ye here? Billy wasna any friend of yours. Ye're barely eighteen, still a boy, even if ye did go up tae University early. He was a man. We buried a man here today, a man who fought for his country, a man who was tae be my son-in-law. His is a great loss for many people. Wha' did he have tae do with the likes of you'?

Jeremy had a smirk on his face.

'Nothing,' he said. 'My father made me come. He forced me to leave my mates in Edinburgh, to make an appearance. He said it was high time I took on the job of the Laird's son. Now, I've missed two football practices and two nights at the pub. By the way, how's your daughter? I thought she'd be here, grieving with the rest of the townspeople. I was looking forward to seeing her.'

Jeremy didn't see the punch coming. Ian's fist landed on his jawbone, narrowly missing the spot under his chin that would have knocked him out. It knocked him down instead. Jeremy looked surprised, but he started to laugh as he got up, rubbing his jaw. 'Old man,' he said to Ian, 'you sure have a temper, don't you? All I did was to ask how your daughter was.'

By this time, Laird MacAndrews had stepped over. He spoke to Ian in a chilly tone of voice. 'Mr. Gilman, I'll forgive you this one time, for laying a hand on my son. I know that Billy was to marry your daughter. You must be grieving for her loss and the loss of his parents. But, you'll never again lay a hand on my son, do you hear me? I'll have you arrested and thrown in gaol.' He turned and said to his son, 'Jeremy, we'll be going now.' He grabbed Jeremy's arm and led him away. Jeremy was still smirking."

"Oh no, Helen, I feared that sooner or later my father's anger toward Jeremy was bound to get the best of him."

"You were right. Your father must be very frustrated that he couldn't protect you from Jeremy, or from Billy's dying. He seems to have gone a bit daft."

"I agree. He's been very angry at Jeremy since I told him and my mum about the rape. Normally, he would have ignored Jeremy and kept himself under control. I can't believe he picked a fight with him. He knows better than to anger the Laird. MacAndrews knows my father is one of his best tenants, the tenant who always produces a high profit. We can only hope he'll not pursue this issue. Surely, he knows what Jeremy is like."

"We all got a look at what Jeremy's like, Fiona. He obviously doesn't think he does anything wrong, ever."

"It's worse than that, Helen. William and my father caught Jeremy stealing, many times, as a young boy. Laird MacAndrews was always in London, and it did no good to report Jeremy's stealing to the housekeeper who looked after him. She seemed hardly able to cope with him as it was. Twice, when they notified the Laird about his son's stealing, Jeremy left mutilated, dead birds on the steps of the pub and the store. They knew then, that nobody could control Jeremy. My father must really be in really bad shape or he wouldn't have provoked him."

"Fiona, there's one more thing I must tell you. As the two MacAndrews walked away from the graveyard, Jeremy turned and shouted out, to your father, 'Tell your daughter I'll see her in Glasgow.'"

"What? He threatened to come here? He knows I'm here, at your place? How . . ."

"Fiona, his father sits in the House of Lords. They have access to any information they care to get, about anyone. While it seems that Edward MacAndrews knows his son is not a model child, he doesn't appear to have given up on him. The town gossips know you and Billy went to Glasgow. It would have been easy from there, to find out where you are. MacAndrews would have no reason to suspect Jeremy of raping you. He probably wouldn't believe it anyway, if he had heard the rumors. You'll need to be cautious, that's all. You're not going too far from home just now anyway. And I'll be with you whenever you go to one of your client's homes."

Fiona's mind was churning. Of course, he could find her. Normally, she'd have known this, but the emotions of the past few weeks had shaken her. She'd need to be careful, very careful. This is just what she didn't need, something else to worry about, to go with her fears about a life without Billy, about what she would do for money, about where she would live, and about who would love her now that he was gone.

The only news of Jeremy came from her mum, who wrote that after the funeral he went back to Edinburgh for the rest of the university year. They hadn't heard anything from him or his father. His comment about seeing Fiona in Glasgow was probably just his way of getting back at Ian, for punching him. Following Kathleen's report, both Fiona and Helen relaxed, relieved that they could resume their routine at Helen's home in Glasgow, while they waited for the birth of the baby.

14 ... Stalked

A few days after describing the turmoil surrounding Billy's funeral, Helen surprised Fiona with a new, "Singer 66" sewing machine, an early 21st birthday present.

"I know your birthday isn't until April, Fiona dear. But, I wanted you to have the new machine to use now. Soon, you'll become too swollen with the child to sew comfortably."

"Thank you! I love it! Actually, next to my Gladstone Kit bag, this is the best present I've ever had! I'm touched, too, by your thoughtfulness. I'll wager you didn't count on me being so much trouble, when you agreed to take me in. I hope you know how grateful I am, for everything. You're a dear friend, Helen."

The new, improved features of this machine would really help Fiona with her fledgling business. She'd be able to produce garments faster, leaving her more time for designing new fashions. Her clients were very pleased with her work. They paid her well for her original designs and continued to order more. She could easily add to her clientele after the baby was born, if she stayed in Glasgow. But, she wouldn't think about that until she had to, one thing at a time. For now, designing and sewing garments distracted her from her constant grief and her thoughts of Billy.

Late March arrived with milder spring weather. Between rainy spells, Fiona managed to get in a walk each day. She enjoyed the West End, taking many strolls on upper Argyle Street, and then along Kelvin Way and into the adjacent park. When the weather was unsettled, she walked through the *Palace of Fine Arts*, an elegant, red sandstone building that displayed equally elegant sculpture, inside and out. Back in Marysburgh, she'd read about its opening in 1901, for the Glasgow International Exhibition. She enjoyed seeing sites such as this elegant building in Glasgow, sites she'd only read about. An added bonus was that the *Palace* faced the park, providing her a convenient escape from sudden downpours.

Over the course of the spring months, Fiona chatted with other young women who were expecting babies or had just delivered them. She'd borrowed Aunt Helen's wedding ring to wear with her sapphire engagement ring, so that the young wives would assume she was married. She felt a bit guilty for her deception but she wasn't up to explaining the complexities of her life to people she knew casually. Eventually, she'd offer to return her ring to Billy's mum, but she couldn't bear to part with it just yet. Some days, she pretended to herself that he was at work, or still away fighting the war. It was easier than facing the truth.

Shortly before Easter, she headed out to the park, happy to enjoy the sunshine and the continuing fine weather. When she arrived at the park, she didn't see any of the young wives. She strolled along toward the area bordering Kelvin Way, where impressive statues of both Kelvin and Lister shared an open space, along with several benches. She sat down to enjoy the view: the red sandstone spires of the *Palace* were visible on her right, through the newly budding trees. A complimentary view of the Kelvin Hall spire rose on her left, in front of the University of Glasgow campus. She relaxed and closed her eyes. She could smell the freshly raked grass and the newly overturned soil where spring bulbs had been planted. She listened to the birdsong from the trees in the huge wooded area behind her bench.

"Hello, pretty Fiona. Don't you look fine."

Startled and terribly afraid that she knew this male voice, Fiona opened her eyes, turned to look behind her, and scanned the woods. She didn't see anyone. As she peered into the dark forest, she concluded that she must have dozed off and had a bad dream. She was about to turn back around and relax, when Jeremy MacAndrews stepped out from behind a large tree and strolled casually toward her.

She froze to the bench, unable to move. But, her fear and the adrenalin surging through her body helped her to stand upright and find her voice.

"Get away from me, you bastard."

He smirked and moved closer to her.

"No, you're the one who's got the bastard. God, you look disgusting, swollen up like a big blimp. I'll wait until you've dumped the kid before we resume our beautiful relationship."

"That will never happen, you despicable prick. If you come near me again, I'll report you to the police and they can deal with you."

"So, that's the way you want it, is it, Fiona, causing trouble for me, interfering with my life? Already, your idiot father's stunt, at your war hero's funeral, set my father to asking questions. He's harassing me about what happened last summer between you and me. Naturally, I denied any involvement with you, but he won't let it go."

As Jeremy's voice got louder, two young mothers, pushing prams along Kelvin Way, stopped in front of the statues of Kelvin and Lister near Fiona's bench.

"Look, there's Fiona!"

Fiona took advantage of this distraction and hurried toward them, away from Jeremy, as fast as her pregnant body would allow. Jeremy, surprised that his prey was getting away from him, shouted after her as she left.

"I'll be watching you, bitch."

Fiona deflected questions from the young mothers, who asked if the handsome, dark-haired fellow was her husband.

"Oh no, she said, he's just a guy I went to school with back home."

"Well, lass, that's a good thing, for I heard what he said, about watching you. What did he mean? Why would he talk to you like that? You'll sure need to tell your husband that this nasty-sounding lad is bothering you."

Fiona couldn't wait for this conversation to end. She walked with the two women to the corner of Argyle Street, feigned a headache, and hurried back to the safety of Helen's home.

Afraid, and exhausted from walking too fast, she gasped for air as she reached Helen's front door. She let herself into the foyer, pulled the heavy door closed behind her, and gave in to tears of frustration and fear. Helen rushed into the foyer.

"He's here! Jeremy's here in Glasgow! He threatened me . . . threatened me . . . at the park! I was lucky to get away from him. Two women I know came by and called to me. Oh God!"

She lost control of herself completely. Helen guided her into the hall chair before she could collapse onto the floor.

A few minutes later, over a cup of tea in the library, Helen and Fiona discussed advising the police about Jeremy's threats. But, they both knew nothing would be done. They agreed that he is, after all, one of the privileged people, the spoiled son of a wealthy and powerful man, whose word would be taken over hers. Nobody would ever believe her. Too many questions would be asked about her connection to Jeremy. The rape would need to be revealed. The police rarely, if ever, believed a woman, especially when the alleged rapist was heir to a title, a fortune, and estates. While they waited for the baby, Fiona wouldn't be able to go out alone.

For the next month, she constantly looked behind her, when she and Helen were out. She was sure she could feel Jeremy watching her. She had nightmares about his following her home and breaking into the house. Sometimes, Billy was in the dream too, fighting with Jeremy. Many a morning she woke up sweating, and afraid.

When will this be over? Why me? What have I done to deserve this continuing visitation from the sick bastard, the animal that Jeremy is? Why has Billy died and left me here to deal with this terrible situation alone?

These thoughts circulated endlessly in her head. Whenever she managed to forget about Jeremy for a while, the child, his child inside her would kick, or roll over to remind her. The best distraction for her was to design and sew as much as she could.

By early May, her burgeoning belly forced her to give up sewing at her machine. She hadn't seen Jeremy again. He must have gone back to the Glenheather estate after the university term ended. Good riddance to him, she thought. More relaxed now, she spent most of her time reading in the library or walking, with Helen, around the block. All she needed to do now was give birth, give Helen this baby, and get away. Maybe this cursed year would take a turn for the better. That's what she hoped.

Early one evening, while Helen was out, Fiona heard a knock on the door. The housekeeper had left a few minutes earlier to run an errand. Fiona moved her blanket aside, slid her swollen feet into her slippers, and forced herself up from her chair. She walked slowly to the door, but rather than unlock it and open it immediately she asked instead,

"Who is it?"

A deep male voice answered. "I'm here to speak with Miss Fiona Gilman. Is she at home?"

"Who wants to know?"

"I am Edward MacAndrews, Baron of Glenheather. I've come to offer some assistance to Fiona Gilman. May I come in?"

Fiona's heart was pounding—it felt as if it were beating in her throat. She began to hyperventilate and she sat down on the chair in the front hallway, trying to get her head between her knees.

What is he doing here? Why has he come? Is he angry? Is

Jeremy with him, here, on Helen's front doorstep? What could they want?

"Are you still there, Miss Gilman?"

"Aye, I'm still here. Are you alone?"

"I'm alone. I must speak with you, Miss Gilman. Please let me in. I would not harm you."

Against her better judgment, Fiona opened the door slowly, just a small crack. She was surprised to see the drastically-changed appearance of Edward MacAndrews. He'd always been a vigorous man who walked straight up with a confident, in fact, an arrogant air. This man on the porch was bent forward and he'd acquired obvious grey streaks in his jet black, curly hair. He had bags under his eyes as if he hadn't slept.

"Come in, Laird MacAndrews."

Fiona was very self-conscious of her huge belly. It could no longer be camouflaged by maternity smocks. She was humiliated by her appearance, in front of the father of her rapist. Logically, she knew she wasn't to blame for the situation, but she was embarrassed, none the less.

"Thank you, Miss Gilman."

MacAndrews stepped into the hallway, removed his hat, and placed it on the hat rack in the hallway. He nodded politely to Fiona.

"We'll go into the library."

As she walked ahead of MacAndrews into the library, Fiona thought she heard Violet come in the back door. She called out, asking her to bring tea for two into the library. She was relieved when she heard Violet reply. She didn't want to be alone with the father of her rapist. Once the haggard-looking man was seated, he began to speak.

"Forgive me, Miss Gilman. I have come to relate to you some recent events that have befallen my family. First, you should know that my son, Jeremy, was found murdered in Edinburgh yesterday. The police are investigating but they haven't yet determined who murdered him."

Fiona was shocked. She was also relieved. But she felt guilty for that, here, in front of Laird MacAndrews. He was a man who had lost a son, however rotten the son had been. She got hold of her emotions.

"I'm sorry for your pain at the loss of your son, Laird MacAndrews. How does this information concern me?"

"Miss Gilman, the second thing I want to say to you, is how sorry I am for the pain and suffering Jeremy inflicted on you and your family. Last fall, I was away in London until Parliament broke for the Christmas holiday. There were rumors about Jeremy's unforgivable behavior toward you, but when I confronted him, he flatly denied having had any contact with you.

Then, at Billy McGinnis' funeral, when your father struck Jeremy, my suspicions were raised again. I tried to talk to your father later, but he wouldn't discuss you in any way. Again, I questioned Jeremy at length and he continued to deny any connection with you.

I can be a blind man, Miss Gilman, where my only son is concerned. I'm sorry, to say to you, that I believed him. However, yesterday I learned from Jeremy's roommate at the University that he had been bragging to his football team mates, about having sired your child. I was able to determine that, regardless of other reports about Jeremy's attacking young women, I'm satisfied that he hasn't fathered any child but the one you carry now.

Miss Gilman, I admit I made many mistakes with Jeremy. We lost his mother when he was born and then I was away in London much of the time. I didn't visit him at school often enough to fully grasp the flaws in his character. I apologize, on his behalf, for your situation. Will you forgive me, for being a bad father, even though I don't expect you to be able to forgive Jeremy for what he did to you?"

"Laird MacAndrews, I have long since made my peace with the reality of my situation. I have the full support of my family and the family of Billy McGinnis."

"You plan to keep the child, then, Miss Gilman?"

"My plans for the child are private, Laird MacAndrews. What are you getting at? Why do you ask?"

"Miss Gilman, I have no heir. Jeremy, flawed as he was, was my only heir. There are no male relations to inherit my lands and title, to carry on our name. But, your child, Miss Gilman, will be my grandson, my heir, the next Baron of Glenheather. If the child is male, he would inherit everything. I am prepared to adopt him, Miss Gilman, in order for this to happen."

"Adopt him! What do you mean? We have someone already adopting the child, boy or girl. Why would I allow you to take the child?"

Fiona was becoming angry now. Do these MacAndrews people think they can simply take anything they want? I can see how Jeremy got that idea.

At that moment, Violet entered the room, set down a tea tray and then hurried back out through the door.

"Please close the door, Violet."

She would need to lower her voice, if she didn't want Violet to hear every word of this conversation. While they waited for Violet to leave, MacAndrews looked increasingly distraught and seemed to shrink down into his chair. He lowered his head and looked at the floor. He was not accustomed to the kind of shame that Jeremy had caused him with this young woman, and now he had upset her. After Violet left, he raised his head and began to speak.

"Miss Gilman, I'm sorry to have offended you. I should have

said at the outset that I'll provide financial support for a female child or a male child. My duties in the House of Lords keep me away in London much of the time. I wouldn't be able to raise a child alone. With my blessing and financial backing, I'd be very glad for the assistance of the family you've chosen to raise the child. In the case of a granddaughter, I would provide her with a significant dowry and an annual income."

As he went on, his voice became softer. He seemed to deflate, looking more haggard the longer he spoke.

"I know I have not much to recommend me as a good father, or grandfather, given the sorry state of Jeremy's behavior and character by the time he died. I'm responsible for the way he turned out. Perhaps, if I'd paid more attention to him, he might not have lived such a wayward life. I promise you, Miss Gilman, I'll be a far better grandfather to this child, boy or girl, than I was a father to Jeremy. Will you please think about what I've said? I'm not asking you to forgive Jeremy. But, is it possible for you to take into consideration my proposal when you make arrangements for this child?"

By the time MacAndrews finished speaking, Fiona had calmed down somewhat. She responded in a soft voice.

"Aye, Laird MacAndrews, I'll consider what you've said. The baby will be born within the next few weeks. I'll get advice from my family."

"Thank you, Miss Gilman. I can't express how much your willingness to hear my request means to me. As you can see, I'm a beaten man, ashamed of my own son, but mourning all he could have been at the same time. I'm resolved to make up, in any way I can, the damage he caused to others, especially to you. I'll take my leave now and let you get some rest."

He stood up, and held out his hand to assist Fiona to her feet. She wouldn't allow him to assist her, not wanting to feel the touch of any MacAndrews, ever again. He waited while she walked ahead of him into the front hallway. Fiona handed him his hat and opened the door.

He hesitated in the doorway, holding his hat in his hand. She waited for him to leave.

"May I ask if you'll please call me once you've decided on a course of action? Here's my card. I'll advise my staff at the estate and also at my office in London that you are to be put through whenever you call."

"Aye, Laird MacAndrews, I'll call you."

She took his card. He stepped through the doorway, just as Helen came up the steps.

"Madam," said MacAndrews. He nodded to Helen and walked down the steps into the night.

Fiona was emotionally exhausted. She knew she didn't have the emotional resources to relate the evening's events to Helen right this minute.

"Helen, I'll fill you in first thing tomorrow. I'm extremely tired. I must go to bed."

She lumbered toward the staircase and ascended slowly, leaving a flabbergasted Helen behind her at the bottom of the stairs.

15 ... Choices

*F*iona had a restless sleep that night. She wasn't unhappy that she'd never see Jeremy again. But, she had conflicting feelings about his father. She'd always thought of him as cold and unapproachable. But here, tonight, he was a broken man.

How surprising that the MacAndrews' fortune could turn out to be a factor in my decisions about the baby. I had totally dismissed the idea of Jeremy, or anyone else in his family, contributing even one shilling to the upbringing of this child. What will I do now? What about Helen? How will my ultimate decision affect her and her future with this suddenly sought-after child? If only Billy were here to help me with this decision. He'd know what to do.

The next morning was wonderfully warm and sunny. The balmy weather helped Fiona to assume an optimistic mood, as she got up, bathed, and dressed. She put on one of her newest, largest maternity smocks. She'd made this smock to wear in the final stage of her pregnancy, to cheer her up when she'd need it the most. It was deep blue, with tiny white flowers embroidered along the neckline. The color brought out the blue of her eyes and contrasted nicely with her masses of dark, wavy hair. She secretly hoped the baby would have her eyes . . . the eyes of her mother's Irish people. There, she thought, as she finished dressing, this is probably the best I'm going to feel all day.

She started from her thoughts when she heard Helen call to her from outside the bedroom door.

"Are you alright, lass?"

Fiona walked to the door and opened it. Helen looked worried.

"Aye. Sorry I couldn't talk to you last night. You must be curious about that visitor I had. Come on, let's talk, over breakfast."

The two women walked downstairs and into the sun-filled breakfast room where Violet had made their porridge and set the table, before leaving for market. Violet knew from Fiona's angry voice the previous night that the gentleman who called on her had upset her. She gave the women their privacy, in spite of her curiosity. When they were seated, Fiona began, cautiously, to relate her news from the evening before.

"I don't need to tell you, Helen, that the man in your doorway last night was Laird Edward MacAndrews. He came here to tell me his son, Jeremy, was found murdered in an alley in Edinburgh. The police forced the newspapers to hold the story until today, when everyone will learn of it."

"Oh! That's a shock, isn't it? It explains his changed appearance. He looked much older than the last time I saw him . . . not at all like the powerful, arrogant man he was at Billy's funeral."

Helen had a sinking feeling in her stomach. They were discussing the murdered father of the baby who was soon to be hers. She knew there must be something else coming. She steeled herself for Fiona's next words.

"Helen . . . Helen, no matter what else happens, you will raise this baby... be its mother. . . . I promise you that. But, there's complicating news. MacAndrews has no heir. He wants to provide financial support for this baby—boy or girl. If the baby is a boy, he wants to adopt him legally, so he'll inherit the MacAndrews title, fortune and lands."

Helen was shocked. She replied quickly, her voice betraying her anxiety.

"Adopt him? But . . . but, how would that work? How can I be his mother if MacAndrews adopts him? Where would he live? Who would raise him? How would this grandfather, who lives most of the year in London, be able to provide a loving home for this baby?"

"He told me he realizes he can't be there all the time for the child. He agrees that the child would be raised by the family I've chosen. By you, dear Helen. I didn't tell him you'll be the baby's mother. Only that the baby will be adopted."

"Well, at least I'm glad to hear you say that. But, he'll know eventually, won't he? And how do you feel about all of this, Fiona? Are you sorry that you're giving the baby up, now that MacAndrews will provide financial support? Will you change your mind?"

"That won't happen. Ever! It's still Jeremy's child. I made a promise to you. I truly believe you're the best mother for this child. But, to answer your other questions, I don't know exactly how Laird MacAndrews thinks a joint adoption would work. Maybe he's thinking he'll see the child on school holidays and in the summers. We'll need to work out the details, legally, before we agree to anything. The Laird did admit to me that Jeremy's upbringing, in his own absence and without a mother, probably contributed to his character flaws, maybe even to his ultimate death. But, we won't know that until the police find out how and why he was killed. Meanwhile, we need to get more information."

Helen listened carefully, her facial expression somewhat more relaxed.

"Do you think he would interfere with decisions I want to make about the child's welfare, Fiona?"

"I would hope not, Helen. He seemed very sincere in his concern for his grandchild, regardless of how he was conceived. And, you'll be his mum, legally. Laird MacAndrews won't have any more say about the child than do you. We'll need to work out the details. We'll need to get legal advice. But, I'm thinking that if the baby's grandfather wants to contribute to the welfare of this child, to provide opportunities otherwise unavailable, we'll want to consider allowing him to assume at least some of Jeremy's responsibilities. Don't you agree?"

"I agree, that's the best thing for the child."

The two women finished their tea and went out into the sunshine for a walk. As they strolled along, Helen was fearful that her longed for role as a mother wouldn't unfold in the way that she'd imagined. Her child's grandfather was a powerful man. But, then, many powerful men ignored their illegitimate children and grandchildren. It was admirable that Laird MacAndrews was willing to assume his son's responsibilities for either a boy or a girl child. Helen was financially comfortable, but she didn't have the huge resources or connections of Laird MacAndrews. She was determined to remain calm while they worked out the details of this arrangement. Admittedly, she was hoping for a girl.

That evening, Fiona and Helen discussed the practical aspects of MacAndrews' proposal. Helen would contact her Solicitor for an appointment first thing tomorrow, to discuss joint adoption papers, if the child were a boy. Financial provisions would also need to be drawn up, in case the child was a girl. Fiona would give birth soon. They wanted to know their options and have the appropriate paperwork in place.

In the next several days, Fiona reminded herself she'd need to make plans, for after the child was born. Once adoption papers were signed, she'd be free to leave Glasgow, go home for a while, or consider other options for her life. She wasn't accustomed to making such important decisions on her own. She'd always been able to count on Billy for support. Now, she'd have to take care of herself.

The next day Fiona and Helen met with the Solicitor. Fiona stayed on the tram afterward, while Helen went home. Now that Jeremy was dead, she wasn't afraid to go out on her own. She got off the tram at the nearest stop to Jack and Jeannie Murray's home. Since Billy's death, she hadn't seen them, although they'd called on Helen's phone several times, to see how she was holding up. Fiona missed them, the warmth of their home, and the antics of Geordie Murray, who'd soon be four. They all missed Billy. Jack told Fiona on the phone he had a question for her. She was anxious to hear it.

Jeannie greeted her with a hug and several kisses on each cheek. "My, my lassie, dinna ye look just ready tae pop? Ye've such a glow on those cheeks! Auch, I see ye've got the swellin' of the ankles too. Here, come in an' sit ye doon."

As Fiona walked toward the living room, Geordie's excited, high voice rang out, followed immediately by the sound of his feet rapidly hitting the floor. It seemed he ran all the time. When he spotted Fiona, he tried to stop himself, skidding toward her on the wooden floor. He looked at her curiously for a moment.

"Wha' ha' ye got under ye're shirt?"

He was pointing at Fiona's huge, protruding abdomen. His limited experience had not included the sight of a pregnant woman at nine months. Jeannie explained.

"Remember, Geordie, tha's the wee bairn in there, Fiona's baby. Now, go play in your room."

Geordie played with his new model ship, while the two women enjoyed some peace and quiet. They spent a pleasant afternoon reminiscing about Billy. They had a few laughs, as they recalled some of the conversations they all had when Billy was alive. Jeannie talked a bit about losing her son, Geordie's father, and how painful it was for all of them. Each woman shed a few tears and both agreed that life wouldn't be the same without their lost young men. The two women talked late into the afternoon, as Jeannie prepared a stew and put it in the oven for supper.

When Jack arrived home from work, he was glad to see Fiona at the table with his wife. He leaned down to give Jeannie a kiss.

"Well, now we'll ha' everyone here for supper. Tess and Taylor are right behind me, draggin' their bags. I'll just get changed and join ye at the table. The gels willna be botherin' us for a wee while. They'll take forever tae get settled."

Jack returned, poured himself a glass of his favorite whiskey, and sat down at the table.

"Fiona, Jeannie and I'd like to offer you a home, here with us, until you decide what to do with yerself, after the wee bairn is born. Jeannie's been thinkin' on this since ye told her ye'd feel a wee bit awkward goin' home tae Helen's with the babe. Will ye stay with us for a wee while?"

Fiona was silent, touched with emotion by this very kind offer. She'd been putting off as many decisions as possible, just trying to get through each day. First, Jeremy had threatened her, then, he got himself killed, and now, Edward MacAndrews had intruded in her life, on Jeremy's behalf, with adoption plans. It was all too much for her. Her eyes overflowed. She leaned her head on Jeannie's shoulder, while she struggled to get control of herself. Finally, she spoke.

"Jack, Jeannie, I'm very grateful for your offer. But, where will you put me? Tess and Taylor have their things in their room. I know you've rented Billy's old room to your new apprentice. I'd just be an imposition, wouldn't I?"

"Well, lassie, we've had some startlin' news, ye see. Jeannie promised me she'd nae tell ye before I did. Tess and Taylor ha' been laid off from their jobs at the mill in Dundee. It seems they'll be emigratin' tae Canada, if ye can believe it! I did my best tae talk them out of it, but they ha' been coaxed into this monumental decision by some work mates at the mill. There'll be a group of them goin' together, for the work is plentiful there. I remember tha' you and Billy looked into the possibility of emigrating tae Canada, before his terrible accident.

What do ye think, lass? Will ye consider comin' here? The gels will be cleanin' out whatever they won't be takin' with them.

They'll be gone in the next two weeks. Move in whenever it suits ye."

Before Fiona could respond, Geordie came bounding into the room. Jack reached out and grabbed him as he rushed by. He gave the boy a stern look and pointed to the doorway. Geordie took the hint, turned, and walked back out of the room.

Geordie's grand entrance provided a convenient distraction for Fiona. She gained some thinking time before she replied to Jack. She relaxed, as she considered the offer from Jack and Jeannie. This was a very kind offer from the Murray's. Life with them would certainly be interesting. And, if she stayed with them, even temporarily, she'd be able to stay in touch with her dressmaking clients, even take new clients, in order to pay her way. Whatever happened with Edward MacAndrews, the baby would be well taken care of and loved by Helen. She was free to do as she wished.

"You're right Jack. Billy and I did look into going to Canada. As you know, many of the lads from Clydebank have moved to Canada or America. Billy probably told you that a good friend of ours from Marysburgh has a daughter who went to Western Canada with her new husband. She writes of wide open spaces, no industrial blackness in the air, and plenty of sunshine. Your Tess and Taylor will certainly have new opportunities over there."

As Fiona spoke, Tess and Taylor entered the kitchen. They squeezed in side by side through the doorway, dressed exactly alike, as always.

"Wha's this, then? Did we hear Canada? Are ye comin' with us, then, Fiona?"

Tess, as usual, blabbed on and on, while Taylor watched. Jack, winking at Fiona, loved to tease his daughters.

"Gud God, my gels! I dinna think ye wud actually flee the country! I kept hopin' ye'd find work here in bonny Scotland, not sail off into the Wild West! It's halfway across the earth tae a God foresakin' country tha's less than a hundred year auld! We thought ye'd ha' come tae ye're senses by noo.

Besides, surely ye canna ignore the dangers of such a voyage. We all know tha' the Titanic sank in spite of the best plans. Why, ye canna even count on changin' ye're mind and comin' back, if ye do get there. Our young cousin, Peter Murray, was a trimmer on the Empress of Ireland, returnin' to Scotland in 1914 when he had to be rescued before the ship left Canadian waters, where it sank! And that ship was built right here on the Clyde! Ye're riskin' ye're selves both comin' and goin', if ye ask me."

Tess, silent for a change was grinning by this time. As her father spoke, she was aware that such teasing and fun at the kitchen table would end when they left the country. She walked over and stood behind Jack's chair, leaned down, and put her arms around his neck. Loudly enough for everyone in the room to hear, she said,

"Wha's for dinner, then?"

Everyone enjoyed her abrupt change of direction, except Taylor, who remained serious. She'd already considered how much she'd have to support Tess, once they were in Canada. Blabby as Tess was, with much bravado, she wasn't as independent as Taylor. She'd probably be quite lost, without the moral support of her closely-knit family. Taylor made herself feel better about Canada, by thinking about finding herself a nice husband—some farmer who wouldn't be surrounded by these half-staffed, or empty Scottish factories—some farm near a nice, quiet, rural town. She kept her thoughts to herself, for the moment.

Fiona decided not to discuss Edward MacAndrews proposal to her and Helen. She'd told Jeannie about Jeremy's murder earlier in the afternoon. She'd leave it to her to pass that news along to her family, as she chose. She gently declined Tess's offer to go to Canada with them, at least for the time being. She accepted gratefully, the Murray's offer of a room. Jack would arrange to have her furniture and her sewing machine moved while she was in the hospital having the baby.

The evening was filled with the usual good cheer, good food, and a performance of old Scottish tunes after dinner, accompanied, as always, by Jeannie's pounding on the piano. Helen sent a taxi for Fiona, who arrived back at Helen's feeling more relaxed than she had for several months. It had been just the kind of evening Fiona needed, before the events of the next two weeks unfolded.

16 ... Beginnings

*E*dward Daniel Brody MacAndrews was born on May 24, 1919. He was a healthy boy, exactly eight pounds, with soft brown hair on his well-shaped head. Fiona was exhausted, having been in labour for most of the night before. But, she was relieved to be free of her interior reminder of Jeremy.

Several hours after the birth, Fiona realized she held no grudge against this tiny boy. She watched Helen murmur endearments as she gazed lovingly at the baby. Fiona was convinced that Daniel would be very much loved. And, it would be Helen who'd contend with Laird MacAndrews, with complications from the joint adoption, if there were any. Fiona looked forward to detaching herself from the MacAndrews clan for good.

A massive floral arrangement arrived for Fiona the following day, delivered by a courier. It was accompanied by a legal sized, sealed envelope. Fiona was surprised that there could be more documents for her to sign. She and Helen had been busy the past two weeks, going from Solicitor to Advocate, where Helen signed the joint application for adoption, along with Edward MacAndrews, before it was to be processed through the Sherriff Court. Fiona signed away her maternal rights to the child. Now that Daniel had arrived, the papers that had been prepared for a girl child would be destroyed. Helen Brody and Edward MacAndrews would share legal responsibility for Daniel.

Fiona opened the envelope and removed a handwritten note.

Dear Miss Gilman,
Congratulations on the birth of your son. He'll be loved and

cared for by Helen Brody, and by me, his grateful grandfather. I'm at a loss for words to describe the joy I felt when I heard that Daniel is healthy. I trust that you, too, are well.

I understand from Mrs. Brody that your future plans are not yet firm. She said you've considered emigrating to Canada. Whatever you decide to do, I've enclosed an account book, for an investment in your name. The annual interest on the investment will be deposited to your account.

Miss Gilman, I beg you take this gift. It is not intended, in any way, to excuse Jeremy's reprehensible actions toward you. Rather, it's a sign of my gratitude for your allowing me to enjoy and support my grandson, along with Helen Brody.

I wish you the very best and remain, gratefully yours,
Edward MacAndrews, Baron of Glenheather
May 25, 1919

Fiona was astounded. She looked in the envelope and saw the account book. It was there, neatly identified with her name on it, along with a signed and sealed legal document that outlined the amount of the annual interest that would be deposited to her account. She noticed there was already a balance in the account, for the amount of one year's interest. Edward MacAndrews wanted her to have access to these funds immediately. A signature card from the bank was also enclosed. The bank manager had included a personal note, paper clipped behind the card, welcoming her to the bank and asking her to come in at her convenience, to provide a sample signature.

She inserted the notes, the bank book, and the document back into the envelope and placed it on the bedside table. She let her head fall back onto several, propped up pillows behind her and closed her eyes, slightly overwhelmed by this unbelievable development in her life.

I can't believe it. Laird MacAndrews, giving me money! Surely, he's hoping I'll use the money to move away from his grandson. Oh, God, I'm ashamed of myself for questioning his motives. He seems a changed man. I should let him off the hook, let bygones be bygones, where he's concerned.

Certainly, the money would be very useful, whether she decided to follow Tess and Taylor to Canada, revisit her plan to go to University, or expand her design and dressmaking business. With this modest annuity, she'd be able to pay a proper rent to the Murrays, while she made up her mind about her life. Thoughts of a visit home to Marysburgh, to visit Billy's grave and see her parents floated into her mind as she drifted off to sleep.

When she awoke, Fiona thought about her peculiar role as a mother. Technically, that's what she was, even though she'd given the baby away. She'd never be able to erase completely the experience of Jeremy's forced entrance into her life. She'd only been able to bear the pain of childbirth, because it was the end of the daily presence in her life, of a child who was half Jeremy's.

Her body continued to remind her that she had given birth. Due to a miscommunication within the nursing staff, nobody wrapped Fiona's breasts before her milk came in. The evening nurse assumed she would nurse her baby.

"Are ye ready to feed your new babe, Miss Gilman?"

Fiona, shocked that she was faced with this situation, replied firmly.

"Certainly not. The baby's new mother, Helen Brody, has arranged for a wet nurse to feed him. He'll have the advantage of mother's milk."

Satisfied with Fiona's explanation, the nurse returned the baby to the nursery and returned to wrap Fiona's breasts. This painful process added to Fiona's on-going resentment of Jeremy; it had also made her feel guilty about not giving the baby her milk. She resolved that she'd trust Helen's good judgment. He'd be fine, with a wet nurse.

Fiona hadn't gained excessive weight during her pregnancy. Already, she'd lost most of the baby weight. But, her abdomen was loose, compared to what it had been. She was determined to become as active as possible, as soon as possible, so she could return to her physically fit body. She thought this restoration of her body might make her feel like her old self, the self she was before she was raped.

But I can't really go back, can I? My life will never be the same—Billy was in my life before the rape and the pregnancy. No matter what I do, I can't undo that rape or Billy's death. I'll have to carry on: a mother with no child . . . a fiancé who will never marry the man I love.

A few days after Daniel's birth, Helen Brody left the Women's Hospital with Fiona's new son in her arms. In spite of her resolve, Fiona felt a sense of loss. She missed the feeling of life inside her. She knew, however, that she'd done the best she could for the baby. She needed to move forward without reminders of Jeremy. She'd also miss her friend, Helen, and the close friendship they had developed. They had agreed that Fiona would come for a visit, after everyone was settled.

Jack Murray collected Fiona from the hospital and took her to her temporary home at the Murray's. They no sooner got in the door than Geordie came running and threw his arms around Fiona's legs.

"They're here Nanny! Here they are! Auntie Fiona, Nanny said I could welcome you for the whole family, but I canna say anythin' aboot a baby, nae, not one word aboot a baby."

He carried on, digging himself a deeper hole, as he shook his blonde head. Jeannie turned the corner into the front hall as Geordie spoke, raised her eyes upward with a sigh, and shook her head slowly as she reacted to the well-meaning words of her incorrigible grandson. Fiona smiled, but she didn't engage with the little boy. She wanted to lie down with a minimum of delay.

Jeannie showed Fiona up to the twins' room, where her belongings had been installed the day before. She recalled that the first hours at home after giving birth could be overwhelming. She was sure Fiona would want to lie down, before supper.

As she rested on Tess's bed, Fiona noticed how quiet the house was without the quick-paced chatter of the twins. They'd be in Canada by now. She'd decided to put off any decisions about emigrating, until she had a chance to see how her life unfolded. There were too many new things happening for her to rush her decisions. The most important thought in her mind was visiting Billy's grave.

During her first week at the Murray home, Fiona rested, read, went for walks, and enjoyed conversations with Jeannie Murray. The two women were constantly entertained by Geordie's lively antics while Jack was at work. Fiona was glad that the Murrays had rented Billy's old room to a new apprentice. She wouldn't have any need to go in there where memories of Billy were too painful. They used to sneak kisses in that room.

The next week, she began to address the issue of MacAndrews' money. She took the tram to the bank, met the bank manager and provided a sample signature. The first amount she withdrew would cover the cost of her rent at the Murray's for the next three months. She also withdrew enough to apply for a telephone for the Murray home. It would be her gift to them for their continuing support. They'd be able to keep in contact with their friends, and Jack could keep in touch with his apprentices on the evening shift, at his Glasgow shop, where he'd installed a telephone. When she paid the rent and showed the Murrays the paperwork for the telephone, they were reluctant to accept such a gift. But, Fiona insisted she help them in this way, so that they, too, would benefit from Laird MacAndrews' unexpected generosity.

In their letter this week, Fiona's parents relayed some surprising news. Her best friend, Katie Montgomery, had fallen in love and was getting married. Fiona could hardly believe it. Apparently, at Billy's funeral, Katie met Charlie Jones, a young Welshman who had recovered from war wounds in the bed next to Billy, in the London hospital. At the post-funeral wake, Katie and Charlie had talked for hours, sharing stories about Billy, while they stood at the bar in *The McGinnis Drinking Establishment*. It appeared to everyone now, that they must have shared a mutual admiration, not just for Billy, but for each other too.

Kathleen went on to write that Katie and Charlie began to date. Their relationship blossomed into love. Charlie stayed on, in Marysburgh, long after he originally planned, in a room above the pub. Many evenings Charlie and Katie visited with Billy's parents, sharing their experiences about Billy and getting to know each other. Sometimes, Katie's mother joined them, obviously happy to see her daughter in love. The wedding was set for the end of August, after which Katie would return to Wales with Charlie.

Now, Fiona had a reason to appear in Marysburgh, beyond visiting Billy's grave. The happy occasion of Katie's wedding would give the gossips something else to talk about, besides Fiona's business. She was nervous about her return home, worried, that she might not be able to hold her temper, in the face of inevitable interrogations from nosy townspeople. Big-mouthed Brigit had seen to that, when she spread the news of Fiona's pregnancy around town before she left last year with Billy. Her parents reassured her that Brigit had been warned to keep her mouth shut, but, Fiona didn't trust Brigit to do that.

In her third week at the Murray's, Fiona received a request to design and sew a new outfit. The client lived in the West End of Glasgow, near Helen Brody. Fiona would have time to make the intricate sketches, measure, select fabric, and complete the dress, before she and the Murray's left for Marysburgh, to attend Katie's wedding.

Alone, one afternoon, after Jeannie left to take Geordie to the park, Fiona sat down at the Murray's dining room table, to work on her sketches. She was annoyed at having to get up to answer a knock on the front door. When she opened the door, she was surprised to see Violet, Helen's housekeeper.

"Miss Fiona, I was nearby visitin' a friend. I told Mrs. Brody I didna mind stoppin' by in person, to invite you, Mrs. Murray, and Geordie to see the baby on Thursday this week at 2 p.m. Wee Daniel is simply darlin'. He's feedin' so well and growin' every day."

"Thanks, Violet. Please tell Helen I'll check with Jeannie. I'm quite sure we can come on Thursday afternoon. Jeannie's been asking when she could see him."

After she closed the door and went back to her design sketches, Fiona couldn't concentrate. She had mixed feelings about Helen's invitation. On one hand, she was curious to see whether or not Daniel looked like his father, Jeremy. On the other hand, she'd like to see how he was doing, yet, she didn't want to risk becoming attached to him. In the end, she decided, in spite of her own trepidations, it would be a kindness for her to allow Helen to show off the baby. Perhaps, Helen also wanted to reassure Fiona that he was in good hands. If seeing Daniel made her uncomfortable, Fiona could leave to visit her nearby client, while she was in the vicinity.

On Thursday, when Helen opened the door, Geordie raced past her into the library, where Daniel lay in his cradle. The baby was an immediate hit with Geordie, who asked excitedly if he could hold him. When Helen placed the baby carefully on his lap, he compared the size of their fingers. Then, to Jeannie's embarrassment, he one-handedly worked off a shoe and sock, so he could compare his toes to the baby's. Geordie's antics broke the ice for everyone and smoothed over what could have been an awkward situation.

Very soon, Geordie became bored holding the sleeping baby in his arms. Helen picked up Daniel and offered him to Fiona, while she looked for some games to keep Geordie amused. Fiona took the baby carefully. She settled into the comfortable chair she'd used so often when she was pregnant with him. As he slept, she noticed he looked very much like a MacAndrews; his thickening hair looked darker, and he definitely had the solid build of a MacAndrews. Suddenly, he opened his eyes and looked at her. She noticed, as she looked back at him, that his eyes were now quite blue, like her people. Fiona hoped so. Other than that feature, he looked like a MacAndrews to her and he reminded her of Jeremy.

Perhaps, Daniel sensed her sudden discomfort. He screwed up his face, opened his mouth, and began to howl. Helen hurried back into the room, took the baby gently from Fiona's arms, and explained that he was just hungry.

"He's taken immediately to his wet nurse. That's who he needs now."

Fiona was relieved when he was gone. He made her nervous. She hurried with her tea and a short visit with Helen, anxious to leave. Her conflicting emotions were too difficult to deal with. Maybe she should stop seeing the boy. She'd done what Helen needed. Enough. She must move on with her life.

Desperate to leave Helen's and her MacAndrews baby, Fiona went with Jeannie into the kitchen to fetch Geordie, so as to avoid any delays in getting out of this house. From there, they heard a loud pounding on Helen's front door. What was behind that door would not only stop Fiona from leaving here immediately, but would result in new, terrifying circumstances to interfere with her chances for a new start. They heard Violet open the door.

17 ... Legalities

Fiona heard her name spoken. Next, she saw Violet, looking uneasy, in the doorway of the kitchen. A middle aged man in a civil service uniform stood behind her. Violet pointed toward Fiona.

"That's Miss Fiona Gilman, there."

The man walked into the room and stood in front of Fiona.

"Are you Miss Fiona Gilman?"

"I am."

He handed Fiona a folded piece of paper.

"Good day, tae ye all."

He followed Violet out of the kitchen to the front door and left.

Fiona, Jeannie, and Helen sat down at the kitchen table, while Fiona opened up the folded paper. It was addressed to her at Helen's address. With the birth of the baby, and her move to the Murray's a few weeks ago, she hadn't gotten around to changing her address with the National Postal Service. It was just by chance that this official-looking document arrived for her while she was paying her first visit to Helen's home since she moved out.

Fiona read: **Subpoena to a Court Proceeding**.

"I'm being summoned to court, the High Court of Justiciary!"

She read further, aloud, so Jeannie and Helen could keep up. She was being called as a witness by the Advocate for the defense, for a man named Ned Smith, who was on trial in Edinburgh for killing Jeremy MacAndrews.

"No, no, no! Will I never be rid of these constant visitations in my life by Jeremy MacAndrews, and now by his ghost? Why can't I escape from him?"

Overwhelmed by frustration, she crossed her arms on the table, lay her head down on her arms, and wept. Geordie, who looked anxious, spoke out.

"Nanny, wha's the matter wi' Fiona? Why is she cryin'?"

Jeannie nodded to Violet, who took Geordie out of the room. Helen put her arm around Fiona and waited while she wept out her frustration.

Helen was concerned. She was beginning to realize that life attached to the MacAndrews clan would be challenging. She resolved, though, to concentrate on how much she already loved her new son. She knew she'd bear whatever came, to keep him in her life. After a few moments, she spoke softly to Fiona.

"Fiona, dear, we'll support you, whatever comes your way. Jeannie and Jack, your Mum and Daddie, and Billy's parents— my own sister, Meg, and her William—all of your friends and family will stand by you.

My guess is that the Advocate for the defense plans to use your testimony to show that Jeremy was disreputable, even despicable, in his behavior toward women. We all know that's true. His own father admitted to you that Jeremy wasn't honorable, to say the least. Laird MacAndrews wan't hold it against you for telling the truth about Jeremy in court."

"But . . . but . . . my reputation! If I testify in court, everyone will know for certain. I was raped by Jeremy. I had a baby out of wedlock. There are always people who think rape is the woman's fault: she must have let it happen, she asked for it. Once everyone knows, I'll lose my clients, along with my reputation, won't I? I don't see how I'll be able to tolerate the snide looks and snickers, once this nightmare becomes public!"

Helen took Fiona's hand. Jeannie placed hers on top. They sat like this for a few minutes, until Helen spoke.

"Let's make a pact. No matter what happens, we'll remember that Fiona is the victim of a despicable action. She was violated by Jeremy. But, we have our beautiful Daniel, as a result. Can we agree that while we detest Jeremy's actions, our Daniel is a blessing?"

They all nodded. Helen turned to face Fiona.

"Fiona, Daniel's the only person who's been able to make me feel whole again since my Robert was killed. Your sacrifice in carrying him, taking care of yourself, bearing him, and generously giving him to me is one that I can't ever repay. As far as your clients go, they pay you for your unique designs and your expert sewing. They know you. Any woman who holds Jeremy's crime against you, isn't worth having as a client."

Jeannie nodded and contributed her support.

"Fiona, lass, ye're the bravest young woman I know. Ye've stood tall in spite of Jeremy's torments and Billy's death. Ye're strong, gel, ye'll get through this. We'll all help ye because we all love ye. And as for those gossiping folk, we ken tha' they're small-minded busybodies, who dinna ha' satisfyin' lives themselves. They spend their days with' nothin' better tae do, than pick on folks with troubles. They're na worth troublin' yerself aboot."

Helen got up. She went to her desk in the library for her telephone list. She'd call the Advocate who worked with her Solicitor. Fiona would need legal advice to protect herself, within the court system, when the trial began next week. Helen returned to the kitchen.

"Fiona, I'll engage a legal advisor for you, at my cost. It's the least I can do."

"No, Helen. I'm alright there. I have MacAndrews' annuity."

Jeannie Murray piped in to the conversation.

"But, my sweet gel, ye've already given away money, some to us . . . the telephone. It's a generous gift, but, we'll cancel the application. We dinna need it, if ye need the money to protect yer'self."

"Fiona," Helen added, "Laird MacAndrews' money is neither for cleaning up the messes made by Jeremy when he lived, nor, is it intended to pay for court appearances now that he's dead. I insist on paying for legal help, Fiona. Now, dear, why don't you go ahead and visit the client you mentioned, while I feed Geordie his tea?"

In the spirit of carrying on with her own life, Fiona agreed with her friends. She went to her client's home. Thinking about her business would be a good distraction for her. She'd do that, until the very moment she left for Edinburgh, and her court appearance.

By the time Fiona returned, Helen had already called her Advocate in Glasgow, who'd recommended an excellent Advocate in Edinburgh, to look after Fiona's interests. Helen asked Fiona if she'd like to telephone her parents, while she was here. Geordie was having a nap, the baby was sleeping, and Jeannie, too, had decided to take a nap in Fiona's old room upstairs. Fiona agreed that this quiet opportunity to relate her news might not repeat itself.

"Hello, Mum."

"Why, Fiona, darlin' I thought you weren't callin' until the week end. 'Tis a grand surprise to hear from you."

Fiona thought how comforting it was to hear her mum's voice, with its familiar remnants of Kathleen's Irish accent. Hers was the soothing voice she had heard all of her life.

"Mum, I've some news that couldn't wait. I want you and Daddie to hear it from me, before anyone else tells you. The fact is, I've been summoned to testify for the defense of a man named Ned Smith. He's on trial in Edinburgh for killing Jeremy MacAndrews. I'm to be a character witness against Jeremy, I think. I'm sure my court appearance will bring my entire, sorry situation to the forefront, at least in Edinburgh. Sooner or later somebody will repeat the news in Marysburgh, or, worse yet, it'll appear in the newspaper. Hopefully, the story will be on a back page, with no photographs of me. I thought you and Daddie should know, before the local gossips begin reveling in my latest notoriety."

"Oh dear, my poor darlin'. Daddie and I were hoping to spare you from our own news about this trial. But, now you'll need to know. The Edinburgh paper carried the murder story with a picture of Ned Smith being hauled into gaol. They made much of the fact that he confessed to killing the son of a Peer. You were giving birth at the time of the arrest. We tried to keep you out of it.

Fiona, Daddie's been called to testify too, by the defense Advocate for Ned Smith. He was interviewed by the police when Jeremy's murder was first discovered. You see, there were so many people there, at Billy's funeral, when he lost his temper and punched Jeremy. Any one of them could have mentioned this fight, when the police came here to interview townspeople, soon after Jeremy was killed. We didn't want to worry you, just as you were about to give birth. The detective said the interview was just routine, while they attempted to pin down the one person, of so many, who despised Jeremy enough to kill him. They told Daddie they'd get back to him, if they needed to talk to him again. And now, suddenly we have this call to the court."

"Oh, Mum, Daddie couldn't be a suspect in the murder of Jeremy, or he'd have been arrested, wouldn't he? Just to be sure there isn't some trickery taking place, he needs to hire an Advocate, to make sure his interests are taken care of. I've already done that. Helen contacted her legal firm and they're setting me up with an Advocate in Edinburgh. Helen insists on paying. She won't consider letting me use my annuity from Edward MacAndrews. She says that money is for my new life, not the old one that was spoiled by Jeremy."

"That's very kind of Helen. But, you're not to worry about us, darlin'. We already have an advocate, from Edinburgh, who called and offered to stand with Daddie. When we said we couldn't afford the fee for his services, he assured us the fee was being covered by an interested party, who'd remain anonymous. It seems there are a number of secrets and partial information in this case. We can only hope the police have the right man and the trial will be over soon. We're going to Edinburgh next week. When do you testify, Fiona?"

"Next week, as well."

They discussed accommodation plans for Edinburgh and decided on a hotel near the North Bridge, close enough to walk to the Law Courts in Parliament Square. After she hung up the phone, Fiona couldn't help but worry about her father. It was because of her, that he'd struck Jeremy. She'd fret about next week, until it was over, hoping it would be her last forced involvement with Jeremy MacAndrews and his clan.

18 ... The trial looms

Kathleen and Ian Gilman met Fiona at the hotel in Edinburgh, where their rooms were across the hall from each other. They arranged to meet for tea after Ian and Fiona returned from appointments with their respective Advocates. Fiona insisted that Kathleen go with Ian. She said she'd be fine meeting alone with her own Advocate, a Mr. Scott.

At supper that evening, they discussed what they'd learned. Fiona would be called to testify ahead of Ian. He was alerted to the fact that once he was on the stand to tell his story, as the father of a raped, impregnated daughter, he'd also be questioned by the prosecutor, about punching Jeremy.

The morning of Fiona's testimony she heard a tap on her door, as she was preparing to leave for the court. The voice of a hotel clerk replied from the other side of the closed door. A gentleman waited to see her in the lobby. Thinking her Advocate must have changed his mind, decided, after all, to pick her up, she grabbed her shawl and hurried down to the lobby. She knew no other men in Edinburgh, except her father.

She was shocked to see Edward MacAndrews waiting for her when she entered the lobby. What was he doing here? Her whole life she'd been wary of MacAndrews. She couldn't help being wary still, in spite of his recent, generous behavior toward her. But, these were trying circumstances for them both. Wanting to be civil, she accepted his outstretched hand as he approached her.

"Good morning, Miss Gilman," he said.

"Good morning, Laird MacAndrews."

She attempted to keep emotion out of her voice. She was

acutely aware that this trial about his son's death must be very difficult for him. She was benevolent enough to mask her relief that Jeremy was dead and could never again torment her.

What could Jeremy's father want with me now? What does he expect of me? Do I act a toady, because of his financial gift? I'm grateful my parents aren't in the lobby to witness this exchange, whatever MacAndrews has in mind.

"How can I help you, Laird MacAndrews?"

"I'm hoping, Miss Gilman, that you'll allow me to help you. I'd be happy to escort you to the Law Courts and walk with you into the courtroom when you're called. I think you'd agree with me that our joining forces, at this time, might prevent the newspaper people from presuming that there is bad blood between our families. I wish it to be known that I support you. I don't blame you, in any way, for what Jeremy did to you. I'm sure the reporters will try to sensationalize our relationship, in the most negative way possible. They'll certainly sell more papers if they speculate there's animosity between us. What do you say? Shall we band together to keep them from having that satisfaction?"

Fiona was stunned. She hadn't expected this powerful man to support her publicly. Then again, her misfortune had resulted in Laird MacAndrews having a new role as a grandfather, with a second chance for a loving relationship with his heir. He must be thinking of his grandson, who'd benefit from harmony between the two sides of his family, in spite of the reprehensible actions of his dead father. These thoughts tumbled through Fiona's mind as she formulated her reply to the Laird.

"Thank you, Laird MacAndrews, I'm happy to accept your support. Neither of us needs to prolong the negativity of this public trial. I understand you and Helen Brody want to shield Daniel from the upsetting circumstances of his father's death. When he's older, of course, he'll be able to read about this trial in the newspapers. I agree, let's not give the scandal-seeking newspaper sellers an opportunity to take advantage of us."

MacAndrews looked relieved at Fiona's response.

"Thank you, Miss Gilman. I admire your concern for Daniel's future. I realize a public airing of the circumstances of his conception will be difficult for you. I can see you're willing to set aside your own feelings, about my son, for the boy's sake. Shall we go, Miss Gilman? I have a driver waiting."

The car pulled up to the front of the Law Courts building. Fiona and MacAndrews saw reporters with cameras, poised to take photos of anyone who was potentially a part of this trial. Naturally, they recognized Edward MacAndrews, Baron of Glenheather. They took immediate notice of the young woman who stepped out of his car with him.

Flashbulbs popped, as Fiona took MacAndrews' arm. They walked toward the entrance to the building. Reporters shouted questions.

"Laird MacAndrews, is this young woman one of your son's conquests? How will you feel when she incriminates your son? Rumour has it she'll testify for the defense of Ned Smith. How will that help you get justice for your son's murder?"

MacAndrews, a seasoned politician, was practiced at dealing with the press. He smiled as he responded.

"Miss Gilman and I are old friends. I'm here to support her as she describes some difficult circumstances in her life. Other than that, we have no comment."

Once Fiona was shown to the waiting area, Edward MacAndrews said he'd return to escort her into the courtroom, when she was called. As he was about to step away, he spoke a few final comments to Fiona.

"Miss Gilman, I hope you don't mind that I spoke for both of us out there. Some of these reporters are scoundrels. They'll do anything to force a bit of gossip from anyone."

"I understand, Laird MacAndrews. I'm grateful you were there. My Advocate will join me soon. And my father, too, will be waiting in this area later. I have much support to help me through this ordeal."

MacAndrews had been gone just a few minutes when Fiona's Advocate, William Scott, arrived, followed by Ian and Kathleen Gilman and their Advocate. Fiona explained to her parents how Edward MacAndrews had stepped up and eased the situation, how they put on a united front, for the press. Ian and Kathleen were surprised and grateful for MacAndrews' support. Daniel was their grandson too, whether or not Fiona was willing to have him in her life.

Mr. Scott drew Fiona aside, directing her to a bench out of earshot.

"Miss Gilman, are you in agreement with Edward MacAndrews escorting you into the courtroom? He asked me about doing that. I thought it was a good idea, but I told him he'd need to ask your permission. I represent you, not Laird MacAndrews, in this case. Are you comfortable granting his request?"

My God. What's the world coming to when Laird MacAndrews is told by anyone that he must ask my permission? I suppose I've suffered enough at the hands of his son, to have earned this one small privilege.

"Definitely, Mr. Scott, I'm comfortable. He's already fended off reporters on the way into the building. I think an alliance is important, for Daniel's future. You know, Edward MacAndrews is a changed man since the death of his son. His sole concern now, seems to be to protect his grandson, and, by association, until this latest nightmare is over, me as well. I won't be able to deny to anyone, after today, that I'm Daniel's mother. The boy will need to know that, eventually. He can do without further scandal."

"How are you feeling about giving testimony, Miss Gilman?"

"You mean, besides being terrified, Mr. Scott? I'm already

humiliated about having to expose the intimate details of my attack for public consumption. I'm also concerned for my parents. My mother, Kathleen, will be in the courtroom to support me. She'll watch the Advocates take advantage of my misfortune. Watching me being interrogated, no matter how upsetting it is for me, will be painful for my mother. But, I'm grateful my father won't be in the courtroom to hear my testimony. A father tries to protect his daughter from the likes of Jeremy. I know he feels he let me down, even though he couldn't have prevented what happened. I'm afraid for him. What if Ned Smith is found 'not guilty' and the police turn back to my father as the next likely suspect?"

"Miss Gilman, Ned Smith has confessed. Your father is not a suspect. You'll be fine in there. Just tell the truth."

"I'll be glad to get this over with."

They both turned as a man's raised voice carried through the waiting area.

"The court calls Miss Fiona Gilman to the stand. Miss Fiona Gilman."

Fiona walked over to where Ian was waiting and hugged him. Edward MacAndrews appeared from around the corner, nodded to Ian and Kathleen and offered Fiona his arm. As the clerk opened the huge, dark, wooden doors to the courtroom, MacAndrews reached over and patted Fiona's hand, silently reassuring her. Mr. Scott stood behind them, ready to take his place in the courtroom. Fiona took a deep breath as they stepped forward through the open door into the huge chamber. The heavy doors closed behind them.

19 ... Testimony

The trial had started the previous day. The Advocate Depute for the Lord Advocate presented the case for the prosecution. He produced and read Ned Smith's confession. It stated that he had, indeed, killed Jeremy MacAndrews, son of Edward MacAndrews, Baron of Glenheather, patriarch of the wealthiest family in western Scotland. The prosecution left no doubt that Ned Smith was the self-confessed assassin of "poor" young MacAndrews, having bludgeoned him to death in an alley off Waverley Square in Edinburgh. The prosecutor dwelled on the fact that Jeremy's head had been unrecognizable, by the time Smith was finished with him. Photos of the gruesome, bashed in head were passed around the jury box, where the fifteen jurors gasped and grimaced at the brutality of the crime. The emotional reaction to Jeremy's death photos prompted one of his football mates, to race up from the back of the courtroom, grab one of the photos before anyone could stop him, and lead his teammates in a chant:

"Justice for Jeremy, hang Ned Smith, Justice for Jeremy, hang Ned Smith!"

The emotional intensity of the chanters provoked an equally-loud response from a group of working men who also stood at the back of the courtroom. They responded.

"MacAndrews, the rapist, deserved to die, MacAndrews, the rapist, deserved to die!"

The noise of the crowd almost obscured the sound of the gavel, pounded repeatedly, by the Judge. The Lord Justice-General shouted.

"Order, I say, I will have order!"

Constables assigned to the courtroom waded into both groups of chanters, waving their truncheons as they went. One of them grabbed the football player who'd snatched the picture and held his arms behind his back, as he led the young man from the courtroom. The constables forced the noisy crowd out onto the street, where the waiting press began to snap pictures as fast as they could.

Back in the quieted courtroom, the prosecutor called his first witness. He was a friend of Jeremy MacAndrews, with an equally-wild reputation for drinking, gambling, and womanizing—especially with young, inexperienced girls. He testified that he and Jeremy had been gambling and drinking for a few days, when Ned Smith appeared in the pub and threatened Jeremy. When the prosecutor asked this witness if he'd seen the murder, the young football player said he'd passed out before Jeremy left the pub and was attacked in the alley by Smith.

The prosecutor paraded a long line of witnesses before the jury, all claiming that Jeremy was an excellent football player, with lots of friends. He was, they claimed, a normal, free-spirited lad.

Next, it was the defense Advocate's turn. He called Ned Smith to the witness box, and began by asking Smith why he'd killed MacAndrews.

"He killed ma wee lass, ma daughter, ma sweet dearie, and along wi' her, ma only gran' babby."

"Do you mean he sought out your daughter and her child and murdered them? Is that what you're saying?"

"Nae, I didna say tha'. But he as good as murdered her. He raped her and she died givin' birth to his wee bairn. She was only thirteen year auld! Havin' his babe killed them both. He had to pay . . . he had to pay," the now sobbing Smith declared.

"Mr. Smith, are you saying that you planned to make MacAndrews pay by beating him to death in an alley?"

"Well, I did beat him and he did die, but I didna plan it. When he left the pub, I tried tae reason with him, get at least a 'sorry' from him, get him to admit tha' his rapin' and leavin' ma wee gel wi' his child, killed them. But, he laughed a' me. He said it wasna his problem. He said she was nothin', lucky tae ha' the likes of him make love tae her, lucky he bothered tae pay her any attention. He . . . he said she was so sweet, he could still taste her sweet skin on his lips . . . he could still feel himself inside her tight, young body, with her silky smooth skin. He said he did her a favor, breakin' her into lovemakin' which, she'd surely be doing soon, with some grubby young boy of her own class. I just couldna take it, ye see, he was so disrespectful, speakin' like tha' aboot ma innocent young gel. When he started tae laugh again, I just couldna hold back. I grabbed a pipe tha' was lyin' there in the alley and ran at him. If he hadna been so drunk, I wouldna ha' been able to overpower him. Next thing I remember, I was running through Waverly Square, and then I was home, with MacAndrews blood on my clothes. I admit it, I killed him and he deserved every blow! But it wilna bring back ma daughter, or my gran' babby, will it?"

Smith paused, gathering power in his voice. Fuelled by the injustice of the situation for him and his family, he shouted:

"MacAndrews was the cause of two lives lost. He paid wi' only his!"

Hearing this statement, his working class friends shouted out their support for him and the Judge, once again, called for order.

"Thank you, Mr. Smith."

His Advocate sat down and turned the witness over to the prosecutor for cross examination. But, the prosecutor said,

"I have no questions for this witness. He said all we need to hear."

Today, the second day of the trial, Smith's defense Advocate would call witnesses to attest to the warped character of Jeremy MacAndrews. He hoped Fiona, her father, and his other witnesses would convey to the jurors, a true description of Jeremy MacAndrews. He'd been cruel, heartless, held no regard for other people, and never exhibited remorse for anything he did. Hopefully, leniency would be granted for the distraught Smith. Anything would be better than hanging.

Fiona, holding onto Edward MacAndrews' arm, walked toward the witness box, in the crowd-packed room, to the tune of the Judge's gavel calling for order. The atmosphere was charged. The crowd started chattering when they saw the two of them together. Yesterday's near-riots were public record, reported on by the enthusiastic press and headlining today's papers. Now, here was the Baron of Glenheather, father of the murdered son, walking into the courtroom arm-in-arm with a young woman rumored to be one of the dead rapist's victims! As Fiona stepped into the witness box, Edward MacAndrews sat in a front row seat that had been held for him.

The man who must be Ned Smith, Fiona assumed, was sitting in the prisoner's box. He was small, and very thin, with straight brown hair. She could see he worked with his hands, which were blackened around the edges and red with scrubbing. He was wearing workman's pants. It looked as if someone had loaned him a jacket that was too large for him, to make a good impression in court. So, thought Fiona, this is the man I owe for my freedom from Jeremy.

Behind Ned, Fiona could see his large family, including a pale-faced woman who must be his wife, with a worried expression that didn't quite conceal her former prettiness. Strung out along the bench beside her were half a dozen children of increasing size, with rosy-cheeked faces that looked well-scrubbed. The Smith family clothing was worn, but neatly mended.

Smith's Advocate stood up and began his questioning with the usual name and address part of Fiona's testimony. Then he began his questioning.

"Miss Gilman, what is the nature of your relationship to the deceased, Jeremy MacAndrews?"

"I had no 'relationship' with Jeremy MacAndrews. We're from the same area. My father works for his. He was two years younger than me. We weren't friends."

"If you didn't have a relationship with the deceased, Miss Gilman, how did you come to have his baby? Was it a miraculous conception?"

"No. I came to have Jeremy's baby after he raped me. That's how."

"How did he manage to do that? We hear you were a top field hockey player at school. You coached the women's field hockey team until this year. For a woman, you're especially fit. We also know the deceased was a football star at University. Was it his superior strength that allowed him to rape you?"

"Yes. I was alone by the Loch, when he surprised me, grabbing me from behind. I wrenched myself from his grip and tried to outrun him, but it seems football players can outrun field hockey players, at least in my case. When he first grabbed me, I was shocked. I didn't know who'd grabbed me or what was happening. Running was the first thing I could think of. But, he caught me, and pushed me to the ground from behind."

"What did you do next?"

"I struggled to get free, yelling at him to stop, to get off of me, to let me go. He had the advantage of weight and position over me, pinning me to the ground. When he started fumbling with my clothes, I knew he intended to rape me. He rolled me onto my back. I closed my eyes, afraid to look him in the face. I thought he'd kill me if I saw his face."

"So then, how do you know it was Jeremy, if you didn't see his face?"

"He spoke, as he was ripping off my knickers. He said, 'Ah, lovely Fiona, you know you want me.' I opened my eyes and saw Jeremy MacAndrews, smirking as he overpowered and raped me."

Fiona noticed that Edward MacAndrews hung his head with either shame, or sadness, or both, if he believed her, or rage, if he thought Jeremy was innocent of rape. Fiona couldn't tell. He looked at the floor the whole time she described the despicable actions of his son.

"Was that the only time you had relations with MacAndrews?"

"Relations! Do you call a brutal rape, relations? He raped me. I made sure I was never alone again in Marysburgh, from that day onward. He had no chance to get near me."

"Did you have relations with anyone else, before or after Jeremy? We know you were engaged to a Billy McGinnis. Often, young people don't wait for the wedding, do they?"

Angry now, Fiona raised her voice.

"Well, we did! Unfortunately, he didn't live long enough for us to marry."

"We're sorry to hear that, Miss Gilman. But, you are under oath here and I want you to swear that you did not have relations, with anyone, except when Jeremy MacAndrews raped you."

"I swear."

The defense Advocate addressed the court.

"We have Miss Gilman's testimony that she was forcibly raped by Jeremy MacAndrews. Yesterday, we heard testimony that the very young daughter of my client, Ned Smith, was also raped by Jeremy MacAndrews. She died giving birth to the child that resulted from that rape, along with the child."

"Objection!" shouted the prosecutor. "Other than from the accused, we have no verification to that effect."

Ned Smith leaped up out of his chair and began shouting.

"She wasna fourteen, just a schoolgel. MacAndrews killed her . . . he killed his own babby too!"

"Order, order" shouted the Judge, repeatedly banging his

gavel. The crowd shouted out comments too. The Judge had a difficult time bringing the noise level down. Finally, everyone quieted. Smith slumped back down in his chair, his Advocate hurrying over to keep him under control. Fiona glanced at Edward MacAndrews. She saw both pain and rage on his face, at this public incrimination of his son. She saw, too, that Ned Smith's wife had tears streaming down her face, as did their older children. The youngest children looked frightened and confused.

The Judge's voice cut into Fiona's thoughts.

"The objection is sustained."

"I have one last question, Miss Gilman. You've sworn that you had Jeremy MacAndrews' child, as a result of his rape. Where is this child now?"

"He's with his adoptive mother, who will raise him, along with the help of his grandfather."

"Thank you, Miss Gilman. Oh, sorry, one more question. When was the last time you saw Jeremy MacAndrews?"

"He began stalking me in Glasgow, a few months before the baby was born. He cornered me in Kelvingrove Park, where he told me how disgusting I looked, swollen with child, and how he'd wait until I had the child before we resumed what he called, cruelly, our 'beautiful relationship.' When friends of mine saw us and called to me, he slinked off, right after he said, 'I'll be watching you, bitch.' I made sure I didn't go out alone again."

"So, not only is MacAndrews a rapist, he's also a stalker who threatened you."

"Objection!" shouted the prosecution. "Where's the question in that?"

"I'll rephrase. Miss Gilman, is it your testimony that your rapist, Jeremy MacAndrews also stalked and threatened you?"

"Yes."

"Did your friends see and hear Jeremy MacAndrews threaten you?"

"Aye, they did."

Fiona knew that the young wives she'd met in Glasgow would be brought into court or at least interviewed to verify her testimony. With the publicity from this trial, her new Glasgow friends would learn that she was an unwed mother, a fraud, not one of them. She couldn't help that now.

"Thank you, Miss Gilman, said the Advocate for the defense. Turning toward the Advocate Depute he said, "Your witness."

The prosecutor stood up to take his turn questioning Fiona.

"Miss Gilman is it true that your son is the sole heir of Edward MacAndrews, Baron of Glenheather?"

"Yes."

"And who is to say that you, as the daughter of a merchant, whose prospects in life are nowhere near those of a Baron's son, didn't lure Jeremy MacAndrews into the woods to seduce him? You are known as a "looker," Miss Gilman, as we can all see here in this courtroom. Why should we believe that you were the victim of a rape, when you could just as easily have offered yourself to young MacAndrews in order to tap into the MacAndrews fortune?"

Fiona was fuming. Now she was glad she hadn't worn the shorter skirt that was coming into fashion. It would have shown off her shapely legs. Instead, she had carefully piled her thick, dark, wavy hair up under a stylish, but conservative hat, anticipating that her good looks might be used against her.

"Well, Miss Gilman, did you lure a younger, impressionable young man into the woods to seduce him?"

"Certainly not! I had a scholarship to attend the University of Edinburgh, to train as a teacher. I had plans before I was raped by Jeremy, plans that would have given me a good living. I didn't need to marry someone like Jeremy. I resent your questions in this regard. I've already told you what happened."

"So you have, Miss Gilman."

The prosecutor turned to the Judge and said he had no more questions for this witness. The Judge excused her and told the Advocate for the accused, that he could call his next witness.

Ned Smith's Advocate said, "The defense calls Mr. Ian Gilman to the witness box."

Fiona passed her father in the aisle on the way out of the courtroom. He looked nervous, but he smiled at her as she left the room.

Edward MacAndrews rose and followed Fiona out of the room. They joined Fiona's Mum. MacAndrews, in a professional, controlled voice, explained to the two women, the strategy that Ned Smith's lawyer was using, to get leniency for his client. Fiona was impressed that the Laird could maintain a businesslike tone when he spoke to them, about the question of leniency for his son's murderer. She was certain he was suppressing his emotions. She'd seen earlier in the courtroom, that he was not matter-of-fact about Jeremy's murderer. He went on to explain further.

"Ian's physically attacking Jeremy at Billy's funeral is being used as an example of a father's natural reaction when coming face to face with his daughter's rapist, particularly when that rape results in a pregnancy. Smith's Advocate expects the jury to empathize with your father, Fiona, and even more so with Smith, because the rape of his daughter led to the deaths of his daughter and grandchild. The prosecution will point out that a murder, nonetheless, has been committed. He'll say that we can't allow people to take the law into their own hands, to get justice. The prosecutor tried to discredit your testimony so Smith wouldn't have the excuse that Jeremy was in the habit of forcing himself on young women. Smith will hang, either way."

"Do you agree with this punishment, Laird MacAndrews?"

"Yes, Miss Gilman, I believe that an eye-for-an-eye is the correct punishment for murder, regardless of the circumstances. Vigilantism is not the solution to violent crime. However, I'm sorry for Ned Smith, given the circumstances that caused him to murder my son."

Ian Gilman approached them, having completed his testimony. He was relieved that he wasn't a suspect. Ned Smith had pled guilty at the beginning of the trial. Ian was sorry for the man.

A handsome young man accompanied Ian. He was tall and slim with a mop of wavy, reddish-brown hair and the smoothest looking skin Fiona had ever seen on a man. He strolled, rather than walked, obviously self-confident, with one hand in his pocket and the other arm swinging along by his side. When Ian introduced him to Fiona, his green eyes seemed to look right through her. Ian introduced him as Sean Talbot, a law clerk, who worked for the firm representing Ian in this proceeding. He looked to be about twenty-three, or four, old enough to have served from the beginning of the Great War. He shook hands with the men. He smiled a greeting at Fiona and her mum.

Kathleen focused in on Sean's Irish accent. The two of them began a conversation, with Kathleen sounding more and more Irish as the conversation continued. Ian noticed Fiona's somewhat tongue-tied, atypically shy reaction to the handsome Talbot fellow. She seemed to be attracted to this young man. He was relieved to see this reaction from his daughter, having watched her grieve deeply for her lost Billy. Perhaps there was hope yet. But, surely not an Irishman! What was wrong with a fine Scotsman?

Laird MacAndrews took note of the young Irishman immediately. He, too, observed Fiona's reaction to Talbot. Good, he thought. Maybe she's getting ready to move on with her life. The sooner she gets out of the picture, the sooner I can stop worrying about her potential interference with my grandson.

MacAndrews had come to know Fiona's strength of character and her determined way of dealing with challenges. The last thing he needed was for her to remain in Scotland and change her mind about being in his grandson's life. If he was lucky, this Talbot character, or some other young man, would marry her and take her away.

20 ... Going home

Kathleen and Ian Gilman returned to Marysburgh, Edward MacAndrews left for Glasgow to visit with Helen and Daniel, before travelling to his London office, and Fiona went back to the Murray home in Glasgow. Everyone read in the paper that Ned Smith was hanged for murdering Jeremy MacAndrews.

Fiona longed to visit Billy's grave. Now that the trial and Daniel's birth were over, she thought constantly about Billy. She thought about the life they should've had. She found it especially difficult living at the Murray's, where Billy had been living when he died. This is the house he left to go to work that fateful day. This is the house he returned to after he gave her the sapphire and diamond engagement ring. She imagined him in the rooms of the house and remembered sadly his quiet, loving support when she first came to the Murray's home, pregnant, and nervous to meet the Murray clan last Christmas Eve. So much had changed. She needed to see his grave to be able to come to terms with her own life—a life that would never again include him. In a few weeks, she'd travel to Marysburgh for her friend's wedding. She'd sew like a madwoman to keep herself busy until then.

The week before the trip, Fiona finished an elegant dress for a client, Miss Hilary Burns. She was moving to Canada, where her parents had arranged for her to stay with friends who'd emigrated several years earlier. Hilary had known their son, Duncan, since they were children. He and his parents lived in Victoria, a city on Vancouver Island, off the west coast of Canada. Hilary chatted about her trip, as Fiona made final adjustments to the trim of the dress. She seemed most impressed that the city she'd live in was named after Queen Victoria. More impressive, to Hilary, was the Prince of Wales' visit to the City of Victoria this year.

"Why don't you come with me, Fiona?"

"It's a tempting thought, Hilary, given recent events and the worries of my life here in Scotland. I'll need to make some decisions soon. I'm putting them off until after I visit my hometown next week. I need to be around my family now."

"Will you consider it? I'm serious. A new country and a new city will give you a chance to start over. Nobody'll know about your past. And, Victoria is so Scottish, so British, you'll hardly notice the difference between there and here. Apparently, they do have their share of Chinese, and quite uncivilized Indians, living near the harbour. But, Duncan's parents write that everyone gets along well—the classes simply don't mix too much—you'd be safe enough. Besides, you could set up a dressmaking business there, just as well as you could here. My parents' friends say it's been difficult to find good dressmakers, of our own race, let alone clothing designers with your talent. And, didn't you tell me that you and your fiancé had looked into the emigration process already?"

"We did consider moving to Canada, but we hadn't finalized our paperwork, when Billy died. You've raised an interesting option, Hilary. I'll think about it, seriously, but not yet."

"Good! I'll give you my address. Write to me, when you're ready to come."

At the time of this conversation, Fiona didn't know how important this particular client would be in her future. For now, she had to get home to pack for the Marysburgh visit.

Early the next week, the train rolled along toward Marysburgh, while Geordie slept between Fiona and his nanny, Jeannie. Jack, along with the rest of the clan, was in the club car, having a wee drop as they enjoyed the beginning of a few days off work.

Fiona had already told Jeannie Murray about her sister, Brigit, and her attempt to ruin Fiona's good name. Now was a good opportunity to relate the latest news.

"Mum wrote that Brigit left home to become an apprentice missionary at Calaba, in Nigeria, Africa, at the mission there. Apparently, she was mesmerized by a travelling missionary from the United Presbyterian Church. He talked about women's roles as educators of young African girls. Brigit became so zealous about her mission that some customers wouldn't come into the store when she was working.

Mum also said Brigit was especially eager to take the missionary apprenticeship training when she learned it takes place at Moray House, at the University of Edinburgh. I won a scholarship to Moray House where I would have taken my university teacher's training, before Jeremy MacAndrews spoiled my plans. Brigit is quite smug, apparently, about her getting to Moray House, rather than me. She's already moved to Edinburgh. She'll leave for Africa late in the fall."

"Ye're well rid of her meddlin' and jealousy, dearie. Do na fret. Sometimes bad blood between sisters canna be fixed. Think on ye're lovely friend Katie, and the chance for ye to say goodbye to Billy at his grave. We'll be there soon."

The train arrived in Marysburgh on a deliciously warm, late August day. The entire Murray clan preceded Fiona off the train. The clan was made up of Jack, Jeannie, wee Geordie, one of Jack's brothers who had worked with Billy, along with the brother's wife and three children. Fiona held back. She was nervous about coming home after all that had happened to her. She hoped the noisy Murray clan would distract anyone from focusing on her. She wasn't disappointed.

Jack stepped off the train and reached out to shake hands with William McGinnis. The unhappy day of Billy's funeral had been the day they met six months earlier. Jeannie Murray went directly over to Meg McGinnis and hugged her. The two couples had each lost a son. They had that, and their shared, deep regard for Fiona, in common.

Billy's Mom noticed Fiona coming down the steps off the train. She disentangled herself from Jeannie's friendly embrace and walked over to Fiona, thinking sadly that Fiona was never to be her daughter-in-law or the mother of her grandchildren. The two women hadn't seen each other, since they stood side by side at the morgue in Glasgow, viewing Billy's body. They held hands for a few moments. No words were needed. Meg knew that Fiona would want to go directly to Billy's gravesite. She assured Fiona that William would send her luggage to her parents' home. Fiona slipped away.

The McGinnis and Murray parties talked all at once as they stood on the platform by the train. Gradually, they raised their voices above the whistle, the hissing of the steam engine, and then the 'all aboard' of the conductor, as he announced the return trip to Glasgow. Finally, outdone by the surrounding noise, the entire party began the short walk of a few blocks toward *The McGinnis Drinking Establishment* in the centre of town. William and Meg had arranged to crowd them into the rooms over the pub.

William and Meg McGinnis took an instant liking to all of the Murrays. Meg, especially, enjoyed meeting Geordie, who'd celebrate his fourth birthday while they were there. His softly curled, blond hair and his curious nature reminded her of her Billy when he was young. She was glad to have a child to spoil.

After the men carried the bags upstairs, William McGinnis, Jack Murray and Jack's brother gathered at the bar in the pub. Charlie Jones, Katie's fiancé, joined them. The older men began to tease Charlie about his upcoming life as a married man.

"Ye'll nay ha' a moment wi' the men noo."

Jack landed a light slap on Charlie's back.

"No sir, the women will ha' ye by the nose just like the rest of the married men, just like us, laddie."

Charlie smiled. He knew there was no point in contradicting these men. They enjoyed their jesting far too much.

Meanwhile, Meg showed the women and children up the stairs to their rooms to unpack. They hung up their wedding outfits and their husbands' kilts, shirts, and jackets. Meg had prepared a lamb stew. She knew they'd need to eat before the men downed too many drinks. The aroma of the savory stew drifted up the stairs. It had already permeated the entire main floor. Meg hurried everyone along, helping as much as she could, while her guests changed out of their travelling clothes, freshened up a bit, and put on crisp, quickly-ironed cotton dresses before they descended the stairs for supper.

When William Sr. and the Murray men spied their women coming down the stairs, they whistled, each calling out compliments to his wife.

"Jeannie, ye're just as bonny as the day we met, dearie."

"Meg, darlin' ye're as lovely as ever. That dress brings out the color of your eyes."

With such comments, the men engaged in an all-out competition, each one trying to outdo the other. Jack's brother, pushing the limits, not only complimented his wife, but also hinted that he could hardly wait until tonight to take his 'voluptuous wifey' into his arms once they were in bed. The women, grinning as they went, hurried past the men out to the kitchen to put the biscuits into the oven. They could see that they needed to provide food, as soon as possible.

Katie Montgomery and her mum joined Charlie and the others for supper at the pub. The conversation included plans for the next few days. The following night, on Thursday, the men's bachelor party would take place to celebrate Charlie's last days as a single man. Meanwhile, the women were invited to a bridal shower at the Gilman's. The day before the wedding, on Friday afternoon, the wedding rehearsal was scheduled at the Kirk for 4:00 p.m., with a rehearsal supper for everyone in the wedding party to be held afterward in the basement of the Kirk.

Their discussion about pre-wedding plans helped everyone get to know each other better. They shared their good wishes for Charlie and Katie as well as bittersweet tales about Billy. Supper ended with a delicious dessert of hot apple tart, topped with fresh cream that Meg had hidden earlier, in the ice box. The revelers retired early, to rest up for the events of the next few days.

Meanwhile, on her lonely walk to the cemetery, Fiona missed out on the warm food, warm feelings, soft light, laughter, and friendly camaraderie at the pub, as she made her way toward Billy's gravesite. She wasn't prepared for what she would find.

21 ... A secret

On her way through town, Fiona slowed her pace as she neared the place where Billy was buried. She had mixed feelings of both longing and dread. Here would be the finality of the gravestone. She knew he was dead. She saw his lifeless body at the morgue in Glasgow. But, she had become very adept, over the past long months, at replacing the image of his lifeless face, with images of him when he was alive: the two of them together, laughing, or kissing. Whenever she remembered his pale, lifeless face, she was overwhelmed by sadness.

As she arrived at the gate to the graveyard, she caught a glimpse of a figure disappearing behind one of the large headstones. She had hoped she'd be alone. She tried to ignore the presence of someone else being there, among the graves. She looked for Billy's name among those of the fallen soldiers, thinking how ironic it was that he survived so many battles, only to be killed in the accident at Clydebank. To date, nobody could say for certain whether or not the weakness of his wounded leg had contributed to his fatal accident. They'd probably never know. Either way, he was lost to her.

She found his name and noticed fresh flowers crowding the base of the white cross. She looked only at the flowers for a few minutes, not wanting to reread Billy's name on the cold stone. She sat down in front of his final place on this earth, her memories of him flooding her mind. Her tears came and went as she spoke to him, trying to ease her pain. Her thoughts were interrupted by the sound of a soft male voice.

"Hello, Fiona."

Startled, she looked up. An elderly man walked toward her from the civilian section of the graveyard.

"It's only me, lassie, John Ayr. I didna mean tae startle ye. Perhaps I've aged a wee bit since I last saw ye."

Fiona was shaken, before she recognized the owner of the voice. Any male voice, intruding suddenly into her thoughts when she was alone, triggered memories of Jeremy's stalking her in Glasgow. How long will it take, she thought, to rid myself of Jeremy's grip on my mind?

"Hello, John. You don't look any older to me. I do recall that you and Iona were wonderful friends to my Billy. He told me your dear wife passed away. I'm very sorry to hear that. How are you getting on?"

"I'm fine, Fiona, other than the loneliness."

Fiona nodded, acknowledging his grief over his wife's death. The old man paused, seemingly reluctant to say whatever he wanted to say next.

"Tell me, lass, did Billy tell you he wrote tae my wife, after he left Marysburgh for Inverness, tae take up his apprentice-ship? Did he tell ye they wrote tae each other during the war?"

"No, he didn't mention it, John. Just the news of Iona's passing."

"Tha's just like him, kind enough to write to Iona but never askin' for credit. I want tae tell you something, Fiona. I'll be dyin' soon myself. I didna want to burn Billy's letters. I didna want to throw them away either. I didna want tae risk it."

"What do you mean, risk? What's in the letters that's risky? Tell me, John."

"Well, gel, I think my wife'd want ye to know about a hidden part of Billy's life. He planned tae tell ye, had he lived. Now, Billy and my wife are gone, and I soon will be. Ye can be the keeper of the secret and do what ye like about it."

What could be in the letters that Billy didn't tell me? Why

wouldn't he mention this close writing connection to Iona Ayr? I'll let John give them to me. He seems to think they're important. At the least, the letters will give me a little piece of Billy to take away with me, when I leave him behind here in the Kirk graveyard.

"I'm on my way home to the store, to see my parents. I could come to get them now, if you like. I'm in town just long enough to see my friend, Katie Montgomery, get married."

At the Ayr home nearby, John handed Fiona the packet of letters, held together with a rose-colored ribbon, carefully finished off with a bow. She could imagine sweet auld Iona Ayr, caring for them lovingly. She was surprised at the number of letters in the packet. Billy's connection with these elderly folk must have been stronger than she knew. She thanked John and headed home.

After she unpacked in her old room, she put the letters into her Gladstone bag, on top of her extra clothing. She could see Iona Ayr's rose-coloured ribbon through the open top of the bag. She was excited to get the letters. She'd immerse herself in this delicious, unexpected link to Billy, as soon as she got back to Glasgow. But now, she had to hurry downstairs to enjoy her reunion with her parents.

Over the next two days, everyone was involved in wedding activities. The great drinking celebrations of the men at their party, and the women's sociable, gift-laden bridal shower preceded the serious wedding rehearsal on Friday afternoon. Hung-over men and tired women experienced mild regret, having consumed much whiskey, Jamaican rum, or sugary, baked sweets. Such afflictions, however, would be no excuse for anyone's not paying rapt attention to the Minister's directives at this rehearsal.

Fiona entered the church with her parents to the tune of Mrs. MacDougall's vigorous playing on the organ.

"Mrs. MacDougall, I hear you've got some good news."

"Fiona!"

The plump, smiling woman leaped up from the stool at the organ. She rushed over to wrap her arms around Fiona.

"Lass, it's good to see you. I can tell you've already heard about Johnny McCauley and me. Fancy that, Fiona. My first date with Johnny, when I was cheeky enough to wear the McCauley tartan, has paid off. I'll soon be Mrs. McCauley! He isna' near as shy a man as we thought!"

Fiona held onto Mrs. MacDougall as she spoke. She was glad to have been a part of the serendipitous happiness of her former choir director. It was one of the few good memories of home that hadn't been tarnished by Jeremy MacAndrews.

Fiona enjoyed her reunion with her friends and family. But, she couldn't stop thinking about Billy, especially during the wedding ceremony the following day. Katie and Charlie, the loving couple, looked so very happy. But, their wedding ceremony brought on a great sadness. She and Billy were supposed to be the bride and groom, here in the Old Parish Kirk of their home town. This should've been their wedding. She'd imagined it for years.

She managed to get through the service and smiled at Katie as she signed the register. She didn't want to spoil Katie's day by revealing her own sadness. Once photographs of the wedding party had been taken, she slipped away home to her old room above the store. She needed a few moments to herself, to think about Billy, before the reception started.

She sat on her bed, overwhelmed, missing Billy. Her gaze fell onto her bag where it sat on the floor near the dresser. She spotted the rose-coloured ribbon that bound the large packet of Billy's letters. Unable to resist, she got up, took the packet from her bag, and sat back down on the bed. Maybe she'd feel better if she read a couple of the letters. It might help her cheer up, before she returned to the wedding festivities.

Carefully, she undid the first loop of the ribbon. She was

surprised when a few envelopes fell from the back of the packet onto the floor. She picked them up and noticed right away that there were three of them, each with a letter inside. They were addressed to Billy, with the return address of Iona Ayr, not the other way round, as she'd expected. Why would Billy have returned these three letters to Iona?

Beyond curious now, she decided to read one of the letters. Then, she'd hurry back to the wedding activities. She'd save Billy's letters to Iona for later, when she had more time to enjoy them. She started with the most recent letter, postmarked 1917. Billy was 19 years old that year. He'd been fighting in the Great War for two years. Everyone had expected him to finish his apprenticeship in Inverness, but, when he was 17, he abruptly cut his apprenticeship short, lied about his age, and enlisted in the army.

At the time, he'd told Fiona and his parents he'd enlisted to do his part for Scotland. Thinking that Iona's letters might elaborate on Billy's sudden departure from Inverness, Fiona quickly began to read the first letter.

Dear Billy,

I'm writing to let you know that your young daughter has just celebrated her second birthday and is doing very well . . .

Confused, Fiona read again, 'your young daughter.'

What? Whose young daughter? She rechecked the date, 1917. Billy was in Europe with his army unit. Shaken, trembling, so that she could hardly hold the letter steady enough to read, her heart pounded, as she continued to take in the shocking words.

. . . My sister tells me the child is surrounded by her adoptive family. They're kind and loving to her. She'll never know she wasn't born into this wealthy, childless family. They named her Ellen Rose.

My sister asked me to tell you she's very much like you, dear Billy, with blonde, wavy hair and blue eyes. She's loved and very well cared for.

I hope, Billy, you'll someday be married to your Fiona and have children with her. My lasting regret is the same as yours. I wish I could tell your mum and daddie they have a grandchild. But, I think your mum would be heartbroken to learn about the child and know that she couldn't see her. I'll not ever tell them about Ellen Rose. As always, wealth and power prevail, keeping silent the few people who know you're the father of the child.

Take care of yourself, Billy. Let's hope this wretched war ends soon. John sends his love.

Yours in love and friendship,

Iona Ayr, 1917

My God! This child was born the year Billy left his apprenticeship to enlist in the Army. She must have been conceived, at Inverness, when Billy was only 16 years old! Who's the mother? Was she his employer's daughter? If not, then who was she?

Stunned, Fiona looked up at the clock. An hour had passed. She must go back to the reception. If she hurried, she could pack up her things quickly and be ready to leave on the first train tomorrow. Then she could think and read the rest of the letters, alone. She rushed back to the reception hall. The first person she met was her Mum.

"Fiona. Where've you been darlin'? What's the matter? You look pale. Are you not feelin' well?"

"I'm fine, Mum. I've been thinking about Billy all day. I'm sure I'll feel better when I get away from the wedding. I'm going back to Glasgow tomorrow morning. I'm sure my trips home will get easier as time passes."

"I understand," said Kathleen as she touched Fiona's forearm gently. "But, will you not stay one more day for Geordie's big birthday celebration tomorrow? We've heard that Helen and

Daniel are at MacAndrews' estate. They're coming into town for the party."

"No, Mum. I'll see them in Glasgow. I'm glad to hear, though, that Edward MacAndrews is allowing you and Daddie to see Daniel."

"Well, he isn't, exactly. The Laird leaves town first thing tomorrow. Helen decided it's important to bring Daniel to the party for Geordie. She's his mother, after all."

With this information, Fiona realized that the tug-of-war between Helen and Laird MacAndrews, for Daniel, had begun. She was glad she wasn't a part of that struggle. She turned her attention back to the wedding at hand, not wanting to think about Helen, Daniel, Laird MacAndrews, or anybody else. What she wanted was to be done with this wedding and get back to Billy's letters.

After many grand toasts and good wishes, Katie and Charlie left for their short honeymoon. Fiona was very happy for her best friend. She'd always be grateful, especially, for Katie's support the night she was raped by that MacAndrews bastard—the worst day of her life, until Billy's death. Tonight's news about Billy's daughter was now running a close third.

As of this day, I must contend with Billy's betrayal of my trust. He only let me think he told me everything. All along, he had this secret. Why didn't he trust me enough to tell me about his child, especially when I told him I was expecting Jeremy's child? Now, I see why he was so quick to help me deal with MacAndrews' rape and that baby of his. Billy must have helped me out of guilt about his own secret. He knew he was deceiving me. He let me believe I was the only unmarried, pregnant young woman in his life, the only one between the two of us, with an unwanted child.

Fiona's mental turmoil finally put an end to her participation at the wedding reception. She left as soon as the bride and groom were gone, planning to get to bed, rise early, and escape from this new nightmare. She was glad the Murray clan wouldn't return home when she did. Already, she'd resolved to look for her own place to live, starting tomorrow. She needed some privacy and somewhere that didn't expose her to constant reminders of Billy.

Fiona's intention to go straight to bed was lost the minute she got to her room. The rest of the letters awaited her. She bathed, got into bed, and began to read. The remaining two letters from Iona Ayr to Billy confirmed that Billy had enlisted the year his child was born, with the encouragement of his employer. The mother of the child was his employer's niece, two years older than Billy. They'd been intimate while he lived with the family. He'd offered to marry her, but she refused. Their child was quietly adopted by the Earl of Hopewell, Donald MacPherson and his wife. After giving birth, the niece took up nurses training, hiding the fact that she was an unwed mother. She was sent to France. She died while attending to a wounded soldier in an ambulance near the front lines.

Billy's earliest letter to Iona described his surprise that anyone back in Marysburgh knew about the child. But, Iona's sister worked for the adoptive family. She'd learned that Billy was the natural father of Ellen Rose. The most poignant of Billy's letters to Iona touched Fiona deeply.

Dear Iona,

I hope you won't be too surprised that this letter isn't full of war news. I've some other thoughts to share with you. First, I can't get used to calling you by your Christian names. For so many years, I've called you Mr. and Mrs. Ayr. I was only a child when my father sent me to help you with the yard work, after John's first stroke. I loved it when you and John taught me how to maintain a home and grounds. It was such a nice change from helping my parents with the pub.

None of us could have known we'd be bound together by a secret, many years after we got to know each other.

I hope you won't mind if I explain myself, my situation, to you. You know I've loved Fiona Gilman since I can remember. I made a serious mistake when I found comfort in someone else's arms. I've no excuse, except I was lonely for Fiona. I miss her joking and her advice about how things could be. She always knows what she wants. She has great strength of character. That young woman, the mother of my child, isn't near the person that Fiona is. I shouldn't have eased my loneliness for Fiona with her. I regret it very much. We're both lucky that Laird MacPherson and his wife were desperate for a child.

After the war, I'll tell Fiona about the child. I'll probably wait until we're married. I know she's saving herself for me. I only wish I'd done the same for her. But, there's no undoing that now, is there?

Thank you, both, for keeping my secret. If your sister hadn't told you, nobody in Marysburgh would've known about the child. I know I can trust you to be silent, until I can tell Fiona when she's my beloved wife.

I know this explanation comes after many words have passed between us. But, here on the front lines, in this awful war, every day could be the last for me. If I survive this war, I'll look forward to both of you dancing at my wedding to Fiona. Until then, I remain,

Your loving and grateful friend,
Billy McGinnis
January, 1918

Hurt, disillusioned, and angry, Fiona decided she'd, later, burn all of the letters except the two that identified the natural parents of Ellen Rose, and the Earl of Hopewell, Donald MacPherson. Her experiences with the MacAndrews clan had taught her that being drawn into contact with people of wealth and power could be dangerous, or unpredictable, at best. She'd be cautious about destroying anything that might be needed later.

She couldn't dismiss from her mind, the heartbreaking, but infuriating image of her Billy, in the arms of the mother of his child. She was ashamed, too. Between them, she and Billy had forsaken two children. She was tormented by this thought, as she finally fell asleep just before dawn.

The next morning, Fiona and Ian were about to walk out the door toward the train when the phone rang. Ian put down Fiona's bag and went to answer the phone, while Fiona, impatient to get going, waited by the door. A few minutes later, father and daughter walked to the station while Ian explained that the call was from Sean Talbot, the handsome Irish law student they'd met at Jeremy's murder trial.

"What did he want?"

"Well, Fiona dear, he very politely asked to speak to ye. But, when I told him we were rushing to get you onto the train, he said he'd call once ye were back in Glasgow."

"Call me? Why would he do that?"

"Fiona! You're at the beginning of the next part of your life, lass—a lovely young women with a future. It's time for ye to try to move on."

"But, he knows I was raped. And that I had a child. My life is a mess. Why would he want anything to do with me?"

"Fiona, nobody can force ye to see him, if ye dinna choose. But, at some point, darlin' you have to put your unpleasant memories aside, and start to live your life. I ken that you'll grieve for Billy, but the hurt will soften over time. I hope you'll give life a chance to make ye happy, my lovely gel."

"I'll try, Daddie."

She hugged and kissed him goodbye, knowing that he and her mum were her strongest supporters.

Maybe, someday, I'll tell them what I know about Billy. But, I doubt it. What's the point? He's dead. He betrayed my trust. I'll just have to live with that.

22 ... Hope

Back in Glasgow, Fiona began searching for a room to let. She found a small, clean but pricey flat near the University of Glasgow. She paid the deposit and the first month's rent. Apparently, the only reason the flat was available was because a student hadn't shown up. She could move in the next weekend. She was looking forward to being surrounded by people her own age. Before she left the building, she used the telephone in the hallway of her new place, to call her parents and give them her new address.

When Jack and Jeannie Murray returned from Marysburgh, they were surprised she'd already made arrangements to move out. They'd miss her, but they understood her need to get on with her life. At month end, Jack and his apprentice would move her things into the flat for her.

Two weeks after she moved into her flat, Fiona heard a tap on her door, followed by a female voice. She'd been working on a new garment that she designed for one of her clients. She didn't need any interruptions or she wouldn't finish the garment on time.

"Who is it?"

"Fiona, there's a call for you."

She walked down the hall and picked up the dangling receiver. "Hello?"

"Hello, Fiona. Sean Talbot here. Have I called at a good time?"

Surprised, she recalled the handsome, lean face and the tall, well-built body that went with his smooth voice.

"I'm working just now. How can I help you?"

"I was wonderin' if you'd care to have coffee or tea with me. I'm in town for a few days. I don't know too many people here in Glasgow."

"Um . . . well . . . when were you thinking?"

"Now, if you like."

"I can't go now."

"What about tomorrow afternoon?"

"I can't. I have an appointment with a client to deliver a dress then."

"Friday morning? Are you busy then?"

"Well . . . no, I suppose Friday morning would be alright. I'll meet you somewhere."

"That's fine, Friday is just fine. I'll give you the address of a nice coffee house. It's not too far from your place."

"How'd you know where I live?"

"I don't, exactly. When I called the Murrays today to speak to you, Mrs. Murray gave me this number. She told me you'd moved somewhere near the University. The coffee house is *The Thistle*, on the corner of Kelvin Way and Argyle Street."

"OK. Well, I'll meet you at ten on Friday morning then."

"Grand! I'll look forward to it."

What the heck. I've got nobody else and I'm so angry with Billy, who's dead anyway. Why not meet with a great-looking Irishman? What can it hurt? I'm not looking to marry him, after all. It might be nice to have some company and conversation.

Fiona enjoyed her cavalier thoughts until she began sewing again in earnest. Now, the garment definitely had to be finished.

She found out on Friday, that Sean was the ultimate gentleman. He held Fiona's chair for her, paid for their drinks, and didn't raise awkward subjects of conversation.

"How's your mum?"

"Oh, she's fine. She talked about you after we all met at the court building."

"I'm not surprised. We have a common, Irish heritage, as you know. She seemed to enjoy what's left of me Irish way o' speakin'."

His putting on an exaggerated Irish accent made Fiona smile. She recalled that her mum had sounded much more Irish, after speaking with Sean.

"Yes, I noticed Mum's fascination with you. What're you doing here in Glasgow?"

"I'm using the law library at the university to check for precedents in a particular case. I'll write my exams soon. My Da was an Advocate. I'm expected to live up to the family tradition. I lost some time while I was in Europe with the military. When I'm finally called to the bar, I'll be the oldest new Advocate that ever was, in my family. These things happen in wartime, don't they?"

"Yes, they do. Actually, I, too, know what it's like to wait for schooling. I'm still waiting. I was to be the first university graduate in my family. The mess you found me in at the trial is the reason I didn't get to the University of Edinburgh as I planned."

"Have you thought about applying for next year?"

"Yes, I've thought of it. I'm still trying to decide what to do. I've started a design and dressmaking business, which I enjoy. I'll need to decide if that will be enough for me, in the long run. I was an excellent student, though. I still read a lot. In fact, I'm surprised I haven't run into you at the library these past weeks. Most days, I go there to escape from my sewing machine, for a bit."

Fiona relaxed, encouraged that Sean didn't seem to expect more than conversation. It was nice to chat in a coffee shop, with someone who didn't press her for too much information, or for sex, either. The admiring looks she'd gotten from men since she was in her teens were no longer flattering. They were threatening, after Jeremy.

I like this man. It might be safe to trust him a wee bit. I'd really like to have a friend to talk to, especially one that's so good to look at.

As the last few months of the year passed, Fiona saw Sean when he was in town, visited with the Murrays, and attended to her designs and sewing. Her business was growing. She'd need to decide soon, whether or not she'd relocate to Edinburgh. She might be able to find enough clients there, to supplement the small income she had from Edward MacAndrews. If she saved her money, she'd be able to take courses on a part-time basis, at the University of Edinburgh, starting the following September.

Why not? If she was going to go on with her education, now was as good a time to start as any. Besides, Sean worked in Edinburgh. Being around him whenever he came to Glasgow was having an effect on her. They'd started to kiss each other goodbye, on the cheek. He held her hand whenever they ventured across crowded streets filled with horses, military vehicles, cars, and other pedestrians.

The evening before he left to travel to Dublin for Christmas with his family he leaned down and kissed Fiona softly, on the lips. Her thoughts raced, her body's response rising, immediately and uncontrollably, to an intense level.

Oh, my God! How can this be happening? I swore I'd have nothing more to do with men. I thought Jeremy's rape, Billy's death, and, especially, finding out that Billy hadn't been honest with me, would keep me from desiring any man. But, Sean is so lovely, so gentle. I want to feel all of him, not just his lips.

She responded to his touch by pressing her body against his, shocking both herself and him. She'd never experienced such intense sexual feelings.

"Fiona darlin', take it easy."

She was totally embarrassed. Tears welled up in her eyes as she opened them and looked up at him.

"I'm so sorry, Sean. After all of my grand efforts to protect myself from physical contact with you, or any man, I find myself trusting you to touch me without hurting me, physically or otherwise. I know I said I wasn't ready for anything but a pla-tonic friendship. In fact, I know I've stressed my restrictions for our relationship repeatedly, over these past few months. And, Sean dear, you've been respectful of my wishes, never pushing me. But, now, I feel ready to trust you."

Fiona took his hand and led him into her flat. Neither of them spoke as they took off their coats and then stood, looking at each other.

"If you're sure you want to do this, Fiona, I have protection. It's against my religion, but I can't be fathering any babies."

"You've just said the magic words, haven't you? We both know I certainly can't have another child."

"What do you mean, you can't? Did that criminal ruin your chances to have children later?"

"Oh. No. I only meant I'll be choosing when to have a child. I'll not have another one forced on me."

"Come here, my lovely lass."

With Sean, Fiona learned how spectacular lovemaking could be. Jeremy had ruined her and then Billy had died before they could make love as husband and wife. Sean taught her, gently, how intense and pleasurable her body could be made to feel. His fingers, his lips, his whole body consumed her and taught her how to respond to him. She turned herself over to him completely, losing any sense of herself in the pleasure of the moment.

However, after he left that night, she felt guilty—guilty that she hadn't saved herself, damaged as she was, for her future husband. But, she reasoned, she'd fallen in love with Sean, over the past few months. And, he'd told her tonight, many times, that he loved her. Surely, they'd marry and then the first person she truly gave her body to would turn out to be her husband, after all.

Christmas Eve and dinner at the Murray's the next day were replays of the noise, succulent food, music, conversation, and celebration, of the year before. But, this year, Billy, Tess, and Taylor were absent, while Ian and Kathleen Gilman, along with Helen Brody and her wee Daniel joined the festivities as guests of the Murrays.

Fiona was relieved her parents had travelled to Glasgow for Christmas. She wouldn't have to go home and be reminded of her conflicting feelings about Billy. With Sean in her life, so loving and attentive, she'd be able to move on and grieve for Billy less, as time passed.

Both Jack Murray and Ian teased Fiona about her new love. Her mum also took a few moments to ask her about her new man.

"Darlin' Fiona, did you say your new Irish love is as caring and gentlemanly as he is handsome?"

"Aye, Mum. That he is. We've been all around the town, exploring the museums, riding the tram, sipping tea, and enjoying ourselves. I've been cooking meals for us too."

"Well, it sounds awfully like it's turnin' to love, dearie."

"Aye, it is. I'm out of my mind with love for him. I'll miss him dearly while he's away in Ireland for the holidays. But, we have a date to go to the *Willow Tea Rooms* on January 15th. He says he has something important he wants to talk to me about, Mum."

"Have you met his parents, Fiona, or any of this relations or friends?"

"Not yet. Only a couple of fellows from his law firm in Edinburgh. I suppose that'll come later—maybe in the spring."

"Aye, the spring will bring better travellin' weather, won't it? I'm just glad you're happy, my girl. You deserve it."

"I am, Mum, I really am."

Their conversation was interrupted when Daniel lost his balance as he stood unsteadily, at the end of the sofa. He let out a surprised squeal when he plopped down onto the carpet. At just seven months, he was attempting to walk, already.

Fiona turned from her conversation with Kathleen to watch

the little boy. His light brown hair had streaks of blonde now. She could see that he had her father's square jaw, a sure sign there was some of the Gilman clan in him. She was surprised. She'd been prepared to see only Jeremy when she looked at him. Happily, this wasn't the case.

On this day, Fiona began to experience a vague feeling of regret, for having given up her son. But, it was too late to fix that mistake now. She could see that Helen was the perfect mother, watching Daniel carefully, lovingly, as she pretended to be absorbed in conversations. She obviously loved the boy as much as any mother loves her son. Fiona wasn't about to interfere with the contentment of Helen, or her small son.

I've made the right decision. I have. Yes. He's better off with Helen than he would've been with me, particularly with Edward MacAndrews involved in his life. I'm surprised, though, that Laird MacAndrews has visited the boy a few times, checking to see if Helen needs anything. So far, Helen's impression of the Laird is that of a kindly, concerned grandfather, even though his involvement with the boy has been somewhat limited. And that's fine with Helen.

I hope, for the sake of Helen and Daniel, that Edward MacAndrews will be able to maintain his transformation. Either way, I'll be able to sever my financial tie to him, once I marry Sean. I'm sure he'll ask me soon. As soon as we're wed, I'll stop taking that annuity from MacAndrews. Initially, I really needed the money. And, I accepted his help because I was convinced he owed it to me. His rotten son had ruined my life. But, it feels like blood money, like a buy-off. I'd like to think I could trust him, believe he's changed. However, many years of subservience to him and his son, by my family and every other family in Marysburgh, leaves me with some doubt that his new behavior will last.

That's enough. Enough thinking about Laird MacAndrews. These thoughts are spoiling my Christmas Day. I'll focus on Sean's return, on our date for January 15, in a brand new year with grand possibilities.

23 ... Et tu, my love?

*J*anuary was brutally cold, bringing flurries and blustery winds that blew along Sauchiehall Street. Fiona and Sean walked arm in arm toward the *Willow Tea Rooms*. He'd returned to Glasgow the night before. They spent the night in his hotel, happy to be back together.

As they removed their coats, at the *Tea Rooms*, Fiona noticed that the receptionist was the same middle-aged, surly woman, Doris, who'd been working the last few times she and Helen came here. Then, Fiona had been very pregnant with Daniel. Her fingers were too swollen, by that time, to wear the borrowed wedding ring she used as a prop. She wanted strangers to think she was married and pregnant, not just pregnant. What rotten luck. She hadn't seen this Doris woman for almost a year. And here she was, again, without a wedding ring. Hopefully, the woman wouldn't remember her pregnant state.

"Good afternoon, do you have a reservation?"

"We do, Madam. It's Talbot, for two please."

"Hmm, Talbot, I don't see it . . ."

"Please check again, Madam. My assistant made the reservation a month ago."

As Sean spoke to the rude woman, clad in her ghastly, large-flowered housedress, Doris surveyed Fiona, top to bottom. Apparently, she resented Fiona's good looks, or perhaps she was jealous because Fiona came on the arm of such a good-looking man. Such hostile behavior had been directed Fiona's way, many times, from women who didn't have her good looks and confidence. Doris appeared to be yet another jealous, judgmental person in a long line of such petty people. Or, worse yet, Doris might actually remember Fiona from the last time she saw her, in her unwed, pregnant state.

"Oh, here it is. It was misspelled, 'Tail-butt,' sorry, this way please."

They were seated at a table for two, in high-backed chairs, with strongly defined vertical lines. As always, Fiona admired the extraordinary fabrics and the amazing frieze in the window, that were so much a part of her *Tearooms* experience. She relaxed into her luxurious surroundings.

"What's up with that woman, Fiona? She was outright rude to both of us. And, she certainly gave you the once over, along with her dirty looks."

"Well, Sean dear, if you're going to take me out, you'll learn the way some women treat other women. I was here with Helen, very pregnant, without a wedding ring last spring. It seems she remembers me and has judged me accordingly. She doesn't seem like the well-read type, but she could also have seen my picture in the paper with Edward MacAndrews, walking into Jeremy's murder trial to testify about my rape and pregnancy. Maybe she thinks wealthy, older men and young, well-dressed men pay me to escort them in public."

"Fiona, are you saying she thinks you're a whore?"

"I wouldn't put it past her. Some women look for reasons to put down younger, better-looking women. Other than her age, she reminds me of the disrespectful way my sister, Brigit, treated me, particularly when she found out I was pregnant. She spread gossip around town and purposely tried to ruin my reputation, something I'll never get back in Marysburgh. By the time you and I met, of course, my reputation was long gone, after the humiliating experience of the trial. But, let's not talk of such negative things, shall we? I'm used to such treatment. I refuse to let it get me down, especially when we're together."

"That's what I admire about you, Fiona, your strong character. I love you for that."

They chatted and ordered their tea, before Fiona got up to use the restroom. A few minutes later, as she walked back toward their table, she saw and heard a well-dressed woman, loudly effusing words at Sean in an Irish-accented voice.

"Why Sean, Sean Talbot, 'tis you! Your mum will be so happy I've seen you! She was just tellin' me last week, about your visit home to Ireland for Christmas. She's tickled at how well your young wife looks, all aglow with her pregnancy."

Fiona stopped just short of the table, behind the woman. She could see the devastated look on Sean's face, as he saw her listening to the woman's comments. Before he could react, she turned, hurried to the foyer, grabbed her coat, and rushed out of the building.

Running on the slippery street was difficult, but she managed to put some distance behind her, as she cut over to Argyle Street and hopped on the first tram. When the tram neared Kelvin Way, she got off and ran all the way up the hill to her flat. She raced in and bolted the door behind her.

She couldn't cry. She didn't make a sound.

How could this be happening? Do I attract only rotten men—Jeremy, the rapist, Billy, the secretive fiancé, Sean, the grand deceiver? What's wrong with me? I'm an unwed mother, who's signed away my child. I lost my chance at a university education, and I'll probably never be able to fix that. My only certain income is from a wealthy, powerful man, who may or may not be sincere in his dealings, with my dear friend, Helen, with his grandson, or with me.

Helen. That's where I'll go. Sean's never met her. He probably thinks I won't go near the boy, because he's Jeremy's son. Quickly, she grabbed her Gladstone bag, stuffed in a few clothes and personal things, and rushed out of the flat. Desperate to get away, she hailed a taxi for the short ride to Helen's. She could only hope that Helen would let her in.

Helen answered the door in her robe.

"Fiona? What're you doing here? I mean, I'm very glad to see you but I didn't expect you tonight. Isn't this your big night with Sean, at the *Tea Rooms*?"

Through a sudden gush of tears, Fiona sputtered,

"A big night, indeed. The night I find out that after all of our confessions of love for each other and hints at a future together, my latest disaster is a married lover with a pregnant wife!"

"Oh, no. Come in, come in. We'll get you settled for the night after a nice cup of tea. Give me your coat and bag. You go into the library. Violet's gone home. I'll get the tea."

Here I am, back with Helen. I thought I'd had left this part of my life behind me. Daniel's here, that small, half-Gilman, half-MacAndrews boy, the boy I can't help thinking about. I imagined that Sean and I would marry and move to Ireland, or Edinburgh. I imagined having children with Sean, leaving this first, accidental child in Helen's excellent care. I thought I might visit Daniel now and again, without upsetting Helen, or making her worry I want him back. I must have been desperate to let my imagination run away with me like that.

Helen came in with the tea. She wasn't surprised to see tears streaming down Fiona's face.

"I'm so sorry about Sean, Fiona. Did he tell you about his situation tonight? Is that what he wanted to say to you?"

"If I were to be totally fair, perhaps he would have told me tonight. But, he missed his chance to do the right thing. An Irish woman came over to talk with him while I was returning to the table from the facilities. She spilled the whole, awful truth, loudly. I overheard 'wife' and 'aglow with her pregnancy' and that was enough for me. I ran and never looked back."

"But, you do love him, don't you?"

"Aye, I love him, wholeheartedly, both physically and emotionally. My feelings for him are the most intense I've had for anyone in my life."

"Will you speak to him about this? Are you going to give him a chance to explain himself?"

"What's to explain? It won't change the circumstances, will it? He'll still be married won't he? Divorce is out of the question in his family, his church."

"Why don't you finish your tea, lass, and try to get some sleep? Stay here as long as you like. Daniel and I are happy for the company. He's so cute now, Fiona, tottering around and speaking a few more words than he did when you saw him at Christmas."

Fiona had a restless night, waking often, disturbed by dreams of Sean making love to her, holding her hand, helping her with her coat, laughing with her at the kitchen table in her flat.

Sean, how could this be? You've used me. Do you even love me, or was I just an amusement to you?

The next morning she'd just finished dressing, when she heard voices from Helen's foyer. She stepped behind the door of her room at the top of the stairs, leaving the door ajar so she could hear what was being said, without being seen. Was it Sean?

Helen's raised voice carried up the stairs. "What do you mean, Edward? You won't be visiting? Daniel's enjoyed your few visits. We missed you at Christmas. I thought you'd visit him in your holiday break from the Parliament. What's going on?"

"Here's how it will be from now on, Helen. I've hired a nanny. She'll start as soon as Parliament lets out in the spring. After his first birthday, Daniel will come to the Glenheather Estate, until the fall session starts and I go back to London full time. You know I have equal time with him. I plan to have that time, starting by the end of May. My Glenheather affairs require me to be there as much as possible. I won't be making side trips here—I'll see Daniel at home."

"How can you do that? He's just a baby!"

"I can, Helen, and I will. He's my flesh and blood, the heir to my estate. The more time he spends there, before he goes to boarding school, the better. The tenants must get used to his being their future Laird, from the start. He'll learn the proper attitudes and behavior for a Laird. There's no better place for him to soak that up than with me, at the estate."

"I assume you'll allow me to visit, while you have your time with him?"

"Certainly, you can come whenever you want, but you're not welcome to stay for more than a few days at a time. I don't want the boy confused as to where he belongs. The tenants need to get to know him and show due respect, from the beginning. They can't do that while he lives in Glasgow, or when he's clinging to you in front of them. When he's a bit older, I'll send a governess to live with you. She'll get him ready for pre-school."

"Edward! You're taking away my child! I'm his mother! How can you do that to him?"

"Helen, I think we both know that I'm well aware of my rights under the law. If you'd care to contest that, go ahead. It won't change anything."

"Edward, what happened? What happened to the kindly grandfather you've been, visiting with Daniel here, in his mother's home, the home he knows?"

"I suppose I was in shock, after Jeremy's murder. I've had some time to think it through. I realize I can't ever be repaid for losing my only son. There's nothing I can do about that. But, there is certainly something I can do about my rights to Daniel. He'll not be mollycoddled. He'll learn to step up to his responsibilities as a MacAndrews, a Laird. The best way for that to happen is for him to live at the estate, for my half of each year, beginning in his second year of life."

"What about his other grandparents? Do you plan to let them see him?"

"Of course. They'll see him as their future Laird, just the way everyone else who works for me will see him."

At that, Fiona swung open the bedroom door, sending it crashing against the wall as she pounded down the stairs.

"I knew it! I knew this grandfatherly guise was too good to be true. Are you human only when something, someone, has been wrongfully taken away from you, even though he's a rapist? Have you no heart? You'll contaminate this little boy, with, with . . . your entitled, condescending ways, wielding your power like a maniac, mowing down anyone who gets in your way. You're wicked! An evil man! I hope to God that Daniel hasn't inherited your character or that of your criminal son. You aren't worthy of being his grandfather!"

"Are you quite finished, Miss Gilman? May I remind you that your only steady income comes from me, an income I did not need to provide, an income I can cancel whenever I choose? With enough legal fees, any contract can be undone. Remember to whom you are speaking, Miss Gilman. I'm your Laird and the Laird of your family."

"We'll fight you, MacAndrews. You'll not be allowed to casually corrupt this little boy the way your upbringing did Jeremy. Look how he turned out, for God's sake!"

"That's quite enough, Miss Gilman. Mrs. Brody, I'll send the new nanny to pick up Daniel the day after his birthday. You have until May 25th to spend your first portion of this year with him. He'll be returned in the fall, to meet the conditions of our agreement."

As he stepped toward the door, MacAndrews turned and spoke to Helen.

"Mrs. Brody, I'll not tolerate having my grandson exposed to this woman. If she's living here, she must leave. If she's visiting, she must leave. Either way, she's not to be in this house or anywhere else, with my grandson. You are his adoptive mother, the only legal mother he has. She willingly signed away all rights to him. See that you keep her to that legally-binding arrangement from now on. Good day."

By this time, Daniel was howling, having been awakened by the slamming door, Fiona's pounding down the stairs, and her subsequent, loud raving at MacAndrews. Helen turned and went to him, while Fiona paced back and forth between the foyer and the library. She was furious, on behalf of the little boy and her friend, Helen. She hadn't realized the depth of her "mother bear" instinct for defending her young son and his adoptive mother.

So, here it is. The kindly old grandfather is no more. MacAndrews is himself again. That bastard is going to force Helen to comply with his demands, or she'll risk losing Daniel. There's no way I can stay here now. It would compromise Helen's ability to provide a peaceful environment for the boy, for as long as she can every year.

Fiona went upstairs and packed her few belongings. She leaned into Daniel's doorway to say goodbye to Helen, who had calmed the little boy.

"I'm so sorry, Helen. I couldn't hold my temper. I was already upset by my situation with Sean. I ignored my better judgment when I shouted what is actually the truth at MacAndrews. I know better. Powerful people like MacAndrews become even more determined to subvert the people they oppress, when anyone dares to stand up to them. I shouldn't have done that. But, now we know his intentions. His kindly and considerate behavior toward you and Daniel was temporary. My presence here will only hurt you both. I'm leaving now."

"Thank you, Fiona. I'm so afraid of losing Daniel I'll do whatever MacAndrews wants, so I can keep my boy, even if I must share him with nannies and governesses. I know you understand. You'll let me know what you decide to do, won't you?"

"Aye, I will."

When she arrived back at her flat and opened the door, Fiona saw a note lying on the floor. It was from Sean. He begged to see her, to explain his situation, to apologize. He wrote that his family had forced him to marry their choice, for a wife, not his. Otherwise, he would face the penalty of disinheritance. His wife was only 18, sheltered, naïve, and spoiled. He doesn't love her. His lot is a sorry one, to hear him tell it. Sean's written pleadings didn't move Fiona to call him. She felt numb, wrestling with the complexities of her relationship with Sean, as she unpacked her bag.

I love him. I love him, in spite of his marital state, in spite of his impending fatherhood. He's made my messed up life worth living. I think I hate him too, for lying to me. Oh, but I was always so excited, so thrilled to see him, to feel the comfort of being in his arms, to feel him inside me, rhythmically taking us both into ecstasy. I know his body and he knows mine, better than anyone ever has. How do I give that up?

I'm going to hell for sure now. I have, indeed, become a wanton woman. This time it's my fault. I've given my body and my heart to this incredibly appealing man—yet another man who keeps secrets. I can't marry him, ever. I'm a brazen woman to myself and to all who know of my physical relationship with this married man. My already ruined reputation will be even worse now.

Her thoughts were interrupted by a knock on her door.

"Fiona, are you there? You have a phone call out here."

"Thanks, Angie. Who is it?"

"It's your handsome Prince, that's who. He's been calling since yesterday."

"Please tell him I can't come to the phone, I'm going out."

Resolved to resist all attempts by Sean to reach her, Fiona left her flat and went directly to the Emigration Office. The only way she could think of, to start over, away from Sean, the love she felt for him, the reminders of him here in Glasgow, and, unfortunately, from Daniel and Helen, was to set in motion the plans she and Billy had started. She would emigrate to Canada. Alone, now, she'd escape from the mess her life had become, here in Scotland.

Part 2

24 ... New world

"You're pinching me, you fool!"

"I'm so sorry, Madam. I'm almost finished, if you could wait a wee moment, please."

Lady Bridge-Harris, or, as Fiona silently called her, 'Bitch-Harris,' was the most cantankerous client Fiona had ever designed for, bar none. She was a permanent resident of luxurious rooms here at the Empress Hotel, in Victoria, BC. The Empress was a world class, luxury hotel on Vancouver Island, off the west coast of Canada. The Lady and her cronies had been clients of Fiona's for the past five years, thanks to Hilary Burns, Fiona's young Scottish client.

Fiona should have come to Canada when Hilary first invited her. Instead, she'd stayed in Scotland until June of 1920, long enough for Sean Talbot to break her heart. The past five years had been challenging. But, she was surviving here in Victoria, glad to have escaped from her sullied reputation, Sean, memories of her dead fiancé, Billy, and Laird MacAndrews.

Hilary Burns was sworn to secrecy. She knew about Fiona's rape, her humiliating testimony at Jeremy's murder trial, and, of course, her Scottish son. In exchange for her silence, Hilary treated Fiona as her own, personal fashion designer. Her outfits were given priority. Such treatment was fine with Fiona, as long as Hilary kept her mouth shut. Thanks to their agreement, Hilary Burns had the best wardrobe in town.

Madam removed the cape, handed it to Fiona, and disappeared into the bedroom to change out of her matching dress. While she waited, Fiona began to work on the hem of the exquisite, beaded, black evening cape, an original design of her own. Her thoughts drifted, as she remembered the painful goodbyes to her parents, to her friend, Helen, and to her Scottish son. Leaving them all behind in Scotland was the most difficult thing she had ever done. Kathleen and Ian Gilman had both cried, as her train pulled away from the Marysburgh station.

But, she remembered, too, that by the time she left Scotland, she hated herself for what she'd become: embittered and quite capable of taking advantage of Sean, as payback for his lying to her. If only, she'd been able to remain unwavering in her determination to stop seeing him.

He was waiting in the vestibule of her building, when she returned from the Emigration Office that January day, back in Glasgow. The sight of him made her weep with anger and disappointment. Yet, she let him lead her into her flat. He comforted her, until their mutual passion overtook them. He cried as he told her how much he loved her. After their desperate lovemaking, even more intense for both of them given the threat to their relationship, he said how sorry he was that he hadn't told her about his marriage earlier, before that busybody of a woman shouted it all over the *Tearooms*.

Passionate as his apologies were, Fiona no longer trusted him. She didn't tell Sean she'd been to Emigration, or that she'd completed the papers for her eventual departure to Canada. For once, she'd be the secret-keeper. The emotional scar he'd inflicted on her with his deception would remain. But, it was impossible for her to resist him physically. She decided she'd revel in their passionate physical relationship until the last moment. In the end, she'd break his heart as he'd broken hers.

And, she couldn't get enough of him. After all, he was the person who had so gently awakened and then fed her sexual appetite. They met only at her flat, no more hotels, where the gossips could see them out in public. Each time he came to her, she completely turned her body over to his caresses, his perfect, light touch, and then his manipulation of her body with increasing pressure, until she was in ecstasy. When he entered her, they were both released from almost unbearable sexual tension, oblivious to marital status, or to the world around them. They would lie, exhausted, in each other's arms, until their passion overtook them again. She realized that he might actually love her, but her love for him was altered. Her naive hopes for their future together were a spoiled fantasy.

Each time he left her flat, she hated herself more. Theirs had deteriorated into a sordid relationship: she must be a slut, or she couldn't possibly enjoy his body in the way that she did. It wasn't right, he wasn't her husband. After every encounter, she vowed never to make love with him again. But, then he'd call and she'd let him come over again. She just couldn't help herself. As four, and then five months passed by, she began to anticipate her mid-June departure date. She'd leave Sean and her wanton behavior behind, to begin a new life, where nobody knew about her past.

"Miss Gilman! Here!" Jolted back to the present time, Fiona saw that Lady Bridge-Harris held out money toward her.

"Thank you, Madam."

"I still don't understand why you need these interim payments—no other seamstress demands them."

"We've discussed this before, Madam. I'm a clothing designer as well as a seamstress. My time and your top quality, imported materials are costly. I simply can't afford to wait until my original designs are totally finished. Aren't you pleased with the dress and cape?"

"Yes, I suppose. But, you have no idea how inconvenient it is to arrange for this cash, quite inconvenient."

"Well, Madam, I'll be going now. I'll deliver the finished garments as promised next Friday morning."

Fiona was relieved to leave the wretched woman behind. She took the lift down to the first floor. She'd descend the rest of the way to the lobby down the ladies' staircase. Each time she did this, she imagined herself in one of her own, original outfits, dressed for afternoon tea, meeting an imagined suitor, perhaps someone who'd be just right for her, someone who'd actually be in a position to marry her. He'd be the love of her life, she hoped.

I'm only 27, a spinster, like Jane Austen's heroine, Anne Elliot. Anne eventually landed her Captain Wentworth. If it weren't too late in those days, for a 'spinster' to catch a man, surely it isn't too late, in these modern times, for me to do the same.

She continued with her musings, smiling to herself, as she walked through the lobby toward the huge hotel doors.

"Miss Gilman?"

She stopped.

"It's Angus, Angus MacArthur. I noticed you at Hilary Burns' party."

"Oh yes, Mr. MacArthur. How are you?"

"Well, I'm grand, seeing you again."

He's flirting with me, the cheeky man. He certainly is grand, isn't he? I remember him from the party.

Fiona had been on her way through the crowded room, attempting to leave quietly, when Hilary spotted her. In her half drunk, loud, high-pitched voice, Hilary made a big fuss about MacArthur's not being "caught," as yet, by a pretty woman. "He'll be snapped up sooner, rather than later, Fiona," she'd said. Hilary's emoting in such a way had embarrassed Fiona. She was glad to escape before Hilary could foist an embarrassing introduction on her.

Now, here was MacArthur himself. Such an enigma. He was a big, muscular looking man, over six feet, with a head of thick, dark hair and a stylish, well-trimmed beard to match. His hands were like huge bear paws, but he had obviously-manicured fingernails. He wore a stylish, dark business suit and a bright white shirt with a subtly-colored silk cravat, sure signs of a well-to-do gentleman. Yet, he was open and friendly, displaying a great smile as he greeted her. His deep brown eyes sparkled as he waited for her to speak.

"Miss Gilman, are you alright, lass?"

"Oh, yes. Sorry. I've just finished with Lady Bridge-Harris. I'm anxious to get outside into the garden so I can recover, somewhat."

"Ah. Yes. I know exactly what you mean. The firm I work with allows me the privilege of being their liaison with the Lady. Nobody else will do it. She's a handful, isn't she?"

They were both smiling by then, as Fiona nodded.

"Here, let me carry that large bag for you. I'll walk you out, if you'll let me. Maybe a stroll along the harbour, rather than in the garden will do as well. The harbour's full of sailing vessels, today."

He held her arm as they walked down the front steps of the hotel. They crossed over Government Street to the causeway along the waterfront. They didn't speak for a few moments, each one happy to be outdoors in the beautiful setting, enjoying the warm, August weather.

"Where are you from, then, Mr. MacArthur?"

"Call me Angus, please. My family comes from a small village in the highlands, called Newtonmore. It was a fine place to grow up, playing sports, hiking, hunting, and fishing every weekend. When the war broke out in 1914, I'd just finished my degree in economics at the University of Edinburgh. My parents, and the Laird, hoped I'd come back after university to run the Laird's cattle operations. But, the lure of the numbers, and my rejection by the military led me here. I'm a consultant to a large bank. I help their wealthy clients and some of my own decide how to invest their money."

"That's quite a resumé, Angus. I'd never have guessed you're connected to investment banking. It certainly is an indoor occupation, compared with the outdoor activities of your youth. You must be awfully good with numbers, to keep it all interesting."

"Aye, I seem to be. The market's boomed, since the Great War. It's almost too good to be true. I've been advising our clients to be cautious. But, they seem to want to make as much as possible and then spend everything they've got. Many fortunes have been made here, Miss Gilman, and I've been lucky to be in the right place at the right time."

"Call me Fiona. I know what you mean. I've been in Victoria since 1920. I've heard about families from Scotland who've made great fortunes here. I was amazed by the story of the Dunsmuir family. Imagine building not one, but two castles, with profits from coal mining and other businesses. Their story gives me hope. Someone told me that back in Scotland, their family rented mines from Scottish Lairds. Here in Canada, they're owners, not renters. Imagine making such profits for yourself and not on behalf of a Laird! Until I came here, I'd never have thought that possible. Now that I've heard your story, I can see you know all about the opportunities here in Canada."

"I've been very lucky, here, that's true. What about your own business, Fiona? How are you faring with that?"

"Very well, thank you. I can't keep up with my clothing design and dressmaking orders. Many of my clients have told me they're thrilled to have a local designer who's able to create custom ordered, high fashion designs. These local, well-to-do women and the constant stream of other wealthy women, who visit Victoria from all over the world, will pay dearly, to stay in style.

Local business people help to generate business for me too. A couple of years after I arrived, Jenny Butchart opened up her sunken garden. Visiting the garden has become a popular pastime, an opportunity to show off elegant, garden party outfits.

I hope there'll be many more such events in this area. The trick is, to keep up with the demand."

"How do you keep up? Surely, you can't do all of the designing and sewing yourself."

"I've been greatly helped by a Chinese friend of mine. He helped me hone my tailoring skills. He also taught me how to negotiate with importers. I depend on the importers who bring in high-quality silks from China and finely-woven, brilliantly-coloured fabrics from India. I've hired two, part-time employees, both fourteen. One is my friend's daughter, Ming, and the other is her friend, Lee. They help me with cutting and basting. I've also taught them how to use the beading machines, for the less expensive garments. Both Chinese girls have a strong work ethic. I couldn't be as successful without them."

"Impressive. You've developed quite a business, Fiona. Tell me, before you became a successful Scottish businesswoman here in Victoria, where were you from, originally?"

"I come from a small seaside town called Marysburgh, near Loch Lomond. My parents operate the general store, owned by the Baron of Glenheather, Edward MacAndrews. He's the Laird of everything, near and far. Actually, I had a scholarship to study at the University of Edinburgh, but my plans changed and I couldn't pursue it. It's a long story. I'm glad I came to Canada, glad for the opportunity to make my way here, without a Laird to answer to. I imagine you feel the same way?"

"Aye, I do. My parents and grandparents had fewer choices. My parents considered emigrating, but they were so grateful to the Laird for helping me with University, they agreed to stay."

"So, here we are, then, Angus, two Scots making their way in this land of opportunity. Oh. I see I've run out of time. I'm meeting a new client this afternoon so I must go."

"Before you go, Fiona, let's make a plan to meet again. I've enjoyed our conversation. I find you intriguing and not just because you're a wonder to look at. You're a clever businesswoman as well. It's nice to discuss business with a woman, for a change. Usually, I don't talk so much, unless I've known someone for a while. But, you've managed to get me to talking a lot today, haven't you, Miss Gilman?"

"It seems so. I've not heard a man talk so much, Mr. MacArthur. Usually, it's difficult for me to get a yes or no out of them."

She smiled at him and removed her arm from his. She was sorry to break her slight, but comfortable physical contact with this intelligent, appealing man.

"Will you consider going to tea at the Empress with me sometime next week? I can shuffle my appointments to be available whenever you can get away from your business."

"Next week is very busy with a number of orders coming due. What about the following week? Usually, a Wednesday is the best day for me."

"Grand. Do you want me to come to your place to pick you up?"

"God, no! Thanks to my Chinese friend, Hoy, I live in a small attic room in the Chinese section of the city, off Fan Tan Alley, where I keep a very low profile. Unless you're familiar with the twists and turns needed to find my place, you'll get lost, for sure. Besides, you're too well-dressed, and too white, for that part of town. I'll meet you in the lobby of the hotel, just before three, if that works for you."

"Aye, it certainly does. Until then, Miss Gilman."

He handed the garment bag back to her, smiled, and strolled away. For a moment, she watched him walk back toward the Empress Hotel.

Now, this is a real man, a big, attractive man with a sense of humor. He doesn't grope or leer at a woman the whole time he's speaking. He doesn't make me feel as if he's biding his time until he can get me into bed. He treats me as an equal, as another businessperson. How refreshing.

There's a gap in his story, though. He said he was rejected by the military at the start of the war. Why? He didn't say. It would've been impolite to ask, but, I'm curious. What's the matter with him? Is he defective in some way not readily visible? He seems so robust, so manly. He's not a weakling, that's for sure. I'll have to find a way to get that out of him, now that he's mentioned it. Surely, it's not a serious disability.

25 ... Parents and children

*A*fter stopping at the post office to pick up her mail, Fiona arrived at her place, clutching a new envelope from Helen. She could tell by the weight that there must be new photographs of Daniel included. But, reading it would have to wait for some privacy.

Hers was a very crowded room, with the two Chinese girls, Ming and Lee, sewing in the corner, and multiple bolts of fabric taking up space on every surface above the floor, including her bed in the tiny alcove. Ming, fourteen, was Hoy's daughter, the widowed tailor, who'd befriended Fiona when she first came to Victoria. She remembered vividly that day they met at the docks. She'd been attempting to buy some newly imported silks. Hoy intervened as she was about to be swindled by a local Chinese importer.

Hoy's broken English was almost understandable to her. They discovered they shared a mutual love of tailoring. He told Fiona he'd learned English on his own, for the first seven years he was in Canada. He needed to work all of the time and couldn't take classes. But, he'd been able to improve his English somewhat, by listening under an open window behind the *Le Qun School* on Fisgard Street, when it first opened in 1909. He'd leaned against the building, stitching on garments, while taking in as much as he could, for the limited time he had. His story and that of his daughter's made Fiona appreciate her easily accessible education in Scotland.

Hoy had come to Canada in 1902, intending to bring his wife over the following year. But, the head tax for Chinese immigrants was raised from $50 to $500, making it impossible for her to join him at that time. He saved every penny he could earn, working for laundries and cafes in Victoria's Chinatown, and keeping up his tailoring skills whenever he had the time. He returned to collect his wife in 1910, but by then his wife's parents were ill and she didn't want to leave them. Ming, his daughter, was born the following year. When Ming was four, her mother died suddenly. Hoy's wife's parents sent her to Canada, thinking she'd have a better life here with her father.

Fiona had been renting the attic room in Hoy's building since 1921, thanks to his intervening on her behalf, with the landlord. Initially, she'd felt very isolated in Chinatown. She was accepted only by Hoy and his daughter. Nobody else in their building or in the shops along the street would acknowledge her. One old Chinese woman would spit, whenever she saw Fiona coming toward her. Fiona just smiled at her. Eventually, the Cantonese grocer agreed to sell rice to her. The butcher, who was Lee's grandfather, sold her meat. The old woman stopped spitting.

Whatever the challenges, life in Chinatown was better than living in a cheap boarding house in the seedy area of James Bay. Hilary had found that residence for her when she arrived in Victoria. Dock workers whistled at her, shouted out lewd remarks, and a few drunken workers chased her home more than once. Waiting for acceptance in Chinatown was preferable to that.

As her business grew, she realized she'd need to hire some help. Hoy suggested Ming and her friend, Lee, for part-time work after school and on weekends. Ming had tried working directly with her father, who was so critical of her work, she refused to continue. Fiona provided an acceptable alternative for the three of them.

Some days, Ming was happy while she worked at Fiona's. Other days, she was upset. Chinese students, along with other, non-white students were discriminated against by their white classmates. Ming hadn't been able to start school, according to Canadian law, until she learned English. That restriction put her behind other children her age. They mocked her for being Chinese and also for being behind in school. At one point, the school trustees attempted to force Chinese students into a separate school. Ming lost another year of schooling, when the entire Chinese community withdrew their children from school altogether, in protest. Luckily, the girl had her father's work ethic. She was making progress at school. Fiona was happy to provide her with part-time work. She also coached her in English, whenever she could.

"Thank you, ladies. That's enough for today. It's time to do your homework."

"Oh, Miss Fiona, no, we not want to stop. It just begin to take a shape, to look good."

"Sorry, Ming, I don't want to get you into trouble. And, I can hear that you need to work on your English grammar and pronunciation exercises. I'll check them over tomorrow when you come back. Go home. I'll see you both tomorrow."

Fiona wanted time alone to read her letter. She was always interested in news from home, especially news of Daniel. She last saw him on his first birthday, May 25th, a few weeks before she left Scotland for Canada. Her memories of that day were still vivid. Helen invited Fiona to his birthday party, risking the wrath of Edward MacAndrews, for just this one day. Although MacAndrews had banned Fiona from associating with Daniel, he'd never know she went to Daniel's party. He'd told Helen he wasn't available to come all the way to Glasgow, for a first birthday that wouldn't be remembered by the boy anyway. He'd reminded Helen that the new nanny would pick Daniel up the following day.

The day of the party, Fiona recalled, Helen showed her into the library. The room was decorated with bright streamers and adorned with a pile of presents heaped up on the carpet. Nearly five-year-old Geordie Murray, and his nanny, Jeannie, joined in the birthday celebrations. Violet's daughter, who'd been Daniel's wet-nurse, prepared and served the food for the party. Daniel was weaned, in time for his departure from Glasgow the next day. Everyone was excited for Fiona to arrive. Then, Daniel could open his presents. Geordie, especially, was looking forward to the cake and ices they'd have afterward.

That last time she saw him, Fiona noticed many changes in her son. She sat in her favorite chair, the one she'd occupied for so many hours when she was pregnant with him. She watched him as he tottered over and smiled up at her, showing his baby teeth. She was expecting him, by this time, to be an exact replica of his rotten father. Instead, he was an interesting blend of both sides of his family. His hair was streaked with blond, like her father's. His Irish blue eyes were very much like hers and her mother's. He did have muscular little legs and the solid build of a MacAndrews. Hopefully, that would be all.

Fiona reached over to pat Daniel on the head. He looked up at her and lost his balance. Her instinctive reaction was to steady him. She surprised herself at the strong surge of emotion she felt, as she took his sturdy wee hands and held them while he rebalanced himself. Perhaps, Helen could sense Fiona's growing feelings for the child. She hurried over.

"You be a good boy for Auntie Fiona, Son."

"Shall I give him my present now, Helen?"

"Aye, Fiona. Come, Daniel, take the pretty box from Auntie Fiona, there's a big boy."

She sat him down. They all watched him tear the paper off the box, examine it, and figure out how to open it. He looked curiously, for a moment, at the wide, sterling silver bracelet, adorned with Celtic designs. He picked it up and immediately tried to put it into his mouth. Helen took it from him. She admired it, before replacing it in the box.

"Oh, Fiona, this is too much. How sweet. I see it's engraved 'Daniel, Love from Fiona.'"

"I hope you don't mind, Helen. I'm not sure I'll see him or any of you for many years, after I leave Scotland. I wanted him to have something to remember me by. Is it alright?"

"Of course it is. I'll make sure he keeps this lovely bracelet as a token of your love. I hope you'll let me write to you about his progress. I know you wish us well. In light of my recent dealings with Edward MacAndrews, I'll want to express my feelings to someone who understands how frustrating MacAndrews can be. His initial grandfatherly temperament is much altered, replaced by a growing indifference toward the emotional needs of a small boy. He seems concerned only with Daniel's future duties as a Laird."

"I know, Helen. I'll look forward to your letters, and photographs too, please."

"Wha' aboot us, the Murray folk? We luv ye too, Fiona. We dinna ken how we'll get along wi' no Auntie Fiona for wee Geordie either."

"I know, Jeannie. I'll miss all of you too. But it's time for me to make a fresh start. I think Canada's the best place for me. Hilary Burns has promised me that, in addition to her, several of her high-class women friends will order fashionable clothes from me. I'm hoping they'll become walking advertisements for my designs. I have MacAndrews' small annuity, too. I should be fine. I'll write to you all and let you know how I get on."

That last meeting with Daniel, five years ago, had been unsettling. Fiona realized then, that her stubborn insistence on giving away Jeremy's son had blinded her to the fact that she had, indeed, given away her own son, not some exact copy of Jeremy MacAndrews. It was all she could do to stop hugging and kissing the wee boy, Helen, and the Murray's, before she left that day. She cried many tears, feeling that she was leaving her family, when, actually, these people who felt like her family were her dead fiancé's Aunt, her dead fiancé's former employer's wife and grandson, and her own, rejected child of rape: a sorry situation, indeed.

She'd started over again in Canada, escaping from Glasgow when Sean was away in Edinburgh, before anything else could complicate her life. Other than her growing regret at having given away her Scottish son, it had been a good five years.

I've spent enough time today dwelling on these sad memories. I'm glad to be here, in Victoria. I've managed to live with my regrets about Daniel, helped by Helen's wonderful letters and the photos of their lives. I'm becoming quite a successful business woman, in a lovely location, where nobody, except Hilary Burns, knows that I was raped, or publicly humiliated as an unwed mother in court, and in the newspapers. Not even Hilary knows of my sordid affair with that lying bastard, Sean. And they certainly don't know I carried on a heated, intimate relationship with him, after I knew he had a wife. Thank God, this handsome Angus MacArthur, this new and interesting man, knows nothing of any of this. I hope I can keep it that way.

She opened Helen's letter and looked at the photographs first. Daniel was six years old now. He was still blond. His piercing blue eyes were obvious, even in the black and white photograph. He'd retained his muscular build. His sturdy legs were visible below the short pants of his school uniform. His cap covered the top of his head, but she could see his hair curling, where it stuck out below the cap. A second photo showed Daniel with his mates, a football placed on the ground in front of them. It looked as if he would follow in his father's footsteps, in the athletic department. Hopefully, that would be his only similarity to Jeremy.

Another photograph showed Daniel sitting beside Helen. It was taken at a studio: *M. Monapenny, 243 Sauchiehall St., Glasgow* was stamped in the corner. Mother and son were seated on an upholstered bench. Daniel looked up at Helen while she looked down at him. Their hands were joined. It was a very touching photograph. Fiona could see much love between them, from the expressions on their faces.

I long for the pictures of this little boy. No matter how busy I am, I think of him. I had hoped these feelings would fade in time, but they haven't. Helen's kindness, her keeping me informed, has made me regret even more that I can't see him, or have him back. I do know, though, that Helen speaks kindly of 'Auntie Fiona' to him. He might not hate me, at least not yet, until he finds out that I purposely gave him away. I'll just have to deal with that later.

Helen's letter was full of news about Daniel's activities and her time with him when he wasn't away at his Glasgow school, or at the Glenheather estate. He wouldn't be sent away to boarding school until he was eight years old. But, the happy tone of the letter changed, before Helen signed off.

Fiona, I've had some other news. I haven't been feeling quite well for over a year. I've had some tenderness, along with a thickness in my breast. I finally allowed the doctor to examine me. He did some tests and then gave me some terrifying news yesterday, in his office. I was quite emotional, at the time, but here's what he said, as closely as I can recall.

'I'm afraid, Mrs. Brody, you'll need surgery. The reason you've been feeling poorly is because your body is fighting disease. The only way to stop the spread of the disease is to remove the affected breast and lymph nodes. We're hopeful the cancer hasn't spread further. You should make a full recovery.'

So, there you have it Fiona. I'm having the surgery tomorrow morning. It'll be over by the time you get this letter. At a time such as this, I'm grateful that Robert left me financially secure. At least,

I won't need to worry about paying the bills. Now, you mustn't worry. I'll be fine. It's not too advanced, the doctor thinks, and I can live quite well with one breast. Thousands of women do it every day. Wish me luck.

 Your loving friend,
 Helen

Cancer! Nobody close to me has ever had cancer. And now, my dear friend, Helen, my boy's mother, is stricken with this terrible disease. This is horrible. I must send a cable, immediately. She has to survive this.

Fiona raced out of her room and down to the telegraph office. She checked every day afterward. Finally, she got a cable three days later.

HELEN FINE STOP SURGERY WENT WELL STOP WILL WRITE NEXT WEEK DO NOT WORRY STOP VIOLET FOR HELEN

Helen must have written only days after her surgery. Fiona got a letter the day before she was to meet Angus for tea at the Empress Hotel.

Dear Fiona,

 I'm fine. Thanks for your cable. I'm sitting in your favourite chair in the library. The surgery was bearable but I'm quite sore, especially my left arm. The surgery involves muscles as well as everything else. I'll need to do physical therapy to get the strength back in my arm. It's a good thing Daniel is at school during the day, while I regain my strength. Jeannie Murray comes over after school, to keep him busy while I rest.

 I felt I had to tell Laird MacAndrews about my surgery. If I hadn't survived it, he would have needed to make arrangements for Daniel. He sounded businesslike on the telephone when I told him.

He's probably thinking up a grand scheme to take Daniel away from me, if he can. But, my doctor knows the situation. He's written a letter about my prognosis. MacAndrews has no reason to pounce on my disease as an excuse to get Daniel for himself. So far, I've been able to offset the influence of his nanny and then his governess. Neither one of those women has changed the boy. He's still sweet-tempered and kind. You'd be proud of him, Fiona.

Love and good wishes for now,
Helen

This is scary. Helen doesn't need emotional wrangling with MacAndrews, at a time like this. And, she might not be safe yet. Breast cancer isn't always easy to beat. That poor little boy: one mother rejects him and the next could be dying of cancer. I hope he doesn't realize that this disease could still threaten Helen's life.

Fiona longed to be there with Helen, to help her when she was in need. Helen came to her rescue when she was a raped, pregnant young woman. She'd always be grateful to Helen for taking her into her home, treating her with respect, and accepting her unwanted child to raise him as her own. People like Helen are rare. She doesn't deserve this.

Fiona felt helpless. She was a world away, just the way she'd planned it. She couldn't have known Helen would get sick. Nor could she have known that she'd live with increasing regret for giving away her son. Helen was the only reason she could bear her regret. If something should happen to Helen, Fiona wouldn't be able to stand by and watch her son follow in the footsteps of his father, living without the love and tenderness a mother could provide. All she could do was pray that Helen would continue to survive for Daniel's sake and, selfishly, for her own.

26 ... Unknown territory

"My, Miss Gilman, you look especially lovely today."
"Why, thank you very much, Mr. MacArthur, you're not looking too bad yourself."

Angus took Fiona's hand as she stepped down from the last stair of the ladies' staircase. She'd taken the elevator up to the first floor of rooms, in order to make this grand entrance into the lobby. She hoped Angus would be amused by her obvious attempt to imitate her upper-class clientele, when they both knew where she came from.

She certainly looked the part. She wore her own creation—a slim cut, Nile green and sand-colored silk dress with hand beading encircling the bottom six inches of the skirt. The weight of the beads caused the dress to sway with each step. It outlined her shapely body as she moved. The matching three-quarter jacket was finished with silk-covered buttons. Her trendy, shorter skirt allowed anyone who was lucky enough to see her, an appropriate view of her one pair of silk stockings and stylish heels. From beneath her close-fitting hat, a few loose tendrils of her dark hair escaped to frame her face. A few long, wavy tendrils trailed down her back. She had contemplated cutting her hair, bobbing it, complete with bangs the way modern women did these days, but she was reluctant to part with it. The styles would change. She didn't want to spend years growing it back.

Fiona was sure she'd chosen the right outfit by the look in Angus' eyes, as he smiled and greeted her. Angus offered his arm and escorted her to the tea room. They were glad to see each other after a busy two weeks. Their conversation drifted into business, once they'd started on their delicious cucumber sandwiches and exotic tea. Angus described his trips back and forth between the bank's clientele on Vancouver Island, where he spoke with people from various walks of life, including miners, mine owners, railroad administrators, and merchants who made their money from expanding businesses in the southern and middle regions of the island.

"Have I gone on too long, about my work, Fiona?"

"No, of course not, I enjoy hearing about your business life. But, I was wondering if you miss Scotland, at all, Angus?"

"Not too much. I don't think my mother ever expected to have a 33 year-old, unmarried son living in a foreign country. She'd have liked me to stay in Scotland and she isn't shy about saying that, in every letter."

"Have you been back to Newtonmore?"

"Aye, when my father passed away three years ago. He had two heart attacks in the last few years of his life."

"Is your heart the reason you weren't accepted into the military?"

"Aye. I was very disappointed at the time. I wanted to do my share. But, they wouldn't have me. Unlike my father, I had rheumatic fever as a child. It has resulted in a damaged heart. I have a condition called Mitral Valve Stenosis.

"Can it be fixed?"

"No, I'm afraid I just have to live with it. I get short of breath sometimes, but it usually doesn't bother me. As long as I haven't inherited the type of heart disease my father had, I'll be fine for years to come. What else did you want to ask me about Newtonmore, Fiona?"

"You mentioned your Laird expected you to run some of his businesses. What happened when you told him you weren't coming back?"

"Well, lass, that's a long story. But, the bottom line is that

I paid him back for the cost of my university. Once he realized I was determined to emigrate to Canada, he loaned me the money for my passage. I paid that off too, with interest. Now, I'm a free man, so to speak, debt free, that is."

"The important thing is that you were able to get the loans in the first place. Your Laird sounds unusual, at least in my experience anyway.

By the way, where do you live? I imagine you've got a fancy, custom-designed home here in Victoria, what with all the money you must be making in the banking business."

"Actually, I'll have ye know, lass, that I live quite humbly. A person gets used to watching expenses, when all of your life and that of your family depends on a Laird. Old habits are difficult to break."

"What does that mean? Do you live in a hovel in the park? Or, is it a shack down by the water? Where would you hang those fancy clothes, then, Mr. MacArthur?"

"Hah! That's good, that's really good. For your information, Miss Gilman, I live in Mrs. Fraser's Boarding House, just past the harbour in a nice area of James Bay. I'm happy for the company of a variety of other people and the home-cooked meals every night. We enjoy much good conversation on a weekend, when everyone's in town. It's a nice way to avoid being too lonely."

"May I ask why you haven't married, Angus?"

"Well, it's taken me a good amount of time to move here and establish myself in the business community. Many of those dull, decorative women who call themselves friends of Hilary Burns have made attempts to get close to me. It's comical, really, to see the way they maneuver themselves into my vicinity, or manipulate their male friends into suggesting I invite them to tea or dinner. I've seen a couple of them a few times, for the female company. But they can be insipid, much more concerned with how they look than how the world runs. Those I've met, so far, seem to concentrate on impressing each other with their latest new clothes.

Auch, Fiona. I'm sorry. I know you make your living designing and sewing those lovely clothes. I didn't mean to imply that there's anything wrong with looking good . . ."

"Ah, Mr. MacArthur, you've insulted me now, haven't ye?"

"Forgive me. I do tend to have strong opinions. Truly, it's refreshing to speak to a woman who also uses her brain for something creative and self-sustaining, a productive woman. You don't seem to be on a quest to snag a husband."

"I forgive you. I know what you mean. Thanks for not thinking of me as a shallow society woman, even though I try my best to look like one."

"Why haven't you married, Fiona? Or, have you?"

"I was engaged, once, but my fiancé was killed in an industrial accident. It was only a few months after he came back from the war."

"I'm sorry to hear that, Fiona."

"I've survived his death, partly, by running away from Scotland and my memories there. Since I came to Victoria, I've been too busy getting established and supporting myself, to pursue a serious romantic relationship. What I really need is to rent some working space, but I haven't accumulated enough cash. Nor can I predict my costs quite well enough to take that chance, just yet. As I mentioned the last time we met, I work out of the room I live in."

"Well, lovely lass, we'll see if . . ."

"Excuse me, Madam, sorry to interrupt. There's one of those Chinese here, asking for you. It must be one of your servants, I think . . ."

Fiona looked up at the tearoom hostess. "Where is she?"

"Naturally, we don't allow her kind in here. I've asked her to wait in the kitchen until it's convenient for you to speak with her."

"I'll have you know, Miss, that 'Chinese' is a serious student and industrious worker that anyone would be glad to know. I'll thank you not to insult her again. Now, please go and get her and take her into the lobby. I'll speak with her there.

I'll be right back, Angus. It must be something important. Otherwise, Ming would never have come here where she's sure to be insulted."

Ming stood in a poorly-lit corner of the lobby, head down.

"What's the matter, Ming? Are you alright?"

"It's Papa, Miss Fiona. He come in late, not get up. He sick. I not know what to do."

"Never mind, I'll come. Wait here."

Fiona returned to the table. She told Angus she had to leave right away.

"Do you need help, Fiona?"

"It's my friend, Hoy, Ming's father. She says he can't get out of bed. I'm going with her. Are you sure you want to come?"

"Aye, let's go."

Angus hailed a taxi. The three of them rode the short distance to Chinatown. He smiled at Ming, but she kept her eyes lowered after glancing quickly at him. He paid the driver, who refused to take them right into the heart of Chinatown. Instead, he dropped them off at the entrance to Waddington Alley. They hurried through the cobblestone alley, crossed over Pandora Street and entered Fan Tan Alley, winding their way through passages. At last, they ascended the stairs up and up again to the top floor of the commercial/residential building. Fiona noticed Angus was breathing harder by the time they opened the door to Hoy's room. Ming pointed to a curtained-off area.

"Papa in there."

Angus went in first, in case Hoy wasn't covered. But, Ming had piled blankets on him. Angus called Fiona. They could see that Hoy's eyes were closed and his forehead was beaded with sweat. His breathing was raspy and uneven. Fiona noticed that his saffron-colored skin had turned ashen.

"Fiona, is there a doctor closeby, in this part of town?"

Before Fiona could reply, Ming nodded.

"Go and get him, Ming, right away. Hurry!"

The young girl left. Fiona wiped Hoy's forehead. His eyelids fluttered, as he struggled to open them.

Angus stepped to the other side of the curtain to wait at the table, hoping the Chinese doctor was very close. He assumed Hoy had a weak heart, judging by his breathing, but he was anxious to get a doctor in here.

Ming showed the Chinese doctor into the room. He gave Angus a dirty look on his way by. When he saw Fiona, the doctor raised his voice and waved his arms, shooing her away from Hoy's bedside. From the kitchen, Angus and Fiona could hear the doctor asking Hoy questions in Mandarin. They waited.

The doctor called for Ming. After a minute or two, she peeked back around the curtain and beckoned.

"Papa want speak to you, Miss Fiona."

Fiona squeezed by the doctor, who was going through his bag. Impatiently, he took himself and his bag out to the table while she stayed with Hoy. His eyes were open. He looked right at her and spoke.

"My friend, Miss Fiona, my only white friend, who care for my Ming. I gone soon. My time come."

"Is it your heart, Hoy?"

"No, I stabbed. See?"

He pulled back the blankets to show Fiona that he was practically floating in a pool of blood. The Chinese doctor's bandages were soaked through already.

"Oh! How awful! Who stabbed you? Why?"

"Bad man who try to cheat me. But, you listen now, my white friend. Doctor owns building here. I talk him into renting to you when we first meet. He say he let you stay if you pay double. You can afford this?"

"Don't worry, Hoy. You'll be fine. We'll get you to The Chinese Hospital."

"No, Fiona. Leave me. Just promise you look after my Ming— she have nobody else. Tell Ming, too, not forget what I tell her about hiding place. Not forget what I say to her before Doctor came back in here. Tell her, promise?"

"I promise, Hoy. I promise."

The doctor finished digging in his bag, stepped back inside the curtain, and elbowed Fiona away from the bed so he could continue his efforts to save Hoy. Fiona was no doctor, but she could see Hoy was very severely injured. It didn't seem possible that he would live.

When she emerged back into the room, Angus wasn't there.

"Ming, where's Angus, the white man I brought here?"

"Doctor tell man to leave. The white man ask me tell you he get his doctor to come here, help Papa."

"I hope he hurries. Your father is very severely injured."

Soon, they heard footsteps on the stairs. Angus entered the room with a man carrying a medical bag.

"Fiona, this is Doctor Logan. He'll look at Hoy."

When the Chinese doctor saw Dr. Logan, he was obviously insulted. As he left the room, he snarled in Mandarin to Ming, who translated. He wanted his rent, for both rooms, or they could move out now. Fiona ignored his hostility, keeping calm for Ming's sake.

The prognosis was dismal. Hoy had lost too much blood, before any of them got there. The Chinese doctor had bound his wounds, but the knife had done far too much damage. Hoy died in the next few minutes. He was stoic in the face of his death, perhaps because Fiona had agreed to look out for Ming. That was all he cared about, at the end. Ming had a few moments to kiss her father's forehead and weep silently over his body, before Angus sent her up to Fiona's room, in the attic of the old building.

Dr. Logan and Angus covered Hoy's body and waited for the medics to carry him downstairs. Logan arranged for the ambulance to take the body to the medical examiner, something that didn't always happen after a death in Chinatown. But, Dr. Logan insisted that this brutal murder be investigated. The wounds looked as if they were intended to cause the most pain and damage possible. As Dr. Logan left, he told Angus and Fiona the police would be sent to investigate. They'd have to leave Hoy's room until the police were finished. Fiona thanked the doctor again, as he left. She turned to thank Angus for his help, but he spoke first.

"Here, Fiona. This is the telephone number at Mrs. Fraser's. Please call me tomorrow and let me know how you and Ming are getting along. I heard what Ming told you about the doctor demanding his rent on the two rooms. Try not to worry about that, if you can. I have access to resources you can use temporarily, if you need them. We can talk about that in a few days."

"Goodbye, Angus. Thank you so much for your help today. It certainly isn't how I imagined our date for tea. I'll let you know how Ming and I get on. Thank you again."

Hoy was respected and influential in the community. But, there was a limit to the community's tolerance for white people. Fiona hoped the community's respect for Hoy would help them honor his wishes to have Fiona care for his daughter.

Ming. God must be determined for me to care for a child. He keeps foisting them on me—first Daniel, now Ming. But, I won't be able to care for her alone. I know a few Chinese women who might help me with her. They'll make sure she stays involved in her own culture. I'll make sure she stays in school and has marketable skills. That's the least I can do to honor Hoy. Without his support and kindness, I wouldn't have been able to build my business, or rent acceptable lodgings.

Now, I'll need to see if I can borrow enough money from the bank to rent a workspace. I'll have to. Ming can move in here with me and we'll work somewhere else. The doctor can rent Hoy's room to somebody else, unless the police actually show up to investigate. If they do, he won't be able to charge me rent for a room that can't be occupied.

As she lay there, thinking, she could hear Ming's breathing coming from the small sofa where she lay, not three feet from Fiona, sleeping restlessly. Listening to Ming, Fiona suddenly remembered Hoy's telling her to ask Ming about 'the hiding place'. What hiding place? She decided they'd sneak into Hoy's room first thing in the morning, to get whatever was in the hiding place and get out before anyone showed up.

Several hours later, Fiona was awakened by flashing lights and the sound of heavy footsteps on the staircase, accompanied by authoritative-sounding male voices. Police raids on illegal opium dens were normal for this part of town, as were fights and arrests for prostitution associated with Fan Tan Alley's gambling rooms. But, this night, Fiona heard the distinctive sound of nails being hammered into wood. She was too late—Hoy's room was sealed.

27 ... Financial politics

Following the medical examiner's investigation, Hoy's body was released. He was laid to rest at the Harling Point Chinese Cemetery. Many Chinese community members attended his funeral, paying their respects to the well-known and well liked man. The Doctor glared at Fiona across the gravesite. Afterward, he approached her.

"Due now" he said, as he pushed a rent increase notice into her hand.

She smiled at him and then walked away with her arm around Ming's shoulder. She knew she'd have to deal with him eventually, but for now, there were other things to take care of.

She had already written to Ming's grandparents in China, expressing her sympathies and explaining that Hoy had been murdered. Ming translated for Fiona, carefully drawing the Chinese characters that spoke to her Grandparents. Fiona reassured them she was caring for Ming and she'd do so as long as she was needed. The letter also confirmed that, in the specified number of years, Hoy's bones would be exhumed, cleaned, dried, and sent back home by the Hoy Sun Ning Yung Benevolent Society for burial in China, as was the custom. Fiona assured them that the investigation into Hoy's murder was ongoing.

It was after the funeral, back in her room, that Fiona remembered her "hiding place" conversation with Hoy.

"Ming, when your father and I last spoke, he told me to remind you about his "hiding place." Do you know what he meant?"

"Oh! Miss Fiona. I forget to tell you about that."

"I learned about it from your father the night he died, but the police came and nailed the room shut, before I could ask you about it. We're probably out of luck, now. Whatever he had was probably taken by the police. Do you know what it was?"

"It is okay, Miss Fiona, I have it. When he first give it to me, he tell me to hide it up here, in your place. He say nobody will think of looking for important Chinese documents in room of poor, white seamstress. He right, nobody did, even you!"

"Well, I guess your father knew what he was doing, didn't he? Where did you hide it?"

Ming went over to the cutting table that sat alongside the wall. She bent down, reached under the table, and felt around for a minute or two. Fiona heard a ripping sound, as Ming tore away the tape that held a large envelope to the underside of the table.

"Here documents. Money, too, lots of money."

Fiona was astounded. The envelope contained both Hoy's and Ming's passports, a smaller envelope with wads of cash, and lastly, a sealed letter, with Chinese writing on the outside.

"Ming, please open the letter and read it to me."

"It say: 'I leave all my belongings to my daughter, Ming, along with the cash here. The money is to care for Ming until she . . . she . . . .'"

"Why are you stopping, Ming? I must hear your Papa's words. I don't want to ask someone else to translate. It's none of their business. Go on, please."

"It say 'until she go back to China, to live with her relations, her maternal grandparents. Reader of this document must contact Ming's grandparents and make arrangements to send her. Without father to protect her, here in this bigoted country, my Ming not have chance for good life. She better off in China. Parents of my wife agree they take Ming, if anything happen to me.'

The document was signed and then witnessed by one of Hoy's friends, a Chinese lawyer. By this time, Ming was crying, unable to believe what she read. Her father had told her never to open the envelope in the hiding place unless he was dead. She had obeyed. He gave it to her the year before, when he first began to have trouble with some Chinese thugs, down at the docks. His sense of danger was validated it seemed, by his violent death.

"Oh, Ming dear, please don't cry. He wanted the best for you. He knew how cruel people can be toward Chinese immigrants. He was trying to protect you."

"You send me back? He say you care for me. Did he mean only 'til you read letter? You think he still want send me back to China? He ask you to care for me!"

"I don't know, Ming. Let's wait and see what your grand-parents have to say. I'm sure they'll write back immediately, when they learn of your father's death. Try not to worry. I don't know what the legal situation would be in your case. But, I can see you want to stay here. I promised your father I would care for you. We'll carry on. And, we'll begin by getting more room to work."

Fiona called Angus at Mrs. Fraser's. They agreed to meet at the bank, to arrange for a loan to pay for leasing a work space. Fiona arrived first. She was shown into the office of the loans manager, a Mr. Wilson.

"Miss Gilman, we do not offer loans to women, especially unmarried women. For goodness sake, Miss Gilman, here in Canada, under the British North America Act, you're not even a person, under the law. We, here at the bank don't care how much fuss that Emily Murphy woman makes to have women declared "persons." Under the law, you're not a person. It's impos-sible to lend money to you. How would we recover our loss if you couldn't pay us back?

Why don't you find yourself a good husband instead? You're not bad looking. Why have you waited so long? You'll never get anywhere without a husband."

These words came from Wilson's pudgy, pasty-white face

that stretched across the front of his large, balding head. He had a short, stout body, encased in a custom-tailored, tight fitting suit of fine quality wool, the lines of which were spoiled by the gaps between the buttons on the front of his vest. They looked as if they were about to pop.

So, the bastard has money enough to get his suits tailored, but no manners, and certainly no self-restraint where indulging himself or insulting a woman is concerned. I know all about the valiant efforts of Emily Murphy, first winning the vote for Alberta women, and then tirelessly campaigning, to have women declared as "persons" under the law in Canada. Wilson's technically correct, about the "persons" issue. But, he must detest women or he wouldn't enjoy bringing it up and throwing it in my face. I must keep calm.

"Thank you, Mr. Wilson, for your opinion. Mr. Angus MacArthur will be here in a few minutes. I'm sure he can ease your mind about loaning me the money. While we wait, would you mind checking over the loan application to be sure I've filled it out according to your requirements? I'm only a woman, as you've pointed out. We wouldn't want you to sign anything incomplete, would we, Mr. Wilson?"

"I don't plan to sign anything today, Miss Gilman. I simply don't lend money to non-persons and that's final."

Angus strolled into the office, smiled at Fiona, and sat down in front of Wilson's desk. Another man in a beautifully tailored suit sat down next to Fiona. Angus spoke first.

"Sorry I'm late, Miss Gilman. Mr. Wilson, you know Joseph James, our bank President. Mr. James, meet Fiona Gilman, one of Victoria's successful entrepreneurs."

"How do ye do, Miss Gilman? I understand this isn't your first trip to our bank."

"Aye, Mr. James, only my first trip to the loan department. I do have an account here, where my annuity is deposited.

Normally, I see only the tellers, when I make deposits from my business income."

"Well, Miss Gilman, Angus has probably told you that bank policy prohibits us from making business loans without sufficient collateral in place to cover the cost of the loan."

At this statement, Fiona noticed Mr. Wilson gloating, probably anticipating that she'd be humiliated again.

"Is that the only condition for lending, Mr. James? For example, does the fact that I'm a woman asking for money to invest into my thriving business make any difference?"

"Not in my book, Miss Gilman. I'm interested in people who have business potential and the collateral to offset the risk we take. Can ye get the collateral in place by, say, Monday?"

Angus spoke. "Perhaps I can help, Mr. James. I know Miss Gilman and the success she's achieved against the odds here in Victoria. I'll top up whatever she needs to have added to her account to cover the total amount of the collateral, if she'll allow me. I've every confidence she'll be able to repay us both, given her record of success and her prospects for the future."

"Angus, Mr. MacArthur, I thank you. This is a surprise. I accept your offer. You won't be sorry you invested in my business. I'm sure we can agree on a suitable interest rate."

"The bank's interest rate is fine. I'm happy to be involved with your business. I know you have more than enough work. Extra space will allow you to expand."

Angus thanked Joseph James, who addressed Fiona on his way out of the room.

"Good luck, Miss Gilman. The bank is always interested in making money, along with its clients. Best wishes for a very successful venture. I'm sure Angus will let me know how you progress. Mr. Wilson, have the loan papers on my desk by Monday afternoon for my signature."

Fiona stood up and looked Mr. Wilson directly in the eye.

"I'll be in on Tuesday morning to withdraw some operating funds, Mr. Wilson."

Wilson didn't meet her gaze, remaining silent, as he looked down at the loan application papers. Angus stood, looking down at the pudgy man.

"I'll take those loan application papers, Wilson. I'll check them over and give them back for you to finish, before you send them for Mr. James' signature."

As they left the bank, Angus and Fiona smiled. They were laughing aloud by the time they reached the noisy street. Angus knew what Wilson was like. He agreed with Fiona that Wilson used his position to further his misogyny. Nobody was sure why he hated women so much. Some of the customers and a few female staff members had complained about Wilson's attitude. But, he was careful not to display his hatred of females whenever his superiors were around. Angus was happy for Fiona that she fared well, in spite of Wilson.

They went to see two suitable workspace locations. The first site was on Government Street, so named, because the Colonial Customs House and the Post Office had been located on the street for decades. Going north, the street ran on past Chinatown, while in the southerly direction, it ran in front of the Empress Hotel, continuing past the harbour into the James Bay district, where Angus lived.

Fiona's clients, including wealthy residents of Victoria, both married and widowed, as well as residents and visitors of the great hotel, would have easy access to this location. If the space worked well, Fiona planned to open a store front facing the street side of the space. That way, her customers could come to her to select fabrics. She'd install a fitting room, giving her the ability to make adjustments to garments in her own space. All she had to do was convince her clients to meet her there, rather than in their homes, or in their suites at the Empress Hotel.

"You know, Angus, many of my clients, such as Lady Bridge-Harris, wouldn't think of coming to me, wherever I locate. They're accustomed to having personal service at their locations. They simply wouldn't consider inconveniencing themselves. That's fine, for them. But, I'm hoping that new clients, perhaps those with slightly less money at their disposal, would enjoy coming to my place. I think they'd like browsing through my exquisite, richly-coloured silks from China and the artistically-designed fabrics from India. Even my top quality wool crepes from Europe, could lure some clients here. At some point, I could offer tea to encourage some of the wealthier women to leave their homes and the rest of their cossetted lives, to visit my shop. What do you think?"

"You're asking me to guess what those spoiled women might or might not do? You know much better than I do, lass. I do have a question for you, though. Have you ever considered sewing sturdier clothing? I'm thinking of uniforms and such for the servant class, or work clothes for tradesmen. You wouldn't get so much for each garment, but there must be plenty of people, single men, I'm thinking, who can't sew their own clothes and would pay for well made, store-bought clothes, if they could get them."

"I have wondered about doing that, Angus. It's a good idea. The very skilled Chinese tailors, now one less in number, with Hoy gone, have more work than they can keep up with. That might be an area Ming could help me explore. She knows many people in Chinatown who had respect for her father. As long as she keeps up with her schooling, we could see about expanding a bit in that direction. She's already mentioned a few ideas for practical clothing, made from sturdier materials. I'll talk it over with her."

"It's good of you to involve Ming. She's lucky to get this type of experience from you. So, shall we tell this landlord we'll think about the space and go look at the next one? After that, you can make a decision."

Fiona linked her arm in Angus' as they walked one block over to Store Street, then further north, away from the inner harbour. The next available space was more spacious than the first one, but it was in a rougher part of the town. She was sure her wealthier clients would never come here. The rent, however, was ten percent less than the space on Government Street.

"This is going to be a tough decision, Angus. I'd like to take the first space for its great location and the possibilities to expand to a store front. But, this second space is more reasonable, closer to Chinatown, for me and Ming, and it fits my budget better."

"You're right, Fiona, the dearer space has far more potential in the long run, doesn't it? On the other hand, this cheaper space would allow you to stretch out the loan money for longer. You'd have more time to turn a profit while you build up your client base."

"I know. This cheaper space is more practical for right now. However, in addition to the loan money, I've saved some money. I have an annuity. I mentioned it to Mr. James at the bank. You're probably curious about that."

"I admit that I am. I'm away on bank business for the next two weeks. Why don't you come to supper at Mrs. Fraser's Boarding House, two weeks from Thursday? We'll enjoy the company and talk afterward. There's a nice big fireplace in the parlour, where we'll have a wee drop and celebrate your new business location, whichever one you choose. What do you say?"

"Thanks, Angus, I'd love to come. About the supper, will this suit I'm wearing be too casual? Shall I wear an evening dress instead? I've not been to supper on the fancy side of town. Do they dress quite formally, or not?"

"There are no tuxedos at Mrs. Fraser's. You always look nice, Fiona, whatever you're wearing. I'm proud to be seen with you any time we're together. I can see other men admiring you, except, Mr. Wilson, of course."

Fiona laughed at that remark and took her chance to tease Angus about his comments.

"Why, Mr. MacArthur, do you consider me to be some sort of prize you've won? A good looking woman to show off, hanging on your arm? Am I just about the looks, then?"

"Oh, God help me. I've insulted you, again. Of course I don't think of you as a prize. You do recall I'm topping up your loan? I wouldn't do that if I didn't have confidence in your business abilities. But, I must admit you're simply stunning, especially when you get worked up about your designs: your cheeks flush, your blue eyes flash, and you emphasize every point by talking with your hands. It's enchanting, Fiona. I'm fascinated by you. I'm only sorry that poor Wilson will never see you like that. You'd scare the devil out of him—all that beauty and intelligence in one, dynamic, female package."

"Thanks for the compliments, Angus. It's hilarious to think how Wilson would react. I don't think he knows what to do when an intelligent woman stands up to him. He gives me the creeps, though. I hope I won't need to deal too much with him, once the loan is signed and I've started to pay it back."

"Don't worry, lass. Wilson knows better than to take on anyone backed by me or Joseph James. He'll behave from now on. You can count on that.

Now, Fiona, when you're ready to move into your new space, go to Leeds Brothers Moving Co. on Wharf Street. I'll tell William and John you'll be coming. They'll bill me for the cost. Consider it a small gift of congratulations. They're reputable and won't damage any of those expensive fabrics, the sewing machines, or your fancy new beading machine. You can trust them to do a good job."

"That's a thoughtful gesture, Angus. Thank you, again, for your help."

"It's not purely altruistic, Fiona. We are, among other things, business colleagues now. The sooner you get settled, the sooner you'll be able to expand your business. I'm sure Ming and her friend will enjoy having less cramped working conditions too."

Angus leaned down and kissed Fiona on the cheek as they said goodbye. She was surprised and thrilled at the rush of sensual feelings she experienced, when his lips touched her skin.

My God! I'm blushing. I can't believe it. How embarrassing. I feel like a schoolgirl. I hope he hasn't noticed. What have I gotten myself into? These feelings complicate things, but they are so, so welcome. It's hard to believe I'm this lucky. I hope my luck lasts.

28 ... Chinese art

Mr. Wilson did as he was told. By the time Fiona got to the bank on Tuesday morning, her funds were available. She purchased a bank draft, leased her new space, the one on Government Street, and applied for a business license. She'd deliberated briefly about the two available spaces in relationship to her budget. The Store Street location was cheaper, but she knew the best location was critical for a successful storefront business. Her father had taught her that. As soon as she could, she'd set up the front portion of new space as a storefront. Already known for her unique clothing designs and high quality garments, she was sure she could cover her rent with increased orders from the storefront. The bank loan would pay for the costs of setting it up. She was very excited when she moved into the space at the end of September.

After the Leeds brothers had left, on moving day, Ming and Lee came over after school to help Fiona organize bolts of fabric, sewing supplies, and furniture in the new space. Both girls were impressed by the size of the space. No more bumping elbows as they walked around the cutting tables. They found a few old wooden chairs out behind the back door. They'd been left by the last renter. The girls hauled them in and arranged them around the smaller cutting table. They spread a nice tablecloth over the surface and placed a small vase of fresh flowers on the table.

"There, Miss Fiona, the first bouquet for your new business. Add colour and smell nice too. Lee's mother send, I mean, sent the tablecloth. She is happy we not working in your tiny room."

"Thanks very much, girls. And thank your mother, too, Lee. What a sweet thing to do."

While they waited to hear from Ming's grandparents in China, Ming constantly reassured Fiona that the sofa was comfortable enough for her. She'd stay there forever, she said, rather than go back to China. But, Fiona was concerned about providing enough supervision for Ming. A young woman living outside her family residences, in Chinatown, needed supervision for her own protection. After all, Fiona had been a strong young woman of twenty, when Jeremy MacAndrews managed to overpower her. Ming was only fourteen and very tiny. Many drunken or drugged young men frequented brothels and gambling rooms, in their vicinity near Fan Tan and Dragon Alleys.

Now that Hoy isn't here to help keep an eye on her, I need to be more involved in Ming's life. I can't lock her up, so I'll ask Ming about an idea I've come up with.

"Ming, why don't you ask a few of your classmates over to the workspace on Friday? Do you think they'd come?"

"What for, Miss Fiona?"

"Well, I was thinking I could tutor them a bit in English, along with you, by showing them a few of my design steps and one or two tailoring skills. We could feed them too, make a social evening out of it."

"Hm. . . maybe. I ask my two girlfriends at school and also a boy who is nephew of some cousins. He lives in building with rest of my father's relatives. His aunt just move in. She watches young people my age who live there. Maybe we ask her too"?

"Sure, that's a great idea."

By Friday, Fiona managed to get a few more chairs to place around the largest cutting table, where Ming and her friends could meet, talk, and eat. Fiona cooked enough food for six people and hoped that the five guests would show up.

Aunt Woo, accompanied by her nephew, Yen, along with

Ming, Lee, and another girlfriend, Lily, arrived after school. Fiona guessed that Woo was sent gladly, by the family's Benevolent Club members. They wanted her to check up on Ming and put pressure on Fiona to release Ming into their care.

Hoy had told Fiona he was pressured, constantly, to let Ming stay in the family residences. He flatly refused all such attempts to envelop his daughter into the larger family fold here in Canada. He was fiercely independent, insisting on keeping Ming with him. Now that her grandparents hadn't responded to the letter, local relatives made a renewed effort to convince Ming to live with them. Fiona wasn't sure how long she or Ming could resist the pressure of the community. So far, Ming seemed reluctant to move in with the family. Fiona decided she'd adhere to Hoy's wishes for his daughter, as long as Ming was happy.

Aunt Woo was very polite, bowing and smiling at Fiona as she was introduced. They all sat down around the table. Fiona, speaking in English, proceeded to show the students some of her design sketches. Next, she demonstrated, using a simple, but elegant design, how a garment idea went from sketch pad to pattern and finally to a finished product. Aunt Woo and the young people were suitably impressed when Fiona produced a finished garment for them to examine. She ended the session by providing sketch pads for everyone. She encouraged them to try their own designs, while she got the meal ready. Fiona could hear Ming translating a few times for the benefit of the others. Most of their table talk, though, was in English. Fiona was pleased with that.

As they ate together, Woo, in her halting English, told Fiona she'd been an artist in China, before she came to Canada to live with her sister's family. She was a widow, who resisted all pressure to remarry, so she could concentrate on creating her delicate, water colour paintings. She kept the family happy by helping to supervise their maturing young adults.

Aunt Woo asked if she could return the next Friday night, with the students in tow. She offered to demonstrate the process she used to create her paintings. Fiona accepted Woo's offer gratefully. She was enjoying the company of this gentle, artistic woman. Fiona was relieved that Aunt Woo approved of her first Friday night session. She agreed that socializing with and teaching Ming's friends was of benefit to her and the students. As Aunt Woo left, Fiona asked her if anyone in their family could check with relatives in China, about Hoy's in-laws. Surely, something must have happened to them, or they would have, at the least, responded to Ming's letter. Woo said she'd do what she could.

Fiona was so involved with setting up the workspace, visiting clients, designing and sewing, she barely had time to prepare for her next Friday night session. She hadn't had much time to think about Angus. The day before he was due back, in Victoria, he walked into the workspace on Government Street, unannounced.

"Why, Mr. MacArthur. How nice to see you on this fine, Wednesday afternoon. Have ye come back a day early to check up on your investment, then?"

"Now that ye mention it, Miss Gilman, I've been curious about how the business is going."

Angus was glad that Ming and Lee hadn't yet arrived from school. He'd have a few minutes alone, with Fiona. She was lovely, as ever, working on a large piece of brilliant red silk that was draped over a cutting table. A few dark tendrils of her wavy hair fell forward around her face, while the rest of her glorious hair fought to escape from the ribbon that tried to tame it. Each time he saw her, he marveled at her looks. Theirs was a game of him looking at her with admiration in his eyes followed by her pretending to brush off his admiration. He knew she could see his desire for her seeping into his gaze. He found it exciting to spar with her verbally, as she pretended to be insulted by his comments. All the more exciting was the intensity in her blue eyes as they danced around their admiration for each other.

"I've come to remind you of our supper at Mrs. Fraser's tomorrow evening. We've a full house just now, with interesting new guests, she tells me. Are you still free, Miss Gilman?"

"Well, I'll have to recheck my social calendar. I'm so busy and popular, you know. It's a wonder you caught me here at all, with my hectic social schedule."

Angus grinned while he waited for her to sort mentally through her pretended full social calendar, until Fiona spoke.

"I'm happy to say I haven't had an invitation from a fine gentleman since you escorted me to tea several weeks ago. I definitely plan to come."

"Grand. I'll send a taxi over for you here, at five, if that's convenient. There's no point in alerting your neighbors you've gone away in a taxi for the evening, leaving Ming alone. We two could have a drink together first, before we go into supper. We usually eat at six- thirty."

"Yes, here would be best. Thanks for thinking about Ming."

As Angus was preparing to leave, Fiona told Angus, about her new sessions, naming them 'Fiona's Friday Night Dinners for Underage Chinese Students and Friends'. She described the first meeting and said how impressed she was with the students, as well as Aunt Woo. Angus listened carefully, his admiration for Fiona growing as she spoke.

"Fiona, this is a generous thing you're doing for Ming and her friends. Your friend, Hoy, must have known how responsible and unselfish you are. I think he'd be very grateful you've shown such concern for Ming's welfare. I'm impressed. These youngsters don't know how lucky they are."

"Thanks. I do think Hoy would like the idea of Ming's having some supervised social activity. And, to be honest, I'm grateful to Ming for suggesting I meet some of her relatives.

I'll need some help from somewhere to look after a young Chinese girl properly. I don't want her to be alienated from her family or her culture. When Hoy wrote out his will, he couldn't have known his in-laws wouldn't respond. The political scene in China's been very unstable for years and it worsens, as time goes on. Surely Hoy wouldn't want his young daughter living there now. She's much safer here, where I'll do the best I can for her."

Angus agreed. He left Fiona to finish her work. Both of them looked forward to seeing each other again the next day.

Late Thursday afternoon, Fiona walked home from work, changed, and saw to Ming's dinner before she walked back to her business to await the taxi. Ming would stay in their room, lock the door, do her homework, and go to bed.

When the taxi pulled up in front of Mrs. Fraser's in the James Bay district, Angus met her at the street, opened the car door and offered Fiona his hand. He paid the taxi. They walked up to the large house and through the front entrance together.

"Well, Mr. MacArthur, who's this young woman? Ye've not brought an attractive young woman tae dinner here as long as I've known ye. Come in, darlin'. I'm Mrs. Fraser. I welcome ye tae the best meals, at the best boardin' house outside Scotland. My ye've got on a beeootiful outfit! Where does a person get such a gorgeous thing?"

"Hello, Mrs. Fraser, I'm Fiona Gilman, a friend of Angus. I made the outfit myself. I'm a clothing designer and tailor, by trade."

"Where've ye been hidin' this lovely thing, then Angus? Nary a word's been spoken by him, about you, Miss Gilman. He's very much closed mouthed, he is."

Fiona smiled, noting the grin on Angus' face, as their eyes met. He decided to save Fiona from further questioning by Mrs. Fraser.

"We're going into the parlor until supper is ready, Mrs. Fraser. We'll come when we hear the bell."

He ushered Fiona into the cozy room, where a crackling fire blazed in a large fireplace. A circle of overstuffed chairs, arranged in a three-quarter arc, faced the fireplace. A large chesterfield sat between bookshelves along the wall. They were grateful for the fire—early October weather often included chilly evenings, dampened by the ocean air.

Angus offered Fiona a glass of wine, pouring himself a whiskey. Fiona refused the wine. She was afraid it would go to her head too fast, without food in her stomach. He sat down in the chair next to hers. They watched the fire for a few, relaxed moments. She asked him about his trip, hoping she could draw him out a bit, about his interests. They'd spent so much time involved in her life—Hoy's murder, her business, Ming. It was time she listened to him. After a few minutes of discussion, he said he could hear the familiar sound of Mrs. Fraser plunking down her heavy casseroles and meat platters onto the dining room table.

"Apparently, we'll be eating a bit earlier than planned, Fiona. That blasted dinner bell will ring any minute now. Why don't we have our discussion about your business finances after supper? Then you can tell me all about your annuity and the first weeks of business in your new location."

"Sure, Angus, I'm starving."

The gong, gong, of the dinner bell, followed by Mrs. Fraser's laughter, broke the calm of the room. Angus smiled, rose, held out his arm, and escorted her into the dining room, to meet his fellow boarders. It would be but a few moments before Fiona would dearly regret not having had the wine. She could never, in a million years, have imagined who awaited her at the table, or how this evening would change her life.

29 ... Caught

Mrs. Fraser bustled around the room, ushering people into their places. Steaming dishes of delicious-smelling food covered the table. Fiona's gaze lingered for a moment on vases of colorful fall flowers on the sideboard. Angus held her chair and she settled into it, anticipating a nice meal and interesting company.

Before introductions could be made, Mrs. Fraser piped up.

"Now, lads and lassies, I'll say the grace while the food's still hot. We'll meet each other while we pass the plates."

Fiona bowed her head and listened as Mrs. Fraser recited in her Scottish brogue:

'Some hae meat and canna eat,
And some wad eat that want it,
But we hae meat, and we can eat,
And sae the Lord be thankit.'

Waves of homesickness swept over Fiona, as she heard her favourite grace, attributed to Robert Burns. While she was growing up in Scotland, her father said this grace before the evening meal. Unexpectedly, her eyes welled up with tears. She knew she must raise her head and open her eyes or she'd draw attention to herself.

"Is something wrong, Fiona?"

"No, Angus, just a touch of homesickness."

She raised her head, her eyes still teary. She glanced toward the head of the table where two people had slipped into the last two chairs during the grace. She blinked a few times to clear her vision, not believing what she saw.

This can't be! HE can't be here, here in Canada, the only person in the world who knows the whole of my sordid past—the rape, the trial, the baby, the affair—everything.

"Let me introduce everyone, starting a' the head of the table, with Mr. Sean Talbot, and his young wife, Eileen. The Empress Hotel didna get their room booking straight. They're here for two nights, and then off tae the Empress. Wouldn't ye ken tha' the English gentry ha' filled the hotel until the weekend. Sean and Eileen have two wee bairns, left wi' her parents while they visit us in Canada."

Fiona nodded at them, fighting to keep her composure. Mrs. Fraser's introductions of everyone else filled all of the available talking space. Fiona had a few minutes to recover, somewhat, from the shock of seeing Sean. He spoke to her first.

"How do you do, Miss Gilman?"

"Very well, thank you. And you?"

"Eileen and I are enjoying our visit to Canada."

Sean's wife was a delicate redhead, with porcelain-looking skin covering her perfectly oval face and her elegant, long neck. She nodded, looking at Fiona from deeply set, green eyes that were framed, surprisingly for a fair skinned person, by long, dark lashes. Her slight body was encased in a somewhat old-fashioned gown.

"Eileen, Miss Gilman designed and made her own outfit! D'ye like it? Isn't it just grand? She's a clothing designer and tailor. Ye might ask her if she could make ye some of the latest clothes."

"Thank you, Mrs. Fraser, the outfit is truly lovely, 'tis. Miss Gilman, I'd like to discuss my wardrobe, when you have the time. I'm afraid I haven't kept up these past few years. The children have taken much of my time."

"Certainly Mrs. Talbot, I'd be happy to speak with you.

Perhaps you'll come to my workspace on Government Street, while you're here. I could show you some of the beautiful silks, organdies, and other exquisite fabrics I've imported from China, India, and Europe."

Eileen's eyes lit up, if that's possible, thought Fiona, given that they're the brightest, most wonderful green colour to begin with. She turned to her husband.

"Sean, this is a mighty opportunity for me to catch up with the wider world. I must see these fabrics—and Miss Gilman's designs too."

Sean smiled. He patted her hand as it rested on the table between them. Fiona could see that he cared very much for her—perhaps he'd grown to love her.

Mrs. Fraser made the rest of the introductions. One man, who was an avid investor, engaged Angus for much of the suppertime, discussing the robust stock market. Fiona was glad he was kept busy. She avoided making eye contact with Sean. It helped that Sean had been involved in his family's considerable investments over the past few years, in Ireland, and in London, so that he, too, was drawn into the men's conversation.

But, Angus had already noticed the shocked look on Fiona's face, as well as her struggle to keep her composure, after she seemed to recognize Sean. He'd ask her if she'd met him before, when they had their discussion later.

In spite of the horrible shock of meeting up with Sean, Fiona enjoyed other aspects of the dinner at Mrs. Fraser's. She felt at home there in the boarding house where her memories of Scotland rose to the surface. She hadn't realized, over the past five years, she'd been suppressing her thoughts of home, except when she wrote or received mail from her parents or Helen, about Daniel.

Now, thoughts of her Scottish son came flooding back as Eileen Talbot spoke of her children. Fiona wished she could share comments about her son with someone, anyone, in this new life she'd carved out for herself. These days, her thoughts of Daniel resided just below the surface of her everyday life, slipping into her consciousness whenever she saw, or heard about a child from his mother. No matter how much designing, tailoring, or lately, teaching other children she did, her abandoned son was still in her thoughts.

I thought once my poor child of rape was out of my sight, he wouldn't occupy a permanent space in my heart or my mind. I thought I wouldn't feel like a mother—but I do, I still do. I'm his mother. He's my son. No amount of rationalizing will undo this fact. I love him whether or not I can see him.

Sooner or later, I'll need to tell Angus about Daniel, if our relationship is to grow. I can't deceive him any longer. It'll be better for me to break the news, along with the horrible circumstances behind it, than have somebody like Sean Talbot, or even Hilary Burns tell him anyway. I'll just have to be honest and hope our relationship survives.

But, the opportunity to speak with Angus alone didn't present itself that evening. The meal conversation carried on longer than usual. Fiona had to get home. Ming was alone. She didn't like to leave her alone, after 11:00 pm when the police raids in Fan Tan Alley usually began. Before she left, Fiona gave Eileen Talbot her workspace address on Government Street, arranging for her to see fabrics on Saturday afternoon. Angus sent Fiona home in a taxi, after they agreed to meet at the workspace on Sunday, when Fiona could update him on her business. Once that was done, she'd begin to fill him in on at least some of the details of her past.

Friday evening, Fiona was grateful for the distraction of planning and hosting another dinner and educational session with Aunt Woo and the Chinese students. The same group as last week arrived after school, along with another boy who was a friend of Woo's nephew. Yen must have been uncomfortable as the only boy last week. Now, he had a friend, too.

Woo's English was halting. Fiona gently guided her along whenever she asked for help. The students were keenly interested in Woo's art demonstration. In fact, they became so enthusiastic they started slipping into Mandarin, forgetting that these evenings were intended to improve their English. Fiona could understand some of their words, but she asked them to re-state their questions and comments in English, as well. Each of the students made an attempt to sketch a floral design, with Woo's help. After they ate their meal, the students left. Aunt Woo hesitated on her way out.

"Miss Fiona. Thanks you very much. I hear my language then yours, same idea, from others' questions. It help me much. May I come back next week?"

"Of course, Aunt Woo. Please call me Fiona. Our ages aren't that far apart. I feel old when you call me 'Miss.'"

"Many thanks. I have request too. Okay with you, if I take Ming to family residence tomorrow morning, to speak to elders about her tailoring?"

"I think so, Woo, if Ming wants to go. We haven't heard back from her grandparents. She's stuck with me for the present."

"Sorry, no word for you from grandparents. You know Hoy's family want Ming live in residences?"

"I do. I promised Hoy I'd look after her, but I don't want her to lose her own culture. A young woman needs to fit into her community. I'm so busy with orders for my new designs and with fittings. I can't supervise her as well as I'd like. Keeping track of her by myself is much more difficult than when I was just helping Hoy with her. Let's see how she does on a visit with you. It's a good first step in my getting some help from the community. I want her raised acceptably, as a young Chinese woman. I'll definitely need some help."

"Thank you, Fiona. I try smoothing way and getting help from Chinese community. You need her to keep working with you after school?"

"I've been very grateful for her help, and for Lee's. New immigrants are arriving in Victoria, including quite a few young Scottish women who are looking for full-time work. I could get other help. But, you can assure Ming, if she moves in with the family, I'll still offer her work, after school and on weekends, for as long as she likes."

"Good. Ming tell me she likes making her own money. I glad she wouldn't have to give that up, if she decide to move in with the family. Tomorrow, I promise I keep her away from stern, bossy mothers of her classmates. They talk much about Hoy's bad decision to leave Ming with you. We know he want send her back to China. But, if no grandparents there, then family think he might say OK for her live in residences."

"I agree. Hoy couldn't know there'd be no response from China. You're right. He didn't intend for her to live with a white clothing designer until she grew up. Let's see what happens when you take her to visit the family."

Saturday morning, the gossips in Ming's family residences were very frustrated when Woo held fast to her promise to keep Ming away from them. Woo was very proud of Ming's discussion about clothing design and tailoring. Fiona and Hoy had taught her well. Afterward, Woo and Ming went with a few family members to the Tam Kung Temple on Fisgard Street, where Mr. and Mrs. Leong cared for the altar, restocked incense, and greeted worshippers. After tea, Ming dropped by the workspace, on her way home, lively and talkative as she told Fiona what a wonderful day she had. Her elated mood and the obvious sense of belonging that Ming felt inside the Chinese community led Fiona to think that Ming's days with her might be numbered.

Meanwhile, Eileen Talbot was to arrive by 2:00. Fiona

carefully selected some fabrics and possible designs in preparation for her visit. Sean's lovely young wife arrived exactly on time. Her green eyes looked gently into Fiona's as she walked through the door, alone.

"Good day, Miss Gilman."

Thank the Lord she's alone. Sean's had the good sense not to show up here.

"Welcome, Mrs. Talbot. Please call me Fiona."

"I will do just that. And you call me Eileen, please. Himself is supervising the move into the Empress Hotel—he sends his thanks to you for fitting me into your schedule. He's told me to enjoy myself and order anything I like. He'll be happy to pay. How's that for a grand invitation?"

Fiona was surprised at Eileen's self-confidence when Sean was not around. She was much stronger than she looked.

"That sounds just fine to me, Eileen. Let's sit down and you can fill me in on what type of garments you'd like. Then, we can look through the fabrics that would be suitable and go from there. Alright?"

"Yes, please."

After a brief discussion, Fiona showed Eileen some fabric choices. She could see the younger woman was thrilled. Together, they selected appropriate materials. Next, Fiona showed Eileen to her new fitting room, a small curtained area behind the shelving, so she could take her measurements. A client had paid Fiona with a soft, Persian carpet, which Fiona had placed over the cement floor of the dressing room. She'd made an elegant curtain, with a remnant from one of Mrs. Bridge-Harris' gowns, and strips of a few other high-quality materials. Eileen admired the space. She took off her outer clothing, while Fiona waited outside the small room.

Once Fiona began measuring, Eileen became perfectly relaxed and comfortable. She began to chat.

"Can you keep a secret, Fiona?"

"Of course I can, Eileen."

"I'm expecting again. We'll be havin' our third child late in the spring. This one just has to be a little girl, to carry on my side of the family. Our boys are both like Sean. Is that going to be a problem? Can you make a few outfits for now, and some motherly, yet stylish clothes for later on in my pregnancy?"

"Of course. I'll make a few of the outfits adjustable. Nobody will be the wiser. You'll be the best dressed, barely expectant woman in Victoria, and look equally as lovely closer to the time of the baby's birth."

"Thank you so much, Fiona. Sean likes me to look nice, especially in the bedroom, which is how I got into this state again. Do you make undergarments too, delicates, slips, nightgowns, and such?"

The conversation was now becoming uncomfortable for Fiona. Images of Sean in her bedroom back in Glasgow came flooding into her head. Controlling herself, she answered,

"Yes, I have been making some delicate things for the dowagers who live upstairs at the Empress Hotel. I'll tell you a funny story. In the evenings, these ladies wash their smalls and hang them near the window to dry. They don't like the commercial laundries to see or touch their delicate things. But, some mornings, especially after a strong wind has been blowing across the inner harbour, these delicate items can be found lying on the grass, or caught in the branches of trees, many stories below, at the front of the hotel. The hotel staff gets very annoyed. The ladies don't always tip, when they get their garments back. So, the short answer is yes, I'd be happy to make you a few undergarments, as long as you don't hang them out to dry at the front of the hotel!"

By this time, Eileen was laughing at the story, enjoying her time with Fiona very much. She didn't have an older sister, only many brothers. However, the three year difference in their ages seemed like much more. Fiona had been independent these past five years, while Eileen had been cossetted at the family estate, out of the social mainstream. She was kept busy with her children and not invited to accompany Sean over to England and Scotland, when he travelled several times a month. This was her first trip out of Ireland. Here, with Fiona, she was really beginning to enjoy it.

Fiona could see why Sean loved this delicate creature. Her naiveté, along with her delicate skin and ethereal appearance evoked protective feelings from anyone who looked at her. Fiona was no exception. She resolved never to hurt her and hoped that Sean planned to do the same.

"So, Eileen, here's the result of our discussion today. I'll make the fall suit first, so that you'll have it for outings in Victoria. We'll use the medium weight wool you chose for that one. Later, I'll add an extra skirt of a fine, warm wool, in a complementary colour. You can pair it with the silk blouse that goes with the suit. A sturdy, wool cape will coordinate well with the skirt and blouse. Second, I'll start on three dressy outfits, with coordinating, longer jackets over sleeveless dresses with dropped waists and shorter skirts, using the silks, organdies, and beads. These dressy outfits will be useful for parties and evening events, especially toward Christmas time. The dropped waist is the latest style. It's also very convenient for concealing an early pregnancy. The jackets will drape nicely over your middle, camouflaging your waist over the next few months. Of course, you'll wear all of these things after the baby comes too. Finally, I'll make you six sets of smalls, four shifts, and six nightgowns. Four nightgowns will be made from delicate fabrics, with lace, and two from warmer materials, with a warm dressing gown to match. What do you think?"

Eileen's eyes had filled with tears.

"Oh, Fiona, I've never felt so spoiled. This is all just grand."

Fiona acknowledged the young woman's gratitude, offering her hand to complete the transaction in a business-like way. Eileen clasped Fiona's hand in both of hers and agreed to come by the workspace at the end of the following week, to pick up the first new garment. When she left, Fiona watched her stroll back toward the Empress Hotel, after dismissing the waiting taxi. She seemed so happy she practically floated down the street.

Now, Fiona's feelings of guilt about her lust for Sean, a married man, were resurrected. Sean's betrayed wife was no longer faceless. She was a beautiful young person who didn't deserve the treatment she got from Sean, or from Fiona. After all, Fiona could have stopped taking Sean into her bed as soon as she found out he was married. But, she hadn't.

Meeting Eileen is a just punishment for my lust, for those many, heated nights and sexual indulgences with Sean. I hope my selfish past won't cost me a promising future with Angus.

30 ... Confession

The sun streamed into Fiona's workspace through two leaded glass panels on the double front doors. The skylight high above the entrance also admitted warm, yellow light into the space from above. Angus admired these pleasing features as he knocked on the front door at precisely 10 a.m. Sunday morning. Fiona had certainly chosen the best space.

When she heard the door, Fiona stepped out from behind the built-in shelves that held her many bolts of multi-colored fabrics. These shelves covered the left wall, starting just inside the front entrance. They continued along the length of the huge space, stopping twenty feet short of the back wall. There, they sprouted legs, turning to form a square corner, and continued across a third of the width of the large room. By now, Angus thought, the fitting room would be set up behind the shelves. The previous tenant had tucked a water closet discreetly in the far back corner, for the convenience of clients and employees. Angus guessed that Fiona must have been inspecting and tidying every corner of the space, in preparation for his visit.

As she approached the locked door, Fiona could see that Angus held a huge bouquet of fresh flowers. She couldn't help smiling, as she unlocked the door and accepted the lovely bouquet.

"Why, thank you, Mr. MacArthur. Please come in. Welcome back to my world—you'll see a few changes, I hope."

"Thank you, Miss Gilman. I see you've already decorated the railing on the staircase with some expensive looking fabric. Do I see a desk up there, in the loft?"

"Aye, Ming found it at an antique shop nearby. She and Lee hauled it up there, so I could keep my accounts somewhere other than right out in the open. I've purchased a small safe as well. The Leeds brothers put that up there the day I moved in. I forgot to mention it when you dropped in last Wednesday."

"Good idea. You'll be taking in cash here. You could, if you want, place a sign in the corner of the window that says 'no cash is kept on the premises' anyway. Have you been making a bank deposit every day?"

"Aye, but some days clients come in after banking hours to pay a bill, or they give me cash when I'm at their location, as does Mrs. Bridge-Harris, for example. I can't always get to the bank on time. That's why I thought a safe would be a good idea. I'll give you the combination before you go today, just in case you ever need to get in there if I'm out."

"No, need to do that, Fiona. Your money is yours."

Fiona led Angus toward the smaller cutting table, where she'd draped a table cloth and set out two tea cups. She put the flowers in a vase and set them on the table. She'd decided they would sip tea and eat biscuits while they discussed the business, before she broached the subject of her annuity, and other details of her past.

Angus could see she was nervous. He didn't think it was because of anything to do with the business. He'd be careful not to press her.

"First, Angus, I want to thank you again for investing in my little business. I couldn't have done this without your help. I've written out my accounts as they are to date. I'd be happy to show them to you."

"Fiona, I don't need to inspect your accounts. You're resourceful and talented—the exact traits necessary for a successful business owner. You've built a loyal clientele without any help from me. I trust you to run your business. Speaking of your clients, how did it go with Eileen Talbot yesterday? Did she like the fabrics and order plenty of clothes from you?"

"She did. I'm designing multiple garments. I'll need help from Ming and Lee, all of us working at top speed, to create and finish a few things for her to wear while she's still here in Victoria. She seemed very happy with her choices. I might need to send the last of her order to Ireland, if I don't get everything finished before they leave."

"I got the feeling, lass, that you recognized the Talbots. Did you know them, or him, in Scotland? I heard him say he spent time in Edinburgh and Glasgow. Perhaps you met him there."

"Angus, you're asking me about a very painful part of my life; the final calamity that led to my fleeing my own country. I hope you won't press me for details. I'll share with you the part of my past that you need to know, if we're to see each other socially, which I hope we'll do. It concerns something that happened to me seven years ago, when I was only twenty. I'll just tell you what it is, along with the consequences, which include my life being made very public in the newspapers of Scotland. After I've told you, I sincerely hope we'll be able to remain friends, or more, as well as business partners.

"Fiona, lass, I'm not a perfect man. Just tell me. Why don't I pour us a wee drop, in case either of us needs it? I've brought one of my finest bottles of Tomatin highland whiskey, to toast your business success. We might as well have some now."

"Oh, Angus, you've reminded me that a Scot uses a wee dram of fine whiskey, in much the same way the English take to their tea: to fortify or to soothe themselves. Thank you, a wee drop would be very nice."

With their whiskey installed in the bottom of two of Fiona's water glasses, they raised their glasses, clinked them together, and downed the whiskey. Angus poured each of them another shot, to hold in reserve. Either or both of them could need further fortification as Fiona's story unfolded. She took a deep breath and began to speak.

"Here goes, the short version. My annuity is for my lifetime, set up by the Laird of my hometown. It's his way of compensating me for providing him with his only heir. His son raped me. I had the baby. I gave up my prized scholarship at the University of Edinburgh and my plans to become a teacher. My fiancé, Billy, was away at war when I was raped. Later, he helped me find a loving mother, his Aunt, to raise the baby. Her name is Helen Brody. She lives in Glasgow, with the boy, when he's not at his grandfather's estate. He's six years old now. His name is Daniel.

The rapist was murdered—he was rotten to the core. It turned out that my child of rape was the only living spawn of the Laird's line. The murder of his son, temporarily, caused the Laird to consider somebody besides himself; he co-adopted the child with Aunt Helen, and set up my annuity. I wouldn't have been able to start over here in Canada, without that annuity. I'm grateful to him for that.

The Laird's later behavior has led me to conclude that the annuity was his way of ensuring I could afford to leave town forever, after signing away my rights to the child. He exercises his rights to the child by taking him away from Helen to his estate, as soon as he can every year, according to the terms of the shared adoption.

The rape, the child, and my connection to the MacAndrews clan were made spectacularly public, as I mentioned earlier. The Scottish newspapers ran a photograph of the Laird, himself, walking arm in arm with me when I testified at the trial of his son's murderer. He claimed, at the time, to be supporting me publically to show the world that he accepted my child as his only grandson. He told me, at that time, that he'd be much more involved with Daniel, than he had been with his own son. He said he felt guilty that he hadn't recognized the kind of person his son had become.

Unfortunately, it's turned out that MacAndrews is absent from the boy's life most of the time, just as he was absent from his son's life. According to Helen's letters, he's usually in London, when the boy is at Glenheather, his estate in Western Scotland. By the time of Daniel's first birthday, MacAndrews had hired employees to look after the boy, a nanny and then later, governesses. Helen tells me the boy spends far more time with the housekeeper and the ghillie, at Glenheather, than with his grandfather. Yet, she writes that Daniel is a thoughtful child. He has a wonderful temperament, in spite of being ignored by his grandfather. It seems that her influence keeps him grounded while he lives with her and attends his primary school in Glasgow. Thank God for Helen."

"Well, lass, I never would have guessed all of that. May I ask you, did your fiancé consider raising the boy, with you, as his own child?"

Fiona's eyes filled with tears at the question.

"Billy would have done that, had he lived, if I'd been willing to keep the baby. But, Angus, he was a child of rape. I was very concerned that I would hate him, that he'd remind me of his despicable father. I was so filled with hatred for Jeremy MacAndrews, I refused to consider keeping his baby. I moved to Glasgow and stayed with Billy's Aunt Helen until I had the baby. Billy died, the rapist was murdered, and I, so to speak, took the money and ran, sure that nothing could ever convince me to go back to Scotland, ever."

"Do you still feel that way, Fiona?"

"No, I don't Angus. I guess I've matured somewhat. I saw the boy, Daniel, for the last time, on his first birthday. But, Helen writes to me and sends me photos. He's built like the athletic MacAndrews' clan, but, oh God, Angus, he's quite fair. He looks a lot like my father, with my mother's Irish blue eyes. I don't hate him. I long for him, but it's too late. On his account, I hate myself and I'm quite sure he'll hate me too, eventually."

"May I ask you another question?" She nodded.

"Are these the reasons you were so upset at dinner on Thursday? Does Sean Talbot know of your circumstances? Are you concerned that he'll tell someone here, about your past?"

"Well, I wasn't going to go into Sean's connection to the whole mess, but I'll tell you this much. He was an articling student, with a law firm that was involved in the trial of Jeremy MacAndrews' murderer. My parents and I met Sean while the trial was in progress. A couple of months before Jeremy's murder, my father punched Jeremy, at my fiancé's funeral. Because of that, my father was considered, temporarily, a suspect in Jeremy's murder. It came to nothing, but that's how I met Sean Talbot."

"Will he be discreet, in terms of your reputation here? Do you think he'll keep what he knows to himself?"

"For reasons I won't go into, I'm sure he'll keep anything about my notoriety in Scotland to himself. That's all I'll say about that."

"Well, darlin' you've surely led a most interesting life. You are as strong a woman as I've ever met. You've had the tenacity and perseverance to build yourself a new life, here in Canada. And, Fiona, I don't think you need worry about the people of Scotland, where your notoriety is concerned. They'll have found plenty of other people to gossip about by now."

"I have a question for you, Angus."

"Wait. Have another wee drop, I'm going to."

"Are you disappointed in me? Did you think I was some kind of Nun? Does this news, especially the part about my having a son, upset you?"

"No, Fiona. I'm only upset at the suffering you and your family must have endured at the hands of the MacAndrews' people. As a man, I can relate to your father, who must have felt powerless to remedy what happened to you. I can understand him punching your rapist."

As Angus spoke, tears filled Fiona's eyes. She was relieved she'd told somebody, finally, about her past, even if she hadn't told Angus the part about her torrid affair with Sean. That could wait. He wasn't stupid. He could see that Sean was extremely good looking and considerably older than his sweet young wife. He might even be able to guess that she and Sean had known each other, in the Biblical sense. As she relived these painful memories, her tears overflowed. She was grateful when Angus got up, came over to her chair, helped her stand, and folded her into his arms. She quietly wept out five years of bottled up tension from concealing her secrets here in Canada. She wept, too, for her six years of anguish and regret, over giving up her Scottish son.

Finally, she stopped. Angus lifted her chin and kissed her cheeks, tears and all. She turned her mouth toward his. Their first, intensely emotional kiss brought with it a feeling she hadn't felt before. Deep, deep emotion surged through her body, causing her knees to buckle. Angus supported her and helped her back to her chair.

She struggled to regain control of her emotions. Angus spoke to her gently, and then suggested they walk over to Mrs. Fraser's for lunch. She nodded. It wouldn't hurt her to have some company, a distraction, before Ming and Lee showed up for a few hours of work this afternoon. Sean and Eileen Talbot had already moved into the Empress Hotel. Good thing. He was the last person she needed to see today. She splashed some water on her face, fixed her hair, and they left the workspace.

They strolled, arm in arm along the inner harbour, in the sunshine. Fiona reflected on her situation. So, this indescribable feeling she had with Angus, must be mature love. She'd loved Billy as a girl and she'd lusted after Sean. But, neither of those men took her to this deep, emotional place. Now she knew why it was called 'falling' in love. Was this, finally, her time to be happy?

31 ... Improvements

Angus would be away from Victoria on business until the end of November. He had business in New York and Toronto. He'd take a ship to the United States and travel by train to the east coast. As well as conducting business for the bank, and his own clients, he told Fiona he'd be arranging for a Christmas surprise for the two of them.

They said goodbye after lunch, inside the door to her workshop, that Sunday afternoon more than three weeks ago. He kissed her, again evoking an intense emotional and physical response. She hoped he couldn't tell that she was almost squirming. Along with the love she felt for him, he had also reawakened her body to intense sexual feelings, feelings she'd suppressed, after her affair with Sean. This newfound intimacy with Angus, the feel of their bodies pressed together, changed their relationship. Theirs was a complete love, both emotional and physical. This big, gentle, handsome man was the love of her life and she knew it.

Before he left, Angus told her he'd been intrigued when he saw her at Hilary Burns' party the previous year. He said he knew for certain that he loved her, from the time of their chance meeting in the lobby of the Empress Hotel, when she described her episode with Mrs. 'Bitch-Harris.' She'd replied, wholeheartedly, 'I love you,' wishing that her intense feelings of that moment would go on forever. Reluctantly, the two friends and newly professed lovers separated before the spell could be broken, with the arrival of Ming and Lee for work.

Over the next few weeks, Ming was quieter at home with Fiona in their attic room and also at the workspace. She and

Lee usually chatted as they worked. But, Ming hadn't been very verbal lately. Finally, at dinner one evening, Fiona asked Ming about her unusual silence.

"Ming, what's the matter?"

"I miss Papa. That's all."

"Are you sure, Ming? What else, is there? You seem sadder than usual."

"I do not want hurt your feelings, Miss Fiona."

"I'd rather know what's bothering you than save my feelings. What has you so upset?"

"I worried you hate me."

"Ming, I couldn't hate you. You're the beloved daughter of my most important friend in this new country. Without your Papa, who knows how I would have gotten by? I would most certainly be broke. I wouldn't have my booming business or my new workspace. I owe him for his support. By extension, I owe you, Ming. I owe you the care he asked me to give to you. I'm honoured to provide it."

"But, what if I want move in with the family, at the residences? What if I live with Aunt Woo, who take care of me and protect me? Would you fire me from my job? Would you be mad at me?"

Fiona got up and put her arms around the young girl, whose eyes were teary.

"Of course I wouldn't be mad at you. And how could I fire you? You're my very best employee. You have great ideas, great skill, and you speak two languages—a benefit for my customers. What better person could I have to help set up my new storefront when I open it next year?"

Ming's eyes showed surprise. She couldn't believe Fiona was including her in plans for her business expansion. She'd be just fifteen next Spring.

"But, won't you miss me?"

"Of course, I'll miss you. But, I'll get my space back, won't I?

Also, I've had an offer to take a room at the boarding house where my friend Angus lives. A room is coming up after Christmas. I'll take it, if you're sure you want to move in with your family."

"What about the mean doctor and his rent? He be mad. Your high rent would not be paid by Chinese person. He swindle you, you know."

"I know. I just wasn't ready to leave before now. Thanks to your help, and Lee's, I've been able to design and sew for enough clients, even nasty people like Lady Bridge-Harris, that I could afford the Doctor's exorbitant rent. He had no problem renting your Papa's room when he had to. He'll just have to take advantage of someone else when I leave. When does Aunt Woo think you can move in with her?"

"She say, anytime is fine, but before Chinese New Year, if okay with you."

"It's settled then. I'm very happy for you, Ming."

Fiona kissed Ming on the cheek. She'd discuss the timing of Ming's move with Woo the following night, after their Friday evening dinner with the students. Woo's nephew, Yen, would give the presentation in English, describing his interest in engineering and showing everyone how he constructed a model bridge. Yen's model was fashioned after Victoria's uniquely designed, Johnson Street Bridge, which had opened with much publicity in 1924.

Woo agreed that Ming would stay with Fiona until the week after Christmas. She'd move in with Woo then. That way, Ming would be surrounded by her family in the weeks leading up to the very important Chinese New Year. It was the perfect time to welcome the young woman into her larger, cultural community.

That evening, the Friday night group planned topics for their next few sessions. Yen's friend, a young man of fourteen, would talk about fishing, Lee would prepare a talk on the history of Chinese cooking, and the serenely beautiful Lily would speak about her favorite topic, medicine. Fiona was looking forward to Lily's talk, particularly. She knew how difficult a road would lie ahead for a young Chinese woman living in Western Canada, who wanted to study medicine. She'd been shocked to learn from Woo, in confidence, that Lily was the niece of the mean Doctor who owned her building. Lily would have a very difficult time if he had any say about his niece's career plans.

When Woo and the students had gone, Fiona reflected that these Friday evening sessions with her Chinese students and Woo, in the workspace, were the best part of each week. They reignited her passion for teaching. They made her feel she'd recovered a tiny bit of herself—the self she was before Jeremy MacAndrews screwed up her life.

She also thought about Lily's predicament. The only person in her family with any influence or wealth was her uncle, that Doctor. Lily had already told him women had been training as doctors in Canada since 1883, when Emily Howard Stowe's daughter, Augusta Stowe-Gullen, graduated from the University of Toronto. But, her uncle was disdainful of the Canadian medical system. He said he'd never help her get accepted to a medical college, even if they'd let her in.

Well, if he won't help her, maybe I'll give her some work modeling, discreetly, to earn some money. I've been asked to hold private showings of my designs, by wealthy female clients in their spacious homes. These clients, who employ Chinese house staff, wouldn't object to a Chinese model. If her uncle realized she could earn her own money, rather than accepting one of the many proposals of marriage he constantly thrust at her, maybe he'd reconsider. Surely, there was a modicum of flattery in the fact that she admired his profession and aspired to be like him.

I can just see the ethereal, delicate Lily, in my designs, lending an exotic flavor to the clothes. Her exquisite, Oriental beauty would be appreciated by both Caucasian and Chinese clients. I'll ask her, too, if she'll allow me to have her photographed in one of my designs, for the display inside the front of the new shop. I have a suspicion that modeling is strictly prohibited for innocent young women, probably akin to prostitution, in the eyes of the most conservative members of the Chinese community. But, if nobody else will help finance her plan to study medicine, I'll do what little I can to help her. I'll ask Woo about my ideas next Friday.

I think I'll also ask Woo what she thinks of another of my ideas, about the young Chinese students. Their presence, charm, and participation in my Friday night sessions have meant so much to me over the past few months. I'd like to make the three young women an outfit each, for Chinese New Year. I could also make the two young men traditional hats and vests. Sharing my design and tailoring skills, in this way, would show my appreciation for their lively participation in my teaching adventure. I'd be thanking them for the interesting and entertaining company they've been. Young as they are, they seem to see that I, too, am a foreigner, here in Victoria. I'm a Scot, not a Canadian by birth. They seem to understand that I'll always miss my homeland, just as their parents must miss China.

November was glorious, in spite of a few very wet days. The day that Ming said she'd be moving out, Fiona walked over to Mrs. Fraser's Boarding House. She'd accept the offer to rent the upcoming room, as of the last week of December. She returned weekly, after that, for lunch with the current tenants, at Mrs. Fraser's insistence. Over delicious stews, scones, and crisp, green salads, they reminisced about Scotland, and the things they missed from home. Fiona could certainly understand why Angus had stayed here, rather than getting his own place. She was looking forward to his contributions at the lunch table, once he returned.

Meanwhile, she'd gotten Aunt Woo's agreement that her New Year's gifts to the Chinese students were appropriate. She worked like a dog in the evenings, after Ming and Lee went home. She wanted to finish the outfits before Angus returned. Meanwhile, she and the girls were well on their way to completing Eileen Talbot's Victoria outfits, ahead of schedule.

Eileen's pregnancy was beginning to show. Fiona showed her where to find the hidden adjustments on her new clothing, to use as her waist expanded. Fiona was grateful that Sean hadn't appeared at the workshop—she had no desire to see him. But, she very much enjoyed getting to know his sweet-tempered wife. Eileen was especially kind to Ming and Lee when she came to the shop for fittings, bringing treats for them from the kitchen of the Empress Hotel.

With her huge volume of work under control, Fiona could spend her time in December planning for and setting up the storefront section of her workspace. She was a natural entrepreneur; she knew exactly what to do next. She'd received excellent training for running a shop, from her father, at their store back home. As well, she'd gained confidence in her ability to survive in the business world, as she'd slowly built her client base in Victoria, over the past five years.

At the back of an old furniture warehouse on Store Street, she found a once-beautiful oak counter that spanned twelve feet. It featured a thick top, slightly curved along the front and sides. It was supported by a solid base on the four corners, and at several points along the span. An indecipherably thinner modesty panel covered the front and wrapped around the two ends. Eight ornately-carved wooden feet, designed as animal paws, gripped the floor. The feet were visible just below the front and side panels, giving the piece an old world appearance. She'd place the counter just to the right of the front entrance of the shop, at a slight angle. This positioning would suggest an open, welcoming feeling to her clients, while blocking their direct access to the back part of the space.

She arranged to have the huge counter picked up and delivered by the Leeds Brothers Moving Co., to a local cabinet finisher's shop, where it was sanded, stained, and varnished, bringing out the original colour and texture of its fine hardwood. The existing nicks and dents in the top attested to the age of the piece and gave it a warm, well-worn, yet elegant appearance.

Fiona had been very lucky to find this wonderfully-designed piece of furniture. She could hardly wait to see it placed in her new storefront. She'd been careful to ensure that the space had large delivery doors, when she leased it. She'd anticipated needing a large counter to anchor the storefront part of the space. She could never have afforded to pay for such a large, important item to be built in place.

Woo agreed to design an artistic sign for the shop: called *Fiona's Clothing Design and Haberdashery*, to be placed inside the front window. Giant-sized photographs of models wearing Fiona's designs would be suspended from the high ceiling, facing the entrance and reaching low enough to create a hanging "wall" that would divide the front storefront space from the workspace behind it.

The last day of November, Fiona glanced up from the large cutting table. She was surprised to see Angus walking toward the door, arm in arm with a young, blonde woman, almost as tall as he was. Curious, she walked toward the door. He announced, as he opened the door for the woman,

"Fiona, meet Jenny, Jenny MacArthur."

32 ... Interruptions

Fiona smiled as she replied, wondering whether or not the mutual love between her and Angus had been a fantasy. Surely, he hadn't married this attractive young woman.

"Welcome back, Mr. MacArthur. Hello, Jenny—Mrs. MacArthur, is it?"

"Hah! I knew, lass, if I told you this lovely last woman's last name, you wouldn't be able to resist a comment. But no, she's not my new wife, she's my cousin. Jenny, this is Fiona Gilman, entrepreneur extraordinaire."

"How d' ye do, Miss Gilman?"

"Very well, thanks. Welcome to Victoria. It's nice to meet a member of Angus' family. I think I know your cousin well enough that you can call me Fiona, Jenny."

"Thanks. I'm dying to see your exquisite fabrics. Angus told me all about them."

"Help yourself to a look around, Jenny. I'll catch up on the news with Angus."

As Jenny went over to look at the fabric shelves, Angus smiled at Fiona and put both his arms around her. He murmured in her ear, "I've missed ye, lassie, I've most certainly missed ye."

"And I you, my love. But, what happened to your beard? I've never seen you clean shaven. You look different, I must say."

"It's one of the looks of prosperous bankers of the twenties, my dear. Some I dealt with in the East were clean shaven. I thought I'd update myself. Do you like my new suit?"

"It's very well-made Angus. You look extremely handsome in it."

"Thanks for that. It's a great compliment to the tailor, coming from you."

"No trouble at all, Mr. MacArthur. Now, tell me about Jenny."

"The bank forwarded a cable from my mother, telling me Jenny would arrive from Scotland while I was in the East. She took the train to Toronto from Montreal. I met her there. I was glad to have her company on the long way back to the west coast, and the short sea voyage up to Victoria. She's a lovely, well-educated young Scotswoman. She could have gone straight up to university. Instead, she worked and saved her money, to earn her Canadian adventure, before she takes on more studying. Would you consider giving her work in your storefront, Fiona?"

"Are you sure she wants to work in a shop, Angus?"

"She has experience working in the village store, ordering goods, waiting on customers. You'll see she's personable, well-spoken, and, I think, quite presentable."

"Indeed she is, Angus, more than presentable—that silky blonde hair, and blue eyes, along with her stately height. Let's sit down in the workshop—Ming and Lee won't be here for an hour or so. I'll talk with Jenny about my plans for the new storefront."

Fiona left Angus to seat himself in the workspace while she approached Jenny. The young woman had strolled along the whole length of the built-in shelves, admiring the quality of the fabrics.

"Do you like them, Jenny?"

"I most certainly do! We stocked a few high-quality fabrics in the shop where I worked back home. None were so fine as these. Where do they come from?"

"The woolens of various weights come from Scotland and other parts of Europe. As you know, the woolen mills back home are some of the best. The silks are from India, or China, depending on their designs and weights.

"I'm particularly interested in the colours. I have a good eye for colour, according to my teachers. I hope, eventually, to become an art teacher, sharing my own interests in colour and texture, with students."

"Ah, Jenny, you remind me of myself. I planned to teach, but things didn't work out that way for me. However, I've found a way to teach young people here in Victoria. You might find it appealing for now. Every Friday night, I arrange a dinner and discussion group, here at the workspace. Some of my Chinese friends, young students, and the lovely Aunt of one of them, meet here every week for a demonstration and a discussion on a pre-selected topic. I hope you'll join us, once you're settled. It'll give you a chance to plan a lesson and work with young people."

Jenny couldn't believe she'd be involved with any kind of teaching so soon. She was a bit stunned by Fiona's offer. She nodded, a bit tongue tied, for the moment. These Scottish immigrants were so kind. She hadn't expected such a warm welcome.

"I think Angus is finished his inspection of the place. We'd best join him. He told me you'd like to get involved in my store-front. You can learn about my plans for it now."

The three Scots spent the next hour discussing Fiona's plans. Angus and Jenny liked her idea of having models photographed, wearing her designs, for the huge, four-part, suspended wall. Jenny was flattered when Fiona asked her if she'd consider being photographed. They agreed that Fiona, Jenny, and Lily were different enough in stature, colouring, age, and race, to reflect variety and give an international flavour to the wall display, while showing samples of Fiona's designs. With that decided, Angus surprised both women with news of his own.

"I visited the General Motors factory in East Oshawa while I was in Ontario. I've ordered a new McLaughlin-Buick roadster. We'll drive around town, in style, Fiona. They're shipping the car early in the New Year. A successful businesswoman such as yourself, Miss Gilman, especially one dressed smartly in her own designer clothing, will look grand, riding around the city in such a car. You'll learn to drive it, too, of course. I hope you approve of my surprise."

Fiona stared at Angus, temporarily unable to speak. She was overwhelmed. Jenny, too, was surprised. Angus hadn't mentioned a word about the car on the way back to Victoria. Fiona finally found her voice.

"Angus, this is very exciting. I can't wait to see the car. But, surely you don't intend to drive the car from Mrs. Fraser's to the bank. It's only a few blocks."

"Aye, you're correct there. That brings me to another piece of news. You'll see how necessary the car will be in the future. I'll need your help, though, to put this next plan into place."

"For heaven's sake, Angus, what else could you have been up to? Tell us!"

"Before I left for my trip to the east, I took out an option to purchase land in the exclusive residential area called The Uplands, in Oak Bay. I assume you've heard of it, Fiona?"

"Yes, more than that. I've done a few design presentations and fittings in some of those lovely homes."

"Well, I plan to build a house there, while land and building costs are still manageable. Unlike cars, getting cheaper with assembly line technology, land isn't getting cheaper. The better the economy does, the higher the cost of land will be. I think now's the time to buy, before land prices go any higher. I need to select a site and I'd appreciate your help with that. How about it? Will you help me?"

"You've truly shocked me, Mr. MacArthur. I'd be thrilled to help you choose your land. I can't believe I'm saying that. It's an experience I thought I'd never have. We've lived on land owned by somebody else, the Lairds, all of our lives. I'd love to help a fellow Scot select his land, especially a highlander, from the wee village of Newtonmore!"

"Grand. I'm grateful. I hope you'll give me your views on the design of the house too. I have an architect in mind, but it never hurts to have the opinion of an artistic designer, such as yourself, does it?"

Fiona was still in shock, flattered that he valued her opinions to this extent. It was all too much. What were his intentions? Was she to help him just as a friend? Or, did he have something else in mind?

"That's enough about me, Fiona. I commend you on the progress you've made with your workspace, while I was away. I see you've found the perfect piece of furniture, to introduce your clients to the storefront space. How clever. Did the Leeds brothers help you with the moving?"

"Aye, they did, from the antique store, to the cabinet finisher, to here. I can't thank you enough for that contact."

"Excuse me, Angus and Fiona. I think I'll go up to the front and take a closer look at that counter."

Jenny left. She could see that these two people needed some time alone. She was thrilled for her cousin; he and Fiona got along so very well. Fiona continued.

"By the way, Mr. MacArthur, I'll be using the Leeds brothers services again, at the end of next month. I've rented a room at Mrs. Fraser's, starting the final week of December. Ming's moving in with Aunt Woo, at the family's residences. I'll be leaving my attic room off Fan Tan Alley, at last. Life hasn't been the same there, since Hoy was killed. I've already been having lunch at Mrs. Fraser's a few times a week. I'm surprised she hasn't blabbed this news to you by now."

"Well, she hasn't really had a chance. Jenny and I just got here. We went directly to her new lodgings, to meet the parents of her school mate. She'll stay with them while she's in Victoria. I haven't been home yet. I sent my bags to Mrs. Fraser's by taxi. She knows I'm back in town and she's probably bursting at the seams to spill the news that you're moving in. She'll hate that I've found out before she could tell me."

Before Jenny left with Angus, Fiona asked her if she'd like to help set up the storefront over the next month. Then, she could work there after it opened. Jenny said she was glad to have something useful to do. But, she wouldn't accept a wage until the storefront opened. The next month would give her a chance to learn about the fabrics and various haberdashery items, before she began to wait on clients. Then, when she could make a useful contribution to the business, she'd gladly accept a wage.

"Great! I think you'll like the work here. I'll ask Ming to teach you to operate the beading machine. I'll teach you, myself, to hand sew beads and sequins onto my highest quality outfits. You'll learn a few new skills and the hand beading will keep you amused at the counter between clients."

"Fiona, thanks very much for this opportunity. I truly appreciate it. And, I gladly accept your invitation to join you for your Friday night teaching sessions. I'd love to come, starting this week."

"You're welcome, Jenny. I'll see you here this Friday at 4:00."

They shook hands on their agreement. Jenny smiled, nodded and stepped outside, while Angus kissed Fiona goodbye, pulling her close to him.

"I've missed you more than I can say, lass, more than I can say. I've an important question to ask you the next time we're alone. Would you like to go the Empress Hotel for tea, tomorrow afternoon? They've already put up the Christmas lights. The place looks grand."

"Thank you, yes. I'd be delighted. I'll meet you there at 3:00. Will we ask Jenny too?"

"Not this time, Fiona, I want to be alone with you, only you."

The following afternoon, the Empress Hotel looked absolutely lovely, and so did Fiona. Angus watched her walk into the tearoom. He stood, his eyes telegraphing admiration. The strength of his emotion was reflected in his eyes.

"Sit here, lass, beside me. You look just lovely this afternoon, Fiona."

"Why, thank you Mr. MacArthur, so do you. I'm still getting used to your clean-shaven look. I do miss your soft beard, though."

"Your approval makes it worth the effort I put into shaving every day, then, doesn't it?"

"You're very handsome, indeed."

"Is that another new outfit you're wearing, then, Miss Gilman?"

"Thanks for noticing. I . . ."

"Noticing? The entire room full of tea drinkers here today is noticing!"

As he finished speaking, a middle-aged woman cautiously approached their table and addressed Fiona.

"Excuse me, Miss, I don't mean to be rude. But, I must tell you I haven't seen such an attractive outfit since I was in Paris earlier this year, at the *Exposition international des arts decoratifs et industriels modernes*. Yet, your outfit is different, in a subtle way, nicer, in fact. Do you mind if I ask you where you got such wonderful designer clothes?"

"This is my own design, Madam. I designed the dress and made it up. Thanks for your compliment. If you're interested in this type of garment, I'll be opening *Fiona's Clothing Design and Haberdashery* a few blocks up from the harbour on Government Street, on January 15th. I've many exquisite fabrics and accessories that could make up such an outfit for you. Would you like the address?"

"Well . . . normally, tailors come to me and bring fabric samples. I don't go to shops for such things."

"I understand, Madam. Perhaps you'd be interested, instead, in a private showing of my designs. I've been asked to arrange a showing in mid-February. Are you acquainted with Lady Bridge-Harris, perhaps, or Miss Hilary Burns?"

"Yes! I was recently introduced to the Lady, through a friend of my husband. I'll make sure I'm there to see your designs."

"Good. Meanwhile, if you happen to be on Government Street earlier in January, do stop in to see the fabrics."

"Thank you. I'll let you go back to your tea, but . . . would . . . would you mind if I just felt the edge of your jacket, before I leave? It looks so touchable. Would you mind?"

"I'd prefer not, Madam. The server is just behind you, waiting to pour our tea. I hope I'll see you again, at *Fiona's*, or perhaps, at the private showing."

Fiona smiled. Madam finally got the hint and moved along. Fiona dismissed the woman from her thoughts, preferring to focus on Angus. But, Angus could hardly contain himself, at the audacity of the potential client.

"The nerve of that woman is unbelievable, Fiona! She was preparing to grab at your clothes here in public. Yet, she gave the impression she was too good to be seen in a shop. Which is she: respectable, moneyed, and reserved, or gushy, classless, and clambering to get next to somebody who looks like you, to the point of pawing your clothes?"

"I know, I know, Angus. In one way, it's flattering she likes my designs enough to forget herself, here in public. My guess is I'll see her at the shop in January. You know, I'm not sure I'm going to like being recognized, all that much. We're here to have a conversation, not to promote my business. I believe you asked me here on the pretense of asking an important question, didn't you?"

"Aye, I did. I hadn't counted on that annoying interruption. But, let's look at the positive side of this woman's accosting you in the tearoom. We both want your business to be successful. Perhaps a bit of recognition is the price you'll pay for that. And now, about the question. Are you ready?"

"Let me have it. I'm ready."

"Fiona, my dear lass, you know I admire you. I also love you, more than I can say. You've told me about your past experiences. Trusting me, with your hurts and disappointments, attests to your courage and your strength of character. I've also witnessed your generous care of Ming and her young Chinese friends, and your concern for your great friend, Hoy. You demonstrate compassion and a resilience that I aspire to. I have my strengths, but so far, I've not been required to suffer the kind of setbacks you've experienced.

Sweet lass, I'm almost thirty-four years old, with a heart condition. I can't see spending any more of my life without you. Another man might be physically healthier than I, but no other man could love you more than I. Fiona, my love, will you marry me?"

"Well, hello there, Angus and Fiona! Fancy meeting you here, at our hotel, the grandest hotel in Victoria. I'm surprised we haven't run into you before now!"

33 ... Scots wae hae

Sean and Eileen Talbot, arm in arm, stood over them, forcing them to abandon their conversation, Angus' romantic proposal, and Fiona's chance to answer. Sean carried on in a loud voice, too loud.

"Won't you invite us to join you? Eileen has some great news to share with Fiona. She hasn't had a chance to get over to see her."

"Sit down, please."

As Angus replied, he stood and held a chair for Eileen. Sean plunked himself down beside Fiona. Sean was acting far more cavalier than he had the last time they saw him, months ago, at Mrs. Fraser's.

"Well, tell them, Eileen! Tell them the news!"

Eileen didn't seem as eager to share whatever the news was, taking a few moments to blush and stammer the beginning to a sentence.

"We . . . we . . ."

Sean blurted out the news, seemingly unable to contain himself.

"We're having twins!"

Fiona hadn't seen this side of Sean. She knew, of course, that he wasn't the most steadfast of husbands, from her personal experiences with him. But, she thought he'd settled, happily, with Eileen. What happened to the calm, mature, loving husband she'd seen at Mrs. Fraser's in the fall?

Suddenly, Sean rose quickly from the table and rushed out of the tearoom. Eileen carried on with the conversation the best she could. She was obviously embarrassed by her husband's raised voice and sudden exit. Both Angus and Fiona ignored Sean's display of bad manners. They congratulated Eileen on the expected twins. Fiona told Eileen that the last of her garments were almost done. She'd send them over to the hotel in a few days, with the final invoice. Minutes later, Sean reappeared at the edge of the tearoom. He hesitated, seemingly confused, as he looked from table to table, apparently unsure which one belonged to his wife and their friends. Eileen stood up, walked over to Sean, and placed her arm in is. She guided him back to the table, where he sat quietly, gazing forward, before his head slumped forward.

Angus suspected what might account for this great change in Sean. He'd seen it too many times before. Wealthy young men came to Victoria and went out at night, once their wives were in bed. They were drawn to the gambling and opium dens of Victoria's Chinatown. No matter that opium was illegal. It was imported nonetheless and available for a price. It seemed, to Angus, that Sean might be a victim of his own indulgences. It was a shame for his lovely young wife, and their soon to be four young children.

Angus asked Eileen if she'd like him to help her and Sean to their rooms. She nodded and handed him the key. Fiona waited for Angus at the table, curious about what might account for Sean's odd behavior. He was obviously not in control of himself. That made her very anxious. Whatever was wrong with him, he couldn't be trusted to keep her secrets to himself. How could she be sure, now, that he wouldn't blurt out the details of their affair, or her rape, or her son? As soon as Angus returned, they left the hotel and crossed the street to the causeway along the harbour. Angus asked Fiona if she had any idea what the matter was, with Sean. When she shook her head, he told her of his suspicions.

"Oh! How awful for Eileen, an opium addict? Are you quite sure, Angus?"

"It's entirely possible, Fiona. I've seen this happen many times, with visiting, wealthy young men. The only other thing I can think of is that he has an addiction to alcohol instead. He's definitely impaired, in some way, today."

"I certainly see opium addicts in Chinatown. They just aren't people I know."

Fiona's nerves were getting the best of her. Addicted people she might have come across didn't know secrets about her past. Sean did. His discretion about their heated affair back in Glasgow had been much appreciated to this point. Now, there was no guarantee that he wouldn't talk.

I must tell Angus, now. He's just asked me to marry him! Not only has Sean spoiled the moment of the proposal, he's forced my hand. I'll have to tell Angus about the affair. It's too risky to ignore that part of my past. I'd be deceiving the love of my life. He deserves better.

"Angus, my lovely man, I'm very grateful for your complete acceptance of me, and my past. I'm honoured you've asked me to be your wife. I love you dearly, more than I can express. I'm dying to accept your proposal, wholeheartedly. But, this new development with Sean means I've got to tell you about a final, embarrassing part of my past, before somebody else beats me to it. Where's the best place for me to make my confession to you?"

"Let's go to Mrs. Fraser's. The upstairs sitting room is quite private. Most tenants are out in the afternoons. Mrs. Fraser makes so much noise coming and going, we'll hear her. I've a set of plans for the Uplands development. We'll look at those afterward."

"That's fine, as long as you'll still want to marry me. What's it like to be so sure of yourself, when you don't have all the facts?"

"Stop it, Fiona. You're too hard on yourself. Let's go."

Those are the first sharp words Angus has spoken to me. I feel like a schoolgirl who's been reprimanded by the teacher.

Who does he think he is? I'm just trying to be honest, honest about what he's getting for a wife.

"I should think you'd appreciate my honesty!"

She unhooked her arm from his and stopped dead in her tracks, as she snapped at him. He waited, while she gathered steam.

"And don't tell me how to feel. I'll hate myself as much as I like!"

So, here it is. Our first argument. Well, that's too bad. He'll not tell me how to feel about myself. Some bad acts can't just be brushed away. I'm so humiliated by my lust for Sean, regardless of his being married, which I knew. Angus has no idea how intimidating it is when he dismisses my feelings. If we get through this, he'll find out how angry that makes me. I only fight harder, when somebody makes me mad.

They walked side by side in silence, until they reached the boarding house. Angus held the door for Fiona and they headed upstairs to the sitting room. Angus lit a fire, to offset the December humidity in the room. They sat down in two comfortable chairs by the fire.

"I'm sorry, Fiona, that I've upset you. I know I don't have all the facts yet. But, I'm not sure you know how deeply I love you. I doubt you could tell me anything that would keep me from marrying you. I only want you to be confident of my love for you. It saddens me when you don't give yourself credit for who you are, for your strength of character. Sins are sins. We've all got them. Now, shall we carry on? Are you alright to tell me what's troubling you?"

"I'm sorry I snapped at you, Angus. I'm extremely sensitive, as you've seen, when somebody dismisses my feelings so quickly. Obviously, I'm not good at handling humiliation, where my past is concerned. I know you were trying to reassure me, but I think you should hear what I have to say, before you dismiss the embarrassing nature of my relationship with Sean.

I'll start with a bit of Sean's background. First, his family has unlimited money, which means he can afford as much opium as he wants, for as long as he wants. Hopefully, the Talbots will leave as planned and he'll get some help back home. Now, as to my relationship with him, I . . . um . . . I'll start by telling you . . . "

"Excuse me, but, will I be needin' a wee drop, to absorb this news, Miss Gilman?"

"Mr. MacArthur, by the time you hear the end of my sordid background, you could be a problem drinker, yourself."

"I'll chance it. Here, have a glass too, in case you need it."

"Thanks. I'll just get it out, then. After I met Sean, at the courthouse, I went home to Marysburgh, for a visit. Sean called me there. When my father told him I was just leaving to catch the train, he asked for my phone number in Glasgow. Knowing what I know now, I can't believe he had the nerve to act as if he weren't married, especially, when he was speaking to my father! No hint of a wife, to any of us. How far does he think Ireland is, from Scotland, anyway? What's wrong with him?

When I returned to Glasgow, I moved into a flat near the university. Every day, I sketched my designs and sewed in my room. I wanted to make enough money to supplement my annuity, while I built up my client base. Sean telephoned me there. If only, the building hadn't had a telephone in the hallway, the next part of my story might not have happened.

But, I met him at a coffeehouse that week, and for months afterward. He was attentive. He never touched me. He was respectful. He listened to my business plans. He also told me about his family history in Ireland. Because he'd worked on the trial of my rapist's murderer, he already knew all about Jeremy MacAndrews and the baby.

Eventually, we developed a close friendship. One night, before he was leaving for Ireland, I lost control of my best efforts to resist him. I thought I'd found somebody to be with. I thought he was the man for me, after the mighty loss of my Billy, earlier that year. This false dream died one evening before Christmas, when we were at the *Willow Tea Rooms*.

Luckily, I was away from the table, when a loud woman from Dublin spotted Sean. Just as I returned to the table, she effused a stream of remarks at him, about his young, pregnant wife back in Ireland. I bolted, grabbed my coat, and ran out into the street. I caught the tram, raced to my apartment, and locked the door.

I refused to speak to Sean. I ignored his repeated attempts, to get whoever answered the hallway phone, to talk me into speaking with him. One day, a few weeks later, he waited for me outside my building. He begged me to let him in, pleading for forgiveness. But, he was married, he'd deceived me. He'd broken my heart. I'd never forgive him for that.

Yet . . . , oh Angus, with Sean, I'd learned to enjoy a complete physical relationship that didn't involve rape. Billy and I had never made love, we were waiting until we were married, which, of course, never happened. The only intimate physical experience I had, before Sean, was Jeremy's awful rape. I can't tell you how grateful I was, to Sean, for showing me that making love could be gentle and pleasurable.

I'm ashamed to say, starting that day, I let him in, let him think I'd forgiven him. We continued our physical relationship. The tables were turned. I used Sean, just as he'd used me. I hoped he was at least a little in love with me. I was determined to break his heart, the way he'd broken mine.

And, there you have it, the vindictive side of my strength. Without telling Sean, I applied for my emigration papers and fled the country. My parents, my dear friends, the Murrays, and Helen, swore not to tell Sean anything about where I went. And I've been happy for these past five years, trying to stop hating myself for carrying on with Sean, after I knew he was married."

Fiona's voice shook with emotion. Tears filled her eyes as she finished her story.

"Don't worry, lass. I can see you feel guilty and ashamed of yourself. Who, among us doesn't have embarrassing times, in our youth? You've had much to bear Fiona, beginning with that rape. I can understand why you'd want someone to hold you who wasn't going to attack you. Can you see the doomed relationship with Sean, as a good thing, in terms of getting past Jeremy MacAndrews' treatment of you?"

"Aye, I can. But, I'm so ashamed of myself, not so much for giving in to Sean physically, but for continuing to see him, when I knew about his wife, and I was long past loving him. What does that make me, Angus?"

"Young, and hurt, that's what it makes you. I think you should forgive yourself for using a user, for dropping to his level to get revenge. Sometimes, that's the only way to move past such a hurt. Don't you agree?"

"Yes, I agree. Now you know another folly of my youth, one that's followed me here, to my new life in Canada. What'll I do if he tells people about our relationship?"

"As I recall, the Talbots are leaving for the east, at the end of December. I think you should avoid them, if you can, and ignore any references to the past, by him. He has much bigger problems to deal with. I imagine much of his time will be spent buying and using the drug. If he does that, most of what he knows will fade or lack credibility, if he does speak of it."

"Does your offer still stand, Angus?"

"Of course, it does, my love. Will you, or will you not marry me?"

"I'll happily marry you, Angus. I'd be proud to be your wife."

He rose and stepped over to her chair, kneeling down on one knee in front of her. He took a ring box out of this pocket, opened it, and held it out toward Fiona. She was wide-eyed, stunned, by the size of the large diamond. She held out her ring finger while Angus put the sparkling ring on her finger. He helped her up, embraced her, and then kissed her, just as Mrs. Fraser tapped on the door.

"I see we'll need our own place, as soon as we can get it built." He winked at Fiona as Mrs. Fraser came in.

"Come in, Mrs. Fraser, it's only myself and Fiona, my fiancé."

"Wha', ye're engaged? How lovely. My God, what a rock tha' is Fiona. Congratulations to the both of ye."

"Thank you, Mrs. Fraser. Do you have any of those delicious scones left from this morning? We're both starving."

"I do, Angus. They'll tide ye over 'til we eat. I assume the newly engaged couple will stay here for their dinner?"

They both smiled and nodded. Now that they'd survived their first argument, and become officially engaged, they'd welcome a chance to celebrate. Meanwhile, there were new home plans to discuss, and Fiona would get a message to Ming, that she'd be out for dinner.

That evening's dinner was the best in Fiona's experience, since leaving Scotland. Everyone toasted the couple. After dinner, they sang old Scottish tunes. As the liquor flowed, the tunes got louder, finishing with a rousing rendition of *Scots Wae Hae*, reminding everyone there, of the homeland they'd left behind. Angus called a taxi to send Fiona home, where she found Ming asleep. Thank heavens, she thought. She wouldn't want the young girl to see her tipsy. She fell asleep, with her diamond ring on her finger, glad to be alive.

34 ... Life changes

*F*iona woke with a headache, the tune of *Scots Wae Hae* running through her head. Ming tried to be quiet, knowing that Fiona had been late the night before. She was already making their breakfast, lost in her thoughts, when Fiona opened her eyes.

It good I know how to make my own food—Fiona and Papa teach me well. I study, like a good girl, too, so I pass my exams at end of term. I think Friday night meetings help me a lot, with my English. They are fun, too. I hope Fiona ask us over on Fridays, even after I move into Chinese residences. I sure hope . . .

"Ming, you're very quiet this morning. Are you feeling well?"

"Yes, Miss Fiona. I just thinking. You have good time with Mr. MacArthur last night?"

"Aye, I sure did, Ming. Look, look what he gave me."

"Oh! Miss Fiona, you marry Mr. MacArthur?"

"Yes, I'll marry him. We're making plans for a summer wedding next year, after our house is built. Meanwhile, I'll get my storefront going. The next year will be very exciting Ming, starting with your move. By the way, what do you think about my plans for the new space at the front of the workshop?"

"Lee and I think it be very good, Miss Fiona. We think you have plenty work for us, for long time."

"Ah, yes, that's very true. You two have work after school or on weekends for as long as you like. Aunt Woo tells me, though, that you'll have quite a few activities within your own community. You'll want to spend some of your time with your friends. Whenever you don't want to work with me anymore, promise you'll tell me. I hope to keep our Friday night dinners going whether or not you work with me. I really enjoy the company of you and your friends, and Aunt Woo. This week, I invited Jenny, Mr. MacArthur's cousin, to join us. She loves the idea of teaching. She'd like to help you and your friends with your English, too. Ming, I told Jenny she could learn to use the beading machine. Would you like to teach her how to do that?"

"Yes, please, Miss Fiona. I so glad, I mean, I am so glad to have help with that part of making clothes. It take, I mean takes, so much time for hand sewing on the really expensive clothes. If she help with beading machine, we have more time for hand sewing."

"That's grand, Ming. Thank you. I'll teach her how to hand sew as well, to save everyone time."

Angus was preoccupied over the weeks before Christmas, arranging for an architect and collecting information on reputable building contractors. The new Buick hadn't arrived yet, so Joseph James, the bank manager, loaned Angus his car. He and Fiona looked at a number of sites in the Uplands. They chose a lot with a mix of evergreen and deciduous trees on a road lined with Garry Oaks. These unique oak trees sported gnarled trunks, with huge crowns. They grew to over 100 feet tall, when mature. Their house would have a view of the bay, adding to the beauty of the spot.

Fiona was finding it difficult to take in her good fortune. She had a man she loved, land, plans for a new house in a lovely community, and a McLaughlin Buick on the way, to top it off. She'd never experienced so much in the way of many things going well, at the same time. She was enjoying her later twenties, enjoying them far more than she had any other time of her life. And, now that Angus knew about Daniel, she could finally share stories and pictures that Helen sent. It was such a relief to be able to talk about her son with someone. She'd be cautious, however, about how much she went on about the boy to Angus. She didn't want to take advantage of his good nature and tolerance.

The only complicating factor in her life, at the moment, was her constant worry about her business. While it was very exciting, making plans and getting the storefront ready, she felt the pressure of responsibility, as she organized every part of the process. With each step, there were costs. The photographer, for example, needed to be paid right away. He was a Swede, Mikael, who spoke English with a pronounced, but charming accent. He came highly recommended by a friend of Angus. His work was spectacular. He visited the space on Government Street, envisioning Fiona's idea of the suspended "wall" of huge photographs, as she explained her idea. He agreed that the oversized photos would make an effective backdrop, when clients looked past the impressive counter. They arranged for Fiona, Lily, and Jenny to come to his studio to be photographed.

Fiona was able to adapt one of her new designs for Lily's tiny frame, creating an exquisite garment to complement the Chinese girl's exotic beauty. Lily would also be photographed wearing the new outfit Fiona made her for the Chinese New Year. Fiona would be photographed in her two favourite dresses, one sleeveless and one with its matching three quarter jacket. She made a new, stylish outfit for Jenny that would serve for the photos and for Christmastime.

The day of the photo shoot, Lily and Jenny met Fiona at the shop and they loaded all of the clothes, carefully, into a taxi. They chatted for the short drive, excited about the prospect of such an adventure that not one of them could have imagined, even six months earlier.

Mikael had a small studio, with an adequate dressing room and appropriate draping, against which the photos would be taken. He began by taking pictures of each model, reserved poses, looking away from the camera, and other photos with each of the women looking toward the camera. Fiona wanted some of the photos to give the impression that her clothes were delightful to wear, in keeping with the "roaring twenties" they were living in. She had extra photographs taken of a few exquisite fabrics, draped over an elegant chair. She planned to include these in a flyer that she'd distribute, naming the business and the location. No pictures of the models would be distributed, only pictures of fabrics and a few shots of originally-designed outfits.

Mikael was tall, muscular, very blond, blue-eyed, and handsome. Jenny had a very difficult time displaying herself, even fully dressed, in front of him. Obviously, they found each other quite attractive. He was equally professional with all three models. He made a few comments to Fiona, about her talent for design and tailoring. The mutual attraction between Jenny and this blond photographer would need to wait for another day, but Fiona enjoyed noticing their mutual admiration. She smiled to herself, remembering, wickedly, how she must have looked at Sean, when she was younger, at the beginning of their doomed relationship. At least, Jenny wouldn't need to deal with such deception.

The proofs would be ready the following week, in plenty of time for the photos to be hung early in January. As a nice surprise, Fiona got invitations, from Mrs. Fraser, for Jenny and Mikael to come for Christmas supper at the boarding house. Great company and a fine supper would be a nice way to thank Mikael for his work. And, it was a perfect way for him and Jenny to see each other again.

Ming began to pack her things in preparation for her move out of Fiona's attic room, which would happen right after Christmas. She was at home less and less, as Aunt Woo ensured she was included in activities of the Chinese community. She shed more than a few tears, sometimes when Fiona was home to comfort her, about Hoy's death and his absence from her young life. They shared stories and memories of Hoy. Fiona would look back on these last few weeks of living with Ming, as a very sweet time. Caring for Ming had been her first actual mothering role. She was very glad for having had it.

Fiona's final session of the year, with Jenny, the Chinese students, and Aunt Woo was held on the Wednesday, two days before Christmas. Earlier, after consulting with Fiona, and getting opinions from the whole group, Aunt Woo had designed the new storefront sign. She presented it, formally, to Fiona. Everyone applauded. They made a ceremony of hanging the sign inside the left front window. Later, as they had their tea, Fiona tried to pay Woo for the design work on the sign. Woo refused to take money for it.

"Please, it is gift, Fiona, for your kindness, teaching skills, discipline, and caring for lucky Chinese students. You always be our friend, Fiona. We wish you well with new storefront."

Aunt Woo bowed, formally, and sat down.

"I thank you, my friends, and I wish you well, too. I hope you'll come to our next meeting the first Friday of February, in the New Year. I'm sparing you the discombobulating that will go on right before and right after the opening of the storefront space on January 15. I hope Jenny and I survive that effort!"

Jenny spoke up. "I'd like to say something, too. Thanks to everyone for making me feel a part of your group. I've really enjoyed helping you with your English. I admire each and every one of you, for the persistence and discipline it takes to learn a foreign language. The limited French I learned at school doesn't compare with the differences between Mandarin, or Cantonese and English. You've reaffirmed my desire to teach. Maybe someday, I'll teach your children."

At that comment, the girls giggled. Any inference to their bodies, especially to giving birth, or partaking in the act of lovemaking was of great interest and embarrassment to the young girls. The two boys rolled their eyes. Aunt Woo gathered up the students, including Ming, and left Fiona on her own to enjoy Christmas celebrations and pack up her belongings.

Angus arrived in a taxi at Fiona's building, to escort her to Mrs. Fraser's, for Christmas day celebrations. Fiona watched out the tiny window under the eave, ready to run down the stairs, rather than have him climb up the six flights to her room.

I'll be so very glad to get the heck out of this place, to see the last of that landlord. I'm sick of him traipsing potential renters through my place. He's trying to rent the room, at the same exorbitant rate I pay. He reminds me of the Lairds of Scotland. Are they all the same, regardless of country of origin? Squeeze the last bit of rent out of people who look only for a fair price? Well, I can see he isn't having much luck getting a new tenant, at his prices. I'm glad I installed the new lock so he can't show the place when I'm out. He's all the more annoyed at having to wait 'til I'm here to let him in. I'm sure, when I move out in a few days he'll be thinking good riddance, which is fine with me. Oh! Here's the taxi.

Angus got out of the taxi, took her hand, and helped her into the back seat, where he joined her. He whispered in her ear.

"Happy Christmas, my soon-to-be-wife, the love of my life."

"Happy Christmas, my highland laddie, my handsome, husband-to-be."

As they settled in for the short ride to the boarding house dinner, Fiona could feel her leg touching his, all the way from her hips down to her knee. She moved her foot closer to his, so she could feel the side his muscular calf against the side of her own. He took her hand, massaging the top of her hand with his thumb, using gentle strokes. Both of them were thinking the same thing.

God! This is so erotic, much more so because he's agreed to wait for our wedding night before we make love. What sweet torture!

Fiona hadn't been sure that Angus would agree to wait, before they consummated their love. But, she convinced him that her great shame, about what she thought was her wanton behavior with Sean Talbot gave her the strength to resist. She was determined that the next man she made passionate love with, would be her husband. She loved Angus in a way that she hadn't loved anyone, more deeply, a mature form of love, with surging waves of deep emotion, especially when their skin touched. She knew it would be worth the wait.

Angus, too, was finding this taxi ride very erotic.

I love her without reservation. Her past isn't important, the present is. She was needing affection and friendship when she first met Sean Talbot. He provided that. The fact that he's a scoundrel finally pushed her to emigrate, the only way I could have met her. I'm grateful for that. But, to be near her, and not have her completely, is driving me mad!

They were both emotionally and erotically charged by the time the taxi pulled up to the front of Mrs. Fraser's. Fortunately, they were distracted from their sexual tension, by the excessively festive appearance of the house. It was laden with bright Christmas lights and decorations, almost more than it could accommodate. Angus paid the driver, giving him a large tip, and escorted Fiona into the vestibule, where they could already hear the noise of conversation, filled with various degrees of Scottish brogue, and breathe in the delicious scent of turkey, roasting in the oven.

Mrs. Fraser had adopted the Canadian way of celebrating— no goose here. But, she kept to the sausage meat stuffing recipe of her Scottish grandmother, and traditional suet pudding, loaded with rum and topped with vanilla sauce. Angus had learned all about the menu, whether he wanted to or not, when Mrs. Fraser caught him as he left for Fiona's earlier in the afternoon.

Fiona wore a red silk blouse, and a black, beaded silk skirt that ended just below the knee. She'd draped a shawl, in the MacArthur tartan, over her shoulder and held it with the glorious kilt pin she got from her parents on her sixteenth birthday. She'd made herself a small, tartan tam to go with it all, tucking most of her long, dark, wavy tresses up under the tam. She looked a Scot, through and through. Angus wore his complete kilt ensemble for this occasion.

Anyone observing this happy group through the front window would have thought they were in Scotland. The whole place fairly oozed Scots tradition, clothing, food, and hospitality, the hospitality of the Clans, long ago, when everyone was welcomed and invited to share in the food and entertainment. Throughout Victoria, Canada, on this occasion, a Christmas not marred by war, or by a bad economy, or prohibition, houses full of people, both wealthy and poor, shared the traditional Christmas of their homelands in England, Scotland, Ireland, or Wales. Important cultural celebrations, such as those of the winter solstice, took place in the homes of other peoples, including Aboriginal peoples, who had lived here on this westernmost piece of land, at the far side of Canada, for millennia. Everyone, including Angus and Fiona, wished everyone else a happy season, thinking that life would go on as it was at this moment, for the foreseeable future.

Part 3

35 ... Homeward bound—1929

"Fiona, have you got everything? The ferry will be leaving without us, dearie."

"I'm coming, husband. I had to make sure I had those sketches for Mrs. Wharton, for when we get to New York. And, Angus dear, I need to stop off at the post office, one last time, before we leave the country for months. Jenny's a wonderful partner in the business. I know she'll keep up with the mail, and the bills, and keep the clients happy. But, I can't expect her to mail me my letters back to Scotland as well, can I? I'm sure Helen will have written by now. I want to read her letter before we get to Scotland."

On the way to the dock, Fiona hurried into the post office. Helen's last letter had an ominous tone. Almost four years had passed, since her cancer surgery. The unusual tone of that last letter, a sense of urgency, suggested to Fiona that something was not quite right.

The post office box contained mail for the store. But, tucked into the bunch was a letter with a Glasgow postmark. Fiona left the business mail for Jenny to pick up and hurried back out to the car.

I'll save the letter for the train ride to New York. It's such a long way to go, before we board the ship for our Atlantic crossing. It'll be nice to have the latest news from Helen on the way. I haven't seen her for nine years. That's far too long for me to be away, regardless of how well I like Canada. I can hardly wait to see Daniel, to show him off to Angus. The latest pictures show a tallish, sturdy, nearly ten-year-old boy, with hair still blond like my father, and the bluest of eyes, like my mother. Their brightness shines through the sepia-coloured photographs.

When she and Angus boarded the train, Fiona was reminded of her train ride long ago, on the Dumbarton Line with Billy. She'd been pregnant with Daniel, fleeing from her hometown in shame, to begin a new life in Glasgow. On that trip, in December of 1918, she'd sketched clothing designs, accompanied by the steady rhythm of the wheels as they rolled along the tracks. Now, eleven years later she'd do the same. But, this time, her travelling companion was her beloved husband, Angus, the love of her life. He'd gone to their sleeping car, to have a rest. His heart condition was bothersome, but it didn't prevent him from doing most of what he wanted. Fiona stayed in the day car, comfortable in her seat by the window.

She thought about their wedding night, three years ago. She'd experienced the most fulfilling lovemaking of her life. Angus knew about the violence of Jeremy's attack, he knew of her lust for Sean Talbot, and their repeated, sexual encounters. He knew she was no virgin. Yet, he was gentle, as he made love to her for the first time. He believed in satisfying a woman before he satisfied himself. Fiona had never experienced such selfless lovemaking. Experimentation with Sean had had its benefits. With him, she was always orgasmic, but afterward, she experienced an empty feeling. No love lingered in their bed after the ecstasy. That's what was missing with Sean: real love. With Angus, she learned that ecstasy and deep love were possible in the same bed, with the same man.

Before she opened the letter from Glasgow, Fiona thought back to conversations and events that had brought her here, on her way back to Scotland for her delayed honeymoon. One such conversation was last year, with Mrs. Emma Wharton, of New York City. They'd met at one of the private showings of her clothing designs. Mrs. Wharton had raved about the originality of Fiona's designs.

"Mrs. MacArthur, I haven't seen anything like these designs in New York. You're definitely ahead of your time. Would you be willing to come to New York, to hold a showing for my friends?"

"Well, Mrs. Wharton, I have the business to run, a new business partner just taking over some of my accounts, and a new husband, all in these past two years. I'm afraid I'm not free to travel just now. The two outfits I've made for you look wonderful on you—you'll be, in effect, modeling them back home, won't you?

I will tell you, though, that my husband and I are planning our belated honeymoon trip to Scotland for early next summer. We'll be sailing from New York. I could write to you and let you know when we'll pass through, on our way overseas. I could bring some sketches and sample fabric swatches for you to look at while we're away. And, my husband has business in New York, on our way back home. You might let me know what you or your friends might like to order, at that time. Will that do, Mrs. Wharton?"

They had agreed on that plan. And now, a year later, here she was on her way to New York, where she'd meet with Mrs. Wharton.

This quiet time on the train was perfect for reading her letter from Helen. When she dug it out of her purse, she noticed the return address was Helen's, but, the handwriting was not Helen's. Curious, she opened it and began to read.

Dear Auntie Fiona,

This is Daniel. Mummy tells me about you and lets me read your letters. I can read very well for myself now. I don't remember when we met at my birthday party. I was only one year old. I still have the silver Celtic bracelet you gave me. Mum won't let me wear it out of the house. I'm almost ten now.

Mum is sick. She was sick before, but now she's sicker. She won't write to tell you about her sickness. She said you have a honey moon or something. I'm not sure what that is, but it's why she won't tell you how sick she is. But I'm telling you because she says you love me too. Nana Murray is here with Mummy every day, helping Violet look after Mum. I have a short break from school. Geordie Murray comes over and takes me out to meet his mates when I'm here at Mum's. I go back to my school next week. Will you be here by then?

Love, Daniel

Oh no! Helen's cancer must have returned. Good thing we'll be in New York soon. I'll send a telegram to Helen to tell her we'll come directly to Glasgow. I'll also send a telegram to Jeannie Murray. What a sweet woman she is. What a good friend she is to Helen. She and Jack will be in their mid-sixties by now. It's just like her to pitch right in and help when someone's sick and needing emotional support too. Thank God, she's involved in Helen's care. I've got to go and tell Angus as soon as he's had enough rest. I suspected something like this, but I didn't expect I'd be hearing it from that sweet boy. It will be awful for him, if Helen dies. I can't bear to even think that terrible thought. Her health might improve . . . maybe . . . I hope.

When they arrived at the port in New York, Angus went immediately to send the two telegrams. He'd also see that their luggage was loaded onto the ship. Fiona waited for Mrs. Wharton at a dockside café. She ordered tea for two. When she looked up, here was Mrs. Wharton, hurrying along the pier toward her right on time. She was a tall woman, dressed smartly, in one of Fiona's spring outfits, from the year before. Apparently, that suited her, regardless of what anyone else thought. She had updated the outfit slightly, with a new hat, and some expensive jewelry, obviously from the Far East. They had just enough time for tea together, before the ship boarded.

Mrs. Wharton and Fiona agreed to meet, when she and Angus returned to New York on their way home. At their parting, Mrs. Wharton mentioned she'd arrange for them to visit one or two speakeasies when they came back through New York City, to hear the latest American jazz music, and get a "wee drop," regardless of this inconvenient prohibition. Fiona would look forward to doing that.

The Atlantic crossing was a pleasant time for both Angus and Fiona. She had almost enough lovely distractions, to keep her from worrying constantly, about Helen. They spent their time lovemaking, engaging in interesting conversations with other passengers, and enjoying the delicious meals made by the ship's world class chef. They'd been hoping for a baby since they married, but Fiona was not yet pregnant. Maybe, being away from the business would relax her enough to conceive. It wasn't for lack of trying that they weren't parents by now. After making the mistake of giving Daniel away, she was especially anxious to have a baby she could keep.

Many people on board speculated about the stability of the stock market. After so many years of prosperity, throughout the twenties, there were signs that all was not well, for anyone who was paying close attention. Angus had been warning of trouble to come—everyone was over-extended, he said. Some of the bank's biggest customers had defaulted on their loans. He made sure he paid in full for their land, and their house, before they married. Angus was also a great saver—he had stores of cash and bonds that would see them through any fluctuations in the market and allow them to pay their property taxes, if the economy got worse. They had decided on this trip now, regardless of how busy Fiona was with her business, because travel would certainly be more difficult in a bad economy. It was now or never.

Fiona had more clients than she could handle, which had led to her taking on Jenny as a partner in the business. Jenny had married the Swedish photographer, Mikael, last winter. They were financially secure in their own wee house in the James Bay area. The store was doing very well. Ming, Lee, Lily, and Yen entered their final year of high school last fall. The students were too busy to carry on with Fiona's weekly Friday Night sessions. They had heavier course loads and they were already balancing their studies with part-time jobs. They met for the sessions once a month, instead.

Fiona enjoyed the ocean voyage, even when the ship rocked on the waves of the North Atlantic. She'd grown up by the sea in Marysburgh. She loved the smell of the ocean air. She couldn't imagine living inland again, as she'd done in Glasgow, so many years ago.

After Fiona read Daniel's letter to Angus, they changed their plans about starting their Scotland visit in Newtonmore, in the Scottish highlands. Their visit with Angus' mum, Jessie, would have to wait. Instead, they'd go directly to see Helen in Glasgow.

Jessie MacArthur had been too ill, three years ago, to travel to Canada for their wedding. But, she'd written that she was healthier these days. She wrote that she'd like to meet Fiona, her daughter-in-law for three years now, before she died.

"Mum tends to be a bit melodramatic, at times. She's always been a bit difficult, you know Fiona. She has great energy, which is one of the things my father liked about her. She always had a part in choosing and organizing the village plays, often giving herself the choice roles. But, she also organized many of the charity events that took place in the district. She was a genius at getting the Laird to contribute to worthy causes."

"Will I be meeting your Laird, then, Mr. MacArthur?"

"Only if you wish, Mrs. MacArthur. I thought you'd had enough of Lairds, given your experiences with the MacAndrews clan and the Chinese landlord you put up with in Canada."

"Well, that's true enough. But, it might be nice to meet a kind Laird, one who actually cares about his tenants and doesn't let his rotten son ruin other people's lives."

"I'll send a telegram to Mother, saying we'll be coming later in our stay. I'll mention that you'd like to meet the Laird too. That will give her something to organize while she waits to meet you."

By the time the ship docked in Southampton, Fiona was ready to set her feet on dry land. They disembarked along with the other passengers. She waited in a taxi, while Angus supervised the unloading of their luggage. The taxi would carry them directly to their train.

As she relaxed in the back of the roomy town car, she watched the passengers greet people who met the boat, embracing, crying, laughing, and carrying on, it seemed, as if they had all been away from home for a very long time. It was a heart-warming scene.

She was taken aback when her view from the window was suddenly blocked, by the body of a man leaning down to look into the taxi window. As Fiona looked out, she came face to face with Laird Edward MacAndrews, Baron of Glenheather, returning her gaze from outside the window.

What the devil is HE doing here? I haven't been in this country for nine years—am I cursed? Why is his the first face I see, the face of my nemesis, that unfeeling turncoat, who once pretended to be thinking of my welfare, when all he wanted to do was get rid of me? What's he doing now, shouting and waving at me to roll down the window?

"Excuse me, Sir! What business do you have bothering my wife?"

Angus had raised his voice as he hurried toward the car.

"Pardon me, Sir. I have a document for her. Would you mind giving it to her for me?"

"What kind of document? How do you know who she is and how she came to be here on this day, at this time? What's going on"?

"Allow me to introduce myself, Mr. MacArthur. My name is Edward MacAndrews, Baron of Glenheather. I'm acquainted with your wife, and with Mrs. Helen Brody, who told me of your plans to be on this particular ship. I was in London. I decided to meet the ship, in order to present this document myself, if you'll allow me to do that."

"Well, you seem to know all about us, Laird MacAndrews. What kind of document do you have there?"

"It's a notice from my Solicitor. Your wife will be receiving a subpoena to appear at a custody hearing, Mr. MacArthur, in two weeks' time, in Glasgow. I believe you'll be in the area then"?

"Custody for whom? You aren't making sense, Sir."

"I am applying for full custody of my grandson, Edward Daniel Brody MacAndrews. You see, Mrs. Helen Brody has died. We shared custody of the boy while she lived. Now that his adoptive mother, is gone, I'll take sole custody of the boy."

"Are you anticipating that Fiona will contest your right to full custody?"

"That's very perceptive of you, Mr. MacArthur. Surely, you must know she signed away her rights to the boy, ten years ago, to me and Mrs. Brody. But, as any good lawyer will tell you, she could attempt to make a case for herself, if she's changed her mind about having the boy, based on Mrs. Brody's death. He's legally motherless, but technically, is not. If she, for some insane reason, decides to challenge my application, one never knows what a bleeding heart judge might do, in such a case.

But, since I know your wife was adamant about not wanting the boy, she won't mind signing this waiver now, to reaffirm that she has no intention, or right, to claim the boy, under these changed circumstances. Her signature will ensure that she need not appear in court, or be bothered by me again, as long as she stays out of the boy's life."

Fiona held her breath, watching Angus as he spoke with MacAndrews. She saw Angus take an envelope from the vile man and watched as MacAndrews walked away. This was not how she'd hoped her visit back home would go. She'd stepped right back into the nightmare that her life had become, before she fled across the Atlantic away from Scotland. She began to hyperventilate, as Angus opened the door and got into the taxi.

36 ... Death

On the journey toward Glasgow, Fiona tried to rest. But, she couldn't stop thinking about the two people who'd impacted her life in such significant and opposite ways: Edward MacAndrews, the Laird who'd controlled her life since she could remember, and Helen, her dear friend, who'd accepted her unwanted son and created a loving home for him.

I've been an independent woman now for almost a decade. How is it that MacAndrews can still make me feel exactly as I did when I was under his control? What is it about this man? Does he have so much power that he's lost his perspective of the world below his privileged line of sight? Where does he get off, assuming he can control every single thing? He makes me so very angry. God, I must get hold of myself and control my anger toward MacAndrews for Daniel's sake. I'll need to be in control of my emotions when I see Daniel at Helen's funeral. MacAndrews told Angus it was this Friday.

Helen. I'm so sorry you died, before I could see you one last time. Why couldn't you wait, until I arrived? You were a dear soul who is, most definitely, already in heaven with the beneficent God who gave you to us. You're a great loss to Daniel. You loved him as if he were born to you. You're a great loss to me. I'll be ever grateful for your kindness to me as a raped, impregnated, young woman. You never judged me, you were always concerned for my welfare, and you were always careful to keep me in Daniel's life, when you could see that I regretted my decision to abandon him, even to you.

Fiona and Angus arrived at Helen's in Glasgow. Violet showed them to their room, just as Helen had instructed her to do, whether or not she was still living. She made them tea and settled them into the library, where Fiona had spent so many long hours while she was pregnant with Daniel. It was also the room where Jack Murray had told her of Billy's death. There was so much history in this house, this room.

"Fiona, I mean, Mrs. MacArthur, I've a letter for you from Helen. She asked me to give it to ye the minute ye got here. I'll be in the kitchen if ye need me."

"Thanks, Violet."

"Oh, Angus, I miss her even more, now that I'm back here in her house. I can see signs of her touch everywhere."

"I'm so sorry, Fiona, that your friend Helen passed, before you could say goodbye. Do you think you might find some comfort in reading that last letter she wrote to you?"

"Maybe . . . I'll read it to you."

My Dearest Fiona,

I don't have long now, they tell me. I know you and Angus are on your way over, but I fear I'll be gone before you get here. Our Daniel confessed that he sent you a letter. He's a sweet boy, Fiona. He'll be back at school by the time you get here. I've asked Violet to give you a file that contains information about his school, and the arrangements that govern his time there. Unfortunately, it's late enough in the year, that his grandfather soon will be sending someone to collect him and take him to Glenheather for the summer.

But, Fiona. I know MacAndrews. He's extremely selfish. He'll attempt, I'm sure, to get full custody of Daniel. He tried to get me to sign a document, here on my death bed, to the effect that I willed Daniel to him, so to speak. It was a codicil to my will, drawn up by him, without my permission. I, of course, refused to sign. I think he knows I want you in Daniel's life, especially now that our boy won't have a mother at all, if MacAndrews succeeds in keeping you away from him.

I don't know what you think about trying to spend time with Daniel, to be in his life, for some of the time, at least. Please know that I support you in any efforts you make to stay in contact with your son. Yes, Fiona, your son. I've been privileged to raise him for ten years, and he loves me as his Mum, I know, but he's still your son. I've raised him to know that his "Auntie Fiona" loves him. Someday you'll want to tell him you are his mother.

I've been dictating this letter to my Solicitor, who kindly agreed to write it all down for me. I'm quite weak now. I must stop. I love you Fiona. I've loved you since we became friends, dear friends, while you carried Daniel. Thank you, thank you, thank you, Fiona, for the privilege of raising your son. He's a darling and doesn't know how lucky he is. He'll still have a mother, after I'm gone.

One last thing, you have the name of my Solicitor. He'll be calling on you here, to let you know the details of my funeral arrangements and when my will is to be read. There's a surprise in it for you.

Love, Helen

"Go ahead and cry, Fiona, you've lost a dear friend. It's good she was able to say goodbye to you in some way."

Angus got up from his chair and went over to Fiona. She stood and he held her, while she had a good sob. After a few minutes of tearful relief, she dried her eyes, for the time being, so they could discuss the contents of Helen's letter.

"Fiona, we haven't had the blessing of our own baby, in our three years of marriage. It's possible we won't be able to have children together. But, you're already a mother, Daniel's mother. Do you want to stay in his life? Tell me what you're thinking."

"Well, my dear husband, I am disappointed we haven't had children. But, even if we had a child, or children, I'd like to include Daniel, somehow, in our lives. He's in a bad spot now. His grandfather will ignore him, whether or not he gets custody. He'll be raised to a young man by his school, and by a series of housekeepers, just as his father was raised. He's lucky he's had a stable home and a loving mother in Helen until now. But, he surely must feel abandoned, which might be why he reached out to me. He knows I love him."

"Indeed, my love. I've not met either Helen or Daniel. But, I know you love the boy. Why don't we think about the situation for the next few days? Helen's letter said the Solicitor will be coming here to tell us about the arrangements. For now, you need a good night's sleep."

The next day, Fiona answered the knock on the front door, thinking it must be Helen's Solicitor. She was surprised to see William and Meg McGinnis, Billy's parents from back home in Marysburgh. She should have been expecting Meg, Helen's own sister. But, with all of the turmoil caused by Edward MacAndrews, from the moment she and Angus stepped off the ship, she hadn't thought about William and Meg. William smiled and greeted her.

"Fiona, it's good to see you gel. You look very well."

"Come here, lassie, hug your almost mother-in-law. This is the second time we three have been together because of a death in the family. First, our Billy and now, my lovely sister, Helen, the kindest person I've ever known. I can't believe she's gone. I'm the older sister. It should have been me, not her. And poor wee Daniel, motherless at ten years old."

Fiona ignored Meg's failure to acknowledge her as Daniel's "other" mother. But, perhaps Meg thought Angus, who was just joining them in the foyer, might not know of, or approve of, Fiona's illegitimate child. That would be the generous way to explain Meg's motives.

I remember Meg as quite perceptive. Maybe there's another

reason she doesn't want to acknowledge me as Daniel's mother. The boy is her nephew, by adoption. But, he's not a blood relative. I hope there won't be any more controversies than there already promise to be with Edward MacAndrews. I know my own parents would dearly love to play a bigger part in Daniel's life than MacAndrews has allowed, so far. Maybe that's what Meg wants too.

The day of the funeral, Fiona and Angus were impressed by the beauty of the Kirk. It was draped with many floral arrangements, including a gorgeous wreath atop the gleaming, solid wood coffin, trimmed with polished brass. It sat at the front of the main aisle. The wreath, with a card addressed to "Mummy" placed on top, was from Daniel. He'd written it, with Helen, as she lay on her death bed. Violet had followed Helen's instructions for the funeral arrangements carefully, deviating only when Edward MacAndrews insisted on buying the most expensive coffin available. He'd also insisted on having an extravagant number of flowers and very expensive, catered food and drink for the reception to follow.

"Over here, Fiona. The family is to sit up there. We've been directed toward these seats further back. MacAndrews' hand is all over this event. We're best to go along, for the sake of peace on this sombre occasion. Your friend, Helen, seemed like a gentle soul. I'm sure she wouldn't want a fuss made at her funeral."

"For God's sake, Angus, surely you don't think I'd stoop to such behavior here. He'd win, that way, wouldn't he?"

"Aye, he would. Fiona, you see this situation as a full on competition, between you and him, don't you? I'm sorry. I'm just trying to do my best to protect you."

"Well, you might as well know that being protected from Edward MacAndrews is simply not possible. I've learned the hard way that he usually gets what he wants. However, I have plenty of fight left in me, for when the time is right."

The service commenced, with the minister giving a lovely tribute to Helen. She'd been a member of this Kirk since she married Robert Brody here. When he was killed in the Great War, his funeral was held here, at this Kirk. Another speaker, a woman who'd worked with Helen as a suffragette activist, attested to Helen's dedication to the cause and her tireless work, on behalf of Scottish women. Three rows of pews were filled with Helen's activist friends.

The minister referred to Helen's beloved son, Daniel, but Fiona couldn't see him anywhere in the family pews, from where she was sitting. However, when it was time for the coffin to be carried out of the church, she noticed him sitting in the front pew. He looked quite small, next to the empty space left by Edward MacAndrews. Helen had designated as pallbearers, Laird MacAndrews, along with William McGinnis, Helen's brother-in-law, and four male friends.

The moment MacAndrews got up, Daniel turned around, to look behind him. He was searching for "Auntie Fiona," longing to meet her and certain he would recognize her from the recent pictures she'd sent to his mum, Helen. He finally caught her eye, and smiled at her, shyly raising his hand in a slight wave. He'd be in big trouble, if his grandfather caught him doing this. Luckily, the elder MacAndrews had already started back down the aisle with the procession, toward the church doors.

Later, at the graveside, Fiona caught a quick look at Daniel. MacAndrews kept a close watch on the boy, steering him away from Fiona's direction. It was at the reception back in the church basement, where Helen had insisted it be held, that Fiona had the chance to meet up with her Scottish son. He came up behind her and tapped her arm.

"Hello, Auntie Fiona. Here I am. Mum told me to make sure I introduced myself to you. I'm ten now. I had my birthday while you were on the ship."

"Hello, Daniel. Happy Birthday. We're very sorry about your mum. This is my husband, Angus MacArthur. He's been looking forward to meeting you too."

Daniel held out his hand. Man and boy shook hands formally.

"It's grand to finally meet you, Daniel. Fiona's told me all about you. She showed me the pictures you sent to her."

Angus had already enjoyed meeting Ian and Kathleen Gilman, the day before, when they dropped in at Helen's house. They were staying at the Murray's, who were also here at the funeral. Fiona had explained to Angus the great part that the Murray's played in her life in Glasgow. He knew she loved them and would always be grateful for their support of her and Billy.

But the boy, the boy was a treasure. He looked so much like Fiona's father that Angus couldn't stop himself from glancing back and forth between them. He was built like a MacAndrews, tall for his age and muscular. He carried himself with confidence, but, not with the arrogance that emanated from his grandfather MacAndrews.

As the reception was winding down, Edward MacAndrews returned to the room, approached Fiona's group, and ignored everyone as he reached out and took Daniel's arm.

"Come along, Daniel. I have a car waiting to take you back to school, for your final week of the term. You'll need to study for your last examination."

"But, Grandfather, I haven't said goodbye to Auntie Fiona and my other relatives."

Daniel remained where he was, his arm in MacAndrews' grip. Someone must have taken a photo, because Fiona heard a popping flashbulb. MacAndrews pursed his lips and stiffened up. He managed to maintain his composure, forcing himself to be kind to the boy in front of these townspeople from Marysburgh, particularly, because someone was taking photos.

These were his tenants, for God's sake, with the exception of

MacArthur, who was married to Fiona, his tenant for most of her life. Who do they think they are? He forced a smile, pulling on the boy's arm gently, as he began to back away from the group.

"Wait, Grandfather! I need to hug Auntie Fiona. Mum told me to get in lots of hugs while she was here in Scotland."

With that statement, the boy pulled himself away from MacAndrews and wrapped his arms around Fiona. She returned his hug, bending down to give him a kiss on the cheek. Another flashbulb popped. Somebody would have a souvenir of this reunion between the mother and her child, probably one of Helen's friends.

"I hope I'll see you back in Marysburgh, Daniel. I hear you're going there for the summer holiday."

"Is that OK, Grandfather? Can I visit Auntie Fiona when we're back home?"

"We'll see, Daniel, but now the car is waiting. We must go."

"Goodbye, Auntie Fiona. Goodbye from my mum, too. She told me to say goodbye to you from her, the first time I saw you. And, she said she loves you, just as she loves me."

MacAndrews was disgusted by these last words of the boy, becoming even more resolved to keep him away from these people, who had no right to him. Well, I'll see you in court, he thought, as he pulled Daniel away and headed for the car.

I'll show them who has the power here. It certainly isn't them, or her. I paid her off with that annuity. She'd better be careful, if she knows what's good for her. My Solicitor, a specialist at breaking contracts, could make a case to discontinue the annuity, in spite of the clause that specifies 'for her lifetime.' Extenuating circumstances, such as questions about her suitability as a mother, might be used to dislodge such a clause. We'll just see about that, while we're at it.

By the time Daniel was pulled away, Fiona, Kathleen, Meg, and Jeannie Murray had tears in their eyes. Everyone, including the men in this group could see that Fiona loved the boy. It was obvious that the boy was looking for love from her too. At this poignant ending, they withdrew from the reception.

The reading of the will would be that afternoon, at 4:00 p.m. at Helen's house. Everyone in Fiona's party went back there, to wait for the Solicitor. It would be a good afternoon for some of them, disappointing for others, and infuriating for one angry Laird.

37 ... The will

At exactly 4:00 p.m., the Solicitor arrived at Helen's home. Only those people named in the will were invited to the reading. Because Daniel was underage and legally adopted by Edward MacAndrews, the Laird was present to hear the will, on his behalf.

"What's SHE doing here?"

These were the first words out of the Laird's mouth, directed at the Solicitor, when he entered the large dining room where the reading would take place.

"Laird MacAndrews, Mrs. MacArthur is named in the will. She has every right to be here. Please take a seat. We'll begin immediately."

Angus tried to ignore the event in the dining room, for the moment, enjoying his examination of Helen's fine collection of books. Fiona had told him she'd spent many hours in this room, reading from one of the better private collections of books in Glasgow. The few books Helen had given her when she left Scotland were just a fraction of the fine volumes Angus saw here.

From the dining room, Angus could hear the Laird's raised voice. MacAndrews' combative stance would certainly increase the tension in that room, along with Fiona's resolve. Knowing Fiona as well as he did, Angus almost felt sorry for the Laird. MacAndrews had no idea of the strength of this fine woman who was his beloved wife. As he surveyed the wonderful collection of books, Angus smiled to himself, when he spotted a worn copy of Jane Austen's *Pride and Prejudice*. Whenever MacAndrews got her down, Fiona would repeat the words of Elizabeth Bennet:

'My courage always rises with every attempt to intimidate me.' By now, MacAndrews should realize Fiona will never, ever back down from him.

The group assembled in the dining room heard Helen's last wishes. She left her clothing, and family heirlooms, such as her fine jewelry, to her sister, Meg McGinnis. Meg wept silently, as she heard her sister's bequest. Helen left 1500 pounds sterling, to Jeannie Murray, personally, thanking her for her very kind care, during her illness, and for her wonderful friendship, over the past eleven years. Jeannie shook her head in disbelief. She hadn't expected anything for her efforts. She had loved Helen.

When my Jack comes tae get me this afternoon, he'll nae believe wha' Helen left us. Maybe noo, we'll get tae see our gels in Canada.

Next, the Solicitor described Daniel's inheritance, from Helen.

'I leave my home and my property to my son, Edward Daniel Brody MacAndrews, to be held in trust for him until he is twenty-one years of age, by my dear friend, his natural mother, Fiona Gilman MacArthur . . .'

"What? She can't do that. I'm the boy's legal parent. I control all estate matters for my grandson!"

"No, Laird MacAndrews, you don't, in this case. I have the legal documents here. The will is very clear. It states that Mrs. MacArthur has the right to occupy the home whenever she likes. Her son is to have his home maintained by Helen's estate, just as it was while she lived. All furniture is to remain, along with the boy's things. Violet is on a retainer, to be called upon whenever Mrs. MacArthur or the boy is in residence. Taxes on the property will be paid by the bank, from Helen's estate, each year until the boy is of age."

The expression on the Laird's face was fierce, unmoving, as if set in stone. His eyes looked straight into Fiona's. He raised his voice and spit out his words at her.

"You knew about this, didn't you? What are you trying to pull? You signed away your rights to the boy! I've the papers to prove it. You should be ashamed of yourself, Fiona."

"Laird MacAndrews, my only shame is in ever thinking I could give up my son. While Helen lived, I would never have dreamed of interfering in the legal arrangements for him. But, in spite of your vigorous objections to Helen's wishes for her son, know that I have every intention of carrying out her wishes. She loved the boy as much as any mother could love her son. His home here, with her, was the happiest he knew. Why would we deprive him of the memories and environment of his happy childhood? I'll follow Helen's wishes to the letter. Daniel will always know his home is still here, even though the mother he knew has gone."

"Is your memory that bad? I told you to stay out of his life! Let's be clear. The annuity I provided for you is proof you took money, money from me, when you agreed I would adopt the boy, along with Helen. I saw to it that you got the money, I got the boy. Effectively, Fiona, you sold me your son!"

Fiona ignored the Laird's intimidating falsehood. She remained calm, fortifying herself silently, with 'my courage rises, my courage rises,' rolling around in her head. She controlled her response to the Laird's insulting comments.

"Laird MacAndrews, you know very well that isn't true. I had already signed the papers for the joint adoption before Daniel was born. You set up the annuity later. You've made it clear today, that you considered the money as a payment for my son. That isn't what your note said, when I received the documents for the annuity, and you know it. I still have the note, if you'd like to review it.

Circumstances have changed. While Helen Brody lived, you had joint custody of my son with her. Now, she does not. It was never my intention for you to have sole custody of my son.

Let's be reasonable. He already knows me as his "Auntie Fiona." Now that he has no mother, I can, at the least, fill that role in his life. Would you deprive him of that, Laird MacAndrews?"

"Pardon me, Mrs. MacArthur. I'll stop you here. If the others will leave the room, please, we'll continue. The remainder of our business, today, deals only with Mrs. MacArthur and Laird MacAndrews."

Jeannie Murray and Meg McGinnis left to join Angus in the library.

"Now, Laird MacAndrews, I had planned to wait a few days, before proceeding with some additional instructions left to me, by Mrs. Brody. In light of this discussion, and the fact that Mrs. MacArthur is here in Scotland now, I think we should get on with it.

Helen Brody asked me to prepare and present a petition to the court, to have Fiona Gilman MacArthur, the boy's natural mother, replace Mrs. Brody as the legal mother of Edward Daniel Brody MacArthur. All that remains, for me to file this petition, is Mrs. MacArthur's signature. I had hoped to give her a few days to discuss the matter with her husband, but you have forced my hand, sir."

MacAndrews pushed back his chair. It screeched loudly, like nails on a blackboard, as the legs of the chair scraped along the gleaming, polished hardwood floor. He stood, glaring at Fiona, who sat across from him at the table, shouting his response.

"Go ahead and file your petition! I'll never agree to it! I've already filed for sole custody of my grandson. You'll never get him!"

With that, he turned, walked out of the room, and out of the house, leaving a surprised Solicitor. Fiona wasn't surprised. She knew MacAndrews too well for that. He'd fight for full custody, just as he said he would, from the moment he'd accosted her outside the taxi window, in Southampton.

"Mrs. MacArthur, there's another bequest from Helen, for you. She left you her library, which you can choose to move to your home, or leave here. She hopes you'll leave the collection to Daniel, in turn. I'll leave that up to you. There is a lot to decide right now, certainly, too many important things for a young woman on her belated honeymoon."

Hearing the Solicitor's last remark, Fiona smiled. Yes, she'd almost forgotten this was supposed to be her honeymoon. It certainly didn't feel like it. Did everyone have this kind of distress on their honeymoon?

The Solicitor gave Fiona his card and asked her to call him, once she'd discussed the adoption application with Angus. After he left, she sat alone, in the large dining room, not sure what she should feel. A few minutes later, Angus came in.

"Fiona, darlin', I've been waiting for you. Are you alright? I saw MacAndrews stomp out. The Solicitor has left too. Everyone is waiting for you to come into the library for tea, or something stronger, if you need it."

"Angus, I don't know what to do. Helen instructed her Solicitor to file for joint custody of Daniel, in effect, me replacing her as Daniel's mother. I feel that I, we, should fight for the boy. He has no mother now. Why would we let him be raised exactly as his father was, risking the same, or a similar outcome? What do you think, about that, my love?"

"Fiona, I knew you loved the boy before I married you. Neither of us could foresee Helen's death, or our childless state. I'll support your decision to apply for joint or full custody of the boy, whatever you wish. We could take him home with us, if you get full custody, and if you think that would be best for the boy.

But, let's not get ahead of ourselves. MacAndrews is powerful. He has enough money to hire the best Solicitors or try to buy favours from whomever he needs, to get full custody. The best you might do is get visiting rights with Daniel. Meg and

Jeannie told me about Helen leaving Daniel the house, with you as trustee. If you don't end up with full custody, Helen's house is here waiting, whenever you come to see Daniel. It's difficult to predict what the family court would allow, in this complicated case."

"Angus, do you think you could treat him as a son, or, at least, be his Uncle Angus? He's not your blood, after all, and I know how clannish some Scots can be, with regard to blood lines. What about your mother? Would she be willing to accept him?"

"Don't worry about Mother, Fiona. She's been after me to provide her with a grandchild since I reached adulthood. She'd be glad to get a grandson. Your parents, too, would be thrilled to be a bigger part of Daniel's life."

"Yes, it is Daniel's life, isn't it? We must consider what will be best for him. He's a bright little boy who will realize that something's missing from the story of his parentage. He'll be able to figure out, sooner or later, that Robert Brody couldn't be his father, when Edward MacAndrews is his grandfather. Helen told me he knows only that his father is dead. That explanation won't suffice for too much longer, will it? Ultimately, I'll need to clarify his parentage for him."

"You will, indeed. The boy, or his classmates, or one of their parents will put it together, sooner or later. You were, after all, advertised as his mother during the trial for Jeremy's murder. Anyone who remembers that will be able to piece together the rest. In fact, it might not be too soon, to ask Daniel a few questions about what he knows."

"I agree. Let's discuss the possibilities with the Solicitor tomorrow. Now, let's join the others in the library."

The scotch was poured and everyone, including Violet, toasted Helen. They had all loved her, in different ways. They would all miss her. Jack Murray showed up just as the toast was concluding. He was pleased to meet Angus and the two men started a conversation. But, Jeannie, dying to share their good fortune, raised her voice to get Jack's attention.

"Mr. Murray, get ready tae head over to Canada tae see our gels. That's wha' you want, isn't it, to visit our gels in Canada?"

"Wha'd ye mean, love? Ha' there been a windfall, then?"

"Aye, a windfall. Our darling friend, Helen, left us 1500 pounds sterling. We'll visit the gels and still ha' some left over, to retire!"

Jack was surprised. He hadn't expected such a gift. He was aware that Jeannie and Geordie had spent many hours here at Helen's over the past eleven years. They had first met Helen, and the pregnant young Fiona, that Christmas Eve, before Daniel was born. Afterward, Jeannie had taken Geordie over to play with the boy, continuing through his early school years in Glasgow, until Daniel was eight and sent away to boarding school. Even then, the boys remained friends whenever Daniel returned to his home at Helen's, for school holidays.

With the return of Helen's illness, Jack had been worried about Jeannie, an old gel in her sixties, tending to Helen day and night, in the months before Helen died. They'd hired a nurse, but, Helen relied on her friend, Jeannie. It was generous of Helen, to leave that large sum.

His wife wasn't going to get any younger. She'd fretted for years, that they couldn't, or he wouldn't travel to Canada, to see their twins. They had two grandchildren by Tess already. He'd give in, now, leave his beloved Scotland, for a time, to make Jeannie happy.

"Well, Jeannie dear, those wi' money willna say we should spend it. They'll say we should invest it. Isna' tha' wha' people do, Angus?"

Everyone else enjoyed the verbal sparring of the Murrays, especially Angus, who enjoyed teasing Fiona in the same way. He replied, "Aye, that's what I tell the bank's customers every day. Don't spend the capital, invest it and make interest on it."

As he spoke, Angus could see Jeannie's face change from hope to disappointment. He continued.

"Now Jack, don't get me involved. I can see your lovely wife has her heart set on seeing her girls."

"Jeannie, if seein' our gels is wha' ye want, we'll see the gels, won't we? Maybe Angus can advise us aboot investing what's left."

He put his arm around Jeannie and kissed her cheek, noticing they were flushed with excitement. It wouldn't kill him to go to Canada, he guessed. He missed the twins too. All the letters and photographs in the world couldn't make up for seeing them in person.

Meg McGinnis was silent, throughout this merriment of the Murrays. Although she and her sister hadn't been particularly close, she would miss Helen. She understood why Helen had preserved Daniel's childhood home for him. But, she was having trouble accepting the idea that Fiona, not she, a blood relative, would inherit Helen's house and responsibility for Daniel. Helen knew Meg and William didn't have enough money to buy a home in Glasgow. They'd stayed at Helen's whenever they could get away from their pub in Marysburgh. They had gotten to know Daniel, the only child in their lives. Helen knew they'd lost their Billy. They'd never have a grandchild. And now, the way Helen's will was written, Meg would get no property and no access to Daniel. It simply didn't seem right, to her.

Meg realized that Fiona had nothing to do with Helen's decision. But, she resented Fiona's intrusion into their lives. After, all, she had signed away her rights to the boy and left the country. Now, here she was taking over Helen's property, and the boy, whether or not she lived in Scotland. Fiona noticed the dark look on Meg's face.

"What's the matter, Meg? We're all grieving for Helen, today, aren't we?"

"Aye, Fiona. It's a great loss for us, her blood relatives, as well as for her adopted son, who knows no other mother. Of course, William and I are Daniel's relatives through Helen. I had expected to be able to continue to see him. With our Billy gone so young, we'll never have our own grandchild, will we? Daniel's the closest we have to a grandchild, a nephew through adoption. We've lost our son and access to the only other child who knows us as his loving relatives.

"Yes, you've lost more than a sister, I know."

"I've always felt sorry for your parents, Fiona, because Daniel is their natural grandchild. MacAndrews kept him away from them, as much as he could. We, on the other hand, used to visit him here at Helen's, which MacAndrews couldn't prevent. We have a great relationship with him. After today, either you or just MacAndrews will be able to see him. As things are, after the will, we have nothing, not even a well-meaning sister."

"Meg, I'm sorry Helen didn't leave you and William the house. I know you visit Glasgow as often as you can. I want you to know that you're welcome to stay here whenever you're in town, whether or not I'm here with Daniel. I don't know, just yet, what the custody situation will be, but the house is Daniel's with me as trustee, and no matter what else happens, I have every right to offer you this hospitality."

Meg was ashamed of herself for the resentment she'd been cultivating toward Fiona. She nodded and smiled, accepted a hug from Fiona, and resolved to stop wishing for things she couldn't have, including a grandchild. This was her lot in life. She'd stop wishing for things that couldn't be.

Fiona felt sorry for Meg, but she held her tongue about Billy's child. Ellen Rose MacPherson would be fourteen by now. She probably has no idea who her natural father was. How would Meg feel about having a granddaughter, when she'd never be allowed to see her, or know her? And, Meg would be really upset if she knew Fiona had found out about Billy's child over ten years ago.

I'll leave well enough alone. Why bring this all up now, open up another front in the child custody arena? I'm already fighting for custody of my own son. Billy's child will have to wait.

38 ... The highlands

*A*fter discussions with Helen's Solicitor, Angus and Fiona agreed that she'd apply for joint custody, with MacAndrews. If that application was denied, the court might grant visiting rights for Fiona and her parents, Daniel's maternal grandparents. That decision, however, would leave Edward MacAndrews with sole custody of the boy. There would be no way to force him to allow Fiona and her parents into Daniel's life. Whatever the outcome was to be, the courts in Scotland were quick and efficient. A hearing was set for June 25.

"Let's go and see your Mum, Angus. I don't need to be back in Glasgow until the day before the hearing. We could spend a few days in Marysburgh, on the way back."

"Good plan. We'll not allow this vexing issue with MacAndrews upset our plans completely."

They rode the train to Newtonmore, enjoying the stunning views of the Scottish highlands as they went further north. The spectacular scenery gave the honeymooning couple the impression of an eerie emptiness. The Highland Clearings of the past century, and mass emigrations between 1904 and 1913, when more than 600 thousand Scots emigrated to the Americas and elsewhere, left vistas almost devoid of people. They'd been replaced by tens of thousands of sheep that brought more income to the Lairds' estates than rent from their tenants ever would.

Angus' mum, Jessie, was tall and slightly stocky, with quite a handsome face. She was over sixty, about the same age as Jeannie Murray, but she had none of Jeannie's warmth. She smiled slightly as she held out her hand to Fiona. No hugs here.

"So, this is the Fiona you've told me so much about, Angus. I should have thought the gel walked on water, the way you spoke of her in your letters."

"How do you do, Mrs. MacArthur?"

"Well, I'm as good as can be expected, a widow alone in Scotland while my only son gads about the world, avoiding his home and his auld Mother."

Angus had warned Fiona that his mother was a cold and dour Scot, sometimes smiling on the outside, but cold on the inside. Other than her moments on stage, playing a role, her outlook on life tended to be one of tolerance and patience, of putting up with this world until she died and went to a better one. She stiffened when Angus put his arm around her shoulder, as if being touched by others was repulsive to her.

Aha! Now I see why Angus left and will never live here again. This woman is formidable! She might very well be a great organizer. She might very well know everyone near and far. But, to me, she's cold. Or, is she just cold toward me? I'll have to see how she acts around her friends before I decide.

"Mrs. MacArthur, thank you for your hospitality. You have a lovely home here."

"Aye, it's the retirement home my husband had built for us, by people from our Kirk. The Laird let us use this pretty site just at the edge of the village. It belongs to the Laird still, of course. Angus' father loved the view of the highlands from here."

"Mother, someone's coming up the drive. Are you expecting someone?"

"No, Angus. Oh. It's Mrs. Simpson, she's so nosy. I'm sure she just wants to get a look at you and your new wife. Then, she'll gossip with the rest of the women at the Kirk. Don't let her in."

"Now, mother, Effie Simpson is one of the kindest people we know. She's been your greatest friend for decades. She's not a gossip. She's warm and friendly and would do anything for anyone. Have you forgotten how much she did for you and Daddie before he died? Or how kind she was during your illness? How can you not let her in?"

Angus turned and went to the door. Fiona could hear the joy in his voice and in Mrs. Simpson's as they greeted each other and embraced. It was obvious he must have received demonstrable affection from her. Such affection certainly couldn't have come from his mother.

I don't understand how a woman who acted in plays, albeit religious plays, could be such a negative person. She seems to have no tact, no desire to say the right, or polite thing. Angus didn't tell me she was this difficult. Maybe he didn't realize she was acting so inappropriately. I'll wait and see how Effie Simpson deals with her outright rudeness.

"Jessie, why didn't you tell me Angus and Fiona were coming today?"

"I didn't think you needed to know, Effie, that's why."

Effie's face remained pleasant, as she went over to her lifelong friend, Jessie MacArthur, and placed a hand gently on her shoulder.

"I'm sure you meant to tell me, Jessie."

So, that's it. Effie Simpson knows more about Jessie's nature than Angus or I could guess. We'll need to talk to her when Jessie isn't around.

"Hello, lovely Fiona. I'm so very glad to meet you. Effie Simpson held out her hand, not sure how formal Fiona would want to be, but when Fiona gave her a broad smile, she added her other hand and clasped Fiona's outstretched hand in both of her own.

"Oh, for heaven's sake, gel, give me a hug."

Fiona was happy to oblige, having been made to feel less than welcome, by her mother-in-law's coldness. Effie, at least, behaved as if she were glad to see them.

Angus had anticipated the tension surrounding his mother. She'd always been averse to physical contact and somewhat manipulative. Now, she was especially negative. She had always tolerated social occasions, by slipping into a hyper organizational mode. That way, people couldn't get too close to her. In the days when she acted in plays at the Kirk, she seemed happy to be playing the part of someone else, rather than being herself.

Her outright rudeness, toward Fiona and Effie, was new. This isn't like her. She seems to have given up manipulating people, using appropriate social decorum to get what she wants. She doesn't seem to care about that now. I'll speak to Effie right away.

Effie updated Angus in the kitchen, while Fiona gritted her teeth and attempted to carry on a civil conversation with her mother-in-law in the living room.

"Angus, you know your Mum hasn't always been the most sensitive person. But, lately, her outright verbal aggression has caused everyone to worry. The doctor says she might be suffering from some form of senility. She could get worse. Some days, she seems not to be able to make good decisions for herself, such as not eating anything, or eating until she makes herself sick. Other days, she seems fine. The doctor suggested you arrange to have legal responsibility for her, for when she needs assistance. It will depend on how she does, whether or not she'll be able to stay alone here in this house she loves."

"I already have legal responsibility for Mum's affairs. We arranged that when my father died. Effie, I want to thank you for all you've done for her, over so many years. I know she can be very trying. You've been very patient."

"There's no need to thank me, Angus. I'll be grateful to Jessie for the rest of my life. She took over when my husband was killed in the accident, organizing my three children, keeping up with my home and hers, while she continued with her numerous responsibilities at the Kirk. Many people here in Newtonmore owe Jessie MacArthur, whether or not she's been their favourite personality, over the years.

Tell me, Angus, what would you think about my moving in here with your Mum? Could you convince her it would be a good idea for her to have someone around? I think she's too embarrassed to ask for help. In fact, I'm quite sure she'd resent a direct offer from me. In the long run, if not sooner, she's going to need help. My nursing experience during the war has more than prepared me, to assist her. What do you think?"

"I'll suggest that possibility to her, Effie. Thanks. Are you sure you want to take on such a responsibility? What about your children? Are any of them still here in town?"

"No, they've all emigrated, like you. They're all doing well. My daughter has been trying to convince me I shouldn't live alone, as I get older. She'd be very supportive of my moving in with your Mum. She knows we're indebted to her."

"If you do move in, Effie, I insist on paying you to look after Mum. She couldn't know, of course, or she'd never stand for it. From the little I know of diseases of the elderly, especially senility, I understand that, if she gets worse, she eventually won't be able to make good decisions about her own health and safety. The rudeness we've seen today is unusual, even for her. I fear that, too, could get worse."

"I agree. I saw many cases of people who were unable to care for themselves in a healthy way, mentally or physically, after the war. I'm well prepared to deal with whatever comes."

"Thank you, Effie. Mum is very lucky to have such a friend as you. We'll speak again, before Fiona and I leave in a few days."

The next three days were as tense as any Fiona had experienced, since Jeremy's murder trial. Being around Angus' mother was like walking on eggshells. One minute Jessie would be relating a fascinating story, about her time on the stage, and the next, she'd be chastising Fiona for commenting the wrong way, according to her. Fiona became increasingly nervous around her. While she felt sorry for this woman, the strain on Fiona's nerves wasn't what she needed, right before she went to court to fight for her son. She was glad when Angus told her he'd spoken with his Mum's doctor, and Effie, about their arrangements. Everything was in place for Effie to move in, hopefully, with his Mum's consent. Angus did his best to convince her that a roommate was better than having someone she didn't know, or like, helping her. Angus and Fiona moved on, having done what they could for his Mum, for the time being.

The trip to Marysburgh was a welcome relief after the strain of the Newtonmore visit. Ian and Kathleen welcomed them both warmly. The two men enjoyed discussions of commerce and fishing, while Fiona and her Mum caught up on their news.

One piece of Kathleen's news was that Fiona's sister had contracted malaria in Sierra Leone, where she continued with her missionary work. Brigit survived the bout, with medicine that made the episode just bearable. She wrote to her parents that she'd always be susceptible to the illness, but she'd remain at the mission.

"Speaking of our children, Fiona, what have you and Angus decided to do about our young Daniel?"

"I'll go to family court on June 25th, to fight the Laird for joint custody. Failing that, I'll apply for visiting rights to see my son."

"That's quite a change, since you left Scotland after he was born, isn't it, lass?"

"Aye, Mum. I've grown up, I guess. I deeply regret not keeping my son. But that opportunity has passed. Helen was a wonderful mother to him. Now, I have a chance to make up for my decision to give him away, partly, anyway."

"You know, Fiona, Daddie gets along really well with Daniel. They look so much alike, and they walk alike, striding off to fish in the loch, whenever they can each summer. He's an intelligent wee man, smarter, it seems, than his father. Helen used to say, when he was younger, he'd return from the MacAndrews estate subdued, afraid to make a mistake. She said MacAndrews seems to have simply replaced Jeremy with Daniel, gradually returning to the impatient, cold nature he displayed around his son, Jeremy. Any flaws he imagines with the boy's character are blamed on our side of his parentage.

As he grew older, Daniel learned, thanks to Helen's gentle encouragement, to cope with his grandfather's coldness. Now, he's more confident. He's thoughtful, rather than fearful. Helen's taught him to behave properly, rather than acting out, the way Jeremy did. The boy seems to respect his grandfather. He calls him sir, doesn't expect affection, and ignores MacAndrews' impatience with him. He's quite the mature ten-year-old, and we're very proud of him, as his 'Uncle Ian' and 'Auntie Kathleen.'

I only hope we'll be able to continue seeing him. It's through the good graces of Mrs. Brownley, MacAndrews' housekeeper, that we've been able to see the boy as often as we do. The Laird has no idea how close we are to Daniel. He'll surely cut all ties, if he can, now that you're back in the picture and Helen has passed."

"I'm sorry, Mum. I hope it won't come to that. I hope the Family Court will see that Daniel would benefit from having his natural mother and his maternal grandparents in his life. I Iopefully, we'll all come through this hearing quickly and quietly, with a good result for Daniel."

But, Fiona's hopes for a quiet proceeding were not to be. *The Scotsman*, her old media friend, from the days of Jeremy's murder trial, would take full advantage of the class struggle between a raped, unwed mother and a powerful Laird. Notoriety, again, was a certainty.

39 ... Battle for a boy

Raped Woman Fights Peer for her Son
Fiona MacArthur (nee Gilman) testified, in 1919, at the
murder trial of her rapist, Jeremy MacAndrews, son
of Edward MacAndrews, Baron of Glenheather. Laird
MacAndrews supported Gilman MacArthur, when she
testified as to her rape and impregnation by his son.
Gilman MacArthur's child was adopted jointly, by Laird
MacAndrews and Helen Brody, who has died and left
the boy motherless. Gilman MacArthur goes to court
tomorrow to fight for custody of the boy. Now, she wants
the boy and so does the grandfather. Tomorrow's Family
Court hearing will determine how Gilman MacArthur
fares against this powerful Laird."
The Scotsman—June 24, 1929

How do the media do it? How dare they bring up the rape,
again, and again? They've even run the photograph of
Edward MacAndrews walking with me, arm in arm, into the
courthouse in Edinburgh, ten years ago. Then, he was adamant
we be photographed together, giving the impression that he, a
kindly grandfather, supported me, a victim of his wayward son.
In actuality, he was fortifying his case for claiming the child as
his grandson. He'd tried to get sole custody in those days and
only agreed to Helen's adopting the boy at my insistence. Now,
he'll maintain he treated me fairly, never stood in the way of
what I wanted—to give my son away, to him and Helen. That
was true, at the time, but no longer.

Will I never escape the label of a raped, impregnated, tenant? Apparently, not, if it's up to the Scottish media. Now, everyone also knows my married name. I'll never be rid of this connection to Jeremy, the rapist, though he's long dead. Well, what did I expect? I knew there'd be some publicity. It'll be worth it, to get the rights to see my son.

The Judge began the questioning.

"Mrs. MacArthur, Laird Edward MacAndrews is the legal and natural grandfather of Edward Daniel Brody MacAndrews, is he not?"

"Aye, that is true."

"And is it also true that you, the natural mother of the boy, signed away your legal rights to him when he was born? You went along with a joint adoption, by Helen Brody and Laird MacAndrews, his grandfather, at that time, did you not?"

"Yes, but at that time, nobody could have known that Helen Brody would die of cancer, when my son was only ten years old."

"That's irrelevant, Mrs. MacArthur. The fact is, you signed him away. You have no legal right to him."

"That may be true, your Lordship, but I'll not stand by and see him motherless. His father, the rapist, was motherless in Edward MacAndrews' home. Look how he turned out."

"Objection, your Lordship, objection!"

"I hear you. This is not a trial. It's a hearing. I'll decide when to caution the witness. Mrs. MacArthur, please answer the questions and refrain from adding your commentary."

His Lordship, Judge McConnell, had noticed how feisty was Fiona Gilman, long ago, when she testified at Ned Smith's trial, after he murdered Jeremy MacAndrews. The Judge had been a practising Advocate then. He'd admired greatly, Fiona's self-control under very trying circumstances. She was obviously more emotional now, about her child.

"Mrs. MacArthur, why did you not keep your child?"

"At the time, your Lordship, I felt that Helen Brody could be a much better mother to my son, than I could. I had no income, having had to cancel my scholarship to University after I was raped and became pregnant. I couldn't provide for him as well as Helen could. She was a kind, and loving mother to my son. She would have seen that he became a well-adjusted member of society, had she lived."

At that remark, the solicitor sitting with MacAndrews stood up.

"Your Lordship! I would like to ask the witness a question, if I may. Are you inferring, Mrs. MacArthur, that your son won't become a well-adjusted member of society, if he remains in the sole custody of his grandfather, Edward MacAndrews?"

"I am saying that his father, the man who raped me, was motherless. He was ignored by his father, who spends most of his time in London, leaving the care of children to the housekeeper. When Helen lived, my son's time at the Glenheather estate was limited. He knew he had a loving mother to teach him the responsibilities of a good Scottish citizen, not just a good Scottish Laird-in-training. He's a sweet child, accustomed to the affection of a mother, affection that balances his grandfather's influence."

The Judge continued with his questions.

"You have asked the court for joint custody of the boy. Do you plan to shuffle him back and forth between Canada and Scotland, then? Is that the best thing for the boy, who attends a superior boarding school, here in Scotland?"

"No, I don't think that is the best situation. I have asked for joint custody because he has a mother—me, and because his grandfather has done everything he can to keep me away from my son. Edward MacAndrews seems to think the boy should grow up the way his son did, without the stabilizing and loving influence of a mother. He's already lost the only mother he knows to cancer. My son's maternal grandparents and I can help to fill that void in his life. The boy's adoptive mother, Helen Brody, expressed her intentions for the boy when she made me trustee of Daniel's childhood home here in Glasgow, until he is of age. I'll come here to visit with my son, when he's not at school or at the MacAndrews estate. In my absence, his maternal grandparents, with whom he has a close relationship, will provide the love and affection he needs."

"Does the boy know you are his natural mother, Mrs. MacArthur?"

"He knows me as "Auntie Fiona," Your Lordship. Helen Brody wrote to me over these past nine years, sending news and pictures of Daniel. She involved me as much as possible in Daniel's life. With Helen's death, he'll have to be told, sooner or later, that he's my son. I had hoped to spare him the details of his conception, for as long as possible. I think you can understand that, Sir."

"Mrs. MacAndrews, because this is a hearing, not a trial, I can suggest an alternative that could work for both parties. Have you considered simply applying for visiting rights to your son, along with your parents? Do you need to have joint custody?"

"Your Lordship, Edward MacAndrews is a very powerful man. Since I returned to Scotland, he has succeeded in keeping my son away from me. Would any arrangement, other than joint custody, force him to let me and my parents see my son? Who will see that he complies with whatever you decide?"

"Let's hear from Laird MacAndrews, shall we?"

"Laird MacAndrews, what are your feelings about sharing custody of your grandson, with his natural mother?"

"I have no intention of sharing anything with her, Your Lordship. She signed away her legal rights to the boy ten years ago. I abide by the law, Sir, and that's the law."

"However, Laird MacAndrews, Mrs. MacArthur could not have known that the boy's adoptive mother would pass away so soon. He is, in effect, motherless, except for Mrs. MacArthur and his maternal grandmother, neither of which you allow access to the boy. Do you not wish him to have any feminine influence in his life? Do you not think there is some advantage to having the moral compass of a woman guiding him, along with yourself?"

"Moral compass? Your Lordship, what moral compass? This is an unwed mother we're talking about, a tenant, my tenant, who has the misguided notion that she's just as good as her Laird. How dare she?"

"You forget yourself, sir. The law is designed for everyone, not just for Peers. You might consider that the young woman did not choose to have your grandson, as we heard in the court ten years ago. In fact, you were very supportive of her, at that trial, as I recall. What changed your mind?"

"She didn't want him, then. Now she does. If you give her joint custody she'll take him away to Canada. I might never get him back. What's to prevent that, Your Lordship, if you give her any rights to the boy?"

"Mrs. MacArthur has already given her reasons for wanting to stay in the boy's life, at great cost and inconvenience to her, I might point out. It won't be easy travelling back and forth to see him for the next nine years, until he is of age. Do you agree with that?"

"No, I certainly do not. She has an annuity I set up for her for her lifetime, when she signed away her rights to the boy. It was meant to help her get settled in Canada, away from here."

"Yes, I'm aware of the annuity. But, surely, you don't think that small amount would fund repetitive travel costs for almost ten years?"

"Then why doesn't she just go home, and leave me and my grandson alone?"

The judge had heard enough from MacAndrews, and from Fiona. He asked the two Solicitors if they had any questions, which they did not.

"We'll resume tomorrow morning at 10:00 a.m., when I will give you my decision. We're adjourned."

As Fiona stepped outside the courthouse, a flood of reporters accosted her, shouting question after question. The general drift of the questions asked how she felt about Edward MacAndrews, now that he had stated in court he wanted her out of her son's life, regardless of the circumstances. One reporter shouted above the others.

"Fiona, do you think MacAndrews did himself more harm than good, berating your status as an unwed mother and a tenant? This is modern Scotland, after all. Women served near the front lines, in the Great War. They campaigned for the vote. They shouldn't need to put up with this kind of treatment, should they?"

Fiona stopped and spoke.

"No, a woman should not have to put up with public humiliation, with having to fight in court to see her own child because she made a mistake when things were different. The circumstances of my son's conception were not chosen. He's a bright little boy who's lost the only mother he knows to cancer. Now, he could lose his natural mother from his life as well. He deserves to have a mother, regardless of what his grandfather thinks. I can't say any more before we hear the judge's decision tomorrow."

Angus had travelled to London the day of the hearing, due to an unavoidable business commitment there. He telephoned that night, knowing Fiona would want to discuss the court proceeding.

"How did it go, my love?"

"It was grand, I think, Angus. MacAndrews showed his true character when the judge questioned him. He turned it into a battle of the classes, unfortunately for him. The judge cautioned him, saying 'the law is for everyone, not just for Peers.' You should have seen the look on MacAndrews' face then. I think he's added the judge to his long list of hated people."

"It sounds as if you're OK, so far. I hope you, at least, get visiting rights, if shared custody isn't granted. I'll be there by supper time tomorrow. I love you."

"I love you, my husband. Thanks for calling. See you tomorrow. Try to get a copy of *The Scotsman* in the morning. I'm quite sure the hearing will be covered. The reporters took pictures. I'll be adding to my notorious reputation, again."

MacArthur versus MacAndrews—
Merchant against Peer over Child Custody

The saga continues as Fiona Gilman MacArthur fights for her son. MacArthur is a self-made, successful clothing designer, an established entrepreneur in Canada, whose business is currently spreading to New York, USA. She was a formidable opponent today, against Laird Edward MacAndrews, whose class bias, typical of his generation, slipped out into the open, to annoy the Judge at court. A court decision, shared custody, visiting rights, or neither will be given tomorrow morning.

The Scotsman—June 25, 1929

40 ... An enemy for life

The judge had weighed the case details carefully. So carefully, in fact, that he had remaining concerns about the welfare of the young boy in question. The next morning, he began slowly:

"Ladies and Gentlemen, I have deliberated carefully, considering all of the testimony, from both parties. I have decided that to proceed without hearing from the boy, Edward Daniel Brody MacAndrews, would be a disservice to him. Therefore, I have arranged for us to reconvene next week, on July 4, in my chambers adjacent to this courtroom, to hear testimony from the boy.

Laird MacAndrews, since you have temporary sole custody, pending the outcome of this hearing, you are ordered to present the boy in my chambers at 10:00 a.m. on the date mentioned. Do you understand, sir?"

MacAndrews' face had gone pale. He seemed not to trust himself to speak. He appeared to be in some kind of shock. He didn't respond to the judge's question.

"LAIRD MACANDREWS, do you understand me, I say!"

"Yes, Your Lordship. I'm simply surprised that you would listen to the words of a ten-year-old boy. He's been under the influence of a woman who kept Fiona MacArthur in touch with my grandson, against my expressed wishes. These two women conspired against me, to influence my only heir. Thankfully, one of them is no longer able to work against me. And, the other is the reason we're all here, isn't she? But, I'm a law-abiding citizen, Sir. I'll produce the boy, as requested."

With that, the Judge, who was obviously annoyed at MacAndrews' attitude slammed down the gavel, rose, and walked out. Fiona still had hope.

This is a good thing, having this particular Judge, for the hearing. He seems determined to do the best thing for Daniel, which is what I want too. MacAndrews, on the other hand, wants what he wants, when he wants it, whatever the subject. His attitude could go against his getting what he wants here, sole custody and my banishment from Daniel's life. Thanks to this Judge, I still might have a chance to be in Daniel's life.

Again, the media awaited Fiona's exit from the building. This day, some reporters attempted to get a statement from Edward MacAndrews, who swept past them all with disgust, as he headed toward his car. But, he apparently changed his mind and turned to speak to the closest reporter.

"The proceedings have been delayed, thanks to the never-ending trouble I've been subjected to by that woman, Fiona Gilman MacArthur, my former tenant, whose parents owe their livings to me. I'm the rightful, legal grandparent here and I will get sole custody of my grandson, period. I'll be happy to give interviews next week, once the matter is settled in my favour."

This just isn't smart. MacAndrews is normally very shrewd, very astute as to the political climate of any situation. It can't be just me, or the Judge, causing him to lose his emotional control. He must be reading the papers too. The media's been more than fair to me. He's simply livid. If his attitude had been appropriate, the Judge might have gone ahead and given him sole custody, for good. This delay is infuriating him, questioning his entitlement to demand whatever he wants. I hope he keeps this up. I'll stand a better chance to get access to my son.

Fiona needed to stop thinking about MacAndrews for a while. She took a taxi back to Helen's house, to meet Angus. They'd have a nice lunch, maybe a glass of good wine, and relax for the afternoon. Later, they were meeting Jack and Jeannie Murray at a pub near their place, for a bit of fun. It would be a nice break from the strain of this court proceeding.

An evening at the corner pub with Jack and Jeannie Murray was an evening of entertainment with or without alcohol. The Murrays knew everyone. Jack and Jeannie greeted friends. They walked with a bounce in their steps, keeping up with the live music, as the four of them made their way to 'Jack's table.'

"This is just wha' ye need, gel, a chance to get away from the press and enjoy yerself."

"Thanks, Jeannie, it's been quite a strain, I must admit. Angus has helped me get through this drama with MacAndrews, so far. I'm not looking forward to seeing the Laird next week. But, it'll be worth it, to see Daniel. The Judge seems to be fair minded. I'm hopeful I won't get cut out of my son's life."

Well, Lassie, here's for luck tae you both, and here's to wee Daniel. He's a fine boy, tha's for sure."

Jack raised his beer glass, touched it to Angus' glass, and downed half the drink in one swallow. The two women toasted each other, Fiona having decided not to drink spirits tonight. She wanted to be mentally as sharp as possible tomorrow, when the papers came out. No point in giving herself a headache. She'd likely get one from the headlines in the morning paper.

But, she was pleasantly surprised. There, on the front page of the paper was a photograph of her, displayed next to a photo of Edward MacAndrews. Her photo was the one of her kissing Daniel on the cheek, at Helen's funeral. The second photo showed Laird MacAndrews pulling on Daniel's arm to get him away from Fiona's group of people at the funeral. Fiona made a mental note to say a prayer of thanks for the person who took these photos.

The article about the hearing was on page three, where Fiona was surprised to see photos of crowds of people, mostly women, carrying protest signs that included several messages:

Give the mother her son
Children belong with their Mothers
MacAndrews is a tyrant
Peers have no hearts . . . .

My God, these women must have gathered after I rushed away yesterday. They were obviously angry, marching back and forth, with their mouths open as they shouted their lines, on my behalf!

The Judge will certainly know about this. No doubt, he'd prefer order on the streets in front of the courts. It's obvious at least some public opinion falls on my side, supports me, rather than MacAndrews. He'll be greatly annoyed at this latest turn of events. It'll fuel his anger and also his determination not to give in.

I know MacAndrews. He likely has connections at the paper. He'll be doing his best to influence the editor, probably try to get him fired, after these headlines. But, *The Scotsman* is a reputable newspaper, known for its in-depth research and balanced reporting. Even MacAndrews won't be able to swing his weight around there.

What about Daniel? I hope he isn't reading this furor in the papers. If he is, MacAndrews will certainly use the boy to get at me, blame me for the bad publicity and claim innocence from all wrongdoing for himself. I can only hope that the housekeeper, Mrs. Brownley, keeps the papers away from Daniel at the Glenheather estates.

July 4 was to be an important day, for everyone involved with Fiona and Daniel. Ian and Kathleen Gilman returned to Glasgow for the meeting with the Judge, with a document that would be unexpected, by the Laird. Fiona's Solicitor had received permission from the Judge for Angus to attend the hearing. When they arrived, Fiona was surprised to see another man in the room, along with MacAndrews' attorney. He wore a crested blazer, as the Headmaster of Daniel's school.

The Judge introduced everyone. Fiona hoped the Headmaster wasn't in MacAndrews' pocket completely. After all, he paid the bills for Daniel's schooling. Daniel sat upright, looking a bit nervous. He wore his school uniform, even now, during the summer holiday, probably because MacAndrews wanted to emphasize his financial support of the boy's education.

"Let's get started, shall we?"

"Hello, Daniel. I'm the Judge who will decide how to resolve who has responsibility for you. I'm sorry to hear of your mum's passing. You can call me "Your Lordship.""

"Thank you for your condolences, Your Lordship. I miss Mummy, I mean Mum. But, I have Auntie Fiona here now. She misses Mum too. And I have Auntie Kathleen, too."

Everyone, except MacAndrews, smiled at the boy's obvious command of a large vocabulary and his composure, under the circumstances. MacAndrews resented any mention of Fiona's name. The boy defied him, by mentioning her at all. He had warned Daniel not to bring up Fiona or her parents.

The Judge continued asking Daniel questions, attempting to determine his state of mind about the people who surround him. When asked about his time at Glenheather, he talked about the housekeeper. The Judge prompted him to speak about his grandfather, but the boy seemed a bit reluctant. He did say he had respect for his grandfather. He added that lots of boys at school didn't see their fathers or grandfathers very much.

"The other boys go home for their holidays, to their parents estates. Except for the summer holiday, I always go home to Mum's house in Glasgow. I have my things there, especially my books, and I have friends in Glasgow too."

"What do you do when you go to your grandfather's estate?"

"Well, Mrs. Brownley, the housekeeper, plays cards with me.

Declan, the ghillie, takes me riding and hunting. Sometimes, I play with other kids from Marysburgh, as long as grandfather doesn't find out. Sorry, Grandfather."

He looked cautiously at the scowling MacAndrews.

"Please go on, Daniel, what else do you do at the estate?"

"I see Auntie Fiona's mum and daddie. Uncle Ian takes me fishing. And Auntie Kathleen makes the best scones in Scotland. I eat a lot of those, too."

"Do you see your grandfather? What do you do with him?"

"Mostly, he's not there. When he is, I go hunting with him and Declan. He says he's too old to come home and go hunting very often. He has important work in London. Oh, I almost forgot. We eat together at a very large table in the big dining room. He's way down at the other end. Sometimes, I have to shout so he can hear me when I answer a question."

"Does your grandfather not allow you to bring your friends home from school, or have friends over from Marysburgh?"

"Oh, no, Your Lordship. Mum used to drive me to school friends' estates, to meet their parents and brothers and sisters. I really liked that. But, in Marysburgh, Grandfather says I'll be the Laird someday. He doesn't want the tenants to be too familiar with me. He says that about Auntie Fiona's mum and daddie too. But, I just have to go fishing with Uncle Ian! I just have to! It's my favourite thing, outside of my books. You won't make me stop fishing, will you?"

At this point, Daniel was visibly upset. MacAndrews was fuming, after hearing the boy's praises of Fiona's parents. The Judge reassured the boy.

"No, Daniel. I won't keep you from fishing."

"Laird MacAndrews, do you find the energy level of a young boy challenging, at your stage in life? Sometimes grandparents have a difficult time keeping up with exuberant young grandchildren."

"Certainly not, I mean, certainly not, Your Lordship. That's what Declan is for. He's a younger man, who has no trouble keeping up with Daniel. My job is to make sure he's a successful Laird, not to cultivate playmates for him."

"Thank you, Laird MacAndrews."

"Daniel, thank you very much, for speaking with me today. You can go with the clerk and wait outside until we're finished. It was nice to meet you."

"Thank you, Your Lordship. It was very fine to meet you too. Thanks for not taking away my fishing. I'll send you a big fish from the loch!"

The Judge, Fiona, the Gilman's, both Solicitors, and the Head Master were smiling as Daniel left the room. The Judge's next remarks were shocking and infuriating for MacAndrews.

"I have a new petition here, from Mrs. MacArthur's parents. Ian and Kathleen Gilman have applied for joint adoption and custody of Daniel, to be shared with Laird MacAndrews. If granted, this arrangement would mirror the adoption and custody agreement shared by Helen Brody and Laird MacAndrews. The petition also applies for unrestricted visiting rights for Fiona MacArthur, the boy's natural mother."

Fiona was relieved and very grateful that her parents were willing to take on the care of her son, along with the challenges of dealing with the Laird. She hadn't wanted to ask them outright. When she and Kathleen last spoke about custody, Kathleen brought up this alternative, to see what Fiona thought about it. Fiona replied that sharing Daniel with the Laird would be very difficult, almost impossible, for her parents, given their position as his tenants. But, it was now the eleventh hour. Today, the Judge would decide whether or not Laird MacAndrews would get full custody of Daniel. Ian and Kathleen, obviously, had decided to fight for their grandson. It was a brilliant strategy to attach legal, unrestricted visiting rights for Fiona, in the bargain.

Hearing Fiona's name mentioned, again, in this latest attempt to take his grandson from him, the angry Laird stood up, as the Judge was concluding his remarks.

"Unrestricted? What exactly does that mean? Is she moving back, lock, stock, and barrel, into the Glasgow house with my grandson?"

MacAndrews shook, as he stood there, glaring at the Judge. Fiona could see that he had aged. He wasn't as physically vigorous as he'd been nine years ago when she left the country. He'd been over 40 when his son, Jeremy was born. Now, he was almost 70 years old. MacAndrews' Solicitor grabbed his arm and hauled him down into his seat. The Judge ignored the outburst, turning to Fiona.

"Mrs. MacArthur, what are your plans, if I were to grant this petition, for joint custody between Laird MacAndrews and your parents, the boy's maternal grandparents?"

"I would continue as trustee for Daniel's Glasgow home, visiting with him there, as often as I could. My husband and I are established in Canada. We don't believe it's in Daniel's best interest to remove him from Scotland, or from his grandfather MacAndrews. We don't want to disrupt his life totally, just be a part of it, a positive influence in Helen's absence. Between my parents and me, we'll support Daniel as he grows up."

"Laird MacAndrews, what are your views of this arrangement? It is clear that Mrs. MacArthur will continue to live in Canada. She'll see the boy on trips to Scotland, rather than move full time into the boy's Glasgow house."

"I suppose they all think I'll continue to pay the bills, to cover his tuition, provide his food and clothing, horses, guns, and leave him the estate, after he's been half raised by the tenants. If they share joint custody with me, they'll need to come up with their half of his tuition, right through university. Shared custody means shared financial responsibilities, doesn't it?"

"Your Lordship, may I speak?"

"Mr. MacArthur, go ahead."

"My wife, Fiona MacArthur, and I will cover half of Daniel's tuition, if that's the condition imposed by the court. We'll find the means to do so."

"That won't be necessary, Mr. MacArthur. There's no reason the arrangement with Helen Brody, in which Laird MacAndrews covered the full cost of the education of his heir, can't continue as it was. I am granting Ian and Kathleen Gilman joint custody with Edward MacAndrews and visiting rights by the boy's natural mother, Fiona MacArthur. A strict schedule of access time to the boy will be established so that both sides of Daniel's family will be able to remain connected to him."

"This is outrageous, Your Lordship. How will the boy learn his importance, in relationship to the tenants, when he's practically living with them?"

"It's a new world, Laird MacAndrews. Since the Great War, we have seen many changes here in Scotland. I hope this boy will become a new, progressive Laird, one who is compassionate and understands his responsibilities for the estate and the people who live there. He'll have plenty to deal with finding out that he has a natural mother, as well as an adoptive mother. He already has a good relationship with his maternal grandparents. He'll eventually learn that they aren't his aunt and uncle.

Therefore, considering the testimony I've heard, including the boy's, I rule that joint adoption is approved. Custody of Edward Daniel Brody MacAndrews is to be shared, equally, by Laird Edward MacAndrews and Daniel's natural, maternal grandparents, Ian and Kathleen Gilman. Additionally, Fiona MacArthur is granted unrestricted visiting rights to the boy, here in Scotland. As trustee of the boy's Glasgow property, Mrs. MacArthur consents to provide access to Daniel's Glasgow home, for her parents and, if she wishes, other relatives of the boy on the Brody side of his family. Throughout the school year, Daniel will continue to go home to Glasgow, as he did when Helen Brody was alive, where his maternal grandparents will maintain his home, as well as providing a home for him with them, for his time in Marysburgh.

Laird MacAndrews, you will continue to have the boy for half of each summer. But, you will be required to allow him to fish with his maternal grandfather and visit their home during your time in the summer, especially when you are not there with the boy. Your adoption of the boy is intact. He will, in fact, be your heir. However, you must, under the terms dictated by this court, adhere to the written time schedule, sharing custody with his maternal grandparents and allowing access to his natural mother until he is of age, when he can make his own decisions.

Laird MacAndrews, if you violate the terms of this custody ruling and visiting rights agreement, I will have you back here in court. Do you understand the terms of the agreement, sir?"

MacAndrews nodded, mumbled "Yes, Your Lordship." He got up to leave.

"Sit down, Laird MacAndrews. I have not terminated the hearing yet."

Fiona could see that Edward MacAndrews looked somewhat beaten, similar to the way he looked the night he came to Helen's, after his son was murdered. But, she knew that look was only temporary. He'd never settle for less than what he wanted, ever. In fact, by the time they all left the courts, he gave her a look of pure hatred. She knew this wouldn't be the end of it.

41 ... Claiming a son

Gilman MacArthur turns her back on son, again ...
Grandparents, not mother, get custody ...
Boy stays in Scotland; mother leaves him behind a
second time ...

The papers in Edinburgh and Glasgow carried the results of the battle for Daniel, between his grandfather and Fiona. Although given unrestricted visiting rights, Fiona would not move back to Scotland to be near her son fulltime. Once these details were out, the furor about mother and child turned sour. Fiona wasn't surprised. For the second time in her life, she'd be glad to leave the Scottish media behind.

The Judge allowed Fiona two weeks with Daniel, in Glasgow, before he went to Marysburgh for the rest of the summer. Fiona and Angus enjoyed getting to know him. He took them on 'tours' of the neighbourhood. They were astonished, when he gave them a tour of Helen's library, pointing out and commenting on many books he'd read. One afternoon, when Angus was out Daniel and Fiona took their tea in the library.

"I can see how much you enjoy these books, Daniel. I'll leave them here for you, when I return to Canada. Your Mum wanted me to have them, but, I'll get them later, once you're finished with them."

"Thanks, Auntie Fiona. The library at my school is fine, but it doesn't have nearly as many of the books I like. I'm glad you'll let me keep them for now. When I'm in this room with Mum's books, I feel like she's still here, even though I know she's in heaven. When I'm older, I'll go away to university, where they'll have the very best collection. You could get these books then, couldn't you? "

"Aye, I could. Tell me, Daniel, what kind of books do you have at your Grandfather's?"

"He has mostly law books, books on hunting, taxidermy, and other country sports books. He's also got lots of books about running an estate. He says I'll need to learn all about that, for when I'm the Laird. I'm not really interested in those things, Auntie Fiona."

"Well, you might be, when you're older. Meanwhile, you can fish with Uncle Ian, can't you?"

"Aye, I surely can."

"Daniel, I have something to talk with you about. Your Mum told you that your father is not living, hasn't she?"

"Aye, he was Grandfather MacAndrews' son. He was murdered."

"You know about that?"

"Oh, yes, Auntie Fiona. Mum told me when I asked her where my daddie was. I've known that for a long time, ever since I was young."

Fiona smiled at that remark. He clearly saw himself as other than young now. He seemed to know he was mature for his age.

"Daniel, do you know that some lucky people, including you, can have two mothers"?

"How do you mean, Auntie Fiona?"

"Well, your mum, Helen Brody, was Mum, as you know. But, Daniel, I'm another kind of mum to you."

"You mean . . . you aren't my Auntie?"

"Not exactly, I'm called your natural mum, the person who gave birth to you. Your mum, Helen, adopted you from me. She became your wonderful mother. I'm called Auntie Fiona, because you already have your other mum, Helen. We didn't want to confuse you when you were younger. But, now, you're almost a young man. With your mum gone to live in heaven, I think you should know you still have a mum, another kind of mum, me."

"Didn't you want me? Is that why you gave me to Mum?"

"Oh, Daniel, your mum longed for a darling son. She was old enough to be a good mum. She had this house and lots of books. I was very young and I had none of those things. She was very, very, happy to have you for her son."

"Were you sad to give me away?"

"Yes, Daniel, I was very sad. But, I think you've been happy with your mum, haven't you?"

"Oh yes, Auntie Fiona. She's . . . she was the best mum of any of my friends, too. I miss her. . . . a lot."

"I miss her too, Daniel. But, I'm here for you now. I hope you'll let me into your life. I'll visit you here in Glasgow, in the summers and at the Christmas holiday."

"I'm glad you came back to me, Auntie Fiona, I mean, well . . . Should I call you Mum, not Auntie Fiona?"

"You can, if you like, Daniel, whatever you feel comfortable doing. Do you want to think about it, before you decide?"

The boy looked pensive, as he often did, when he was thinking. She'd noticed in these past ten days, that he was a thinker, one of those rare children who thought about things before he spoke.

"So . . . then, what's Uncle Angus? Is he going to be my new daddie, because he's your husband? I don't get all of this."

"I know it's confusing. I married Angus a long time after I gave birth to you. He's not your daddie. But, he's very glad that you call him Uncle Angus. Is that OK with you?"

"Aye, I like him anyway, and I'm glad to have another uncle, to go with Uncle Ian. Next week, when we go to Marysburgh Uncle Angus is coming fishing with me and Uncle Ian. Did you know about that, Aun . . . I mean, Mum?"

Fiona couldn't have hoped for more. The sweet boy seemed happy to call her Mum. She'd never heard anyone call her that before. Her eyes filled with tears when she heard it. He seemed not to object that she and Angus would be going back to Canada, after their visit with him. She didn't want to worry him by discussing her absence when they'd just gotten to know each other. He was a very bright little boy. He'd probably ask more questions, once he'd processed this new information.

Fiona, Angus and Daniel enjoyed their last few days in Glasgow. Their two weeks were up. They took the train to Marysburgh. While the wheels beat out their rhythm on the tracks, Angus and Daniel played cards, while Fiona sketched new designs, as she always did on the train. Her mind wandered back to the day two weeks ago, when Daniel was dropped off at the Glasgow house.

MacAndrews seemed to have resigned himself regarding the situation. The door knocker sounded right on time. MacAndrews didn't show up, sending his driver with the boy instead. Given his behavior throughout the hearings, Fiona was relieved. She preferred not to have a run in with him in front of Daniel.

When Daniel had entered the house, he politely greeted her and Angus, and then took his own small carrying bag upstairs to his room. He came back downstairs immediately, to ask if tea would be in the library, the same as it was when his mum was here. Fiona and Angus had marveled at how well-adjusted the boy was, adapting easily to his new situation. Over the two weeks in Glasgow, they recognized that Daniel was comfortable here, in his Glasgow home, with them. Helen had certainly done a great job with him. And, it seemed that Edward MacAndrews would hold up his end of the arrangements for Daniel, so far, anyway.

The week at Marysburgh was the happiest Fiona had been in her hometown for many years. Daniel seemed perfectly at home, enjoying daily fishing trips with Ian and Angus. Ian and Kathleen had reworked Fiona's old room for Daniel, using a fishing motif. The boy was thrilled. He knew he'd live with Ian and Kathleen for two weeks. Then he'd go to the MacAndrews' estate, until he left for school again. Fiona prayed that MacAndrews would allow Daniel to go fishing with Ian during the rest of the summer, as the Judge had directed him to do.

Everyone in Marysburgh wasn't as happy as Fiona, with the arrangements for Daniel. One evening, Kathleen invited Meg and William McGinnis over for supper. They really enjoyed seeing Daniel again. They'd gotten to know him, in Glasgow, with Helen, and when he visited with the Gilmans, on his clandestine visits from Glenheather. That evening, as everyone began to eat their dessert, Daniel spoke to Fiona.

"Mum, will you please pass me the cream?"

Meg McGinnis dropped her dessert spoon. She looked quickly back and forth between Daniel and Fiona and then at Kathleen.

"Here, Daniel, here's the cream."

Fiona answered casually, as if he'd called her Mum for his whole life. Meg's stunned expression reflected her great surprise. But, she seemed to think it better not to comment. William kept his eyes on his dessert, as did Angus and Ian.

Kathleen smiled to herself. Fiona had told her earlier that Daniel was considering calling his natural mother, Mum. He must miss Helen terribly, she had said to Fiona at the time. Tonight, they could see that he was comfortable with the idea of another mother ready and waiting, after Helen's passing. Most children didn't have that.

At the end of their week in Marysburgh, Fiona said goodbye to Daniel at her parents' home. She made sure he understood she'd be back in Scotland for his Christmas holiday in Glasgow and also for a month the next summer. He agreed that he'd be busy at school, at his grandfather's estate, and at Ian and Kathleen's.

"That's more time than I saw you any other year, Mum. I'll be OK until you get back with Uncle Angus. Don't worry about me. I'm fine."

My son is such an optimist! I'm grateful he sees the situation this way, rather than concentrating on my leaving him again.

There was one last piece of Daniel's family puzzle that the adults decided to leave alone. He was well-adjusted, there in Marysburgh, with his Auntie Kathleen and Uncle Ian. Everyone hoped he'd be happy with things as they were, unless Edward MacAndrews went out of his way to stir up trouble. It seemed unlikely that MacAndrews would get into the complications of explaining another set of grandparents to the boy. He probably wouldn't want to admit the boy's connection with his lowly tenants. If ever Daniel asked about the Gilman's relationship to him, Fiona agreed that her parents would tell him they were, technically, his maternal grandparents.

The night before their departure from Marysburgh, Angus surprised Fiona with an itinerary for a week's holiday in Ireland, before they were to leave for their Atlantic crossing back to New York. Thus far, their honeymoon had consisted of a funeral, a court battle, a mother-in-law who was declining up in Newtonmore, the exhilaration of being granted visiting rights, followed by an emotional reconnection with Daniel. Relaxation and time for just the two of them hadn't been, so far, a part of their journey.

Fiona was looking forward to a lovely holiday, in a country that boasted some of the most unique sights in the world. Angus was very anxious to show her some of his favourite Irish places. He planned to avoid obvious trouble spots, in Northern Ireland, and in the Free State of Ireland. Hopefully, his careful planning would keep them safe for the week. After tearful goodbyes in Marysburgh, they headed off on their long-awaited honeymoon.

42 ... Irish scenes

"Oh, Angus, it's absolutely unbelievable!"

"I knew you'd like the Giant's Causeway, lass. Did you Western Scots learn about the Finn MacCool legend at school?"

"Only in passing . . . probably because it's about the besting of a Scottish challenger to MacCool. It's such a wonderful Irish story. I guess the educational authorities in Scotland didn't want to focus on anyone else beating the Scots. We'd had enough of that from the English!

From up here, the Causeway is a spectacular sight. It looks as if someone has carved and arranged the huge columns and promontories, rather than nature doing the carving and arranging. It's hard to imagine 200 million years of wear and tear turning out like this. It's beautiful. Thank you, my dear husband, for bringing me here."

They had started their Irish trip at Portrush, where they boarded the tram to the Causeway Hotel. Before going in for supper, they viewed the Causeway from the top of the cliffs near the hotel. Later, they joined the other hotel guests in the pub, where the inevitable Irish story telling was in full swing. Each amusing story brought about much laughter and many toasts to the characters and their exploits. Fiona and Angus went back to their room full and happy, looking forward to the next day's closer exploration of the Causeway.

"My God, Angus, these Irish people have such imaginations! I'm really enjoying their lively spirit, and their tongue-in-cheek way of telling stories about leprechauns and giants."

"Me too. They seem to use humour to cope with their troubles.

The partitioning of the country was only eight years ago, leading to their civil war. Now, it's good to see both north and south making progress. Here in the north, they've been getting some economic aid from Britain. In the south, the Irish language is being taught in the schools, a great step forward for the Free State of Ireland. They've also harnessed the Shannon River to produce much needed electricity, for their people. Whatever troubles remain, I hope, we two Scots-Canadians will be able to avoid conflicts. We'll just enjoy Ireland, and each other."

Their lovemaking was especially sweet, that night at the Causeway Hotel. Both of them had relaxed. They enjoyed exploring new ways of satisfying each other, thinking only of each other and nobody else.

Their next stop was in Belfast. They went to see the shipyard where the ill-fated Titanic had been built. That infamous maritime disaster had very much dominated the news before the Great War and well beyond. While they looked at the shipyard, Fiona told Angus the amusing kitchen table conversation of 1919, at the Murrays. Jack had told his twin daughters they were taking their lives in their hands if they sailed to or from North America. He'd used the Titanic as evidence to back up his statement, along with another sinking at the Canadian end of the crossing. At the time, Fiona told Angus, Jack wasn't seriously disapproving of his daughters dreams to start over in Canada, because of one or two maritime disasters. But today, seeing the place where the Titanic was built, the place where hope was carried out to the sea, with the 'unsinkable' ship, Angus and Fiona felt the weight of that tragedy.

After their sobering experience at the shipyard in Belfast, Fiona and Angus travelled to northwestern Ireland, which was covered with peat bogs. They boarded a coach and enjoyed a rollicking experience, as the road undulated, from the weight of the coach. The bogs were an amazing sight. They enjoyed these sights and sensations, until the driver of the coach filled them in on a bit of Irish history.

This area of northwest Ireland was a sad testimonial to tragic, past events. During potato famine times, in the mid-nineteenth century, the Irish poor were herded into this northwest section of Ireland, while better- off landowners farmed arable land further south. The passengers learned that nobody could grow anything, let alone blighted potatoes, in such ground. From the coach windows, Fiona and Angus could see memorial sites remembering famine victims dotting the landscape . . . another sad part of Irish history. They were glad to get to their next stop, further south.

"Here we are, my love, in Sligo. We're lucky to get a room at the Yeats Country Inn, here on Rosses Point. What do ye think of THESE spectacular views, lassie?"

Fiona stepped out from behind the coach, as the driver unloaded the bags. She was amazed by the beautiful vista in front of her, overlooking this point. She was reminded, at this moment, of one of her favourite poets who had a history in Sligo.

Fiona had read that William Butler Yeats spent quite a bit of time in Sligo while he was growing up. His mother's people were from the area. Undoubtedly, the views in this area must inspire him to write such beautiful poetry. Yeats had been a senator in the Irish Free State government until he retired. Fiona hoped she might catch a glimpse of him around the Sligo area, while she and Angus were there. At the very least, she'd check with the museum, to see what information they had about him and his family.

The summer weather and the extraordinary beauty of this spot were highlights of their honeymoon trip, so far. They checked into the hotel and later enjoyed an amusing evening in the hotel pub, again hearing Irish stories. But, they had a few uncomfortable moments, when two men at the back of the pub began to argue about politics. Angus chose that moment to rise, holding Fiona's chair, so they could make their exit quietly. But, the loudest young man noticed them and started shouting.

"Where does himself, in his fine English suit, think he's takin' you, beautiful Anglish girl? Are you from the North, then? What are you doin' enjoyin' our Free State scenery? Your kind didn't want to be a part of it, remember? You Anglish people killed our children while you stole part of our country."

"Have a good evening, lads. We're Scots, also conquered by the English. You've only given up a few counties. We've lost the whole country. Let's leave it at that, shall we?"

At Angus' comments, the barkeep roared with laughter, as did the rest of the people in the bar. The loud young man's friend reached out and patted his friend on the shoulder.

"That's enough, Seamus. Let it go. You can't accost every person you see who might have different politics from your own. Here, have another Guinness. That'll fix it."

Relieved, Angus and Fiona left the pub and went back to their room. Fiona thought about their encounter in the pub, as she undressed for bed.

So, here's the volatile undercurrent of the troubles, just below the surface of this lively Irish culture. The young man's comments were unnerving. Thankfully, though, not everything is bombs and bloodshed. As pretty as the scenery is, up here close to the Northern Counties, I'll be glad to head further south and east, to Dublin. That cosmopolitan city, hopefully, will mask the tension between remaining political factions. Both the northern counties and the Free State of Ireland encourage tourists like us. They appreciate that we're interested in seeing ancient Ireland through its relics: ancient Celtic crosses, and ruined abbey remains, where monks kept literacy alive, in spite of such grand events as the fall of Rome. What a history! It's exciting just thinking about it, as long as we don't stumble into the troubles. She discussed her concerns with Angus.

"Angus, are you concerned for our safety at all? Do you think we'll be able to avoid trouble spots in Dublin?"

"I certainly hope so. We're staying at the Shelbourne Hotel. It's near the National Art Gallery and Trinity College, where Jonathan Swift was once Dean. We'll walk to these sites, and to a few pubs in the area, where some of the authors you talk about get their inspiration, or have, in the past. You've told me you the like the short stories of James Joyce, especially "Araby," from *The Dubliners*. He's long since left the country, but it'll be interesting to see the places he wrote about. We'll have lots to do, within a safe walking distance, and we'll get a good taste of Dublin life, especially in this lovely summer, of this most unbelievably prosperous year.

Actually, Fiona, I am more concerned about this seemingly endless, robust stock market. Some of us, including Joseph James, at the bank, are almost certain it's too good to be true. We've tried to encourage our clients to be cautious. Yet, everyone seems drunk on greed, ignoring our cautions about excessive debt. If the market should take a turn, as it must, eventually, many people will lose a lot of money. They'll be unable to repay their loans. Historically, there's no way this kind of prosperity can continue indefinitely."

"What about us, Angus? What happens if the market does go wrong? My business, for example, relies on mostly wealthy clients. Admittedly, life for me is easier, the more wealthy clients I can keep. Much of my time, I design and create haute couture. These clients generate the most income, for my business.

I do have a few commercial clients, for uniforms and such. I don't have quite all my eggs in one basket, so to speak. If the market does change, I hope *Fiona's Clothing Design and Haberdashery* will survive, with continued employment for six employees, along with Jenny and me. Let's hope, anyway.

What about my annuity from Edward MacAndrews? Try as

he might, he still hasn't been able to undo that, to punish me. Is it a risky investment? And, Angus, what about our own security?"

"MacAndrews has been quite conservative, when it comes to that investment. He isn't cash poor, like some of the Lairds have become, since the Great War. The only way you wouldn't get the annuity is if he finds a way to break the agreement. That's unlikely. I'm sorry I've caused you to fret about this now, Fiona. As far as our own investments are concerned, we're as secure as anyone can be.

So, my lass, let's enjoy our honeymoon. It's July, the sun shines every day, we're in a lovely, green country, and we'll return to an equally lovely place, our home in Victoria, Canada."

"Come into my bed, then, my husband. This place is so romantic. Let's take advantage of these peaceful, relaxing surroundings again tonight." Angus didn't need to be asked twice.

The train took the MacArthurs to exciting Dublin, where they checked into their hotel. They spent the next few days enjoying visits to galleries, Trinity College, pubs, and museums. The morning of their last day in Ireland, Angus surprised Fiona with an interesting side trip.

"I've arranged for us to take a train less than ten miles north of Dublin, to the Malahide Castle, where an interesting project is underway. They've been building the *Fry Model Railroad* exhibit, over the past few months. The gardens of the castle are said to be stunning. We'll enjoy our last day in Ireland, in yet another lovely environment, before we head to our ship and the Americas."

A few hours later, Fiona looked briefly at the model railway exhibit. Angus was thoroughly enjoying the experience. He'd become quite animated as he discussed the progress on the model, with the designers and builders. Fiona left to walk toward the gardens of the Malahide Castle. As she strolled in the sunshine, she was surprised by a woman's voice calling her name. "Fiona, is that you? I thought it was you!"

Eileen Talbot stepped toward her, trailed by four, auburn-haired children. From their appearance, they must certainly be hers and Sean's. The twin boys would be three years old by now. They ran to keep up with their two older brothers.

The women embraced, as well as they could. Eileen was hugely pregnant, surely on the verge of giving birth again. They were happy to see each other and renew their friendship. Those uncomfortable moments at the Empress Hotel four years earlier, when Sean's behavior had ruined their easy rapport were in the past.

"You're married, I see! Congratulations, Fiona. I assume that wonderful man, Angus MacArthur, is your husband?"

"Aye, he is, Eileen. We married the summer after you left. We're on our delayed honeymoon, here in Ireland. We leave tomorrow morning, for our ship, to sail back to North America. How's Sean?"

"Very well, thank you, Fiona. I'm sure you noticed his unusual behavior the last time we were all together. He's recovered very nicely here at home, away from those dens of iniquity in Victoria's Chinatown. He should be along any minute. You can see for yourself."

"So, then, is Malahide the castle he lives in then? Is he TI IE Talbot of Malahide Castle, whose ancestors have resided here since 1185?"

"Oh, no! His direct ancestors didn't own the castle. A many times removed, very distant relative of his father's was connected to that Talbot. We live on another estate nearby. Sean's helping with the new model railroad construction. He's enjoying every minute of it. Here he comes, with Angus!"

At the sight of Sean, all four children ran toward him, shouting 'It's our Da,' throwing themselves at him, the smallest boys wrapping their arms around Sean's legs. Angus enjoyed the sight, as did Fiona. The children helped to offset the tension Fiona normally expected whenever she saw Sean. She was surprised that he had no such effect on her today. She was so happy with Angus. Sean's lovemaking was an obscure, vague memory now. Thank the Lord, she thought.

"Hello, Fiona. Your husband has agreed to join us for a picnic lunch. It's good to see you."

"Hello, Sean. It's lovely to see you and Eileen, and your family. Now, who's who and how many others are there to be soon, Eileen?"

The four young Talbots politely greeted the MacArthurs, as each one was introduced. Eileen said the next baby was due in a few weeks. At that remark, the men realized that talk would continue about babies, and probably clothes. They stepped away and immersed themselves in discussion about the model railroad. Indeed, Eileen and Fiona renewed their friendship, enjoyed the children, and discussed clothing design.

It was a perfect afternoon. Fiona could see that Sean was himself again, obviously very happy with his family. He doted on Eileen, while, at the same time, he seemed to rely on her. This was a very pleasant way to end their Irish honeymoon. Fiona and Eileen agreed to stay in touch with each other. Anything seemed possible, that day.

43 ... Golden opportunities

"Hurry please, Miss. I've parked Mrs. Wharton's car over here, in a temporary drop off zone. I'll need to move it as soon as possible."

Fiona could see Mrs. Wharton waving to her, as she stood beside the long black vehicle. She was wearing an outfit Fiona had designed for her. She looked lovely in the dress and matching jacket. The colours in the outfit suited her complexion perfectly. It was made from desert sand coloured silk, with muted images of a pyramid and a sphinx, woven into the silken fabric. Such King Tut motifs were all the rage, since his tomb had been opened earlier in the '20s. Mrs. Wharton liked to keep up with the trends.

"How was the crossing? Where's your lovely husband?"

"The crossing was wonderful, Mrs. Wharton. Angus took a taxi to a business appointment on Wall Street, for the afternoon. He'll meet me at the hotel later."

"Well, hop in and meet three of my friends. They can't wait to see for themselves, the talented designer I discovered on the west coast of Canada."

The rest of the day went quickly, as Fiona exchanged clothing ideas, samples, and news of the latest styles from Europe, with Mrs. Wharton and her friends. Her return, today, from the United Kingdom was perfect timing, for her discussions with these American women. The latest designs from Paris, including some of those from Madame Vionnet of Paris were on display throughout Europe, including Glasgow and Dublin. She'd been able to spend part of an afternoon in Dublin at Switzer's, a high end women's clothing store. They carried designer clothing as well as styles that had been inspired by haute couture designers from London and Berlin.

Fiona was flattered and surprised at the enthusiasm these New York City women expressed for her designs. The lot of them had, it seemed, unlimited funds at their disposal. They were accustomed to buying whatever they wanted. And if they wanted Fiona's designs, she would certainly see that they got them. Before she left them, that afternoon, she had orders for several outfits. She'd start on them as soon as she got home. It would be the end of September by the time the fabrics were shaped into garments and shipped back to New York. Yet, nobody seemed to mind the delay. The women paid huge deposits, enough to cover the costs of their outfits and the shipping. Each of them hoped to get priority in Fiona's busy schedule.

Emma Wharton was determined to display this talented designer to as many of her friends as possible, while Fiona was in town. Her friends were either married to, or widows of, some of the wealthiest men on Wall Street. Toward the end of the afternoon, Mrs. Wharton, backed up by her friends, suggested to Fiona that she consider opening a design studio in New York, for part of each year. They assured her that many, many women would buy her original designs. Her pieces were finished exquisitely: seams, beads, buttons, hooks, bows, excellent craftsmanship applied to every small detail. If she could be there for a few months each year, just enough to show her newest designs for the season, she'd have plenty of business to keep her going for the rest of the year.

"Thank you, ladies, for your encouragement. I'll certainly think about your proposal. I'll discuss your very tempting suggestion with my husband."

After her friends left, Emma Wharton expanded on her idea, that Fiona should open a studio in New York. She had the details all worked out. She hoped that her taking care of the details would influence Fiona and Angus, as they considered the possibility.

"Seriously, Fiona, please consider opening a modest design studio here in New York. I'll help you get set up; if you decide to go ahead. I own a building on Central Park West, with a suitable suite—enough rooms for you and your husband to stay in when you're here, and extra rooms for the studio. Before my husband died, we lived there. I can't bear to live there with him gone. I don't want to rent it to just anyone either. You'd be doing me a favour, for an extremely reasonable rent. Let's discuss it again tomorrow afternoon, after my next group of friends has seen your designs."

"This is a lot to take in, Mrs. Wharton. I hardly know what to say."

"Just consider the idea for now. I'll see you tomorrow. My driver will take you to your hotel. Your husband's probably wondering what kept you so long."

Fiona was so deep in thought she hardly noticed the taxi ride to the hotel.

I can hardly believe it. A design studio in New York! Me! We're planning to visit Daniel every summer anyway. We'll pass right through New York, coming and going. Angus might think it's a good opportunity for him too. He's told me he always has business he can do in New York, whenever we pass through. This could actually happen!

When the bellman let her into their hotel room, Angus was waiting for her.

"So, my lovely, talented haute couture designer, how did the day go?"

"Stop, Angus. I'm getting really nervous now."

"Nervous, are you? Well, I know you get nervous when something unpleasant is in the forecast. But, my love, you're most anxious when something is too good to be true, or you think it is. I gather from the look on your face that Mrs. Wharton and her friends loved your designs. You must have new orders.

"It's better than that, Angus."

"Better, is it? You'd best just let it out, then, lass."

"First, I have an appointment for another showing at Emma Wharton's, tomorrow afternoon. She's invited another dozen of her friends to see my designs."

"Splendid! That's it, then? That's what you're so nervous about?"

"Nae, it's not, laddie. There's oh, so much more. They want me to open a studio here in New York, for a few months each year. Mrs. Wharton owns a building on Central Park West, with a suite of rooms to accommodate us, when we're here, along with extra space for a small studio. It would be so much more convenient and productive, than working out of someone's living room, as I did today. I'd have my machines and supplies in place . . . and . . . I could hire someone to help me with measurements and fittings at this end. I'd sew like a fiend until we left for Scotland to see Daniel. That's it! What d'ye think, lad?"

"I think it's bloody fantastic, that's what I think! Congratulations, my love, it seems you've arrived! I have one question about the rent, though. Would we be paying for the space all year or just for the months we're here in New York?"

"Just for when we're here. She says it's been empty since she moved out, after her husband died. She'd be happy to have a modest rent for a few months, from me, from us."

"It sounds mighty fine to me. I'm stunned. This is the kind of break that talented, artistic people dream about. You've created this opportunity with your talent, Fiona. And, you've got great business skills as well, not to mention a wonderful husband with some skills of his own. What an opportunity, a well-deserved opportunity!"

"Thanks, my dear husband. It's unbelievable, isn't it? The thing is that we'll be travelling through New York anyway, on our way to and from Scotland, to visit Daniel, and your mum, too."

"Aye, we will. We're three thousand miles closer to Scotland from here. Breaking up our journey from Victoria to Scotland is an appealing thought. It'll make our next few years of travel, while Daniel grows up, easier to do and far more interesting. Now, Fiona, I have some news too. It could fit in very well with your new opportunity here in New York."

"What is it, Angus? Have you been saving some news, or did you just find out about it today?"

"I wasn't sure what would come of this meeting I had this afternoon. I didn't want to say anything about it until I was sure. I've been offered a contract here, in New York, with a company whose management people agree with my misgivings about the market. They're one of a few, powerful firms that predicts a big shake up, sooner or later.

My experience with Joseph James, at the bank in Victoria, my earlier management experience, and my financial success in the coal mining industry on Vancouver Island appeals to this firm. It would be exciting work, dealing with a new set of clients. They sorely need advice on cutting back their debt. The CEO of the firm is John James, Joseph's brother. He came through Ellis Island to the United States, the year before Joseph docked in Montreal, on his way to the west coast of Canada. The two brothers have achieved great success in their respective adopted countries. John James is anxious to have another successful Scot—that would be me—to help him when we face whatever happens with the market. That's my news."

"Congratulations to you, my clever husband! They'd be lucky to get you. But, Angus, does this mean we need to consider moving to New York? There's no way I'll stay in Victoria while you work in New York. But, God! We've our house and my business, in Victoria. And our friends! It'd be very difficult to leave our friends there. I suppose, though, that Jenny might think it a great opportunity for her, anyway. That's one positive thought. "

"Aye, and there are probably lots of other positive things about this chance to move to New York. It's a lot to think about. Why don't we talk about this over some supper? Are you hungry, dear?"

"I'm famished. But I need to change first. I see you've already changed for the evening. You look very handsome, Angus."

"Thank you, Mrs. MacArthur. While you're getting changed, I'll pour us a wee drop to toast ourselves before we go. John James gave me a nice bottle of very old Tomatin whiskey. His brother told him it's my favourite. This prohibition they've got here in the States, something called the Volstead Act, is quite inconvenient. But, John tells me people have found ways around it, particularly those with means. After supper, if you're lucky, Mrs. MacArthur, I'll take you out to one of the hundreds of illegal speakeasy clubs. John gave me a password to get in. We'll hear some fine American Jazz music, while we celebrate our exciting future."

That evening, the couple made a decision that would change the rest of their lives, but not in the way they imagined.

They began to redirect their futures the following morning, when they met Mrs. Wharton at her suite of rooms on Central Park West. The building had been constructed in the Victorian era by a wealthy, former Scot, yet another in the stream of successful Scots who'd become well-to-do Americans. The rooms were furnished sparsely, but tastefully, as Mrs. Wharton had mentioned to Fiona the day before. The view of the park was lovely. The street below bustled with activity. The suite was on a high floor, far enough away from the noise of the street, to allow for a peaceful rest at night.

On his last visit to the doctor, Angus was prescribed a walk, every day. As the three of them toured the lovely suite, he pointed out to Fiona that he could walk in the park, an added bonus he hadn't counted on. The damage to his heart couldn't be repaired. He'd need to look after himself as best he could.

"Mr. MacArthur, Angus, I had no idea you have continuing work here in New York. This is good news. Now, tell me, is the rent agreeable to you both? I don't need to make a huge amount on these rooms."

"Mrs. Wharton, Fiona and I agree. The rent's very reasonable. But, we wanted to ask whether or not you'd consider leasing the rooms to us for a longer term. We were hoping for a lease with the option to buy the suite, if everything works out here in New York."

"A marvelous idea, Angus! Does this mean, Fiona, that you've decided to emigrate to the United States, move to New York? That certainly suits me. And yes, a lease with an option to buy would be fine."

"Great! And yes, we've decided to make the move. We'll be visiting Scotland every year, sometimes twice in a year. Living here will make those trips much more convenient. We're very glad to lease the suite from you. It'll make our transition much easier and give us a way to purchase a home in New York, once we've settled in."

"I'll have my attorney draw up a lease agreement, with an option to buy the suite, whenever you're ready. Fiona, I know you'll be very successful here in New York. I'm happy to have you both as tenants, for the time being. Until I met you two, I couldn't bear to sell the last place my husband and I lived together. Now, I know I can let it go, if you decide to buy it. I'm sure you'll ask me for tea once in a while, won't you Fiona? And, of course, I'll be coming to the studio, to order new designs as the fashions evolve."

The three, satisfied people shook hands all around. They agreed to sign the lease documents before Fiona and Angus left on the train for the west coast, early the following week. She'd take advantage of being in New York, arranging for the studio to be painted, before she left. Then, she could open it immediately, when they returned. Already, she was thinking of having Mikael take some photos of her newest designs, to hang as soon as she arrived back here. There was so much to do.

As the train pulled out of New York, Fiona and Angus tried not to let their high level of excitement affect their usual, relaxed way of enjoying the train. Rather than sketching designs, as she'd always done on the train, Fiona made lists of what she had to do, and what Angus had to do, to get ready for their move to New York. Making up the lists calmed her.

They still had their Scottish citizenship. The next time they sailed south from Victoria, they'd enter the United States as Scottish immigrants, en route to their new home in New York. Lucky for them, the Immigration Act of 1929 allowed for a high percentage of Scots to continue to emigrate. It was based on the fact that there were many Scottish immigrants already living in America. This was one time Fiona was glad she wasn't Eastern European, or Asian, as were many of her dear friends in Victoria. Those groups of people wouldn't have found it so easy to get into the United States. Just thinking about leaving her Chinese friends made Fiona sad. She put down her pen, abandoning her lists.

Angus noticed she'd stopped writing. He reached over and placed his hand on hers.

"Fiona, you look pensive. Are you alright?"

"Yes, Angus. I'm just thinking about leaving our friends. I'll stop brooding about that and work on my lists. Keeping busy will distract me from the upcoming goodbyes."

"Aye, it will. If you'll be fine here I'll just go off to the smoking car, to join the other men. No doubt, they'll be discussing how much they're making on the market. I'll see you for supper, later, my lovely lass."

He bent over and kissed her on the mouth gently. With his gentle touch, she felt the familiar surge of emotion, pure love, ripple through her body, for this wonderful husband of hers. Lately, though, when she experienced these intense emotions of love, the thought of losing Angus intruded, spoiling the moment. She'd noticed he seemed not quite so robust, experiencing shortness of breath more often than he used to. The strain of his work and now, the added pressure of the move could compromise his health further.

I'm going to encourage him to get more rest, especially in the exciting days to come. This long journey has taken a toll on his health. I know he thinks about his mortality. I certainly do. I worry about him much more than he knows. But, I don't want to be a harpie about it and have him feel like an invalid. I'll need to keep his condition in mind, without letting him know how much I worry about his health. It's such a difficult task, when he looks and claims to feel fine. I wish he wouldn't hang around that smoking car. The doctor said he shouldn't smoke. It can't be good for him to sit around breathing it in, either, I think.

Well, at least we can eat properly once we're home. No more rich foods and a lot less alcohol can't be a bad thing. Maybe prohibition isn't such a bad idea, given Angus' heart issues. I won't ever mention that to him either, if I don't want to hear a harangue about it. What a great husband he is: a true partner, friend, and lover. I couldn't ask for more.

Part 4

44 ... Leaving

Pressure on Angus increased, once he and Fiona reached Victoria. Technically, he was a private consultant to the bank. But, he assured Joseph James he would meet with each of the bank's clients, just in case his own forecast was accurate, for a downturn in the market. He wanted to ensure that the bank's clients were in the best possible financial position, before he left the city of Victoria.

One night, soon after their return from their overseas honeymoon, Angus discussed their personal financial options with Fiona.

"I know you love Victoria, Fiona, and this house."

"Aye, Angus dear. I surely do. It's our first home together, as a married couple. Two rooms at Mrs. Fraser's boarding house didn't really qualify as our first home, did it?"

"No, I agree with you there. We weren't making sweet love in our marriage bed at Mrs. Frasers, dearie."

Fiona ignored his inference to their lovemaking. She wanted to get the decision about the house in Victoria over with—to sell or not to sell.

"Ideally, Angus, we'd keep the house and return to it later. It would be a fine place to retire, someday, here on the Island."

"I agree, from a sentimental perspective. I'd like to keep the house. But, it might not be the best decision financially. I'm sure the markets will decline, eventually. If we rent it, we could end up with renters who wouldn't be able to afford the rent. We'd also need to carry the taxes, which would surely go up.

Financially, the best course of action is to sell the house now. We're lucky we built when we did, in this well-to-do area. It's worth far more than what it was when we finished it in 1926. Several of my clients have expressed interest in buying it."

"You didn't tell me that! Who, when, which ones"?

"The Swedish couple the Larsens, the Irish McGintys, and the Muirs of Dundee are the couples interested. The Larsens can't really afford it, given the amount of debt they already have, nor can the McGintys. But the Muirs are very well off."

"Don't you think it odd that the best qualified people share Helen Brody's family name"?

"I do. That's why I didn't mention their inquiry to you right away. You'd suffered through Helen's death on our overseas trip. The Muirs asked me if we'd be selling the house when I saw them at the bank, a few days ago. And, there was no point in telling you about the earlier two inquiries. I couldn't, in all good conscience, entertain the thought of selling to clients of mine who clearly couldn't afford it. We'd be courting disaster. It would be fine for the bank. They'd be owed a huge mortgage, and eventually foreclose on the house. But, that's not what we'd like to have happen to our acquaintances or our lovely home. It has so many good memories for us, doesn't it?"

"Yes, it surely does, Angus. The timing couldn't be better, could it? We have an interested buyer, a Muir, and we can get a high price. We should sell now. The money will help us with the move and later, go toward Mrs. Wharton's apartment in New York, when the time comes."

"I agree. Now, let's go to bed and enjoy every last night, making love, in our first home. If we're lucky, you'll be expecting before we leave. We'd have a child to remind us of this lovely place, especially now that we're leaving it."

Fiona took him up on his offer, that night, and many other nights, while they waited for their emigration documents. Where

lovemaking was concerned, Angus didn't seem to have a problem with his heart. Hopefully, that would be the case for a very
long time.

Angus contacted the Muirs. They rushed over the same
night, toured the house, and paid a substantial deposit on the
spot. They were, in fact, distant cousins of Helen's father's
family, in their later fifties, looking for a suitable place to retire
by the sea in Canada. They knew Helen had died, leaving an
adopted son. They expressed their sympathies about Helen,
and enjoyed hearing about her sister, Meg McGinnis, who
hadn't kept in touch with their branch of the family. The evening ended with the shaking of hands all around, and smiles
on everyone's faces.

From that day onward, Fiona began to sort and pack the
things they'd take, putting the house into chaos, with boxes
bound for New York, the Salvation Army, or the next rum-
mage sale at the Kirk. Now, she was very glad she'd left the
books willed to her by Helen, with Daniel in Glasgow. She
wrote to him at school to let him know their new address and
when they'd be arriving in New York. She told him to look up
New York in one of his atlases, as a way to include him in the
excitement, she hoped.

Jenny and Mikael were married a year ago. They were thrilled
to have the opportunity buy Fiona's business. And, she was glad
to help the younger couple. She'd never have been so successful
without Jenny's talent and hard work. Mikael's artistic photographs, in the shop and in printed leaflets, enhanced the business.
They'd own the haberdashery shop and retain the clients with
contracts for uniforms and soon, ready-to-wear clothing. Jenny
planned to employ more sewers, for the high volume clients.
She'd become a talented milliner, adding hats to the inventory,
while Fiona was away.

Jenny and Mikael got a bank loan from Joseph James. After

much convincing by Fiona and Angus, they gratefully accepted Fiona's price, far below the inflated market price, for the business. It was the only way they could afford to buy it. They resigned the lease with the landlord, for the space on Government Street. The new business name in Victoria was: *Jenny's Haberdashery, Hats, and Practical Clothing.*

Fiona retained the rights to her name, Fiona's Clothing Design, which she would change to *Designs by Fiona*, when she took out her business license in New York. The beading machines, all of the expensive fabrics, and Fiona's best sewing machine would be shipped to New York.

Two years earlier, Angus had helped Mikael arrange a loan for his photography business, which he'd already paid back. He'd done quite a bit of work for the *Victoria Daily Times* newspaper, travelling up and down Vancouver Island, getting well paid for his timely photographs. Some of his photos, particularly those of mining accidents and marine disasters had been used by papers across the country. He was artistic, with a good deal of common sense, traits that had served him well. Together, Jenny and Mikael were well positioned, whatever happened to Angus' predictions about the markets. They would survive.

Oddly, Fiona's Scottish client, Hilary Burns, the person who invited Fiona to Canada, arranged for a huge going-away reception at the Empress Hotel. Hilary had always liked Angus. In fact, she would have liked the handsome, very successful businessman, for herself. But, he was obviously devoted to Fiona. Initially, Hilary was resentful. Fiona was beneath Hilary's social position. But, once Fiona became a successful designer, Hilary came down off her high horse, accepted Fiona as an equal, and accepted the fact that she'd never get Angus for herself.

Hilary kept her promises too. She never betrayed Fiona by gossiping about her scandalous past in Scotland. Their social connection had been maintained for ten years, and now it was she, who'd send Angus and Fiona off in style, to their new life in New York.

The evening of the reception arrived. Fiona and Angus were surprised to see so many people in the stately, Palm Court, with its domed, intricately-worked glass ceiling, at the Empress Hotel.

"Look, Angus! Mrs. Bridge-Harris is here. She's wearing the latest gown I designed for her. Oh! There's the rest of her little group of dowagers, all decked out in my designs! And there's Joseph James, whose wife is also wearing one of my designs.

Oh my God. I see Mrs. Fraser, and Jenny too, both wearing clothing I designed for them. How can this be? I had no idea Hilary would mix social groups like this. I can't believe she's finally given a nod to egalitarianism. Look, even the servers are wearing uniforms that Jenny and her sewers made for the staff of the Empress Hotel. She'll be very proud too."

Seeing these many women gathered together, from different levels of Victoria's society, reminded Fiona that Hilary wasn't the first person to organize such mixed class gatherings. The suffragette movement had drawn together all types of women, winning the vote for Canadian women in 1918, two years after Alberta led the way. Here, in the "New World," it seemed that opportunities for women came earlier and were plentiful, compared with those they had back home.

Obviously, being in Canada has been good for Hilary. It's taught her something. I recall Mrs. Wharton saying that The Temperance League in America has commandeered all classes of women, to work together. Perhaps I'll outfit many of them, as well!

"Fiona . . . Fiona! Are you alright, darlin'?"

"Sorry, Angus, I was just thinking. What were you saying?"

"This display, of your designs, regardless of where folk come from is a lovely tribute to you and your artistry. Everyone is beaming. Hilary certainly is good at keeping secrets, isn't she? She's radiant, looking like the cat that got the canary, as they say."

"I agree. Nobody even hinted that they'd all be wearing my designs. I'm grateful and humbled by this display."

A faint clinking sound was barely audible over the conversation in the room. Gradually, the conversation died down as everyone turned toward the sound. Hilary Burns addressed the crowd, from a dais at the front of the room.

"Ladies and Gentlemen, may I have your attention please?"

"Ladies and Gentlemen, thank you for coming tonight, to say goodbye to our dear friends, Angus and Fiona MacArthur. Each of you, in some way, has benefitted greatly from knowing this fine Scottish couple. I, for one, am happy to take credit for inviting Fiona to come to Victoria, not for her sake, but for mine. I've never been without her talented artistry, reflected in the designs and fabrics we can all see here tonight. Nor, have I been out of style, for even one minute, since she came to Canada, nine years ago.

Fiona's a new breed of woman, a self-made woman. She's succeeded because of her perseverance and tenacity, in spite of many struggles. She's established herself here in Victoria and we've all been the better for having known her. Thank you, Fiona, for accepting my invitation. I wish you the best of luck in your new home in New York. Lucky them!"

Everyone raised their glasses and toasted Fiona. Hilary continued.

"And now, I'll turn the floor over to someone else, who'd like to say a few words."

Lady Bridge-Harris rose. She leaned heavily on her cane, with each step she took, waving away efforts to help her, as she climbed up the two steps up to the dais. Finally, she began to speak.

"Fiona, Miss Gilman, as I first knew you, and now, Mrs. MacArthur, I want to tell you something in front of these witnesses. I never thought I'd say this aloud, let alone, in public.

But, I'm getting old now. There may not be a time to say this to you, after tonight.

Fiona, you've been one of the brightest lights in my life. I know I can be cantankerous. I'm afraid I was unnecessarily impatient with you, when you first started coming to my rooms, here at the Empress Hotel. You showed me your designs, measured me while I fidgeted, and adjusted endlessly, each garment, as I changed my mind, repeatedly. Age is no excuse for rudeness. I apologize.

What I should have told you long ago, is that you were one of very few visitors to this old lady's rooms, one of the few pleasant, attentive, and kind people in my life. I had no daughters. I like to think you could have been the daughter I never had. I'm sure I must have frustrated you many times, as with all mothers and daughters in their relationships. I want you to know that I admire and respect you. I care for you. I'll miss you. I hope you'll think of me now and again, in your new life. I know I'll always think of you."

Tears filled Fiona's eyes and those of many other people in the room. Everyone who knew Mrs. Bridge-Harris was shocked and touched, by the raw emotion she displayed, and by the feelings she expressed for Fiona.

Oh my God. I had no idea she even liked me. And I was so mean, when I spoke of her to Angus, that day he and I met in the lobby. I know I wasn't the only person who called her Mrs. Bitch-Harris behind her back. Now, I'm ashamed to think I did that. I should've been kinder to her. I should've appreciated that she was probably lonely and liked to have company. Why didn't I think about that, instead of resisting the idea of being nice to her?

Fiona stepped forward toward the dais. She offered her arm to assist the old lady down the two steps from the dais and walked with her to her seat.

"Thank you, for your very kind words, Lady Bridge-Harris. Tell me, do you allow hugs, on special occasions?"

"It'll cost you."

Fiona saw an unreadable expression on the old lady's face, so she sat down, instead, in the chair next to the old woman. She placed her hand gently on the old woman's arm.

"Do you call that a hug, where you come from? We English don't hug often, other than our dogs and horses, but when we do, we make the best of it. Here, help me up so we can have a proper hug. It could be my last in this world."

When the two women embraced, shakily, on the part of the older woman, everyone in the room applauded. It seemed they were relieved to see the old lady relax. Perhaps, they anticipated fewer tongue lashings, or sarcastic remarks, being directed toward them in the future. After all, they still lived here, while Fiona would escape. How nice, people were thinking, that we've seen the vulnerable side of this formidable woman.

"My name is Ester, you know. Please call me Ester."

"Why, thank you, Ester. I'll write to let you know how I'm doing in New York, if you like. Would that be OK with you?"

"Yes, that would be acceptable. Thank you."

The evening continued in the same vein, with many wonderful tributes to Angus, as well. His friends and colleagues described how much he'd meant, to people in Victoria, and up the Island, in the banking and mining communities. Joseph James gave a touching speech. He spoke words that many immigrants could relate to about the importance of friendships, with people from home, to those who'd ventured so far away from their families.

A heartfelt tribute to Angus came from Mikael, Jenny's husband, in his much improved English, with its lilting Swedish rhythm.

"Angus is my big brother, not in name, but in spirit, as I see it. He's treated me as such, when he had no benefit for himself.

He befriended me, supported me, as I struggled to make a living with my photography and journalism. He never, even once, laughed at my accent, which, I hear, most people do. His greatest gift, of course, was introducing me to his lovely cousin, Jenny MacArthur, now my gorgeous wife. She'll soon to be the mother of our child."

Mikael was interrupted by "ohs and ahs." Everyone realized he was announcing that Jenny was expecting. Jenny blushed. She smiled as many "congratulations" were spoken aloud. By the time they raised their glasses to toast Angus, Mikael and "brother" Angus had tears in their eyes. Fiona steeled herself for more emotional goodbyes.

God, this is so difficult, more difficult than I thought it would be leaving our Victoria life, leaving these fantastic people we've met here.

A narrow door behind the dais opened, as Mikael walked down the steps into the crowd. Out stepped Aunt Woo. She faced the crowd, holding a large, flat object in her hand. Fiona heard an audible gasp from many individuals in the room. It seemed that some of the privileged, white attendees were unable to suppress their surprise at seeing a Chinese woman about to address them. The room went silent. Aunt Woo began to speak.

"I am Woo, friend of Miss Fiona, Mrs. MacArthur. Some of you do not know she took care of my cousin's daughter, Ming, when her father was killed. She employed Ming and also her friends. She gave weekly lessons, at back of her shop, helping many students with their English. She cooked for them. She also taught them useful skills and gave them chance to learn about their white neighbours. These young people will be going on to university, one in particular, only because Fiona intervened with resistant uncle. The great success of these students might never have happened without Fiona's extra help and kindness, when they need it.

I now ask special guest, my niece Lily, here for her last year before she go to medical school in United States, to present humble gift to Miss Fiona, on behalf of Chinese students and friends."

Lily stepped into the room through the narrow door. She looked exquisite in one of Fiona's custom designed outfits. She addressed the shocked crowd in her soft voice.

"Miss Fiona, my thanks and the thanks of your many grateful Chinese students, for letting us know you. I give you here, a painting by Woo, the latest in her collection, for you and your husband to enjoy in New York. We hope it will remind you of your Chinese friends in Victoria. We are honoured to know you."

Fiona was overwhelmed. She knew that Woo could command a huge sum for her paintings now. She was internationally successful, as Fiona always knew she would be. The painting was exquisite, reflecting all of the delicacy, and intricacy, for which Woo was famous. It was moving to behold, as everyone in the room was learning.

Lily's testimonial was the last, and a fitting one for the occasion. Angus and Fiona walked up to the dais, hand in hand, to receive the painting. Angus spoke first.

"My lovely wife is overwhelmed, just now. She's asked me to speak first. There's only one thing Fiona has never been very good at, and that is accepting credit for how truly caring she is toward the people in her life, both personal and professional. We've heard tonight, tributes from a number of speakers who share love and respect for her, as do I. I'm grateful that a few people here tonight think I'm good enough to be her husband.

Aunt Woo, Fiona still calls you 'Aunt,' just as if you were both from the same family. We're especially humbled by this gift of your wonderful painting. It will remind us, of the friendship and respect we feel, for our Chinese friends, and their community here in Victoria. If enough people like Fiona pass through our lives perhaps our children won't learn to be suspicious of other races, of cultures different from their own. Fiona and I dearly hope that the effect of her involvement with Victoria's Chinatown and its people will resonate for a long while after she's moved away.

"Thank you, formally, to all of you, colleagues and dear friends. I'll miss you all and think of you often. I'll say so long, not goodbye. I'll pour you a wee drop of my highland whiskey, the next time I'm in Victoria. And now, I give you Fiona Gilman MacArthur."

Fiona took a deep breath and prayed that she could get through her speech without breaking into tears, or worse yet, blubbering her way through it. Angus stood by her side, for moral support.

"Thank you, Hilary, for inviting me to come to Victoria in the first place. You've been a loyal friend. Thank you, too, for organizing this wonderful evening.

Everyone's kind words will stay with me for the rest of my life. I'm grateful for the friendship of everyone here. You had faith in me. You supported me as I made my way, on my own, for five years, before I met Angus, and beyond that. Maybe that's the way it was meant to be. I was destined to meet Hoy, Ming, Lily, and Aunt Woo, Mrs. Fraser, William and Joseph Leeds, Joseph James, Lady Bridge-Harris and so many of my wonderful clients. Ah . . . too many people to name. Please know that, in my heart, I have all of you to thank for my happiness among you and for my success at *Fiona's Clothing Design and Haberdashery*.

On that note, I hope everyone will support Jenny. She's renamed the shop, *Jenny's Haberdashery, Hats, and Practical Clothing*. For those of you who own businesses, she'll specialize in uniforms and work clothing. For everyone else, she'll set up the shop for ready-to-wear clothing in the near future. Please let your friends, know she's there."

Just then, a voice from the crowd interrupted Fiona's address.

"What about us, the women who've relied on you for original, custom designs all these years? What will we do, now that you'll be in New York?"

Many of Fiona's wealthiest clients were nodding, waiting for her to answer.

"Well, ladies, I'll send my latest design photos and contact information to Jenny, at her shop. You can contact me after that, if you like."

Fiona hadn't anticipated the slight tone of hostility underlying the question about the loss of a rising haute couture designer, from their midst. It seemed, regardless of the praise that was heaped on her tonight they resented not having instant access to her. But, that was the price of success. They knew it—their husbands are or were when they lived, successful. And that comes with a price. They knew it, they just didn't like it when it affected them.

By the end of the evening, Fiona wasn't quite blubbering, as she hugged goodbye, some of her close friends. And she still had Ming to go. That goodbye would be the most difficult for Fiona. Ming hadn't wanted to be here tonight. It was too sad for her. They'd have lunch together the day before Fiona and Angus left town.

Thinking of Ming, Fiona couldn't deny that she had, indeed, made a great difference to many people in Victoria, in a good way. In turn, she owed them for her opportunity to become a successful business woman. Although she was emotionally exhausted now, she'd think fondly of this evening very often, over the ensuing decades.

One very pleasant experience remained for Fiona and Angus, before they went to bed for one of their last nights in Victoria, British Columbia, Canada. They walked, hand-in-hand, out of the huge, carved wooden doors of the Empress Hotel, into the darkness. They turned left at the street and walked along the inner harbour, toward the Provincial Government Building. It was outlined against the night sky by thousands of electric lights, creating a glow over the grounds that reflected in the water beyond. Queen Victoria, for whom the lights were first lit in 1897, to celebrate her jubilee, would have been as impressed as they were, by this spectacular display. Indeed, Victoria was a city that Fiona and Angus would never forget.

45 ... Angus

"Excuse me, Madam, are you Mrs. MacArthur?"
"Yes, I am."

The conductor looked like he'd seen a ghost. His face was pale. Sweat dripped down the sides of his face from beneath his cap. He placed a glass of water down on the table in front of Fiona. Then, he removed his cap and sat down opposite her. At this point Fiona, became alarmed.

"What's going on?"

"Madam, I've just come from the smoking car. I'm afraid there's been an incident. Would you care for a sip of water, while I tell you what happened?"

"No thank you. Where's my husband, Angus MacArthur? Is he still in the smoking car? What's wrong? Tell me, please, just tell me!"

"I'm sorry to tell you, Madame, that your husband has suffered a collapse. The doctor is with him now, attempting to revive him."

Fiona leaped up from the bench, turned quickly on her heel, and rushed back toward the smoking car. She'd see for herself, rather than wait for this man to get over his nerves and start making some sense.

When she entered the car, she saw a group of men gathered at the far end, near the table closest to the bar, which, of course, was not legally able to stock alcohol. The air was full of smoke, enough that the whole car seemed to be enveloped in a fog. There was no sign of Angus. She approached a tall man with a white handlebar moustache, who had a stethoscope draped around his neck. He reeked of strong drink.

"Where's my husband? Tell me where he is, please!"

"Madame, I'm Dr. Whitely. I attended your husband just after he collapsed. Please sit down."

The doctor reached into his inside jacket pocket. He poured a dram of what looked like whiskey into a glass on the table. He offered the glass to Fiona. She shook her head.

"Just tell me, for God's sake! Where is Angus?"

"I'm very sorry to tell you, Mrs. MacArthur, I couldn't revive your husband. He passed away. I'm terribly sorry."

"Where is he? Where have you taken him? I need to see him."

"Follow me. The staff and I thought that the temperature in the next car would serve your husband best."

Dr. Whitely led Fiona into the refrigeration car. There, in the darkest back corner, on top of a pile of crates, was Angus, the top half of his body covered with a tarp.

"Would you like to see him?"

"Yes," Fiona managed to whisper.

The doctor pulled back the tarp. Fiona swayed at the sight of Angus. The doctor reached out to steady her. Her husband's face bore a peaceful expression, not a grotesque death mask, full of fear or contorted in pain. His colour was washed out, but other than that, he looked as if he could be asleep.

This can't be happening. This can't be Angus, here on these crates. What will I do? I can't bear this. What will happen to me without him?

She reached over and began to stroke his face while her tears fell. It didn't matter that her knees were shaking and her body was freezing. She wanted to touch him. She leaned down and kissed his soft lips, feeling, for the last time, the fine moustache that formed a part of his dark, neat beard. He'd regrown it at her request.

"I'm very sorry, to interrupt you, Mrs. MacArthur. But, we arrive in New York City in just a few hours. The coroner will meet the train and take your husband's body to the medical examiner's location. This procedure is required for any death, on a train, in the state of New York. You'll be able to make arrangements for your husband once the mandatory autopsy is completed. Now, Mrs. MacArthur, do you have a contact number where you can be reached in New York?"

"Mrs. MacArthur, did you hear me? Please give me your contact number in New York. I'll need to write it on the form that will go with your husband's body. Do you have it with you?"

"I . . . I seem to have left my case back in the other car. The number is in there."

Fiona was numb. She allowed the doctor to lead her back to the car, but when they arrived at her seat, her case was wide open. Her purse was gone.

"My purse was in here. Someone has taken it."

Distraught, she sank down into the seat, not sure what to do next. She could hear Dr. Whiteley's voice, muted, as if it were coming from very far away. Seeing that she was overwhelmed, he repeated what he said.

"I say, I have your husband's wallet, watch, and papers here, in this envelope. Would the number be in here?"

Fiona forced herself to deal with the present crisis. She must. There was no option.

"Aye, it would. We had duplicate copies of everything, except the cash, of course."

She found Mrs. Wharton's phone number and the address of the suite in Mrs. Wharton's building on Central Park West, where she and Angus—where she alone, would live. She gave the details to the doctor. He left to alert the railway people about Fiona's missing purse.

As the doctor walked away, Fiona remembered the other important documents that were in her ransacked case. She'd need to have them to be able to live in New York. She rifled through her case quickly, praying that her immigration papers and her passport were still there. They were. Relieved, she allowed herself to think about Angus.

So, this is the end for my wonderful husband, my soul mate, my friend, my lover. I'm alone, again. How lucky I was to have him as long as I did. Four blissful years, four years that didn't include the horrors of my life before I met him: getting raped, giving away Daniel, bearing the death of Billy, and living with the shame and humiliation of my wicked affair with Sean. Only during these last four years with Angus, have I known real happiness. Now, he's gone.

She closed her eyes, hoping to get some rest, but sleep was impossible. She kept waking up, expecting Angus to be there with her, just as he was every day when she woke up. Each time she awoke, the pain of his death reinserted itself into her consciousness.

Fiona gave up on sleeping. There were things she had to do. They'd distract her from the weight of the grief that hovered over her, threatening to drop onto her, at any minute. She made her way through the darkened train cars, to the administration office. The doctor had told her that someone was there 24 hours a day. She'd send a cable to Mrs. Wharton. That way, she wouldn't need to explain why Angus wasn't with her when Mrs. Wharton met the train. She dreaded discussing his death with anyone she knew. That would make it real.

This clear, fall day, October 25, 1929 would have been a glorious welcome for the talented MacArthur's as they set up their new home in New York City. They had such promise for a prosperous and adventurous new life. Angus had been looking forward to working with John James. Fiona had been very excited about her new studio, and designing the latest fashions, for Mrs. Wharton and her wealthy friends. The studio was a huge step up in her career as a designer. But, death had accompanied her to New York, obliterating all anticipation of her new life.

At dawn, the train pulled into Grand Central Terminal. Mrs. Wharton was there, organized, and ready to take charge. She could see that Fiona hadn't slept, as she watched her step down from the train.

"Come, my dear, you'll come home with me for now. I've arranged for a car to deliver the your large trunks to your suite on Central Park West."

The ambulance that would take Angus' body to the coroner's office was visible further down the track. Fiona had spotted it, as she stepped down from the train, looking for Mrs. Wharton. She avoided looking in the direction of the ambulance again. She didn't want to acknowledge that her Angus was in there, dead, never to be with her again. His strong, masculine face, that lovely soft beard, his huge hands, with their manicured nails, and his big arms that encircled her with such ease, each time he embraced her. All of this, and the essence of Angus, was gone. His spirit had flown, his body would disintegrate. She'd never see him on this earth, again.

"Thank you, Mrs. Wharton. I'm sorry to burden you with me. Are you sure you want me to come to your place?"

"Of course, Fiona. You'll need a few days to get some rest and make some arrangements. My driver will see that your trunks are unloaded into your suite. Your studio is ready to go as well. But, you can deal with that later. Let's get you home now."

Fiona struggled to distract her thoughts from her present horror. Fortunately, Emma Wharton, like Jane Austen's Emma Woodhouse, was a take charge type of person, a person who never hesitated to step forward and intervene in whatever was going on around her. When you were on the top of the world, such a person could be annoying. When you were oppressed by grief, she was a Godsend. Fiona was grateful for such a friend, at this terrible time.

As Mrs. Wharton steered her through the very noisy, crowded station, Fiona noticed newspaper hawkers all over the station, waving their papers in the air and selling them as fast as possible to passersby. Their shouts added to the noise and confusion: "Get your paper here. October 24, 1929, Black Thursday, the market has dropped. It's a disaster—we're doomed. Prepare to lose everything."

"Mrs. Wharton, what's happened?"

"Angus was correct, that's what, Fiona. He predicted that our rosy financial picture could turn dark. And, it has. We'll need to see what happens over the next few days. My friend, Mrs. Whitney, says her husband and a group of bankers have the problem in hand. We should be fine. But, you don't need to worry about it just now, Fiona. You've enough to deal with. Here's our car."

On the drive to Mrs. Wharton's home, Fiona thought how perceptive Angus had been about his forecast for the market. They'd gotten a very high price for their Victoria home. They'd built on a particularly impressive lot and added to the value of the property, with Fiona's artistic, decorative flair inside their home and in the gardens. Angus had insisted on leaving their house funds in the Canadian bank of Joseph James back in Victoria, safely stashed in an American currency account, topped up with other cash. The lease they'd signed with Mrs. Wharton stipulated they could buy the apartment at market price, whenever they chose; they wanted their money to be safe and readily available. Angus had said the banks in the United

States were too plentiful, and too many of them operated, especially lately, in the unbelievably robust market, with far too much in the way of unsecured debt. The remainder of his wealth was invested in low risk assets, spread over a number of international accounts. His cautious approach to the market in the past few years had left them in the best possible circumstances. He had continued to predict this burst in the financial bubble, right to his last day, on the train. Now, it had happened, just as he said it would.

Fiona still couldn't sleep when she arrived at Emma Wharton's opulent home on the Upper East Side. She was propelled by the energy of grief, afraid to go to sleep, only to awaken and remember, again, that Angus was lost to her.

Mrs. Wharton took her for a walk in the neighbourhood, to take her mind off her grief and help her to relax. They stopped at a small café for lunch. Tomorrow would be soon enough to send cables to Angus' mother, and Fiona's parents, in Scotland. Fiona hadn't told Mrs. Wharton about Daniel. She'd write to her mum later, to discuss the best way to tell him about Angus.

They walked back to Mrs. Wharton's home, where Fiona finally managed to get some sleep. She awakened to the sound of Mrs. Wharton's voice, calling her to dinner. Lying there in the strange room, Fiona thought about Daniel. He'd now lost "Uncle Angus," on top of losing his Mum, Helen Brody, just a few months earlier. She hoped he had her resilience, as he dealt with these continuing losses in his young life.

I've been in a similar position to this before, haven't I? I was alone in a new country, in a new city, when I first moved to Canada, nine years ago. I was meant to survive, I think, so I could meet Angus, the love of my life, the person I was meant to be with, for the rest of my life. I was lucky to have my Angus, but, only for the rest of his life, not mine.

I have my son. I'll be there to help nurture him, to help him become a man like Angus—kind, responsible, considerate of others, and able to find a path in his life that makes him happy. I've been given a second chance with Daniel. I'll hang onto that thought, while I long for Angus. If this is God's way of intimidating me, my courage will rise, again. I will survive.

✦ ✦ ✦

Acknowledgments

I am indebted to the following people for their encouragement and support:

. . . my husband, Jim, who listened patiently while I read aloud many scenes, as I constructed the story. We laughed together at the funny bits. We wept together . . . well, I wept and he became teary eyed, at points in the story that involved death, or injustice, or poignancy. We cheered together with each victory of the heroine, as she continues, courageously, to rise above the challenges that life deals her. I'm particularly grateful to Jim for taking on the roles of bodyguard, photographer, taxi payer, and dinner partner, as we toured around Glasgow, Victoria, and New York, locating sites that appear in the novel. Jim reminded me to live life, too, as I worked on the manuscript.

. . . Isobel Grundy, who contributed many invaluable suggestions for improvements to my manuscript. Along with other points, she reminded me that modernisms such as "tote bag" needed to be reset into their historical context. Fiona's Gladstone Kit Bag resulted from my additional research, following Isobel's comments. I very much appreciate Isobel's expertise and encouragement.

. . . Patrick Brown, who kindly pulled himself away from his non-fiction and technical reading enjoyment, to read and provide written feedback on my manuscript. I incorporated a subtle refinement to my presentation, of the villain in the novel, thanks to one of Pat's suggestions. As well, the main characters were lucky that Pat was a reader. I had them buying a new Ford,

Model T. At Pat's suggestion, I upgraded them to the more luxurious McLaughlin Buick.

... Audrey Stibbe, who suspended her fiction and non-fiction reading of the Tudor Period, to proofread my novel set in the 1920s. Audrey's written feedback led to my elaborating on the main character's earliest encounters, in Victoria's Chinatown.

... the Jane Austen Society of North America in New York (JASNA), who invited me to participate in a panel for authors influenced by Jane Austen's novels. I am also grateful for the encouragement of the members of JASNA Victoria.

... the following authors, whose unique books provided me with useful background reading for particular points in my story:

Knox, William W. J. *Lives of Scottish Women: Women and Scottish Society, 1800–1980*. Edinburgh. Edinburgh University Press, 2006.

Kinchin, Perilla. *Taking Tea with Mackintosh: The Story of Miss Cranston's Tea Rooms*. San Francisco. Pomegranate Communications, Inc., 1998.

CPSIA information can be obtained
at www.ICGtesting.com
Printed in the USA
BVHW040527101222
653906BV00001B/3